CLIMBING
THE
COLISEUM
A NOVEL

Bill Percy

Black Rose Writing | Texas

ISBN: 978-1-68433-221-2
PUBLISHED BY BLACK ROSE WRITING
www.blackrosewriting.com

Printed in the United States of America
Suggested Retail Price (SRP) $22.95

Climbing the Coliseum is printed in Adobe Caslon Pro

To Michele, my first, best, and most devoted reader, critic, partner, and friend.

ACKNOWLEDGEMENTS

MANY PEOPLE HELPED me with *Climbing the Coliseum*. My thanks to Patrice Jamar, who read the earliest draft and provided enormously helpful suggestions; and to Lorna Lynch, my editor, who helped me shape the story and give it consistency and coherence. David Levine provided the wonderful cover design, and Patti Frazee the interior book design. For their many insights and suggestions, I'm grateful to Mark Nammacher and Mary Kay Stranik, to June and Ken Stewart, to Bob Percy and Sue Haasis, to Sara Wright, to Nancy Larson, to Jen Percy and John Santelices, to Cary and Aaron Percy, to Cathy Johnston, and finally to the crew at Sweet Lou's, who welcomed me, draft after draft (of words and of beer).

CLIMBING
THE
COLISEUM

PRELUDE

On a Sunday in December

S NOWSHOEING UP THE steep trail through heavy snow was backbreaking, but he felt none of that, only a curious numbness. Now and then, he heard himself muttering between heavy breaths, but paid so little attention that it might have been another voice. He hardly cared, or even knew, what the words meant. *It'd be such a relief to be done*, he thought. Done with what? He didn't know or care. All morning, he'd felt an urge to stand on the granite edge of the summit and peer down the long fall.

Below the last switchback, he rested, gasping – the weight he'd gained over the last two years was too much cargo – and stared out and down at the gray granite face of the glacial cirque, an enormous amphitheater of sheer rock. What would it be like to fall? Had finding out been the allure of the cliff?

He'd worry about that some other time. If there were another time.

A raven lifted on air, soared across the face of the horseshoe-shaped cliff, a black line across the void. He felt no consolation, none of the uplift he usually got from this hike, only a far-away sense that he was climbing to the end of something. He'd climbed the Coliseum – the name the valley people gave this glacier-gouged mountain – many times. Always, climbing had buoyed him. Not today.

A half mile back, he had surprised a cow elk and her calf traversing a snow-clogged field. When he'd startled them, the calf had wallowed in a drift, eyes wide and frightened. But the mother had bolted, leaving the little one behind. Absently, he'd thought it odd that the cow hadn't charged. What mother wouldn't protect her calf? He should have helped the calf, but he'd kept climbing, staring ahead. Now, resting, looking out over the cirque, he wondered why he hadn't felt more.

A snow cornice at the other end of the long summit ridge broke off with a gunshot crack, white sheets of snow falling and feathering out against the dark stone. He watched the veils of snow as if he had a kinship with them.

He climbed. At the summit, he walked out to the lip of snow above the cliff and gazed a quarter-mile down the sheer ice-gouged granite. The tiny pool below, Saint Mary's Lake, made a white oval, a pale target. Beyond, the long valley stretched north, fields shining in the winter sun. What would falling be like? Would his bones wash down the Monastery River, to be found by someone fishing? *No need for drama*, he thought – or did he say it aloud? The *black dog* had got him, finally. It had pursued him for twenty-seven years, since his troubles in Minnesota, and at last it had caught him.

He moved closer to the edge, his right snowshoe protruding into the empty air. He stared down through it, into the void.

This – his snowshoe out in the air – satisfied him. *No more listening to patients' troubles*, he thought. No more forcing compassion through a haze of sorrow. An end to being the valley's listener. The space beneath his snowshoe soothed him, an opening in his pain.

Just one more step: out into the air.

The chime of a monastery bell wafted up from below, a pure tone rising on the white air. Again, he stared through his snowshoe, waiting for another bell, but there came only silence, as if a child held her breath behind a locked door. Yet, the bell had wakened something in him. There were monks down there, real people, and people lived down in town, in Jefferson, a darker patch thirty miles up-valley, trees surrounded by the winter-white fields. People. *His* people. The people he took care of.

His attention lapsed. He simply stood, his snowshoe out over air.

Just one more step: out . . .

My people. He no longer wanted that, was weary of people needing his help, draining him, depending on him. Was there no end to being dependable? That's what brought him up here, onto this shelf of snow hanging over the void.

A whisper, down the meadow to the right. He turned his head. A larger elk, the bull, stood quietly under the verge of trees. The father of the desperate calf? The bull gazed at him, black eyes calm, his breath billowing clouds of steam. Ed thought, *Protect your calf.* Did his people, his patients, look to him for the steadiness he envied in the bull? He grunted. *I don't want it.*

Just then, the snow beneath his shoe shifted, sank an inch. He snapped alert, heart racing. Was he on an overhang? If it broke off, if he fell swiftly with it, wrapped in falling feathering ice down the cliff face, he and snow would drop too fast. He felt sick, knowing how his body would try to jerk back but would find no footing, would stretch for rock but grasp only air, his fingers dragged through rootless snow as he plunged. In the moment before the snow fell, he came instantly alive. He jerked upright, then froze, realizing that he stood not on granite but on the wind-blown cornice extending out beyond the rock, a drift his weight could break.

Get off the edge! His mind screamed, but he stayed motionless. Throwing himself backwards, moving at all, could crack the cornice. He remembered the sharp gunshot pop, remembered white sheets of snow cascading against the dark cliff. He stilled his breathing. *Slow. Easy.* Shifting his weight slowly onto his left snowshoe, he edged the right shoe back. Its rear point caught in snow. Holding his breath, he leaned all his weight on the left, gently freeing the caught tip. He dreaded the gunshot sound of the cornice snapping.

At last, his right shoe came free and he carefully lifted it backward, planted, shifted weight, then moved the left. Repeat, repeat, until he stood above granite. Exhausted, he sank into the drift and began to tremble. He lay on his back, looking up at the incomparable blue of the mountain sky. *I almost died.*

His fear gave way to a surge of self-contempt. *How stupid can I be?* He'd hiked these mountains for twenty-five years, knew the dangers of the winter cliffs. Disgusted, he sat up and gazed out over the long valley, down where his patients lived, the people he no longer wanted to help.

The sensation of plunging down through air with no hold to grab swept through him and he began trembling again. *So close!* If he'd fallen, or stepped off into the air, what would his people do without him? *That's nuts*, he muttered, almost aloud. He looked up to the deep sky to calm the trembling. The cold air bit his skin.

A long time ago, when a Minneapolis psychologist had committed suicide, his partner Paul Carlen had said, "A psychologist has no right to suicide. Too many people need us." What did it matter if he resented it? He'd chosen it, hadn't he? They needed him, didn't they? He gazed at the trees lined vividly green against the implacable blue. And waited.

In his pocket, he dug around for the ten-dollar gold piece he'd carried since Minnesota, twenty-seven years, the coin little Elizabeth Murphy had used to pay him. For a moment, he fingered it, rubbing it between his thumb and forefinger, as he always did, soothing himself. "So I'm burned out," he said to the trees. It had crept up on him, year after quiet year, until now. Until he almost threw himself off – or fell by stupidity.

He stood and threw Elizabeth's coin into the void. It curved up, sunlight flashing on the twisting disk, and in a fading arc it fell, a dark speck against the white lake, and then was gone. He watched a long time, then thought, *I don't want to die. But am I ready to live?*

The bull elk had gone. Ed shivered. The sun was declining, the afternoon air growing chill. Why had he thrown away his coin? He'd carried it, fingering it, every day for all the years since Minnesota. Losing it solved nothing: He bore the same burden, felt the same burned-out despair. The *black dog*.

At least there'd be no death today on the Coliseum.

He turned and followed his tracks down the trail as the afternoon sun fell into the west. When he reached the trailhead, the sun had gone behind the rugged Monastery Mountains. He sat in his pickup waiting for the heater to take the bite out of the air. Across the little lake, St. Brendan's Monastery was immersed in shadows. He'd drive down the mountain to town and he'd resume his life, care for his patients, find a way to keep his despair at bay. Nothing had changed, except he'd thrown his coin away.

High above, the rim of the Coliseum reddened in the alpenglow. Ed gazed at it sadly. What would come of this? His belly fat, the thirty pounds he'd gained lately, strained against the seatbelt. He was defeated. Alive, but futile.

Something had to change.

"I'll lose the damn weight," he said aloud.

He snorted. What he needed was to really talk to someone. Maybe Jim?

Ed put his truck in gear and drove slowly out onto the narrow road down the mountain. At the monastery gate, he stopped the truck. For twenty-seven years he'd kept silent about his Minnesota life, quiet as those monks inside. Talk to somebody? After all this time? Silence had accumulated within him like drifts of snow.

PART ONE

ONE

A month later, Wednesday, January 18

FROST LINED THE inside of his front door. Ed groaned and scraped it off the window, then squinted at the thermometer outside. Eighteen-below zero. *I can't run in this*, he thought. He took off his running jacket and threw it against the couch. *Wimping out.* He'd never wear off the fat this way. He poured a cup of coffee and sat in front of the dark wood stove, depressed. He shivered. He needed to lose this damn weight. He shivered again, and realized the room was cold. The damn furnace must've gone off again, even though he'd fixed it before Christmas. The day after the Coliseum thing, actually. He tossed kindling and a couple of logs in the stove and they caught fast, roaring up, taking the edge off the chill. He went to the closet to re-set the pilot light. *Damn furnace.*

While he was doing that, the telephone rang.

"Who the hell?" he muttered, glancing at his watch. Four minutes after six. Who would it be at this hour? They can leave a damn message. He knelt beside the furnace and lit the pilot.

When the answering machine started, he knew her voice at once. Mara, his ex-wife. *This won't be good.* They had only spoken once, no more than five sentences, in twenty-seven years.

Her voice hadn't changed. Crisp, urgent, demanding, although she sounded tired. "Ed, you need to call me. It's important. It's about Gracie. I know you wouldn't lift a finger to help *me*, but you're a psychologist, after all, even if you're hiding out in Montana, and Gracie needs help. Call me."

I need to call you? he thought. *Like I need AIDS.* Who's Gracie? He thought back. Gracie was Mara's daughter, from one of her marriages. He and Mara had married in a blaze of sexual adventure, but after their newborn died, the fire guttered to ash. *There aren't shrinks in Minnesota?* He decided not to call back.

He'd only met Gracie – hadn't she been called Grace then? – once, when she was four. He'd gone back to Minneapolis for a conference and to visit his parents. It had been a bitterly cold January day, like today. Mara, dragging the little girl through the hotel lobby, saw him at the lobby bar and called his name. He'd liked how politely Grace smiled at him, and was astounded when, after awkward small talk, Mara had turned to Grace and said, "You stay here with Mr. Northrup, honey. Mommy will be back in a few minutes." Not a word to Ed, just a nod, simply assuming his willingness to babysit. He retrieved his beer from the bar and sat with the girl in the hotel lobby. Two hours later, long after he and Grace had run out of four-year-old conversation and the child was gnawing her lip and blotting a napkin with his Waterford pen, Mara emerged from the elevator on the arm of a distinguished-looking older man, her business obvious enough. She was laughing too much at something the white-haired man had said. She stopped in the lobby, collected Grace, thanked Ed briskly, and the three of them went out and entered a cab. That was the last time he'd spoken with Mara.

So, Grace is in trouble. He remembered the little girl's patience when they'd sat in the bar together, as if she were used to waiting for her mother, stroking her dolly's hair and playing politely with his pen. He sighed and dialed Mara's number.

No hello, just, "You didn't answer."

"Hello, Mara. You said you needed me to call." He felt defensive, which was not surprising. He was, after all, talking with Mara. How excited he'd been, in the beginning, to talk to Mara. He'd thought that was love.

"Yes, I did say that. Look, I'll get right to the point. Gracie attempted suicide yesterday."

Another kid going under. He felt the brush of desperation. *I can't bear another one.* He collected himself. "You said 'attempted.' I take it she didn't succeed?"

"Would I be calling you if she had?"

"Look, Mara, I don't know why you called me. I'm not there, and I can't do anything to help Grace. Gracie. I'm trying to be nice here – "

Mara interrupted. "You're right, Ed. I'm sorry. I'm just beside myself and I don't know what to do."

He softened. "Have you thought of taking her to a psychologist?"

"She's been seeing one for six months now. This isn't the first time, Ed. It's number two."

"What does the psychologist say?"

"That's why I called you. I need a second opinion. She thinks Gracie is using some drug, maybe meth. She also says that Grace is angry with me, I can't fathom why and the damn shrink won't tell me, some confidentiality bullshit. You would know all about *that.*" *Ouch. Low blow.*

She was going on. ". . . that Grace is doing these things to get my love. Believe you me, if that's the case, it's exactly the wrong strategy, if you ask me." Her voice rose, then she paused. "*Whatever.* I'm sorry, there I go again with my temper. I'm just soooo worried about her. You know how it is for a mother."

"No, Mara, I don't. But what did the psychologist say that you disagree with?"

"She thinks Gracie needs some residential program. Let me ask you, what good is she if she can't help a fourteen year old girl?"

He grimaced. Mara either was deliberately baiting him about what had happened with Elizabeth, or she was oblivious. He decided for oblivion. How others felt had never much concerned Mara.

Mara paused, then said, "Anyway, she wants to put Gracie into some program they've got out in your neighborhood, a school for girls with depression and drug problems and that kind of crap. I hate the idea."

"My neighborhood?"

"Utah? Oregon?"

"I'm in Montana, Mara. Utah and Oregon are hundreds of miles from here."

"Whatever. You're always so... *precise*. What do you think of her plan?"

Ed's annoyance bubbled up. "Hold on, Mara. You thought I was a lousy psychologist back in 1984, and I haven't worked with kids since, uh, Elizabeth died. Why ask my opinion now? Get a second opinion from someone back there. Ask Paul. He'll be glad to help you." Paul had been his business partner and closest colleague. They'd carried each other through grad school and set up a practice together after getting their degrees. Carlen and Northrup, Ltd.

There was a long silence at the other end. Then quiet sniffling. Ed stiffened. Mara's tears had always been a ploy. She said, finally, "I called *you* because I need *you*, Ed. I never really thought you were a lousy psychologist. I just wanted to push you away after the Elizabeth Murphy tragedy. Anyway, Paul won't talk to me."

He grunted. "Well, damn it, find someone else for your second opinion. There's nothing I can do, and I'm not interested." He hung up.

He expected her to call back, but she didn't. Waiting and watching the fire while he sipped coffee, he wondered what Grace was like. She'd been a sweet little girl, at least for the couple hours they'd spent in the lobby. He thought about Elizabeth, who'd been fourteen when it happened. His resentment of Mara faded into a fog of grief and guilt. He went into the bathroom.

Through the bathroom window, the January dawn backlit the still-black eastern mountains. Lodge pole pines on the long slope above the river were emerging in the dim light, frosted gray from the rising mist. He felt sadness ebbing around like fog drifting among cedars.

Ed ran the shower to warm up the bathroom, then stepped into the steam and let hot water cascade down his body for a long while before shampooing. What was Mara's motive? She was intelligent; she knew he couldn't help Grace at this distance. What did she *really* want?

No speculating, sport, he reminded himself, reaching for the shampoo.

Not my business.

As he toweled off, he thought about the morning. No run, no weight loss, the furnace acting up, Mara's damn call. A lousy start to the day.

*   *   *

The phone rang during his lunch break. Ed frowned and put down his leftover ribs and wiped his lips and fingers on a paper towel. "Northrup here."

"Greetings, pal. This a good time?" It was his friend Jim Hamilton, the priest at St. Bernard's.

"Four bites into my lunch," he mumbled.

"Sorry about that. When's better?"

"No time. I'm booked solid till four. What's up?" He looked sadly at the ribs cooling on the plate and the little pile of neatly stacked cookies beside them.

"One of the windows in the church cracked in this cold. Can you repair it?"

"I'm swamped, Jim." He didn't feel like helping, not today. Jim couldn't fix a bent paper clip, and Ed had repaired dozens of things at Jim's church over the years, but not today. He just wanted to go home and climb into bed.

"Hey, it's just a little window. Won't take you a half hour."

"What do I know about stained glass?"

"Not stained glass. Just one of those ordinary windows in the sacristy."

Ed sighed and took a bite of a rib, and mumbled through it, "I'm done here at four. That work?"

"Sure. Beggers can't be choosers, right?"

"Yeah. So go to the hardware store and get a pane of glass, some new glazing points, and glass putty."

"What size pane?"

"How the hell would I know?" he snapped. "Measure it. You can do *that*, can't you?" His harsh tone startled him. "I'm sorry, man."

"No problem. Hard day?"

Ed sighed. "Yeah. Too many hard days, maybe. Anyway, can you measure the window?"

"Yeah. I can handle that. I'll use one of those tape measure things." The priest chuckled.

"One of those." Ed sighed again. "So, four or so?"

"Perfect. Oh, another thing. What do you know about Maggie Sobstak? My organist?"

Ed closed his eyes. *This valley's too small.* Maggie Sobstak was a new patient of his, and he couldn't talk about her. In Monastery Valley, everybody's business was everybody's business. "I guess I have to say I'm not at liberty to say."

"Maggie's your patient, isn't she?"

"I'm not at liberty to say."

"Are you at liberty to give me some advice?"

"No, but that isn't going to stop you from asking."

Ed bit off another mouthful of rib meat and listened. Jim said, "She's been erratic, or maybe preoccupied's the word. Last Sunday, she came late for Mass, and she botched the hymns she did play. It's not like her."

Ed thought back over his three sessions with her. Nothing dramatic, just a middle-aged woman unhappy with her husband, Victor, who she thought was cheating. Even if he wasn't, she'd run short of tolerance for Vic's sudden disappearances.

"I can't say anything, Jim." He swallowed the meat, which thickened his voice. "Has she mentioned anything to you?"

The priest hesitated. "You eating? Watch your weight, pal." Ed held his tongue, annoyed again.

Jim said, "Anyway, no. She hasn't said a word. Maggie's not one to say much about herself. I'll talk to her tomorrow night after choir practice."

Ed felt the weary bitterness rise up. *Another one to worry about.* Without thinking, he said, "Does this stuff get you down, Jim?" The priest always seemed calm and optimistic. "How do you stay so cheerful, listening to people day after day?"

Jim chuckled. "Who listens?" He paused. "You having some trouble, buddy?"

He thought of the Coliseum. "The job's getting to me. There's too much pain going around. I probably need a vacation." He remembered looking into the void through the tip of that snowshoe, felt his heart race, and thought of his promise to talk to someone. "No, I need to talk. You care if now and again I give you a call? Just to share trade secrets?"

"Love to, man. Maybe we can talk after the window?"

Ed's twelve-thirty patient, Glady Allen, cleared her throat loudly in the waiting room. He glanced at the clock: two minutes past her time. Glady did not tolerate even a minute lost from her hour, and he hadn't finished the ribs or even touched the cookies. "Gotta go, Jim. Patient waiting." He sighed as he shoved the unfinished lunch into its bag and opened the door for Glady, who did not live up to her name.

*   *   *

Promptly at four o'clock, Ed tossed the uneaten ribs in the trash, stuffed the cookies he'd missed at lunch in his jacket pocket, and locked his office door. It was one of three on one side of a nondescript building on Division Street, the main street in Jefferson, the county seat and only town in the valley. The Adams County Sheriff's Department occupied the entire other side of the building, which was bisected by a wide hallway. Ed's was the middle office on this side, with Oliver Tweedy's law office beside him to the front, and Ed's accountant Leese MacArdell's to the back. Only the Sheriff's Department had a receptionist, Callie Martin, who doubled as the Sheriff's Department dayshift dispatcher, 911 contact, and overall building mother. Oliver Tweedy's paralegal, Ardyss Conley, came in every day, boxing up the practice. Oliver had died, eighty-seven years old, two weeks ago. Ed wondered what would become of Ardyss. Going out, he waved at Callie through the Department's glass doors. She beckoned him in.

"Where you off to, handsome?"

Ed stuck his head in the door and blew her a kiss. "Off to see the Wizard, Callie." She grimaced and shooed him out. Callie was in her mid-fifties, thin as a sapling, lightly freckled, and given to thick red lipstick and a liberal dose of eye shadow, and she knew everything going on in the office, in town, and in the valley.

Ed went down the hall to the back door, which opened onto the parking lot. Just as he started to pull on the handle, the door burst open and Sheriff Ben Stewart pushed in along with billowing bitter air.

"Damn, that's cold!" Ben growled, slamming the door.

"January runs on the cold side. Don't sheriffs like cold?" Ed said.

"Why the hell would we like cold?"

"Keeps the bad guys home, I'd imagine."

Ben snorted. "Keep dreamin'. When it's cold, bad guys do bad things indoors." Ed smiled, but didn't quite feel it.

"Where you headin'?" Ben asked.

"Over to St. Bernie's. Jim's got a broken window."

Ben grinned. "Jim's a good guy, but he sure ain't the handiest." He stepped out of Ed's way. "You be careful drivin'. It's a bastard out there."

"I'm fine. The truck's in good shape and I've got my phone. I'll call you personally if I break down."

"You do that, and I just might send Deputy Sheriff Pelton out to rescue your ass."

Andrea Pelton was the only female deputy sheriff in the valley. Since she came to the Department eight months ago from Chicago, Ben had been trying to get Ed to take her out. She was attractive enough, Ed thought. Her right ear was disfigured, like someone took a bite out of it. She was too thick for Ed's taste, which ran on the slender side. Like his accountant, Leese, who was tall, lithe, and athletic.

Or like nobody, he thought. *How long's it been since I wanted to be with a woman?*

Looking even more rotund than usual in his parka and huge fur hat, Ben pulled open the door and clapped Ed on the shoulder, then shoved him out into the cold. "We still on the corner tonight at the Angler?" he called to Ed's retreating back.

"Absolutely, Ben. See you there about six," Ed shouted back.

"Over and out," Ben waved and slammed the door.

*   *   *

Same time

As she climbed out of the warm black-and-gold in front of the Angler, the frigid air slapped Deputy Andrea Pelton's face. Since lunch, she'd been patrolling north of town along some of the older roads. Just after four, her radio had squawked.

"Andi? Callie here. You out there? Come in, please."

Andi, annoyed, had reached over and lifted the microphone. "Deputy Pelton here. What's up, Dispatch?"

Callie's informality rattled her; hell, the whole department's informality rattled her. She'd told Ben that without radio discipline, some yahoo might hijack the frequency to lure a deputy someplace and fire a round into the vehicle. "Won't happen out here, Andi," he'd assured her, stifling his smile. But it had happened back in Cook County. She'd been cruising South Kedzie, when the too-casual voice on her radio, not following protocol, reported a child wandering on the road near the Markham Preserve. Andi had switched on her light bar, u-turned, and sped there. A rifle shot from the woods blasted through her windshield and banged around the cab. She ducked, swerved the squad, controlled the skid. The bullet had settled in the back seat, but the fear ricocheted a lot longer.

Then came another shooting, just ten days after her new husband stayed too long in their bed with the other woman she wasn't supposed to walk in and find. After that, she'd pulled the plug on her life in Illinois and answered the ad in *Sheriff Magazine* for the position out here in the mountains. It'll be safer, she'd told herself, but so far nowhere was feeling safe.

Whenever Ben teased her, she blushed. The valley seemed peaceful enough, but she couldn't shake the need for protocol, for procedures, for sharp uniform creases. These were her armor. True, the people – so far – seemed more or less friendly, and, judging from the routine speeders and the minor drug busts, tame as the cattle they raised. Even the drunks were mostly polite, but the informal valley ways hadn't yet softened her starch.

Callie came back, her voice tight: "Hightail it over to the Angler, would ya, Andi? Ted's got hisself a drunk event goin' on. Over."

Andi smiled. A drunk event? "Roger that, Dispatch. The Angler. On my way. Out." *Hightail it?* They'd never believe it back in Cook County.

*   *   *

She moved quickly toward the Angler Bar's big pine door, shivering. This cold wasn't the swirling cocky damp-city wind of a Chicago January, but a chill that flowed down a thousand miles of ice and froze the air. She smiled, thinking *drunk event*, and pulled open the Angler's heavy door. Warm smells from the kitchen blended with the tang of burning logs in the fireplace. The old bar room on the right – the original Angler Bar, low and cozy with smoke-darkened pine – was a nice contrast to the exposed brick and blond beams of the renovated dining room ahead. For a moment, Andi let herself enjoy the contrast – she'd once thought of studying architecture, and this place was pleasing to her eye.

Then, she pushed through the swinging half-doors into the bar. *Here comes the Sheriff,* she thought. Matt Dillon pushing in through Miss Kitty's swinging doors, genders reversed.

Two older men sat at one of the tables near the fire. She hadn't met them, but they were minding their own business, and didn't look drunk. The one facing her touched his cap politely.

The bartender, Ted – Ted Coldry, she reminded herself of his last name – waved her in. He nodded to the end of the bar, near the fire. A figure slumped there. A graying head, hair sticking up, rested on jacketed arms folded on the bar. The jacket was thick, worked-in, elbow-frayed, and a hand-knit scarf bunched around the neck. One Sorel-booted foot had slipped off the bar stool and dragged on the floor; the other hooked on a rung. The pants were gray nubby wool, with rumpled cuffs. Andi thought they looked very old. And very warm. "Sheriff," Ted intoned loudly, more for the figure's benefit than Andi's, "this is Mrs. Margaret Sobstak." He tapped the bar in front of the figure. "Maggie! Wake up. The sheriff's here to talk to you." Margaret Sobstak didn't stir. He turned back to Andi and shrugged. "Out like a light. I served her one drink – "

He gestured toward the half-full glass in front of her. "Half's all she's had. Passed out cold. I think she must've had something before she came in."

One of the old men stood up and walked stiffly over. He extended his hand.

"Afternoon, Miss. I'm Doc Runge, retired. I suggested Ted give your department a call. Mrs. Sobstak here is drunk, or worse. What's unusual is that, to my knowledge, she doesn't drink. I suspect she'll need more than a night in the tank."

Andi smiled. "Now that you mention it, I don't think I've been shown the female tank, Doctor."

"Everybody calls me Doc, and yes, you have – it's the men's. Just the one." He chuckled. "Anyway, thanks for your prompt response, young lady." He patted her forearm sweetly and returned to his table. The other older gentleman was watching curiously, and he smiled and touched the brim of his hat politely. Andi almost said, "Yeah, I *hightailed* it." Almost.

She laid a hand on Margaret Sobstak's arm. "Ms. Sobstak?" Was she breathing? Looking back toward Ted, Andi asked, "What'd she drink?"

"Beam and Coke. She slurred the order a little, so I went light on the Beam."

Andi nodded. More roughly, this time, she nudged the woman's shoulder and said, "Ms. Sobstak! Ms. Sobstak! Margaret!" The woman grunted and shifted on the bar stool, but remained unconscious.

Andi asked Ted, "Who is she?" Not knowing everyone in the valley left Andi feeling vulnerable.

"She and her husband, Victor, own old Charley Wright's spread, just north of town. Vic was the foreman at the CW till Charley got cancer and sold it to them on a contract. It's been, I don't know, maybe ten years now? Doc?"

Doc Runge nodded. "Yep. Charley died about eight years ago now."

Andi tried to get a look at Mrs. Sobstak's face, but it remained buried in her arms. She had graying hair. "How old is she?"

Ted frowned. "I don't know exactly, but probably early fifties."

"Any kids?"

He shook his head. "Not that I know of. They're life-long ranch people, married to cattle." He considered. "Maggie's also the organist over at St. Bernie's. She's been playing the hymns there for, oh, probably eight or nine years. I guess they need the extra income, such as it is."

"Does she drink a lot?" She glanced at Doc Runge, but he and the other man were talking quietly.

Ted shook his head vehemently. "I can't imagine it. She's never been in the bar before, just the restaurant." He gestured toward the other room. "Maggie Sobstak, as far as I know, is one of the nicest ladies in the valley."

Andi shook Maggie's shoulder more roughly, and the older woman stirred a bit and tilted her head up, one unfocused eye half opened. Andi thought of the red-brown eyes of the alkies on South Kedzie. The gray hair was stiff and spiky, as if she'd slept on it wet.

"Who you?" the woman slurred.

"I'm Deputy Sheriff Pelton, Ms. Sobstak. Can you wake up a little more?" Maggie tried to lift herself off the bar but her head rose only a few inches. She squinted sideways at Pelton and growled, "You jus' go as' Ed Northru'." She licked her lips, as if the consonants were sticking to them. "You as' North... u'. He'll... tell ya wha's... goin'... on." Her head sagged down onto her crossed arms and she snored once, then sputtered, and went still. Andi shook her again, and put her fingers on her neck, searching for a pulse.

With her other hand, Andi flipped open her cell phone. "Dispatch, Deputy Pelton here. Can you call the Dew Drop Inn and Buck's Lounge and ask if Margaret Sobstak has been there drinking?"

Callie's voice came back offended. "Number one, Deputy, my name is Callie, not 'Dispatch.' Number two, did you say Maggie? She's a church lady. She don't hardly drink."

Exasperated, Andi looked up at the wooden nude sculpted at the top of the back-bar. "Callie, just do it, please? And call me back." She rolled her eyes toward Ted, looking for support, although he could not hear the exchange.

Ted looked concerned. "She didn't get it here, Deputy."

Andi felt a twinge of loneliness that Ted hadn't used her name. "Call me Andi, okay, Ted? When did she come in?"

"Maybe 25 minutes ago. She walked well enough, but when she sat down and ordered, she was pretty slurry, so I made it real light. Halfway into the drink, she just collapsed."

"She was drunk, but you served her anyway?" She tried not to sound accusatory. Before Ted could answer, her cell rang. "Pelton."

Callie, business-like, rubbed it in. "*Dispatch* here. Buck, 'n then Judy at the Dew Drop, they both say Maggie Sobstak ain't never been in their place. Buck said, and this is a direct quote, 'Maggie Sobstak? Jesus Christ, she's dry as a spinster's pussy.'"

Andi flinched. *Am I a spinster? At forty-six?* She said, "Thanks, Callie. So she wasn't either place?"

"I'm thinkin' that's what I said." Crisp and frosted. Fences needed mending. Andi sighed.

"Okay, then. Thank you. Now, could you patch me through to Ed Northrup's office?"

Callie chuckled. "Ed drinkin' too?"

"No, Callie. Just patch me through." Exasperation tinged Andi's voice; she tried to tone it down.

Callie snorted, frosting up again, and the line went silent. Then a ring, and Doctor Northrup's message answered and she left the details and her number and asked him to call her back.

"Ted, I want to get her to the hospital." She glanced at Doc Runge, who nodded and said, "What I'd do." Ted reached behind the back-bar for his jacket. Together they lifted Maggie off the stool and drunk-walked her toward the door. Her feet dragged.

The cold air outside the big door slapped her momentarily awake. "'s goin' on?" She passed out again as they stuffed her into the back seat of the squad.

"Thanks, Ted." She dialed her cell phone again. "Callie? Would you call Doc Keeley and ask him to – " Andi thought a moment. " – to hightail it over to the ER?" Might as well acclimate.

"Will do," Callie said, ice in her tone. Andi sighed after she hung up.

Ted looked sad. "I probably shouldn't have served her even the one, Deputy, uh, Andi," he said. He shivered.

Andi put her hand on his arm. "Duck back in the warm, Ted.

Whatever happened to her isn't your fault."

Even though it was only six blocks from the Angler to the hospital on the south end of town, Andi fingered the light bar switch. Her snapping at Callie over protocol embarrassed her. She could hear her father's voice: "Nothing worse'n a tight ass cop." Tight ass. She lifted her finger off the switch. Although the light bar was standard procedure for this, she left it off. Loosening the ass a little couldn't hurt.

*   *   *

In the ER, Doctor Keeley came in just as they finished taking blood. Looking at Maggie's body on the gurney, he said, "Betcha we got point-2 or better." Andi frowned.

She called Callie at Dispatch again. "Callie, sorry to bother you again."

"What a dispatcher does. *Dispatches*."

Andi rolled her eyes. "Got it. So can you get me Ed Northrup's cell phone number?"

Callie's voice was cold. "That'd be affirmative, Deputy."

Andi waited a moment before asking, "Then will you?" She paused, then added, "Please?"

A moment of silence passed, then Callie came back with the number.

Andi punched it into her cell and waited while it rang. His message came on.

At the beep, she repeated the message she'd left on his office phone, asking Ed to meet her at the hospital, or to call her.

Matt Dillon brings in a drunk, she said to herself, and sighed. *Alone.*

TWO

That Afternoon

ED'S TIRES, FROZEN flat on one side from sitting in the frigid lot, thumped on each rotation, bumping faster as he picked up speed. St. Bernard's was only a few blocks down Division Street. He decided to run out into the valley, though, to warm the engine and the cab, before stopping at Jim's to fix the glass. As the tires warmed, their thumping faded, but every crack in the highway jolted up through the truck's cold stiff metal to his hands on the wheel. *I'm driving an ice cube tray.* He pushed the speed to seventy-five. The highway stretched south down the valley like a straightedge laid across a rumpled sheet. At the base of Mount Adams, the southern end of the valley, the highway narrowed, climbed, and ended at the Coliseum trailhead, across the lake from the monastery.

The setting sun reddened the cornice of snow above the Coliseum, Mount Adams' gouged upper face, and his mood darkened, remembering that December Sunday. He slowed and turned onto the drive to the StreamSide Lodge, a fishing resort built in the 1980s by Magnus Anderssen, the valley's leading rancher. The Lodge was closed for the season, but the freshly plowed road sloped down to the river, into a grove of cottonwood trees, bare and black in the near-dark. Maybe the solitude would lift his mood.

He stood on the bank for a few moments, listening to water running under the thick ice. He heard his cell phone ring back in the truck, but ignored it. When the cold finally cut through, he felt no better, and climbed back into his truck. Time to fix a broken window.

As he turned onto the highway, the lights of Jefferson sparkled in the distant center of the valley. While he drove toward them, he listened to the message. It was Deputy Pelton, so he called her back. "Deputy Pelton? This is Doctor Northrup. You called about Maggie Sobstak?"

When she told him the situation and asked him to stop at the hospital, Ed winced. "Frankly, I've got no idea what to say," he said, then stopped himself. When she waited him out, he sighed and said, "Look, I'm on my way to do a favor for someone. Can this wait?"

"Sure. How long do you think?" She obviously expected him to come today.

Resentment – another demand, another person with needs – moved inside him like a surly dog, his *black dog*. "Give me an hour." He tried to keep his voice neutral. It wasn't her fault, or Maggie Sobstak's. *I gotta talk to Jim.*

*   *   *

Ten minutes later, he pulled up to St. Bernard's rectory, directly across Division Street from the Community Hospital. *While I fix the window, I'll tell Jim about the burnout.* As he leaned into the back of the cab for his tool box, his heavy stomach strained against his belt. He sucked it in. Jim Hamilton, close to Ed's age, had no paunch. *If I weren't handy, maybe I'd be skinnier.* He smiled at how stupid that was. Jim opened the door as he climbed the porch steps and handed him a cup of coffee. "You hear a good joke?" he asked.

Ed inhaled the savory steam. "No, just laughing at myself." He sipped. "Good coffee."

The priest nodded. "Egg coffee. You put in the grounds, break an egg onto them and boil away. An old Swedish nun taught me. You ready to fix my window?" Ed shook his head. He wanted to talk about his depression.

Jim poured himself a cup and sat down at the table. "While you sip, let me pick your brain."

Ed frowned. *Speak up*, he urged himself.

"Maggie Sobstak's over at the hospital. Alcohol intoxication."

Ed nodded. "I know. Deputy Pelton called me about her."

"Thing is, Maggie doesn't drink. She takes an occasional whiskey and water, but I've never known her drunk."

Ed squirmed. "I can't talk about Maggie, Jim. Anyway, you know more about her than I do."

The priest shook his head. "That's just it. I don't know squat about this."

Ed looked at the gag clock on the kitchen wall – all the numbers were fives. The hands translated to twenty-five past four. "Let's go fix that window."

As they walked through the covered arcade to the church, Ed said, "I was climbing the Coliseum back in December. I went up there to – "

Jim interrupted him. "Save that thought, Ed. You know with Maggie out for a while, I'm short an organist."

Although the interruption annoyed him, Ed felt relieved he hadn't actually said anything about his near-suicide, if that was what it was. He said, "I really can't talk about Maggie."

"Not asking you to, bud. You used to play the organ, right?" Jim held open the church door and pointed behind the altar at the sacristy door.

Ed stopped walking and glared at him. "Don't even *think* about it. I haven't touched a keyboard in thirty years." He hesitated, then forced himself to go on.

"Besides, there's something I need to talk about."

"It's only hymns. *Anybody* can play hymns! Come on, I need help here!"

Ed didn't answer. *I need some help too,* he thought. They entered the sacristy, and he put his toolbox on a counter and pulled off the taped cardboard covering the broken pane. After he'd inspected the old crackled putty, and looked at the other panes, he said, "The putty's gone to hell on all these windows. Better tell your parish council to hire a couple of high school kids this summer."

"About the organ..."

"Damn it, Jim, drop it!" he burst out. He felt himself blush.

Jim looked surprised. "I'm sorry, Ed. I'm not listening. What's going on?"

Ed pulled a putty knife out of his toolbox, scraped off the cracked and chipping putty around the broken pane, and used a long-nose pliers to extract the glazing points. He found it hard to answer. "I've, uh, been a little, uh, down lately. Just thought it'd be good to talk about it."

"A little down? You're poor butt's has been dragging for months. Hell, years."

Ed pulled out the remaining broken glass and scraped clean the frame without saying anything. "Where's that pane?"

Hamilton handed it to him, and Ed bedded it in the frame. "Good fit, you measured right." He tapped in the glazing points. Rolling a ball of putty between his hands to form a rope, he pressed the rope across the top. Repeating that for the other sides, he smoothed the putty and neatly creased the corners. "Done." He wiped his hands on his pants.

Jim had waited, leaning against a big oak cupboard, his arms folded. There was a faint smile on his lips. "Not done," he said softly. "What's bothering you?"

The embarrassment flared again. Ed replaced his tools in the box. *Say something,* he demanded of himself, but he held back. His mother's voice: *Don't whine, Eddie. Whining is unbecoming.*

"Look," he said. "Let's make a date to talk. I've, uh, got to run."

Jim looked skeptical. "Why not right now?"

Ed shook his head. "I'm on the corner with Ben at six, and I promised Deputy Pelton I'd come by the hospital when I got done here. How about sometime next week?"

"You don't see patients on Friday. Let's do it then. I'll make coffee."

Ed felt cornered. "Got an emergency Friday. Can't."

Jim arched an eyebrow. "Uh-huh." He picked up his own cup and Ed's, and said, "Okay, I get it. So, Monday after work?"

"Sure," Ed said, inwardly cursing his cowardice.

*   *   *

Deputy Pelton stood when Ed walked into the ER waiting room. Shaking her hand, it occurred to him something wasn't quite right about her. He'd seen her a few times in the Department, but never this close. Her light hair was cut short and curly, framing a strong face, with an engaging smile and smooth skin, tanned even now in winter. Her looks were fine, although the notch in her right earlobe was hard to miss. She spoke in facts, but her hazel eyes were all smiles. Attractive, but her head seemed – this was it – just a bit too small for her body, which resembled a column from the shoulders down. Deputy Pelton had no waist.

"Thanks for coming by, Doctor," she said. He liked her voice, smooth and calm. The voice of a woman used to handling trouble.

"Please, call me Ed. So what's going on with Maggie?" he asked.

She was filling him in when Doc Keeley bustled into the small conference room. "Blood alcohol's point-one-nine. Not a chance she got there on half a Beam and Coke." He nodded to Ed. "Hey, Ed. What can you tell us?"

"Not much, I'm afraid. Ethically, nothing." Point-one-nine hinted at something ugly, didn't it? Ed thought about it: A non-drinker awash in alcohol, with no known reason. He slumped in the chair. Maybe a suicide attempt? A risk he'd missed? *Damn*, he decided. *This trumps confidentiality.*

"I don't know anything that would explain this. Maggie's mildly depressed, because she thinks Vic's been running around with another woman. She admits she hasn't got any real evidence."

"Vic's the husband?" Andi asked, then put her hand up to stop him. "Wait, I know. Sorry."

He nodded. "I gather he might be under some kind of stress." He stopped himself. This wasn't about Vic. He had no right to speculate.

"Really? What kind of stress?" she asked.

Ed hesitated, but Keeley interjected. "Vic's been a foreman since before God turned Catholic. I've seen him in here a couple times. He thinks he's having a heart attack, but his heart's strong as they come. It's anxiety."

Andi turned to Ed. "What's Vic anxious about?"

"I don't think I should speculate about Vic."

"This might be about him."

Ed shook his head. "Consider the possibility that Maggie tried to kill herself."

Andi looked at him intently. "Do you think that's a possibility?"

Ed felt helpless. "No, not really. And she wouldn't use alcohol to do it."

"So we're back to Vic."

"Why do you say that?" Keeley asked.

Andi turned to him. "When I picked her up at the Angler, there were two vehicles parked in front. One was either Doctor Runge's or his friend's, unless it was hers."

Ed said, "What was the car?"

"Ford Taurus, probably late 80s."

Ed and Doc Keeley shook their heads at the same time. "No, that's Connie Fuller's." When she looked puzzled, he added, "Doc Runge's friend. They have one beer at the Angler every afternoon."

"Okay. And the other vehicle was my squad. Maggie sure didn't walk ten miles in this cold with that much booze in her. Somebody dropped her off. Vic's the obvious guess."

Ed ran his hand over his hair. "Good point. Well, I don't know much else about him, beyond her thinking he's having an affair." He felt terrible saying even that, and whatever was going on with Maggie, he'd obviously missed it. "I know Vic to say hi to, and we've worked a few Fourth of July fireworks, but that's it.

Always seemed like a good guy."

Keeley excused himself. "Gotta go sober up my patient."

Andi looked at her watch. "Almost six o'clock. Time for a visit to Mr. Sobstak."

Ed said, "I thought your shifts end at four."

"Shifts end," Andi smiled. "Work doesn't."

*   *   *

At the Angler Bar, Ben Stewart's haunches amiably overflowed his regular stool at the corner of Ted Coldry's bar, and the ale still foamed in his glass. Ed clapped him on the back and sat down beside him.

He nodded to the bartender. "The usual, Ted."

Ted had started pouring as soon as Ed came in. Ed and Ben had been meeting here for a couple beers almost every Wednesday for twenty years. Ben met on the corner with one citizen or another every weekday evening, keeping his finger on the pulse of the valley. This was his method of campaigning for re-election. "If I spread it out over four years," he'd once told Ed, "and talk to most of the men in the valley, come votin' time, they know I know what they need and they know I'll come through for 'em. Ain't no need to make a bunch of damn speeches. Everybody *knows* what I think, from sittin' on the corner."

But Ben sat on the corner with Ed, Wednesdays, for friendship, not business.

Seven years ago, Ted and his partner, Lane Martin, had bought the old Angler Bar and remodeled the falling-down burgers-and-fries side of the bar into a city-class dining room of brick and blond beams. There, the valley business people and ranchers and cowboys and their wives could get a glass of good wine and lean close and murmur and then eat a good meal and sit back and laugh out loud like the sophisticates over in Missoula. The wives appreciated the civilized feel of the place, and their men, whose hearts were seldom as rough as their hands, appreciated the pleasure the Angler's new dining room brought to their women.

Ted coastered a Fat Tire in front of Ed. Ben lifted his mug and nodded at the bartender. "To the only gay fella whose beer I'll drink in this town."

Ted chortled. "Buck won't like that." Buck DeWitt was the town's other male bar owner.

"Buck don't pour beer, he pours Budweiser. And accordin' to half the heifers in Monastery Valley, he also ain't gay."

Laughing, Ed clinked his glass with Ben's.

Ben asked, "You and my deputy get everything sorted out over at the hospital?"

Ed began to tell him about Maggie Sobstak, but Ben interrupted. "My point is, did you ask Andi out yet? You couldn't get a better chance."

Ed sighed. "No, Ben, I didn't. You know as well as I do I'm not in the market."

"Come on. What's wrong with Andi? I know you ain't gay."

Ed rolled his eyes at Ben. "And you know *that* how?"

"Well, for starters, you ain't hit on Ted here, right, Ted?"

From down the bar, Ted mock-sighed. "I've felt so wounded, Edward."

Ed shook his head and lifted up his hands. "Drop it, can we? Andi's cute enough, but to me she's a bit, uh, bulky. Anyway, I'm not interested in dating."

Ben sputtered, beer spraying on the bar. "Bulky?" He wiped his lips. "Did you say *bulky*?"

"She's got no waist."

Ben looked at Ted; both men grinned.

"*What?*" Ed demanded.

Ben said to Ted, "I gotta go melt some ice. You be so kind as to brief our friend Dr. N. here on the, uh, contours of the situation?"

Ted nodded. "Pleased, Sheriff."

Ben grunted and lifted his weight off his stool and ambled, a bear entering his den, down the small hallway toward the men's room.

Ted leaned his elbows on the bar across from Ed, voice low, personal. "It seems that in Chicago, Andrea was shot at a couple times. It's why she moved out here."

"I didn't know that."

"Apparently, she's still a bit on the leery side. On duty she wears a vest."

Light dawned. "A *bullet-proof* vest."

Ted nodded and straightened and moved down to his end of the bar. "She's slim-and-trim as a lady comes, Edward." He was chuckling, then glanced at Ed's midriff. "And one wonders whether pondering waists might not more usefully start with your own."

"Ouch."

Ben eased back down on his stool, a hen roosting. He turned to Ed. "Ted set you straight?"

"You referring to Deputy Pelton's bullet-proof vest?"

"The same. So how about you just loosen up and take a shot at her."

"Nice choice of words, Ben," Ed said. "But I'm not interested in taking a shot at anybody."

"Whatever happened to that girl up in the capital? The politician?"

"The campaign consultant. We both got tired of the drive. We're friends."

Ben meditated on his beer. "Pitiful. *Friends*. A man needs a woman for something other 'n friends."

Ed bristled, but Ben was only trying to help, so he said nothing.

"So, why not – "

"Just stop, Ben, okay?" he snapped. "Quit pushing it." But the vision of his snowshoe extending into emptiness came to mind. Was loneliness the toxin infecting his depression? Was it that simple?

Other than the job, Ed thought he enjoyed his life. He'd built his own cabin and loved doing it. The place was a pleasure to live in, except for the damn furnace. He and Magnus Anderssen or Ben or Jim hunted and fished in season, and long hikes in the mountains, or climbing the Coliseum, invigorated him. Or used to. He had his books. Through the year, he volunteered on the committees for the many events that made small-town life convivial. And always he went home alone, and read his books alone. Maybe Ben was right. And maybe not.

*   *   *

The long day, the two Fat Tires at the Angler, and the numbing cold added up to deep fatigue by the time Ed pulled into his yard on the crest of the ridge. He'd be glad to climb in bed. He would run in the morning, although morning would come too soon. He felt empty. "Baloney," he muttered. "You're not empty, you're depressed."

The cabin was cold again. *Damn furnace!* But the pilot light was lit. He didn't have the energy to start a fire, so he cranked up the thermostat and the furnace groaned to life. The phone rang. He considered letting it ring, but it might be a patient. He sighed and picked it up, and when he heard her voice, he snapped awake.

Mara, again, despite his hangup this morning. "It was rude to hang up on me."

"What do you want, Mara?"

"I want you to help Gracie."

"No. I'm twelve-hundred miles away. If your psychologist is right and she's doing meth, not to mention depressed enough to attempt suicide, she needs more than I can provide, even if she were here. Talk to Paul."

"I told you, Paul won't talk to me.

"Why not?"

There was another long pause, then the sound of sniffling. "I wasn't having an affair with Marty when I left you; you assumed that when I married him later. I was sleeping with Paul."

Gut-punched, Ed pressed the phone against his chest. Paul! His friend, his partner. He tried to catch a breath. His hand gripping the phone was white. He curbed the hard rage filling him, breathing heavily. The handset felt heavy as a hammer. He lifted it to his ear. "So why this call, Mara? A good night for confession?"

"That's uncalled for. I'm admitting things here. I meant it when I said that I need you, Ed." She paused, and Ed pictured her reading from a script. "If you want to know the truth, I called because I miss you." *Really,* he thought.

She was going on. "I was thinking, if Gracie's shrink thinks the Western air would do her good, maybe we could come out to where you are and spend some time. Maybe get reacquainted."

"Forget it, Mara! I've got a life here. I don't need to mess it up walking down memory lane with you."

"A life? As in a wife? A girlfriend?"

He closed his eyes. Mara would think that. Mutual friends told him she'd had five husbands so far, and when a marriage failed, her preferred method of coping was to turn the latest boyfriend into the latest husband, and in due time, the latest divorce. Over the years, those friends had hinted, she'd become quite wealthy in the process.

"Look, Mara, your psychologist's right. If there's drug use and suicide attempts, and outpatient treatment isn't cutting it, a residential program's the next step. She has to go somewhere. Here's out of the question. I can't treat her and there's no one else here." He thought of Rosemary Rasmussen, the social worker in town, then dropped it. Having Mara anywhere near him in Monastery Valley was not an option.

Mara waited a long moment, then said, "Ed, think it over. You owe me at least that much."

He slammed his hand against the wall. "I *owe* you?" He kept his voice as even as he could, which wasn't very even. "Mara, we had a few good months, then you started your affairs, and when you left, you took our money. I don't owe you a damn thing."

"Well, don't be sour. You're not the sort of man to refuse to help a child."

He took a breath. "No, Mara, I am exactly that sort of man. Listen to Gracie's shrink." And he hung up. But he pictured the little four year old girl, quietly talking to him in the hotel lobby, brushing her dolly's hair. *Little girl, I hope Mara finds somebody for you.*

THREE

Thursday, January 19

DEPUTY ANDI PELTON woke at dawn, and went to the kitchen to make coffee. Through the kitchen window, she watched the sky lighten over the Washington Mountains. The trees were frosted again this morning. Still cold. This morning hour, quiet and untouched, had always been her favorite. After her mother had died, on Andi's sixteenth birthday, being alone eventually became as natural as breathing, even when it grew lonesome. Being alone felt strong, bolstered a quiet confidence in herself. Before dying, her mother had been ill for five years, had lain alone in her darkened bedroom for days at a stretch, and Andi had navigated the early churnings of adolescence without her. As her mother's condition deteriorated, and the days in bed lengthened into weeks and her body shrank and withered, Andi's anguish encased her aloneness with emotional steel.

One evening, her father had said, "It can't last much longer. It just *can't*." Andi took that and the tears in his eyes as confirmation of her own sorrow over her mother's pain. So, when Anne's death finally released them all, Andi took it as her mother's birthday gift. Aloneness, from that time, had become her most dependable memorial to her mom, a source of secret pride.

The sun lifted above the mountains. Across the valley, the western range glowed, rose-colored. Andi smiled. *A beautiful place,* she thought. *Maybe a safe place too.*

*   *   *

Later, at the department, Callie Martin was cool. "Mornin', *Deputy* Pelton." Andi gave an awkward grin. "Morning, Callie. Another cold day."

Callie nodded judiciously. "Ma'am, it is."

Andi clocked in, then returned and leaned on the counter. "Look, Callie, I'm sorry about yesterday."

"Nothin' to be sorry about." Callie's eyes took in the thickness of the vest under Andi's uniform shirt.

"Well, I need to lighten up a bit, and I might as well get started with you." Callie nodded slightly. "That'll be nice." But she didn't smile.

Andi sighed. *This might take some time.* She might be fine alone, but a friend wouldn't hurt.

*   *   *

On morning patrol, Andi's first stop was the hospital. No doubt, Maggie Sobstak would be hungover, but maybe she'd be up to a conversation. When Andi peeked in, though, she was asleep on her back, snoring softly, her mouth open. Andi walked to the nurse's desk and stood quietly while the nurse continued reading a chart, studiously not looking up. *Just like nurses in Chicago. Hell, just like anybody at a desk in Chicago.* After a long moment, Andi said, "Excuse me?"

The nurse looked up slowly. "Yes?"

"I'm Deputy Pelton from the sheriff's office. I need to talk with Mrs. Sobstak, so could I ask you to give me a ring when she wakes up?"

The nurse said, "Doctor Keeley is making rounds about eleven o'clock this morning. Why don't you come back then? We'll be waking her up."

*   *   *

Maggie lay as still as she could. Any move hurt. *I'm a damn fool,* she started in on herself. Even thinking hurt. Her breath was ragged, but she stretched it out to keep her head from throbbing worse. *It ain't like me. Not just the drinking, the whole thing. Thinkin' Victor was runnin' around. It ain't like me to think that about him. He's a good man.*

She stilled herself again, the bile rising in her throat. *Just what I deserve, lyin' here sick as a dog.* She felt a tear run out the corner of her eye. *I don't hardly drink.* A flash of anger at Vic scared her. *Why? Why'd he do this?*

Just then, a knock came on the door. "Who's there?" she croaked, then groaned.

A woman stuck her head in, and after the head came a body in a uniform. "Hi, Mrs. Sobstak, it's me, Deputy, uh, Andi Pelton from the sheriff's office. May I come it?"

"Do I know you?"

"No, ma'am, you probably don't. We met yesterday, but you were pretty, ah, sick."

Maggie grimaced. "Not as sick as I am today."

"I'll bet. Do you feel up to answering a few questions?"

What questions does a deputy got for me? Maggie felt a chill, fear mostly, but nausea too. "Why? I do somethin' illegal?" *None of this is me. None of it. I'm a good woman. I visit the sick in the hospital, I ain't one of 'em.*

"No, ma'am, not at all. It's just that we're puzzled about some of the particulars of what happened yesterday."

That frightened her again. *People are talkin' already.* "Who's this *we?*"

"Myself, and Sheriff Stewart, and Dr. Northrup."

Maggie's stomach belched. She tried to control it, made it sound like a grunt. "Ed Northrup. Ben Stewart. You." Her voice came out disgusted, although she didn't want it to. It just did. "Maybe you all can keep your questions to yourself. Never knew Ben Stewart to get all fussed up over somebody gettin' herself drunk." Her vehemence surprised her. *I'm scared. This ain't happenin'.*

The deputy asked politely, "May I sit down?"

"Suit yourself." Maggie noticed the look in the deputy's eyes. They made a little squint, like she was mad.

"Mrs. Sobstak, what you drank at the Angler wasn't enough to cause the level of alcohol you had in your blood. And we know that someone dropped you off at the Angler because your car wasn't there."

Alarm flickered in Maggie's chest. Her heart began to speed up, and that made her feel like throwing up. *Could Victor get in trouble here?* She tried to toughen herself, but she was too sick.

"Ma'am, could you tell me how you got to the Angler yesterday?"

Maggie looked at the wall behind the deputy's head, toward her name on a whiteboard, next to "Melissa Hanson" written under the "Today's Nurse" sign. She locked her face in a deep frown. "Do I have to tell you anything? Am I under arrest?" She kept her eyes on the whiteboard. Her heart was pounding against her chest. *This ain't me. I want to like this girl.*

"Oh, no, Mrs. Sobstak, not at all. And if you don't feel like talking now, I can come back later."

Later. They want somethin'. This ain't goin' away. She surprised herself, sounding so tough. "It ain't about now or later." Maggie continued staring behind the deputy's head, pretending an edge she couldn't feel. "It ain't about *when* I feel like talkin', it's about me not talkin' to you at all, if I don't have to." She was almost panting with anxiety when she finished. Maggie hated being so mean, but she had to protect Vic.

The deputy waited, and Maggie waited longer, barely breathing. The deputy finally stood up. "Okay, Mrs. Sobstak," she said. "I'm sorry I bothered you. If you do decide we can talk, here's my card." She laid the card on the bedside stand. Maggie kept her eyes on her own name on the whiteboard.

"I don't even know you," she said quietly, as disgusted with herself for saying it as she was for being hungover. "You're new to the valley. I don't talk to nobody I don't even know."

The deputy blinked and her face paled. She murmured a good bye, thanked Maggie for her time, and closed the door quietly behind herself when she left.

*   *   *

As she turned the ignition key, Andi had to take long breaths to recover from the wash of emptiness she'd felt when Mrs. Sobstak said she didn't talk to somebody she doesn't know. The loneliness had blasted her like the cold downdraft before a thunderstorm. Then, something Doctor Northrup had said in the ER came back to her.

He'd said, "Maggie's one of the Welcome Wagon ladies."

"Who are they?"

"Welcome Wagon's a group of local women. When somebody moves into town, they bring over a pie and a street map and a bunch of store coupons, stuff to introduce the new family to the community."

"Hmm, nice. I remember someone doing that when I came. It wasn't Maggie, though. I didn't realize they had a name. 'Welcome Wagon.' Cute."

"Anyway, Maggie's usually the greeter. She likes meeting the new folks."

Driving back to the office, Andi squinted as she thought about that. *The Welcome Wagon lady, eh? She likes meeting new folks? Well, then, she's hiding something behind that "don't talk to strangers" bull.*

She pulled into the parking lot, letting the loneliness fade, displaced by growing curiosity. Doctor Northrup's pickup was in the lot. She suddenly wanted to ask a favor.

Instead of going into the department, she stepped into Dr. Northrup's waiting room. The office door itself was closed, and she made out a low murmuring behind it. *Seeing somebody.* She left quietly, went back to her cubicle in the department, grabbed her cell phone, and dialed.

*   *   *

Between patients, Ed checked his phone; the only message was from Deputy Pelton. He called her back.

"Deputy? You wanted me to call?" he said when she answered.

"Hi, Doctor. Yes, thanks. I wonder if could I ask a favor?"

"Uh, sure. I'm about to go in with a patient, though."

"I'll be quick. I tried to talk with Maggie Sobstak this morning but she says she doesn't talk to outsiders."

"That stings," he said. "And it's not true, either."

"Yeah," Andi said, with a little self-deprecating chuckle. "Anyway, I think she's hiding something. I wondered if you'd stop by and see if you can learn what happened yesterday."

"You're still thinking about Vic?"

"Yeah, I am. He wasn't home when I went out there. One of the employees thought he'd gone somewhere."

Ed chuckled. "We call them *hands* or *cowboys* out here."

She laughed. "*Whatever*. As we say in the Big City."

"Sure, I'll talk to her and get back to you." Ed frowned as he hung up. Another problem to worry about. Where had Vic Sobstak gone? As he opened the door for his next patient, he thought, *She's smart. I'd suspect Vic too.*

*   *   *

After the last session of the day, as he was writing his notes, he heard a knock on the doorframe.

"Come in," he called. Leese MacArdell came in and leaned against the doorframe. Her waist-length down jacket, celadon green, enhanced her trim athletic legs. Leese had been his CPA since she came to the Valley from Denver ten years ago. Exactly Ed's height, six feet, she looked directly into his eyes when she talked, and her forthright voice pleased him.

She moved, he thought, like an athlete, almost on her toes, graceful as a dancer, and she worked out every day. Unlike his, her professional advice was delivered directly, without the caution with which he invariably tailored his opinions, hoping delicacy would finesse resistance. Leese advised with authority and precision. For her, wisdom derived from the data on her calculator, which she played like a pianist, fingers flying, and her advice usually saved him money. He swiveled his chair to greet her.

"Out for a run?"

"Nope. Too cold. It's a high school gym workout today." She straightened up. "Let's get together to talk about your taxes. It's January, you know."

He started to pull his appointment book from his bag, but she said, "Why not tonight? I could join you at the Angler after my workout, around six."

"Uh, yeah, I could do that."

"It's a plan, then." She turned to go, then faced him again. "Rosemary's on the hunt for you. She wants your contribution to Landon Burke's campaign." Burke was the first Black to run for Montana governor.

"It's only January!"

Leese chuckled. "Tell Rosemary that. And tell her this: The Republican'll eat him alive."

*   *   *

Maggie Sobstak was not at the hospital when he called. "She's discharged, Ed," Millie, the operator, told him. He dialed the Sobstaks' number, but there was no answer. After leaving a message asking Maggie to call him, he finished his notes and headed across Division Street to the Angler Bar. Despite the bitter cold, a fine dry snow haloed the streetlights. The Angler's green neon fisherman glowed softly through a powdery gauze. Ed stamped his boots inside the door and gave a brief wave to Ben Stewart, who was ensconced on the corner, listening to Larry Miller complain. Leese wasn't there yet, so Ed sat at a small table near the fire.

"Fat Tire, Edward?" Ted called over the bar. When he brought the pint around, he asked, "How goes the battle?"

Ed nodded his thanks for the beer. "Sweating and slaving over hot psyches is thirsty business, Ted."

Ted assumed a studious look. "Indeed. I don't recall you coming in two nights in a row in a month of Sundays."

"Just business with Leese. Tax time, you know."

Ted lowered himself onto the second chair and his voice into a conspiratorial whisper, looking around as if he were about to divulge a dark secret. "That woman is after your body, Edward. And it's a very nice body, too, I might add, for a man of your years, and, ah, weight."

Ed frowned. "I could lose a few pounds."

"And a few sorrows, my friend." Ted smiled. "You ought to take Ben's advice and date Deputy Pelton. Or Leese, for that matter. It would do you a world of good."

Ed picked up the beer, then put it back down. He felt a momentary annoyance. All these friends trying to set him up with women. "Screw you, Ted. No, scratch that."

Ted chuckled. "Only in my dreams, sadly. Lane would be so annoyed. But I tell you, Leese MacArdell is going after you one of these days."

"Give it a rest, Ted. Leese wants my business, not my body."

Ted patted his knee once, stood, and returned to the bar, shaking his head. "Such a child."

Leese came in, brushing the fine snow from her jacket.

"Have a good workout?" Ed asked her. Over her shoulder, he saw Ted gesture toward her legs, nicely snugged in Lycra tights. His one eyebrow lifted, unmistakably. He might as well have said it aloud: *This is no business suit!*

Leese turned to order a Martini and Ted's face instantly changed, the hospitable bartender. Ed almost laughed. While Ted mixed her drink, she reached into her bag and handed Ed a folder.

"The customary tax information package," Leese said. "I give it to you every January and you forget to fill it out until I nag you to death in March. Then you deliver it to me half-done on April tenth and I kill myself to get your return done by the fifteenth, which is impossible because you leave out half the important information. So we file an extension." She gave him her most piercing stare as she sipped the

Martini Ted had delivered. Her eyes dared him to protest.

"That sounds about right," he managed.

"What do you say we try something different this year? Say, oh, I don't know, like you get your numbers to me by the end of February?"

Ed smiled. "Maybe. But you'll probably have to come over and force me to sit down and get it done."

The challenge in her eyes immediately softened; she lowered her head slightly, looking up at him. "I could do that," she said, her voice pitched down, sultry.

Ed glanced at Ted, who was working a crossword puzzle at the far end of the bar. Ben and Larry Miller were winding up their business. Nobody noticed the change that came over Leese. Ed cleared his throat, feeling awkward.

Leese laughed. "Sorry to make you uncomfortable, Ed." She tapped the packet. "Let's get it done on time this year."

Embarrassed, Ed looked down. Was Ted right? Although he'd kept things scrupulously business-like with Leese, he had always found her sexy. Why hadn't he taken her out? For that matter, why wasn't he responding to her hint now, feeling tongue-tied like a boy? At age fifty-six! He sucked in his stomach.

"Earth to Ed."

"Oh, sorry. Yeah, I was thinking about doing this – " He tapped the folder. " – on time. I'll get on it a.s.a.p."

Leese smiled and took another sip. "It's that *p-for-possible* that worries me."

He smiled back. "February twenty-eighth. In your hands."

She looked, again, directly in his eyes, and further softened her voice. "You can put whatever you want in my hands, Ed."

This time he felt himself blushing. "Ted warned me you were after my body."

Leese looked over at the bartender and lifted her Martini in salute. "Very perceptive, Mr. Coldry." Ted leaned up from his crossword puzzle and tipped an imaginary hat to her. At that moment, Ben Stewart stopped by their table. He rested a hand on Ed's shoulder.

"You two kids havin' a good time?"

"Talking taxes, Ben."

"Shoot. Don't time fly? Well, don't talk *taxes* too late now – that there's a slippery snow out there. We don't want no *complications* on a night like this."

He clapped Ed on the shoulder, nodded politely to Leese, "Ma'am," and left.

"Which translated," she said, amused, "means, don't forget Andrea Pelton."

Ed started to disagree, but remembered Ted's *Such a child.* He looked quizzically at her. "You think?"

"Sure. Everybody knows Ben wants to hook you two up. Don't act naïve." *What the hell*, he thought. *If she can talk straight, so can I.* Ed sipped his beer. "So to what should I attribute *your* come-on?"

She lifted an eyebrow. "To interest. You're single, I'm single, you're good looking – " She looked swiftly at his belly, then back to his eyes. "Except for the paunch. Anyway, I'm interested. And the nights out here get lonely." She smiled.

"You're direct."

"I am. I learned in MBA school that indirect doesn't cut it in the real world. That was the mistake I made with my marriage – I didn't like Robert's ski-bum laziness from the get-go, but I never said anything till the third year and he still wasn't looking for a job. Indirect doesn't work."

He nodded. "Well, your *interest* surprised me. It's so sudden."

"It isn't sudden, Ed. It's just direct."

"Which doesn't answer why *now*."

"True, it doesn't."

He waited, but Leese sipped her Martini calmly, as if to say, *You figure it out.*

FOUR

Friday, January 20

IN THE PRE-DAWN light, the valley nestled in new snow. Outside his window, there were three or four inches. For a few minutes in his warm bed, Ed contemplated sleeping in, but he felt unsettled after the encounter with Leese. And there was a lot to do. Fridays were his day to catch up on paperwork, errands, chores – all the things put off during the week. He'd lied to Jim about having an emergency, and he knew Jim knew it. He was free all day. Calling Maggie would be unpleasant, but Deputy Pelton's curiosity about Vic Sobstak had piqued his own. Besides, if Maggie were suicidal, he'd missed it and he wanted not to miss it again. He pulled himself out of bed and into his cold running gear.

He ran to Milk Creek, almost a mile, and stopped to listen to the water murmuring under the ice. The tinkling sounds soothed him, and during the run home, he felt less unsettled. He fixed his breakfast and coffee. He was hungry, so he added a third egg and another piece of toast. *No marmalade*, he told himself righteously. *Gotta lose the poundage.* On the way into town, he put the truck in four-wheel drive and drove cautiously. He dreaded calling Maggie; he opened the office, watered the plants, and tidied up, delaying it.

*   *   *

When the phone rang, Maggie looked at the caller ID. *Ed Northrup*. She picked up, anxious. What could she say? She wanted to confide in him, but what if she got Vic in trouble?

"Hi, Maggie, it's Ed. How're you doing?"

"Why're you calling? I'm fine." She heard the guarded tone in her voice, the timbre of fear masked with hostility. Didn't like it. But she couldn't help herself. Whatever was going on with Vic, too many people were in it now. *It ain't goin' to be good for Vic if I don't clam up.* But she hated that.

The psychologist was saying, "Well, I know you've had a rough couple of days and I thought maybe – "

She interrupted him. "Did that female deputy tell you to call?" Maggie wanted to soften her tone, but her fear for Vic overrode that. *Get honest with yourself, Margaret Sobstak. You're ashamed of yourself all around.*

He said, "Well, yeah, as a matter of fact, she expressed concern about you, Maggie." She heard a pause, as if he were thinking about something. "Point-one-nine blood alcohol is serious. We're *all* worried about you."

She couldn't reply. *They're all worried. I should relax. Ain't they friends?* Then she thought of the deputy. *She ain't a friend.* "Maggie?"

"I'm here." *Don't say nothin' you don't have to.*

"Maggie, talk to me. What happened Wednesday? You know I'm not out to hurt you." Maggie ached to believe that. It wasn't her nature, was it, to distrust everyone? Ed, he'd always been a good man, and when she'd gone to see him, he was kind and patient and didn't shame her. *But he don't know, does he?* She felt weak, unsure. More than anything, she wanted to talk to him.

She held her silence, as long as she could, wanting and fearing to talk. Then, she broke down. "Vic got me drunk. He knows I can't hold my liquor. He thought if I was drunk, I'd have sex with him." As soon as it blurted out, she regretted it. She heard him sigh. "I'm really sorry about that, Maggie."

"Sorry? He ain't *your* husband." She panicked. *They'll blame Vic.*

Ed said nothing.

Just talk to him. It ain't like me to be so hard. Maggie sighed. "Vic's been randier than a stallion the last few months. Somebody's got him all revved up and he's mad at me all the time for not playing along." Inside, she berated herself. *Don't go on. Stop.*

"Have you any idea who's revved him up?"

Maggie sniffled, embarrassed. "He says he ain't seein' nobody."

"So maybe he's randy because he's *not* seeing anybody." *There's truth to that.*

After a moment, Northrup asked, "How'd you get to the Angler?"

"Vic drove me. He said he was going for cigarettes or some crap like that and he'd be back. I don't remember." *Don't I hate lying? But it's a little lie.*

"Ted Coldry said you ordered a Beam and Coke."

"Did I?" She put demoralization into her voice, and Northrup was silent for a moment. Then he said, "How about coming in to see me so we can talk more about this?"

She said it quick, hating herself for it. "Don't push me, Ed. I can't show my face in town."

Ed said, "Is that why you haven't been to choir practice?"

This time her anger burned away her shame. "That all you town folks got to do, gossip about Maggie Sobstak?"

She heard another sigh from Ed. "Well, if you can't come in town, what if I come out to your place?"

That fired off her fear again, and her breath got short. She kept silent. *This ain't how I am,* she protested to herself, and then she put her finger down on the "End" button.

*   *   *

Ed heard the click and then the dial tone, and looked at the phone for a moment. *Nothing about that call felt right,* he thought. He considered it for a while, then dialed the Sheriff's office.

Callie answered. To his request to be connected to Deputy Pelton, she said, "She caught a surprise midnight shift last night. She's probably home." She gave Ed the number.

He thanked Callie and dialed.

The deputy's "Hello?" was thick with sleep.

"Oh, did I wake you up?" he asked.

"Who is this?" There was more edge this time.

"I'm sorry. It's Ed Northrup." He was embarrassed, then a little annoyed that Callie hadn't warned him Andrea might be sleeping.

She said, "Oh. Yeah, I was sleeping." Rustling sounds, bed sounds. "Give me a minute."

He took a breath, indulging for a moment the image of Andi in bed. In a moment, she was back.

"What's going on?" Her voice was calm, alert. He'd observed Ben and other deputies over the years – they all seemed to have the ability to come instantly awake. Ben called it "cop-alert."

He filled her in on his conversation with Maggie Sobstak. They parsed it together, as far as they could. Andi asked, "Don't you think there'd be rumors if Vic were having an affair?"

Ed thought about it. The gossip lines in the valley provided more coverage than the telephone company dreamed of. "Probably. But there are a lot of barns and empty houses in the valley. It wouldn't be hard to meet somebody on the sly, if you're careful."

Andi said, "I don't know. Does it make sense for Vic to be desperate to have sex with Maggie if he's doing it with somebody else? I'm still thinking she's hiding something else about Vic, Doctor."

"Please, call me Ed. Something other than getting her drunk and dropping her at the Angler?"

"Maybe that's all it is. But think about it. If his motive was to get her liquored up for sex, why abandon her at the Angler?"

"Good point," he said after a moment. That hadn't occurred to him. *Logical mind*, he thought. "The question is, what would something else be?"

*   *   *

As he typed the week's notes, Ed pondered his self-defeat at Jim's on Wednesday. He'd wasted the chance to talk about the *black dog*. He smiled to himself. He preferred calling it the *black dog* to "depression." Where had he first heard that? It was a rough cowboy phrase Magnus Anderssen had once used to describe a foreman's depression. "It's a black dog, Ed, gnawing him like a bone."

He heard a knock at the door. "It's open," he called automatically, thinking, *Damn. I need some alone time.* Leese MacArdell came in.

For a moment, there was an awkward silence, which she broke. "About last night."

Ed stood. "Don't worry about it, Leese. I'm flattered." He glanced at the computer.

She arched an eyebrow. "Well, first, I'm not *worried* about it, and second, I'm angling for a little more than *flattered*. I dropped by to, ah, repeat the offer. I'm interested in getting something going between us."

"Yeah, I got that message," he said. He cleared his throat.

She appraised him, and seemed to conclude something. She picked up a pen from his desk and turned it around in her hands. "Nice pen. This Connie Fuller's?" Fuller, at seventy, was the town's premier fishing guide and tie-er of trout flies. He also crafted beautiful wooden pens for his friends.

Ed nodded.

She handed him his pen. "So, you know where I am; if *you* get interested, use your pen to write me a note. If not, this is the last time we'll talk about the subject."

"Look, Leese, it's not that..." *What was it?* Here was an attractive woman proposing a relationship and he was, what?

She smiled. "No explanations necessary. I'm a big girl and I've put the ball in your court. If you leave it there, I'm glad we're friends and I'm still your accountant. No hard feelings."

She turned to go, then turned back. "And you've got exactly 40 days to get your tax stuff to me." She closed the office door behind her.

He felt it then: A *black dog*, gnawing.

FIVE

Monday, January 23

SNOW HAD FALLEN on and off throughout the weekend. Although the plow had opened the roads, the shoulder was too icy for running. Not the time to twist an ankle. Ed moved up onto the asphalt where his shoes gripped, but even with better footing, he ran uncomfortably, his paunch a yoke. As he shuffled along, odd words came to mind: *Father to me.* Ed wasn't entirely sure what they meant. At the Milk Creek bridge, he stopped and peered down at the rushing water. Suddenly, he knew what the words referred to: Oliver Tweedy's death. When Ed came to the valley in 1987, Oliver, then the valley's only lawyer, had taken him under his wing, introducing him to "the right people." Over the years, the older man had watched Ed from a friendly distance, much as a careful father might. But other than a few tears at the funeral, he'd left the grief for Oliver behind quickly, even if Oliver had been a father to him.

Looking down through the railing of the Milk Creek bridge reminded Ed of looking emptily through the toe of his snowshoe down the face of the Coliseum. *Would my dad have been hurt if I had jumped? Or cared?* It hardly mattered: His father had died years ago.

Oliver would have cared.

Ed turned back toward home, jogging more easily now that he was warmed up. On the road that climbed toward his cabin, he thought about Mara's girl, little Grace, trying to die before her life began. Where was *her* father? Laboring up the hill, still bearing the Oliver-sadness and slowed by his extra weight, Ed glanced toward the eastern mountains. Pale light outlined their crests. Sunrise soon. He felt a moment's comfort.

Would little Grace find an Oliver, as he had, to show her how to live?

The air wasn't so cold this morning, so when he came inside, the cabin felt over-warm. He'd fixed the furnace – again – on Saturday. The repair had required two trips to the hardware store, but would last the winter. He hung his running gear on their hook. On the way to the kitchen, he glanced at the day's appointments. Maggie was coming in at eleven o'clock. The other hours were jammed, only thirty minutes free at noon: another depression-drowned day. His too-familiar weariness flooded him. The *black dog*. Suppressing it, looking out the kitchen window toward the east, he told himself, *Knock off the crap. Sun's up.*

He poured the first coffee of the day and started his usual big breakfast, eggs, toast and jam, bacon. Then, ruefully, he put the food back in the refrigerator and pulled out milk and a piece of cheese, and cereal from the cupboard. Time to attack the weight.

*　　*　　*

During her appointment later that morning, for twenty minutes, Maggie had sat sullen and grim, answering his questions with barely a nod, sometimes a word. Yes. No.

He decided to push her. "Maggie, you've already told me about Vic getting you drunk so he could have sex. Let's quit pussy-footing around. What's going on between you two?"

She glared, said nothing. Then her eyes broke away.

He waited a moment. Then, "Have you confronted Vic about the other woman?"

Maggie'd looked away and down. Ed thought she looked ashamed. "Maybe I'm makin' it all up," she sighed.

Ed waited, but she looked miserable. "Well, let's talk about it."

For a long time she simply stared at the floor. Then, she surprised him. "You don't have to believe me, but I have proof. I got me a matchbook from the Jefferson House motel. Found it in Vic's jeans, doin' the wash."

He waited.

"Least I think that's what it is." Doubt tinged her voice.

"It'd be easy enough to check out, Maggie, if you really want to go that way."

She looked away again, and said softly, "Leave it. It ain't your mess." She gathered her coat and purse and left. Thirty minutes early.

*   *   *

That Afternoon

Andi's shift started with the regular briefing at four, and afterwards, she tackled some overdue paperwork. *Wonder why we don't call it screenwork,* she thought, yawning at the computer. She'd caught an extra midnight shift last night when Pete Peterson's son had been taken to the ER for a broken collar bone; she never slept well during the day, and she couldn't get back to sleep after Doctor, no, Ed Northrup's call. After the pixels wouldn't un-blur and she had written the same sentence twice, she stood up and stretched. Ben Stewart was emerging from his office, ten past five, off to his routine late afternoon meeting with a constituent at the Angler.

"Who's on the corner tonight, Sheriff?"

He stood in his tracks. "Hell! Can't remember! An' I'm only 54." He bellowed the question through the open door to Callie's reception desk.

Callie called back, "When did I get promoted to your social secretary?"

But she was grinning and pulling up Ben's calendar on her computer when he came out in front of her desk, followed by Andi. Callie's smile faded.

"Deputy," she nodded coolly. Then to Ben, "Today it's Cam McGowan. Tomorrow you're on the corner with Magnus Anderssen."

Ben lifted his eyebrows. "Ah, big boys' week." He turned and said to Andi, "Cam owns the paper here and three more in this part of Montana. Magnus – " She interrupted: " – owns half the valley and has the other half on payroll."

Ben, tickled, said to Callie, "Quick study ain't she?"

Callie narrowed her eyes even further. "Some ways."

His big head swiveled between the two women. "It don't take a thermometer to catch the chill in the air. Whatever it is, ladies, patch 'er up." He went out the door toward the Angler to learn what was on Cam McGowan's journalistic mind.

Callie began typing.

Andi almost spoke, but instead turned and went back to her desk.

The valley people had a term for what she needed to do, but she couldn't recall it. She tidied the folders on her desk and pushed her chair up close, getting ready for evening patrol. As she put on her parka, the phrase came to her. *Cowboy up.*

"Okay, Pelton," she said roughly and a little too loud. "Cowgirl up!"

From outside came Callie's cigarette-graveled voice. "You say something to me, Deputy?"

Andi took a breath and went out to Reception. "Naw, just talking to myself, Callie. And, please, call me Andi."

"They say you talk to yourself too much, you'll grow hair on your palms." Smoke-raspy chuckles followed.

Callie was making an opening. Andi took another deep breath. "Look, I'm sorry for my starchiness, Callie. I was trained differently. Protocol and all, you know. I'll get over it."

Callie looked surprised, and then said, "Seems to me, well, you and me bein' the only girls in this department, I was thinkin' we oughta have each other's backs a little better. Maybe try to be friends."

Before Andi could answer, the phone lit up and Callie swiveled to her console. "Adams County Sheriff." She listend. "Roger," she said. "Deputy Pelton's on her way."

She turned to Andi and said, "Got us a cow loose up on Hanson Road. You're up." Andi felt disappointed. She was about to say so, when Callie's board rang again. Andi shrugged and pushed open the door and went out into the evening.

*   *   *

Same Time

Ed parked in front of St. Bernard's rectory. He hadn't called ahead, but Jim's truck was in the driveway. After last week's failure, Ed was determined to tell Jim about his close call on the Coliseum.

"Hey, pal! To what do I owe the pleasure?" Jim exclaimed, wearing a threadbare Rolling Stones t-shirt – the one with the tongue – jeans, and fluffy pink slippers.

"Nice slippers," Ed said.

"*Warm* slippers."

Ed gestured to the T-shirt. "I didn't know you're a Stones fan." Elizabeth Murphy's Grateful Dead T-shirt flashed through his mind. He brushed the memory away like a spider web on his face.

"I'm not, but it's my favorite shirt. Got it from the only woman I've ever had sex with." In the tumbler in his right hand ice tinkled in an amber liquid.

Still on the porch, Ed gave a start. "Wait. Sex while you were a priest?"

Hamilton's smile broadened. "Indeed." He gestured Ed inside. "Come in before my tootsies in these warm slippers freeze. Yes, ordained I was, and thus my delight in my shirt!"

Ed stepped inside. "Isn't that, what, grounds for excommunication?" Then, "Was she good?"

The priest shrugged cheerfully. "Like *I* could judge? The Resusci-Annie doll turns *me* on. All I can say, she was heavenly."

Ed tossed his parka on a chair. "Did you, uh, like, do it in the confessional?" Hamilton scolded, "Hey, hey!" and swooped up the coat and tossed it to Ed. "What is this, you think because I'm celibate I'm a slob? Hang your coat where it belongs." He pointed to the coat rack in the hall.

Ed chuckled. He'd known Jim's fastidious housekeeping rules for so long that dropping his coat on a chair was a tease.

Jim grunted, getting the joke. "And no, we did not do it in the confessional – that's a common layman's fantasy. The confessional is cold, damp, hard on the butt, and a vessel for body odor, broken wind, and boring sins."

"Appealing. No wonder the sacrament's called Penance. So where *did* you meet her?"

Hamilton lifted his tumbler. "If this visit is for priestly show-and-tell, you need one of these – *and* you play too."

'I'm afraid there's nothing all that intriguing on my side, Jim, but I'll gladly accept a drink. That *is* Scotch, right?"

Hamilton tilted his head, offended. "Would I drink *Canadian* whiskey? And nothing *intriguing* on your side? You're more depressed than I thought."

Ed reacted without thinking. "I'm not *that* depressed," he said, and regretted it. He wanted to talk about the damn *black dog*, didn't he?

Taking a glass from the dark mahogany breakfront, Jim called back, "Ice or neat?"

"No ice. One finger. I'm driving."

Jim poured a careful half-inch and handed Ed the glass. They touched their glasses delicately and sipped. Ed sighed. He gathered himself to say something about his *black dog*. He thought again about how the name, silly as it was, appealed to him, sounded less shameful than "depression." *What an attitude for a psychologist,* he thought. He hesitated, framing his words.

Jim spoke first. "Now that I've got your ear, could we schedule a time to change my oil?"

Ed sighed again. "Take it to Bud's. That's his business."

"You're handy, though, and Bud's not the conversationalist you are, even if you are more depressed than he is."

"And I'm cheaper."

"And cheaper. So? How about it?"

Ed sighed again. He *was* handy, and Jim had no qualms about volunteering him to repair things, change his oil, whatever. Still, refusing would be selfish. Priests don't make much money. "Poor as churchmice," his father had described priests. *Hell, they are churchmice.* He grunted. "Next week sometime." He sipped again, and decided he would talk about the depression in a minute. "So, now, dish. Where did you meet this woman? Did you have your robes on?"

"Isn't that bad interview technique, two questions at once?"

"Talk!"

Jim chuckled. "No, no robes. I met her in the grocery store – she was the checkout girl, or as she told me, checkout *person*."

Ed laughed. "The priest and the checkout girl! Could be – "

"*Person*. Checkout person."

"Person. So, what, you asked this checkout person to come over to the rectory?"

Jim shook his head. "It was quite a surprise, believe me. I remarked on her friendliness as she bagged my groceries, and she said that she was off in fifteen minutes and we could get friendlier. I was a goner. I put my groceries in the truck and panted at the door like a puppy. I didn't leave her apartment for thirty-six hours." He smiled. "Missed Mass the next two mornings. When I got back in my truck, the groceries had bloated up so bad they nearly knocked me down." He swirled his glass and pondered it a moment. "My bishop did pretty much the same."

"You lost your priesthood?"

"No, you can't lose that; it's like a pre-existing condition. No, I got sent to Wolf Point, about as far away as they could ship me. The bishop thought it was punishment. He didn't know her parents lived there." Jim beamed. "We had a real nice thing till 1987, when she met her husband-to-be and I got assigned here to St. Bernie's. I've been a good boy since." He'd started a fire in the wood stove before Ed arrived. He looked thoughtfully at the flames. "I'm faithful, very faithful, to two lovers. To the Church, and to Jane." He lifted his glass; Ed lifted his. "To Jane. May she be as happy as I am when I remember her."

For a moment, the two men stared contemplatively at the fire. Ed felt the *black dog* stir. His relationship with his ex-wife had offered no such bliss, only a fruitless struggle to make Mara happy. He wanted to tell Jim about her call, but since coming to the valley, he'd never told anyone about her or his Minnesota life.

Why drag that up now? He sighed.

Jim looked over at him. "You said you've got things you'd like to talk about."

Ed rested his glass on the side table. It was mostly full. "I miss Oliver. I guess it's got me down." But he was thinking of the Coliseum.

His friend said, quietly, "Would I be out of line if I said your sorrow is probably about more than missing Oliver?"

Ed picked up his glass, studied it. If he started, he'd have to dredge the past up. One thing would lead to another. The divorce. Elizabeth. A twenty-seven year wall of silence is hard to push through.

Jim looked over at him, as if pondering what to say now. Finally, he said, "Something tells me you don't want to talk about it."

Ed shrugged. "Very intuitive." After a moment, he added, "I'll be fine."

Jim grimaced. "Your face gives you away. You look like you feel like shit." Ed stood up, the drink unfinished on the table. He pointed at Jim's T-shirt.

"Like Mick says, I can't get no satisfaction."

"Wait, Ed," Jim said, standing too. "You're hurting, man. Talk to me."

Ed heard his father's voice. *A man who whines, I've no respect for him.* He thought, *Bullshit, Dad,* but he shook his head anyway. "I'll figure it out, Jim. Thanks for listening."

Jim just looked at him, his face a mix of frustration and sorrow. "Listening? To what?"

SIX

That evening

VIC SOBSTAK EDGED his F-150 into the farthest parking place in the Jefferson House lot, in the dark shadows beyond the reach of the motel's lamps. Yellow light glowed behind the curtained window of Number 18. Reverend Loyd Crane's black Cadillac Escalade was parked at the door. The only other vehicle in the lot, down in front of Number 4, was that old brokeback Chevy Vega the boys on Dick Polson's place shared for booze and grocery runs, or the occasional visit to one of Jefferson's three whores. Vic curled his lip, disgusted. Any man who needed a whore ought to get married. One of them saints wrote it right: Better to marry than burn. Made him think of Maggie. This tax business bothered the hell out of him because he couldn't talk to her about it, couldn't have her lose faith in him. *A man can't do his taxes right, maybe he ain't fit for ownin' a ranch.* No, it was his problem and he'd solve the goddamn thing.

He concentrated on Number 18, waiting till the others arrived before going in. Reverend Crane could be too much if he caught you alone. If the Reverend had been some slick government asshole or one of them jerks from Cargill or Simplot sniffin' around to sell you seed or some goddamn "best practice," Vic could've held him off. Crane wasn't. He was a smart guy with a college education and he was born-again, whatever that meant. And most of all, he told how government taxes was screwing the little people. He was a powerful goddamn talker. Vic couldn't blow him off, and he couldn't sit in a room alone with those piercing blue eyes and powers of persuasion, either. Vic wasn't stupid, but he wasn't smart enough to resist Reverend Crane for long.

Door Number 18 opened and a short man wearing a big black Stetson stepped out and opened the Reverend's Caddie and pulled out a briefcase. He was some kind of assistant or something. He never said much, but when Reverend Crane wanted them to read a flyer or something, Stetson pulled them out of that leather briefcase and passed 'em out. When he took off his sunglasses, you saw cruel goddamn eyes. Vic sat quietly until Stetson went back inside. He needed to think a little longer.

That business with the Jim Beam last week bothered him, bothered him a lot. Maggie hadn't said a word to him after she came home from the goddamn hospital. She was pissed. Hell, he could see her point. He hadn't meant to leave her at the Angler, but damn. When he came back after running the errand for Reverend Crane, the Sheriff's SUV out front spooked him, after what he'd heard from Crane at the last meeting, that business about the government keepin' an eye on them. He headed out and spent the next couple nights in the bunkhouse with the boys, playing Texas Hold'em and enjoying the whiskey and the wood smoke and the easy male talk. Tell the truth, it was the best he'd felt since they'd bought the goddamn place from his boss, old Charley Wright. Even if runnin' off on Maggie was a weasel thing to do.

Sure, he shouldn't've tried to get her liquored up, but goddamn, who could blame him? Except Maggie, of course, with her way of playing Virgin Mary for three-and-a-half weeks every goddamn month and then, right before her period, have half a drink on a Friday night and climb all the hell over you. She'd acted, lately, like she don't understand the stresses he was under, prices crazy high and cattle selling low, and now taxes due and no cash lying around to pay 'em. And like she don't remember how, all twenty goddamn years they'd been married, when Vic stressed out, he got lustful. It's just his nature and she damn well knows it. When they were young and he was a field hand, even later when he took the foreman job, he'd come home all tense and such, and she'd oblige him, no questions asked. Now they own the goddamn ranch and live in the big house and oh, no, not now, now it's "Go in the bathroom and take care 'a yourself." No sympathy for his stress – which by the way beats the younger years' stress ten goddamn ways to Sunday.

That's why the drinks. A man ain't a goddamn teenager, makin' do with his hand. A grown man's got marital rights. Last Tuesday's meeting with Reverend Crane and the boys, it scared him silly, what with talk of the law bein' against us, and all those statistics the Reverend pulled out of Stetson's briefcase about the illegals, Mexicans mostly, but millions of 'em from places in Central America and goddamn Asia, how they're swarming all over the country. How they'll outnumber real Americans in twenty years. A white man, a good Christian, he works his whole life, he looks to take it easy when he's older, but no sir, Reverend Crane told 'em. "We'll all be sixty years old and beggin' for a decent job from some 5-foot-3 guy named Emilio."

Yessir, this had scared Vic to the marrow, so no wonder he came home with some goddamn needs. Maybe he'd went too far. He'd figured a couple drinks at home after lunch – she'd surprised him by agreeing – then maybe a Beam and Coke or two at the Angler – Maggie liked the Angler since that queer had remodeled it, you gotta give him credit, it's decent. Kind of romantic. He'd figured maybe the Angler'd get her in the mood and he'd get lucky the easy way. Goddamn, though, the sheriff's car outside had spooked him, after what the Reverend said last week.

What was it? "You know, gentlemen," he'd said, looking somberly at each one of them, "they're watching us even now." The men in the meeting murmured – there were nine that time – and Reverend Crane had settled them with an upraised hand. Vic was amused at that.

"I'm almost certain, gentlemen, that someone in our group has been planted to infiltrate us."

Vic flashed to Jesus outing Judas. He glanced at the others, wondering if it was true. Then he'd chuckled a soft cowboy snicker;

couldn't help himself.

Reverend Crane had stared at him. "You find that funny, Vic?" His voice sounded like steel against steel.

Vic had shrugged, suddenly a little intimidated. "I doubt that CIA stuff happens here in Monastery Valley, Reverend."

Reverend Loyd Crane solemnly, slowly, had shaken his head, as if Vic were an ignorant child. "Victor, the guv'ment is everywhere, watching." So last Wednesday, when he'd seen that cruiser outside the Angler where he'd dropped Maggie off, it just plain spooked him, so he drove past, leaving Maggie there. When he'd poked his head in later, she wasn't there. *Goddamn,* he'd thought, and hurried back home, but not there either. He got spooked. He wasn't proud of hisself, but there it was.

Two more pickups glided into spaces and three men got out and went into Number 18. Vic recognized the two who came together, a tall fellow named Jack-something, a foreman at the Double-A's copper mine, and a fat bald guy who had a funny name Vic couldn't remember. The fat guy had something to do with the Anderssen's timber operation. The third guy he didn't know.

"Guess it's time to get my skinny butt in there," he said to the steering wheel.

*   *   *

Number 18 was your standard small town motel room. Cracked porcelain fixtures, a rust-stained tub, a shelf-and-rod to hang a few shirts on screwed in crookedly beside the bed. Over the sagging bed hung a paint-by-numbers picture of an elk bugling on a ridge above his harem. On a narrow, cigarette-burned cabinet facing the bed sat an ancient 19-inch television, old-fashioned rabbit ears bent back against the paneled wall. To Vic, the men looked tense, except for Reverend Crane, whose smile was bright. *Like he's on TV,* Vic thought. The Reverend leaped up easily from the only chair and extended his big hand. "Victor! We're *so* blessed to have you join us again."

"Thanks, Reverend." Vic reached across the corner of the bed and shook hands, hating the silence. He had no idea what to say. Cattle and cowboys don't require chitchat.

"We're not actually started yet, Victor, so you haven't missed a word. Right, gentlemen?" The three valley men nodded. Stetson sat on the far corner of the bed, glaring. His big hat was pushed back. Jack-something and Timber leaned against the wall, flanking the TV cabinet. The stranger, frowning under a tan ball cap sweat-darkened around the bill, sat on the cabinet, his back against the TV screen. The man leaned up and stretched his hand to Vic.

"Gene Autry."

Vic hesitated; then decided to play along. "Pleased, Gene. Call me Lone."

"Lone?"

"Last name's Ranger."

Everyone chuckled, except Gene Autry. The undertone was paranoid. The handshake was harder than required. Vic remembered Reverend Crane's talk of an infiltrator. Did they think it was *him*? He said, "Name's Vic. Victor Sobstak. I own the CW Ranch." Gene Autry pulled back his hand and pursed his lips, but said nothing.

Vic stuck his hand toward Stetson, the Reverend's assistant, sitting on the corner of the bed, leaning back against the headboard. Stetson glanced at the hand, and then looked away. Vic stuck it in his jeans. All of a sudden, Vic didn't like the atmosphere.

*   *   *

Reverend Crane started the meeting with a prayer. "Heavenly Father, You have told us to gather in Your Son's Name and assured us You will be in our midst. So: We are here gathered in his Holy Name, so here You must be with us, for we *require* it and You do not lie. Let our thoughts be righteous and our plans – " Vic glanced up from under his bowed head. Plans? " – be just, and guide our actions to strike true against the evil of our times."

Vic raised his head, thinking the prayer was done, but Reverend Crane went on. Vic dropped his head. The Reverend's rich baritone, with its radio-ready intonations, billowed like the thick brown hair that rolled in waves back from his smooth forehead; Vic stopped listening to the words and tried to enjoy the sound. Still, he worried about those *plans* and that *striking* God was supposed to bless.

"Let us not lose faith in Your Son's promise to bless this great nation. Grace us with the courage and the power to cleanse America – " He drew out the second syllable, A*mur*ica; Vic liked that. " – Your new Promised Land, of those who darken her with their sinful desires and tax her with their Socialist Godless agendas. Amen."

The other men muttered their *amens*. Vic made a noise. The prayer unsettled him. He didn't cater much to the God talk, or to the business about socialist godless agendas. Not the immigrant-bashing, either. He had two Mexicans on his payroll and they were goddamn good workers. They did in a day and a half what took the other boys two. Being against taxes was Vic's thing, not God's plans. Taxes was breaking the ranch's back, truth to tell. Him and Maggie agreed on one thing: Leave God out of it. Sure, she was the church organist, but that don't mean she's a believer, now, does it? He smiled to himself, thinking about Maggie. His anger with her always seemed to waft away during these tax meetings.

"Victor?" Reverend Crane's voice interrupted his memory. "Care to tell us what you're smiling about?"

Vic collected himself. "Enjoying your blessing, Reverend."

Reverend Crane tilted his head slightly, then shrugged and sat down. He seemed to reach inside himself for something. His eyes closed and then he spoke very softly. Vic had to strain to hear.

"Gentlemen, I have good news."

They waited while he communed within.

"I have word that the most recent Internet article condemning us –" *Us* meaning Crane's Idaho church, which had been accused some months ago of sponsoring meetings of hate groups – "has received 73 responses *in our favor*. My friends," he paused to let the number sink in, "this is an extraordinary outpouring of support! The Southern Poverty Law Center, which publishes these abominations, is a Satanic Socialist organization that has targeted us, but our supporters are beating back the liberal lies, thanks to the power of the Holy Spirit!"

Vic hesitated, then raised his hand. The Reverend nodded at him.

"Reverend, good for you all, but you know, us folks here in the valley
– " he looked at the others, except Stetson, who was from God knew
where – "we're on board with your message about taxes, but I ain't sure
about that other stuff. I was wonderin' if maybe we could get back to
that?"

Reverend Crane's smile was entirely friendly, although his eyes were
blue steel. "You're absolutely right, Vic." He lightly clapped his hands.
"So, gentlemen. Let's get to work."

Everyone settled back. Vic squeezed between the bed and the
window and sat down on the pillows opposite Stetson, who followed
him with his dark eyes. Jack-something – ah, Moen, Jackie Moen,
worked up at the Double-A in the copper mine – and Timber, the guy
with the funny name, slid down till they were squatting, their backs
comfortably against the wall, elbows on their knees, cowboy style. Gene
Autry glowered. The Reverend surveyed them.

"You'll all remember that almost all the taxes we pay in this country
are illegal."

Timber raised his hand. "Run that one by me again, would ya,
Reverend? I'm just a little rusty on it. I run it by the missus but she thinks
it's horsesh – , 'scuse me, thinks it's wrong and I couldn't explain it as
good as you."

Vic was surprised to hear the man mention his wife; he envied that
Timber could talk with her about this business. How could he admit to
Maggie how he'd let the taxes get out of goddamn control? Timber's
name came to him: Franky. Not Frank, Franky Concini, something like
that. Up on Magnus Anderssen's logging operation.

"Of course," said Reverend Crane. "Take the income tax. You'll recall
that the Sixteenth Amendment to the Constitution wasn't properly
passed. Nevertheless, Philander Knox, the Secretary of State, ignored
this ignominy and rammed certification down our throats. So income
taxes are illegal. Are we clear now?" There were muttered assents.
Seemed goddamn weak to Vic, some political shenanigans a century ago,
but the taxes were killing him and if there was a legal way to escape
them, he wasn't arguin'.

Crane continued, "And I'm sure you recall that only the *counties* have true and legitimate authority to govern, which includes laying taxes."

Stetson added, on cue, "As our colleagues in the Posse Comitatus have proven." The others nodded.

Vic lifted his hand. "Try that part about poss'bly commies got us again, please."

"*Posse Comitatus*," said Reverend Crane, pronouncing it slowly. "It's Latin, Victor. It means 'power of the county.' Let me create a context for you." His face showing a flicker of frustration, Reverend Crane now spoke as if to a slow child. Vic shrank against the wall. "And then I'll ask you a simple question. That okay with you?"

Vic nodded, avoided the blue eyes.

"First, the Posse is a group of dedicated men and women who have demonstrated an ironclad legal argument that the only legitimate level of government authority in this country is the county sheriff. And how do we know their argument is ironclad?" He looked pointedly around the room, catching the eye of each man.

No one answered. They'd covered this, Vic remembered, though he couldn't remember the logic. It hadn't made much goddamn sense the first time, truth to tell. Crane, for the first time looking annoyed, nodded to his assistant, "Michael?"

Stetson recited, in a monotone, "We know it because of Gordon Kahl."

"Exactly. Thank you, Michael." To the others, he said, "Are you with me?"

Vic shook his head. "Sorry, sir, but I ain't quite. Remind me?"

Reverend Crane sighed. "Gordy Kahl belonged to the Posse Comitatus in North Dakota, where the guv'mint tried to silence him in 1983. In the struggle, he succeeded in killing a couple of marshals before fleeing to Arkansas. There, the county sheriff assassinated him. Gordy's assassination proves that the Posse's argument is solid."

Again, the other men nodded, except for Stetson, whose eyes flicked toward the old TV set, as if he wished he could tune it in and watch news about murders. Vic, however, took off his cap and scratched his scalp. Reluctantly, he said softly, "I think I'm havin' a little bit of trouble workin' that out. How's that assassination prove the idea?"

Reverend Crane nodded to Stetson, who intoned without a pause, "If the government had a legal leg to stand on, they'd have arrested and tried Gordon Kahl back in 1977 when he didn't pay his taxes. They tried to kill him instead – that's why he killed those deputies, out of self-defense. The state took enormous shit for killing him, so why didn't they just arrest and try him? Because a fair trial would have shown that taxes are illegal."

Vic rubbed his face; something didn't seem right about all that. He remembered, now, that Gordon Kahl coverage. The man had weaponed up in an isolated farmhouse, manned it with his son and maybe some other kids, and dared the authorities to take him, dead or alive. When the shooting stopped, he abandoned his boy and escaped to Arkansas. They trapped and killed him in a house owned by some other Posse members who, during the shooting, killed the local sheriff. To Vic's way of thinking, the business maybe proved a few goddamn points, but the Posse's crackpot ideas? Anyway, weren't the sheriffs *trying* to arrest Kahl?

"Victor, you with us?" The Reverend's voice was hard.

Vic nodded.

Crane went on, staring directly at Vic. Vic looked away. "You see, Victor, the Posse's right. We aren't obliged to send all our money to Washington. Gordon Kahl died for that idea, and no one has disproved him to this day. To this moment." He looked at Vic, his eyes now dark. "Are you with me, *sir?*"

Vic nodded. He wanted to be. The mere idea that taxes were illegal warmed him. He'd pay his county property taxes, sky-high as they were, thanks to them needle-dicks in the state house cutting taxes so goddamn deep the counties were strapped. If Reverend Crane was right, lifting off the income tax burden would give the C.W. Ranch real breathing room.

There was something else, though. Maggie had brought it up during one of their arguments, early on, when he'd nervously brought up Reverend Crane's ideas, as if he'd heard them on TV. In fact, her point had shut him up. For good. He raised his hand again.

"Victor, I do admire your Western skepticism." His voice did not sound admiring. "What is it *this* time?"

"I'm sorry, Reverend." Vic felt moisture under his armpits. He wasn't so good at all this questioning. "It's just one more thing. Don't taxes pay for necessary things, roads and prisons and whatnot? My wife thinks, without them the goddamn society'd fall apart. Pardon the French."

Reverend Crane smoothed his thick pompadour with his strong right hand. His smile flickered, as if some far-off power source had dimmed momentarily. He gathered himself, over-friendly. "Victor, Victor." He ended with a long sigh.

Over Vic's years in ranching, branding thousands of calves and castrating hundreds of pigs, he'd learned there came a moment when the animal oughta realize there ain't nothing to do but goddamn relax and let 'er happen. Reverend Crane's *Victor, Victor* signaled Vic's moment. He leaned back into the pillows against the wall and closed his eyes. *Let the goddamn bullshit flow,* he thought.

"Victor, I'd have to agree with you – or your wife, who I guess you're channeling here. I'd have to agree, that is, if your sheriff was the one to decide how much taxation he needed to run things smoothly here in – " he darted a glance at Stetson, who said, "Adams" – "in Adams County." Crane's voice lowered to a fatherly pitch. "But look around you! You run a business." He pronounced it *bidness*. "Does it look to you like this society's doin' all that well? Listen to me." Reverend Crane had stood, and now he shifted into a pulpit resonance.

Vic watched him, nerves jangled.

"Think of it, Victor. The moral strength of our land? Weakened! The integrity of our families? Seduced and corrupted! Do you not see the Welfare Queens and their Drug Lords sucking the lifeblood out of our cities? Do you not see our small bidness owners, our moms and pops, tears in their eyes, wiping their hands on their aprons and boarding up their shops? You are not blind, Victor, to the swarming tide of illegals sweeping into our very homes, eating our sustenance, taking our jobs, polluting our lives with their alien languages and customs, driving out our good Amurican families!" Thundering now. "Victor! *You are not blind!*" Reverend Crane inhaled, a shuddering breath; his passion overwhelmed the small room.

Vic almost felt sick. The *swarming tide* was too vivid, conjuring the brown waves of cockroaches in the sultry apartment in town where he'd grown up with his mother, after his daddy died. He tried to shake loose of the memory. "How can the government – " he tried, and failed, to pronounce it *guvmint* like the reverend did – "stop these illegals if we don't pay taxes?" But under Reverend Crane's now hostile glare, his question melted, a snowflake falling on water.

The preacher lowered his voice. "Contemplate this, Victor, and all of you," looking balefully now at the other men. "If. You. Montanans. Elect." He paused for emphasis. "This Negro, Ter*rell Lan*don Burke" – his voice dripped sarcasm – "who no doubt grew up on welfare, well." His voice faded, as if he were overcome.

Vic could not help feeling stunned as Reverend Crane pounded in the final nail. "If. You. Elect. Burke. Don't blame *me* if this country and if this valley of yours turns into the next Russia and you – " He looked straight at Vic, as if Vic were personally going to be the first to take the blow – "and every good Christian white man and woman in this valley is dragged off to the camps."

Stetson, sounding bored, asked, "Reverend, how could that happen? This is the United States of America, is all I'm saying."

Reverend Crane relaxed. "Thank you, Michael. Good question." The other four were avid for an answer. "It's taxes, men. Suppose your Negro is elected governor." Franky groaned. "No, it could happen, believe me. You've seen what they do. They raise taxes for their socialist welfare state programs. Next thing you know, patriots like us are either in the poorhouse because we pay the tax collector, or we're in jail because we don't. Or can't. The liberals don't care."

No one spoke. Vic raised his hand. "So what do we do, Reverend? Me, I'm a cowboy, not a philosopher, and I need me a job I can tackle."

Reverend Crane was ready. "Two things, Victor. One is for those with courage; one is for the rest. I'll give you the first one first, okay?" Vic nodded. The reverend obviously classed Vic with *the rest*.

"You can just ignore April 15. Don't file, don't pay. It'll take the bureaucrats and the lawyers months, probably years, to do anything. Just send 10% of what you would have sent to the IRS to us in Twin Falls and we'll keep it in our defense fund for you. You can't lose."

Stetson nodded, but Vic and the other men were pensive.

Reverend Crane added, "Or if you haven't got the courage for that, gentlemen, you can start nailing these posters to every tree and telephone pole in Adams County." He gestured to Stetson, who pulled a ream of flyers out of his briefcase and handed them around. Vic took a large handful, glancing at the title: *Do You Want THIS for Your Governor?* There was a paragraph under an ugly caricature of Terrell Landon Burke. The credit line read, *The Church of Jesus Christ of the American Promise.* Centered at the very foot of the page was a faint and tiny cross, so minute that Vic did not see its corners bending into a swastika.

SEVEN

The same evening

COMING INTO HIS cabin, Ed inhaled the aroma of the beef stew he'd started in the slow cooker this morning. He glanced at the clock. Ten hours' simmering: perfect. Although he wasn't really in the mood, he popped the artisan bread out of his pack and into the oven to warm, and uncorked the Shiraz Jim Hamilton had given him. He put the bottle on the table to breathe, and spooned the stew and tasted: Big, bold, beefy – that was the anchovies.

Ordinarily, the beef stew with the anchovies cheered him up. They reminded him of Danielle, who'd taught him to add them to the stew for flavor. Today, the whole rigmarole, warming the bread, setting the table, wearied him. Too many patients had been too depressed, today, and Maggie's leaving early had worried him all afternoon.

He set his table. After Mara had left in 1984, a friend had said, "always set the table. You'll keep your dignity." *Oliver would have appreciated that,* he thought. After lighting a candle and pouring the Shiraz, he made a mental toast to the old man's memory, working to jack up his mood. He was spooning the stew onto his plate when the phone rang.

Damn. The *black dog* stirred.

It was Deputy Pelton. Ed felt a moment's chagrin: He'd called her earlier in the day, but when she wasn't in, he'd promised to call back, then forgotten.

"Gosh, Deputy, I'm sorry I didn't get back to you – busy day. What's up?"

"Hey, if I call you Ed, you call me Andi, okay?"

"Uh, sure. Andi. What can I do for you?"

"Do you have a few minutes to talk about Maggie Sobstak?"

"Well, I was just sitting down to eat." He looked sadly at the stew, torn between wanting to eat it hot and wanting to be helpful.

"Oh, look, call me back when you're finished. Will that work?"

"Sure. Give me twenty minutes." He looked at the Shiraz. "Make that thirty minutes."

*   *   *

The stew was wonderful, and enough was left over for a couple more meals. His mood had definitely been jacked up. He dialed. "Deputy Pelt – uh, Andi?"

"Thanks for calling back. How was dinner?"

He smiled into the phone. "Excellent. Beef stew, artisan sourdough bread, a Shiraz to die for. Did you know that beef stew tastes beefier if you add anchovies?"

"No. Where'd you learn that?"

"A woman I, uh, know up in Helena. She got it from a gourmet magazine, I think."

"Well, business before pleasure. What can you tell me about Margaret Sobstak?"

"Well, look, I have to be careful. Confidentiality, you know."

"I understand that." Andi paused. "I talked with a couple of people here, and they say basically what you said, Maggie's a kind, friendly person, and not a drinker. Her recent behavior makes no sense to them. Can we do this hypothetically?"

He hesitated, then agreed, and they worked gingerly around

Maggie's privacy. Andi played twenty-questions, until she finally got exasperated. "Can't you just tell me what you think? This could be a matter of domestic abuse, after all."

He took a moment before answering. "I don't know anything that suggests that."

"Your impression, then. What's going on with her?"

He sighed. "That's too much, Andi. I can't share professional speculation unless there's a lot more reason to do so, or I have her permission, which I don't."

"So what if her husband's abusing her?"

"If I had any reason to suspect that, I'd report it. That's the law."

"You can't just give me your impression?"

"Stop pushing me on this, Andi."

"I'm a cop, Ed. It's my job."

"And I'm a psychologist. That's *my* job." Andi said nothing, apparently annoyed. Ed was quiet a moment. He felt the *black dog's* nudge, torn between wanting to help and wanting to be left alone. He said, "I *can* say, I don't really *have* an impression of Vic. Don't know him well at all. He doesn't strike me as the unfaithful husband type – I'd peg him as a guy who loves his ranch, his horse, and his wife. In that order."

"Not another woman?"

"Who knows? Maggie thinks so, but I don't know."

Andi said, "Getting her drunk was abusive, Ed."

"If he did." Ed felt suddenly uncomfortable, knowing what Maggie'd said.

Andi's answer was sharp. "You have an alternative?"

He grimaced. "Wish I did."

* * *

Wednesday, January 25

Lunchtime conversations buzzed in The Valley Inn when Ed scanned the dining room. He was meeting Jim for lunch, but the priest hadn't arrived. Ed took a table near the window and watched the street. A young woman brought him a cup of coffee. He introduced himself.

"I'm Henny, Sally Benson's cousin. I'm subbing while she has her baby."

"Henny?"

"It's short for Henriette. It's French."

"Pretty name."

"Thanks. It's better than what they called me in school."

"What was that?"

"Hank." She laughed. "I'll be right back for your order."

His cell phone buzzed. He thought it would be Jim, canceling lunch. Instead, Mara's voice chilled him. "Mara," he said flatly.

Mara said, "You have to help Gracie."

Just then, Jim arrived and sat down at the table. Ed gestured to the phone, and Jim mouthed, "Take your time."

Ed said, "No, Mara, we talked about that. There's nothing I can do for Gracie. If you don't like her doctor, find her another one." He remembered Elizabeth Murphy's eyes, and closed his own. "I can't help from so far away."

"Then I'll bring her there."

Ed exploded, but kept his voice to a fierce whisper. "Damn it, Mara! That's so crazy I won't even answer it!" Jim's eyebrows lifted.

"There's no reason to be profane," Mara said, coldly. "I'm trying to help my daughter here. Perhaps I should have *expected* you to refuse to help a little girl in trouble." She remembered Elizabeth too.

Disgusted, Ed punched the END button and banged the phone on the table.

Jim said, "Whoa! What was that about?"

He wanted to tell him everything, but no. *Never complain, never explain*. He sighed. *Bullshit*. "My ex-wife's daughter is in emotional trouble and she – my ex – seems to think I should do something about it. It's ridiculous, but Mara has never taken no for an answer."

"Mara's the ex-? You've never mentioned her."

"Uh-huh. Very ex-, thank God."

"So you're going to help the child?"

He shook his head, calming down. "No. There nothing I can do. The kid's in Minnesota."

"Nothing?"

"Come on, Jim. I don't need you piling on."

Jim shrugged and waved to Henny, holding up a cup for coffee. "Actually, it was a sincere question."

Ed thought again of Elizabeth Murphy and shuddered. "God. The last thing I want is Mara coming here. Anyway, I don't treat kids anymore."

Jim cocked an eyebrow. "Anymore? Did you once?"

Just as Ed was framing his change-of-subject, Henny brought the pot of coffee. "Ready to order?" she asked. Ed nodded and picked up his menu.

*   *   *

Maggie was in the laundry room doing some ironing for old Mrs. Tolblom up on the *Bar J* ranch. The poor old lady had been sick all winter, and Maggie and a few of the Welcome Wagon ladies had been sharing her laundry and bringing in frozen meals. She heard Vic's truck crunch into the yard, then the cab door slam. She heard his feet stomp three times outside the back door – Vic always stomped his right foot twice but his left foot only once, which she'd never figured out. The mudroom door squeaked. Its hinges had needed oil for years, which was a laugh because the oil can sat in the mudroom cupboard only six feet from the squeaking door. For years Maggie had smiled at that squeak. Today it annoyed her.

She'd been angry since Vic had snuck out to his truck long before dawn. The squeak had wakened her. Four-thirty and he's driving off the place already? *Probably off to see his girlie.* All morning, she'd ricocheted between shame and anger, sure as a cow knows her calf that Vic's affair was known across the valley. Her getting drunk last week only added to the gossip about her she knew the valley women were trading.

She loved this ranch. If it weren't for the ranch, she'd tell Victor Sobstak to go do it with his girlfriend till his old wiener fell off, and then she'd leave this valley and her shame behind. Well, maybe she would.

She heard the mudroom cupboard door click shut and Vic came in the kitchen. "Maggie? What's for lunch?" he called.

Resting the iron at the end of the board, she considered pretending she hadn't heard, but that was being spiteful. Ed Northrup would say she should be direct, not be, what'd he call it? Passive active? That didn't sound right. She called back, "I'm in the laundry room." She smiled. It was a direct answer, just not what he'd asked.

Passive aggressive, that was it. She couldn't figure out what was wrong with that. How else can couples get along without killing each other, for crying out loud? Obviously, Ed was never married.

Vic poked his head in the laundry room. "What's for lunch, sweetheart? Got me a powerful empty spot!"

Maggie did not look up from her ironing board. "Nothing with Jim Beam in it," she said, picking up the iron.

Vic paused and his face darkened. He chewed his lip a moment. "I screwed up on that one, Maggie. How many more arguments we gonna have about it? You already got my word it ain't gonna happen again."

She kept her eyes on the blue shirt she was ironing. "You know what, Victor? I don't need your *word* to know it ain't gonna happen again." Her tone was venomous. "And you know what else? If I have your *word* – " she came down hard on it – "I ain't real clear I got me something that's worth a whole lot any more."

Vic said nothing for a long moment. Maggie saw on his face that he was holding something in. When he spoke, it came out slow and hard. "I was bad wrong last week, Maggie, but I ain't goddamn lied to you about one little goddamn thing. You know damn straight what those drinks was for."

"Oh, yeah, you made that real clear. Poor Vic needed a dip in the honeypot for his 'stress.'" Her sarcasm dripped, but she realized he did not comprehend her larger concern. She raised her voice, as if she were talking to a lazy ranch hand. "I ain't just talkin' about last Wednesday, Vic. I'm referrin' to you and that woman down at the Jeff Motel."

Vic grabbed the doorknob of the laundry room; she saw the vein in his wrist pulsing. Again, she had the feeling that he was holding himself in, which gave her a small moment of satisfaction.

He said, "Maggie, I ain't sayin' this but once more. There ain't no goddamn woman down at the goddamn Jeff Motel nor any other goddamn place. You think if I had a woman stashed someplace – " His voice was getting louder now. " – I'd even *bother* trying to get you drunk so you'd goddamn – " His voice cracked. " – help me feel like a *man* again?"

He turned abruptly and left the doorway.

The plain homegrown truth of it stunned her. The mudroom door squeaked, then slammed. A moment later, his pickup roared. Tires sprayed ice and gravel as Vic swerved out the yard onto the long drive toward the highway.

She shakily pulled the plug on the iron. *No use burnin' down the house. Thelma Tolblom's ironin' can wait a minute.* In the kitchen, she put the sandwiches and the quartered orange she'd laid out for Vic's lunch in the fridge. *That man! So blind he can't see his lunch sittin' on the sideboard.* She felt a sorrow building. Vic had told it true: There was no other woman.

In a kind of trance, half-wondering where Vic had gone, half-not caring, Maggie avoided the obvious question. She thought of the door's squeak. Numbly, she went to the cupboard, lifted out his toolkit, and grabbed the Three-in-One can. She oiled the hinges. She liked the can's quiet click, click, click as she squeezed drops onto the metal.

Maggie tested the hinges. Swinging the door open, she liked the silence, but then, absurdly, felt vulnerable. *Now how do I know Vic's comin' in?* That squeak had always afforded her a moment to collect herself. With all the sneakin' around he's been doin', how'm I gonna know? Was he too angry to love her again? She tried on the thought that Vic maybe still loved her, or short of love, needed her. He *was* a man of passions, after all, no matter what cowboying and being a foreman and now owning the spread had extracted from him. He still had his stresses, as he called them. It had never bothered her before to ease him. Why now? Was she maybe unfair, depriving him of his relief? She glanced out the mudroom window, hoping she'd see his truck turning apologetically into the yard. White snow stretched out to the base of the mountains. She sighed and put the oilcan back in the tool kit.

Lifting the kit box back onto its shelf, she saw the stack of papers

Vic must have put under it. *What are these?* She was about to take one out to read when the phone rang, and she laid the flyer back, replaced the tool kit, and went in to answer it.

* * *

When Ed came into the Angler Bar, five-thirty on the dot, Ben Stewart perched on his bar stool on the corner, intent on a pile of wrinkled papers before him. He held a pen poised over a notebook. The upper corners of the pages he studied were torn. Behind the bar, Ted waved. "Your usual, Edward?"

"Absolutely, Ted. One of those days." He tapped the sheriff on the shoulder.

"Greetings, Ben."

Ben grunted, continuing to read his papers, jotting notes.

Ted spun a coaster onto the bar and set Ed's pint on it. To the sheriff, he said, "What brings out the grouch in you tonight, Benjamin?"

The sheriff only growled and returned to the papers. Ed craned a look over his shoulder; they looked like flyers, text beneath a picture.

Ted leaned closer to Ed. "How are you doing, my friend?"

Ed felt the warmth in Ted's voice. "I'm still in the fray, Ted."

"You're seeming a bit down at the mouth lately."

Embarrassed, Ed lifted his glass. "Burnout. Too many sad people around."

"Well, I worry about you."

Ben growled again, looking up. "We got us, what, a love-in here?"

Ted straightened, winked at Ed, and knocked softly on the bar. "All done, Sheriff. Love-in terminated."

"Good," grunted Ben. To Ed, "What's that all about?"

Ed shrugged. "Been feeling down about Oliver."

Ben nodded. "I'm aware of your attachment to the deceased."

"The *deceased*? We're talking about Oliver here. What's with the cop jargon?"

Ben tapped his finger roughly on his flyers. "I'm just pissed off about *this* crap." He slid a page over to Ed. "Have a look."

The page had a 28-point headline: "Do you want *THIS* for your Governor?"

Below the headline was a crude caricature of Terrell Landon Burke as *MAD Magazine's* Alfred E. Newman. Ed slid it back. "Disgusting."

Ben shook his head. "Picture's just the start." He pushed the flyer back again. "Read the whole damn thing."

America was once the new Promised Land, but a tide of Illegal Immigration and the faithlessness of our racially terrified Politicians have reduced us to this: Our blind Citizenry may be seduced into electing this Descendant of Slaves. With no personal abilities of his own, he has been elected to various Offices purely because of criminal Affirmative Action, given power and positions he has not Earned. He will not admit it, but his politics is race-based Communistical Socialism. Do you want four years of Democrat and Africanistic lies, hate, and disrespect of everything our beloved White Country stands for? If not, pray for our Great Nation's deliverance, work to defeat this Abomination, and send your donations so we can continue waging the battle for the soul of our beloved Country!

Ed tossed it on the bar. "Christ."

"Reaction," Ben demanded.

"Other than outrage?"

"Yeah, other'n that. Who? Who the hell did this?"

Ed tapped the credit line at the bottom. "The Church of Jesus Christ of the American Promise."

Ben slammed his fist on the bar. "No, damn it! I mean who *here*, who in my valley is tackin' this filth up on my telephone poles?"

"How would I know?"

Ben breathed deeply for a moment, then lowered his voice. "You're right. I'm just so pissed." He took a long swallow of beer, put it down hard, and belched. "Let's do hypotheticals."

Ed said, "Really, Ben, I haven't heard about this. None of my patients would get involved with this crap, at least none I can think of."

Ben moved his glass around in a small repetitive circle. "You'd tell me if you learned something?"

"Probably not, Ben, if it's patient information."

Ben's frown was pure exasperation. "Your ethics are – how shall I say it?"

"Unhelpful to law enforcement."

"You think?"

Ed relented. "If I learn anything I *can* share, I'll let you know."

Ben grunted, barely mollified. "Don't do any heavy lifting on my account."

Ed tapped the pile of flyers on the bar. "What do *you* think about this?"

"It's either a lone crazy, or it's the water pullin' out 'fore the tsunami. And unless my intuition ain't as good as it's been, it ain't a lone crazy."

"What are you going to do?"

"First thing in the morning, I assign a deputy to investigate who put these up. Then I find out who this 'Church of Jesus Christ of the American Promise' is and how they came into my valley." He was furious again.

Ted set an un-ordered pint in front of both men. Ben frowned. "I didn't order this. I've had my two."

Ted smiled. "It's been a hard night, Sheriff. Leave it if you don't want it."

"You're pourin' me a beer on the house?"

Ted pretended to be offended. "No, sir! This is a bribe, a blatant purchase of political influence."

Ed and Stewart looked at each other; Ed started to chuckle, and after a moment, Ben followed. Ted beamed. "You two were getting *way* too serious for six o'clock in the evening."

Ed said, "Thanks for the humor, Ted." He turned to the sheriff. "I'm supporting Burke, Ben, and this flyer makes me furious. It's hateful. Do you think you could have your deputy keep me informed about the investigation?"

Ben thought it over, sipping his unheard-of third pint. "Usually we don't, but yeah, I'll keep you in the loop."

"So which deputy will you assign?"

Ted's ears perked. He'd been down the bar leaning over a crossword puzzle, and he straightened up.

Ben grunted, now slightly slurry. He pushed the nearly full glass back. "That'll be for me to know and you to find out." He stood up and donned his heavy jacket. "So long, Ted. Night, Ed."

When the big front door closed, Ted leaned on the bar in front of Ed and whispered, "Guess which deputy will get *that* job?"

"No idea."

"Such a child, Edward. Ben's going to put Andrea Pelton on that assignment, and she'll be ordered to stay in close touch with you."

"Jesus."

"No. Andi."

EIGHT

Thursday, January 26

SOMETIME IN THE deep night, Ed half-woke and drowsily watched light snow drift through the yellow cone of the yard light. He fell asleep again and later awoke from a dream of Oliver Tweedy, his chest aching. Then he slept again, and knew nothing until the alarm clock buzzed him awake at five. He lay in bed a while, remembering snatches of the dream, which drifted in and out of his mind like the snow through the yard light. The lingering sadness kept him abed, until he had time only for a shortened run.

While dressing for the day, he debated reheating Tuesday's stew for breakfast. Poached eggs on toast, with plenty of butter and jam, won the debate; the stew would keep for dinner. He shouldn't eat the toast or the butter. Or the jam. For that matter, he should skip the eggs. Tomorrow. He'd get serious tomorrow on the weight.

He drove into town, watching the snow drifting across the road. It might not be a blizzard, but this slow, steady snowfall would pile up. Snowshoeing on Saturday would be great. He thought maybe he was up to climbing the Coliseum again. Exorcise the demons. Out of nowhere, he wondered if Leese MacArdell snowshoed. *She must, she's in great shape.* Maybe an affair would... what? It'd been a long time since he'd been with a woman. Hell, a long time since he'd wanted to be. Maybe... He decided to knock on her door when he got to the office.

But Ardyss Conley, Oliver Tweedy's paralegal, was just unlocking *her* door as Northrop came in, and he could tell she was suffering. Ardyss looked very old this morning, her eyes red, although her well-kept suit was prim and neat, her modest black business shoes polished. He greeted her and they embraced, and she began to sniffle softly in his arms. Ed invited her into his office. She composed herself, muttering to herself "Oh, shoot, stop this," and they chatted. He asked what her plans were, now that Oliver was gone.

"I'm 82 years old, Ed. Oliver was a wonderful boss, but just my Social Security's not enough. I'll have to move down with my daughter." Her eyes moistened again.

"Where's she?"

"Los Angeles." He saw fear in her eyes. "I'll die of that city, Ed."

"How much is your Social Security?"

"I get nine hundred dollars a month. Oliver paid me six hundred. Without that, I can't pay my rent and bills."

Ed felt sad. "You've lived in the valley a long time."

"My husband Price brought me here sixty-four years ago. I was eighteen." Her eyes glistened again.

"Isn't your house paid for?"

She frowned. "It was, until it burned down in '96."

Ed grimaced, embarrassed. "Sorry. I forgot about the fire."

"We didn't have insurance. Price's memory had been failing for some time, and he forgot the premium. We sold the lot, of course, but Price's nursing home ate all that up. Then, when he died in '99, I about gave up. But Oliver – " She dabbed at her eyes with a neatly ironed white hankie. "Oliver was so kind. He moved me in with him and Loretta, until I could afford my little place."

Ardyss stood up. "Shoot, listen to me! I've plenty to do next door without feeling sorry for myself! Thank you kindly for the visit."

He embraced her lightly, wondering what he could do to help. She closed his door politely behind herself.

He never remembered to knock on Leese's door.

*   *   *

Later that morning, a few minutes free, he stepped over to Ardyss's office, trying to think how to give her a boost. She was packing files in a box, but Oliver's mementoes still hung cheerfully on the walls. The room glowed with his presence. The old lawyer would have smiled kindly at Ed, said nothing about his sadness, and found something to lighten Ed's heart just as he was leaving, a little joke or maybe an invitation to a poker game or a tip on an excellent wine. And it would have worked, though Ed had overlooked these everyday kindnesses. He felt his sadness well up.

"I never noticed that picture," Ed said to Ardyss, pointing to a picture on the wall, of Oliver with Eugene McCarthy, the poet-politician from Minnesota who campaigned against the war in Viet Nam.

"Oh, yes, Oliver was quite proud of that. He worked for Senator McCarthy's campaign here in the valley, you know." She stopped. "Actually, now that I say it, he *was* Senator McCarthy's campaign around here." She chuckled an old lady's chuckle. "He was so proud of that. When the Democrats held their primary, the Senator actually carried the vote."

"I didn't know Oliver was into politics."

Ardyss looked fondly at the picture. "Oliver was a strong believer in political affairs." She blushed. "He was a strong believer in all sorts of affairs, if you take my meaning. But anyway, he was saying to me just the week before he died that he got a kick seein' old Landy Burke – imagine, him calling Mr. Terrell Landon Burke 'old Landy'! – and thought he might get involved in the governor's election. He said, 'Ardyss, let's recapture the spirit of '68!' if you can believe it. And him going on eighty-eight years old! The dear man didn't stop living till the minute he died." She dabbed a small tear, then reached up and removed the picture from the wall and handed it to Ed. "Oliver would love you to have this. He thought the world of you."

Ed chuckled. Oliver was doing it again, giving him a little something to cheer him on his way.

*   *   *

After his last patient of the day, Ed stayed a few minutes, opening the mail, finishing his notes, putting files away. Oliver's picture sat propped against the desk lamp. The old man had been dapper in 1968, with a Clark Gable mustache, hair combed straight back, and a slim pinstripe suit and bow tie. Handsome. Lawyerly. Gene McCarthy looked grim. Ed stared sadly at them, both gone now.

He heard the waiting room door open. *That's odd*, he thought, glancing at the open appointment book. No one was listed for this hour. Maybe the custodian, cleaning up early? Ed locked the file drawer, grabbed his coat from the hook, and stepped into the waiting room.

He was startled to see a woman and a girl, sitting apart. The girl he didn't recognize, but the tilt of the woman's head, or perhaps the way her hand turned a magazine page, tripped a memory. From behind, her neck looked scrawny and gaunt, its skin, like her hands, sallow, and her thinning hair all angles and juts, verging on unkempt. He could not see her face – she sat in the chair that looked away from his office door – but from the back her neck seemed unnaturally narrow and mottled. Once, he had known that neck.

The girl sat as far from the woman as she could, and did not look up when he entered; she peered into a cell phone clutched in both hands, her thumbs flying. Her eyes were edged with black.

He cleared his throat.

Hearing him, the woman turned and he knew her eyes, those hard, demanding brown eyes: Mara. Ed stopped breathing. It was an old, worn-out Mara, gray-faced and gaunt, not the exuberant girl who'd taken whatever she wanted and laughed. This was Mara emptied out. *So the girl*, he thought, *must be Gracie.* The girl had still not looked up, but her thumbs had quieted, and she continued peering into the phone's tiny screen. Ed looked back at Mara's lined and hollow face.

Ravaged but still stylish, she wore exquisite brown slacks and a cashmere turtleneck sweater under an expensive après-ski jacket. *Her idea of Western wear,* he guessed. A string of pearls. The quality of her clothing, though, failed to conceal that she was aging poorly, or perhaps was ill; her skeletal, yellow eyes looked haunted. Grace, on the other hand, wore dirty black jeans with tears in the legs, untied black running shoes without socks, and a torn black hooded sweatshirt, but the skin of her hands and her face glowed. *She'll freeze in the valley's cold,* Ed thought. Tiny white earphones trailed thin white cords into the phone. What hair he saw under the hood shone with grease, or perhaps with some application meant to convey grease. Light acne crawled up her jaw, and a row of small silver rings arced along her earlobe. Her lower lip was pierced with two gray studs. The girl lifted one hand and pulled the hood up, covering more of her head. She did not look up from her phone.

Mara struggled to stand. She grimaced as she pulled herself up out of the chair. "Damn arthritis!" she grunted. Her voice commanded the pain to recede.

Fruitlessly.

The girl pulled the hood further over her head, becoming a small monk.

Surprised, suddenly infuriated, Ed managed a stuttered "How did you get here?" What he wanted to say was *Get the hell out of here.*

"We flew into Missoula."

The hood jerked. "Omigod. What a joke of an airport."

He looked at the girl, then turned to her mother. "That's impossible," he said. "The flight from Minneapolis arrives at 1:50. You can't get here from Missoula in less than three hours. You'd have to arrive…"

"Yesterday," Mara finished. She turned fully toward him, extending her arms as if for an embrace. They faced one another like that, ten feet apart. "It's so good to see you, Eddie, after all these years."

Ed glared into her eyes for a bare moment, then silently walked past her to the perennial coffee pot on the counter. A viscous black sludge an inch thick steamed on the hot plate. This morning's dregs. He poured a half-cup into a mug, then roughly switched off the warmer.

Mara dropped her arms. "You needn't be rude, Eddie."

He gripped the hot mug hard. No one called him Eddie. He'd left the name with so much else in Minnesota, after Elizabeth's death. When he felt himself under control, he addressed the girl, ignoring Mara. "Do you drink coffee?" Chancing it, he added, "Grace?"

Mara interjected. "No! She doesn't like – "

The black hood pulled back. The girl glared defiantly at her mother, then said, "Yeah, I do."

"Mara? A cup for you?" Perhaps hospitality could quell his fury.

"Not that. It looks poisonous."

Ed filled another mug and carried it over to the girl. "Montana coffee. Puts hair on your chest."

Grace arched her eyebrows and shot a glance down at her flat chest. "At least something'll fucking grow there," she said, not humorously.

Mara barked, "Gracie Ellonson, you will apologize to Doctor Northrup for your mouth! And you will *not* drink that coffee!"

Grace looked out from under her hood like an animal in a cave. "I apol-o-gize, Dr. Northfield," she said, drawing it out.

It was a mistake to take sides, he knew. Yet his fury felt reckless. For years, his hurt and rage toward Mara had been locked up like a river under ice, and the shock of Mara's appearance had ruptured that ice, rage bubbling up like black water. He nodded to the girl. "No problem, Grace. And my name's Ed Northrup." He glared at Mara. "Not Eddie."

He turned toward Mara, who had said nothing. The crack in the ice widened. "You flew in yesterday. So your call came from Missoula?" He leveled his voice, as a man levels a rifle.

"From the motel, yes."

Grace burned her lip on the hot coffee. "Fuck!" she grunted under her breath.

Mara snapped, "Gracie, your mouth!"

Grace snorted. "This shit *burned* my fucking mouth!" She slammed the cup on the table, splashing the coffee.

Then, as he poured Grace a cup of cold water, he said to Mara, "So you planned this without asking me."

"I asked. You said no. But Gracie needs your help and I intend to see she gets it." She moved toward her daughter, her arms out, but Grace struck them away. Ed wondered if Mara actually cared about the girl. *Maybe she did.* He restrained his anger. "Grace, what do *you* want?"

"Nothing." As Grace turned her head and stared out the window, her hood fell partially back. Her nose had the same gentle slope and sweet upturn as Elizabeth's. Her chin, set now in annoyance, rounded to a smooth beautiful throat that belied the ugliness of her attitude and her clothes. Studs weren't trendy in 1984, so Elizabeth hadn't worn any, but the profile was the same – the dirty hair, the defiant stare, the rift with the mother. He didn't try to calibrate how much of the pounding of his heart was rage at Mara, how much fear for Grace.

"Nothing? *Nothing*? Nonsense!" barked Mara. "You do *too* want something, Gracie! You told me so yourself. You want somebody to *listen* to you, you said. To *understand* you."

"Not him!" Grace yelled. "Not somebody you *hire*."

"*Someone* has to, Gracie." Suddenly, Mara's voice was pleading; her eyes looking terrified. Ed had never seen Mara afraid, only controlling, only demanding. Even when she'd announced he'd made her pregnant, she'd been accusatory, as if demanding, "Solve this!" And of course, when their newborn died, she'd shown only a sullen anger, as if he'd failed her. He felt the rage-holding ice breaking away and opened his mouth.

But it was Grace who exploded first. She spun to face her mother, the hood falling fully back. "Stop calling me fucking *Gracie*! My fucking name is Grace!"

Then Mara struck like a rattlesnake. "Grace Marie Ellonson! Don't you dare – "

His rage burst out. "Mara! Shut the hell up!"

Grace's eyes widened at Ed's roar, and she looked swiftly at her mother, whose mouth was poised, open, but soundless.

Words, welling up from some dark place of pain, swarmed into Ed's mouth.

Grace wants you *to listen to her, you stupid self-centered bitch!* Long-honed restraint, though, silenced him. But his roar still hung in the air. On Mara's face he saw bitter anger, but also something at war with it. Mara glanced sideways at Grace, then back to Ed.

Unexpectedly, Grace giggled. "*No*body tells Mara to shut up."

Mara slumped, no, fell heavily into the chair, and her voice came raggedly. "Eddie," she began, then looked apologetic. "Ed... please. You have to help her. Help us."

Ed nodded. His roar had settled something in him. "It's not up to me, Mara." He turned to Grace, his voice as soft as he could pitch it. "Grace, do you want my help?"

Grace turned again to face out the window, staring at a car. Her refusal to answer called to mind Elizabeth Murphy's silences. *I have to let Grace be Grace,* he reminded himself.

"Mara," Ed said. "If Grace doesn't want me involved, I'm not going to play games with either one of you." Grace's head turned back to the room, her eyebrows lifted.

Mara fluttered a hand, said, "All right, you win." She restrained the bitterness in her voice. "We'll go in the morning. Do you have a room we could sleep in? We thought you'd let us stay with you."

Ed saw the ploy and stiffened, but it was Grace who said, "*You* thought that, Mara. I'm not staying with him."

"Grace Ellonson," Mara began, but it came out weary, defeated. "That is so rude of you. You apologize this minute."

Grace paused a long moment, looking appraisingly at her mother. Then she smiled tightly. "Shut up, Mara," she ventured, glancing sideways at Ed.

Mara, seeing Ed's grin, sputtered at him, "You're encouraging her! You'll make it all worse. I'll never be able to control her now!" There it was. Even Mara heard it, but Ed saw the fear return to her eyes as well. Or perhaps what he saw was the loneliness of a mother unable to fathom how to turn her daughter into a friend.

He said quietly, "We'll see. And no, I don't have a spare room for you to stay in." It was a lie, but perhaps kinder than saying he would never sleep under the same roof with her again. He asked the two to wait while he called the Jefferson House to reserve them a room. Then, he went out and asked Grace if she'd mind waiting a few minutes while he and her mother "caught up on old times."

"Do you know my mother?" Grace asked, looking back and forth between them, parsing this news. Obviously, Mara had told her nothing.

"Oh, we go back a long way," he said.

"Were you one of my mother's boyfriends?"

Ed looked at Mara, then back at Grace. No use lying. "No. I was married to her."

*   *   *

Ed deliberately rested back against his desk, half-standing, arms folded, looming above Mara in the chair. "Tell me about Paul."

"That's old news, Eddie."

"Not to me. I always thought you were sleeping with Terry when you left. You let me think so, anyway."

She smirked. "It was convenient. I didn't want you attacking Paul."

Paul Carlen, colleague, business partner, best friend. Over the years since coming to Montana, he'd talked occasionally with Paul, who had never let on. He wanted to slap away Mara's smirk, so he kept his arms tightly folded against his chest. He forced himself toward calm.

"Is Grace Paul's daughter?"

"No, the thing with Paul ended when you moved out here. Her father's Larry Ellonson."

"Is he the guy I saw you with that day in the Minneapolis Hyatt? You were getting off an elevator with him, after you left Grace with me."

She took a moment, thinking. "No, Elevator Man was nobody, a diversion."

"Just another affair, then?"

"At first. Larry and I were on the rocks and I needed... hell, I don't know what I needed. Actually, Elevator Man turned into marriage number four, if you count six months a marriage." Mara looked puzzled. "You're awfully calm."

Ed ignored that. "You look sick. What's the matter with you?"

Mara said, "This isn't about me. Will you help Gracie?"

"Does her father see Grace now?"

"Are you kidding? Larry left me when Gracie was five. His parting words were 'I never wanted the little shit.' I was glad to be rid of him and his drug habit."

"How many more?"

"Are you trying to embarrass me?" A faint pink tinged her gaunt and bone-thin cheeks.

"If your life doesn't embarrass you, my questions can't. You asked me to help Grace, so I need to know what her life has been like." His arms were still tightly folded, holding in his anger. He thought momentarily that he ought to let up on her. *The hell with that.* He had an image of the *black dog*, this time snarling at Mara.

Mara glared at him and held his eyes for a long moment, then looked down.

He said, harshly, "So, how many other men, Mara?"

"Leave me alone."

"Let me ask it differently: How many male figures has Grace lost in her life?"

"All right, I give up." Her voice was weary. "After Larry left, I needed somebody. A child isn't something you can do alone."

"*Something*'? Some *thing* you *do*?"

"Fuck you, Ed. I don't need this. Is this about Grace or just your spite?"

Ed unlocked his arms. "You brought her here, Mara. How many men walked out of Grace's life?" He shoved his hands in his pockets, fisted.

Mara sighed. "Six. Six assholes," she snapped. Then she shook her head, looking enormously weary. "No, the last one, John Hertz, he was a decent one. Gracie liked him."

"What happened to him?"

"Do I have to talk about this?"

Ed gave no answer, letting the cruel silence say *Yes, you do, every rotten piece of it.*

She waved her hand, weakly, as if dismissing something. "Fine. I got rid of him. He was too passive, like you. I hate passive men."

Ed waited a moment. He wondered if Mara's bitterness toward him might distort her information, but so far she seemed grudgingly candid. It wouldn't hurt to ease up. "You're right. I was passive. And you hated me."

Mara looked surprised, but before she could speak, he asked, "Was Grace attached to Hertz? Before you *got rid* of him?"

"I suppose."

"You suppose? You don't know?"

She sank back in the chair. "Eddie, Ed, please. Why are you being cruel?"

He stared at her.

"All right, she was attached."

"How do you know?"

"Fuck you." It was weak, exhausted. "I'm her mother, whatever you might think. John loved her and Gracie loved him. It hurt her a lot that I dumped him. He really was the nicest one of all."

It didn't need asking, but anger asked it. "Including me?"

His question hung long in the air. She sighed. "Yes, including you." Then Mara looked feebly away. "No, not including you. You probably were the only one of the bunch who really loved me."

He paused. "No, Mara, frankly, I don't think I really loved you. I needed you to want me, that's all."

Mara's eyes widened, shining with tears. Skeptical, he handed her a box of tissues. *Mara uses tears.* She didn't so much cry, as she took in ragged breaths, dabbed her nose. After a couple of silent minutes, she held out the soggy tissues to him; he gestured toward the trash can. When she deposited them, he asked, "What makes you think Grace is using meth?"

"I don't. Her therapist thinks it."

He thought about that. The girl did not look like a meth user to him, but maybe it had just started. "Grace's two attempts at suicide. When was the first one?"

"After John left."

"How did she do it?"

"Pills. A prescription I had."

"Why did she do it?"

She looked at him sharply. "I have no idea."

"You didn't ask her?"

"We never discussed it."

He stood upright and walked to the window, looked out. "And the second one, how did she do that?"

"Pills again."

He turned back and faced her. "You didn't lock them up after the first time?"

A shrug. "I know what you think of me, and I don't care. Just help her." She lowered her head.

"You maybe wanted to be rid of her?" It was vicious, entirely unnecessary, but he would not hold it back.

Mara jerked upright. She glared at him. "Fuck yourself, Ed. I couldn't sleep. After John left – "

"John didn't leave, you got rid of him."

She sagged back into the chair, her momentary anger dissolved. Her skin was gray. "I was terrified of being alone. It was half a fucking Ambien. How could I know she'd steal them?"

He turned again to look out at the dark. "Did you want rid of Grace, Mara? So you could maybe be free to find a new boyfriend? So you wouldn't have that *something to do* alone?" There was no ice constraining his fury now, though he kept his voice calm.

Mara was quiet. When he turned back again, she was looking at the floor, tears flowing. Her head moved slightly, perhaps a nod, an acknowledgement. "I know what I've done to Gracie. Am I on trial here?"

He softened. His cruelty had run its course, but he said nothing. He came back and sat on the desk.

She kept her head down, wiping her eyes with tissue. "If you'll just help Gracie? Please?"

He stood up. "If she'll let me. Let's go out and see."

"No, not looking like this." She pulled more tissue from the box, found makeup in her bag, and touched up her eyes.

"You don't need that, Mara."

She snarled, "Ed, you have no fucking idea what I need."

He almost laughed. *You never change.* "Let's go get you two settled in the motel."

But Grace was not in the waiting room. Mara looked around wildly. "Where's that little shit gone now?"

*   *   *

Callie Martin, the sheriff's receptionist, glanced up at the short black-clad girl struggling with the heavy glass door to the department. Her clothes were black, she had dirty hair, and those white earphone thingies in her ears. The metal studs in her lip and lining her ear fascinated Callie: *Doesn't she have a mother?* The girl sure was not from the valley.

"You searchin' for somethin', darlin'?" she called out from behind her counter.

"You the cops?" the kid said, her voice sullen.

"Well, yes 'n no. My name's Callie. Callie Martin." She reached a hand across the high counter, but when the kid ignored it, Callie gestured at her name placard on the counter. "I'm Reception." She thought of Deputy Pelton. "And Dispatch." She gave the kid a moment, then added, "And your name would be?"

The girl looked surprised. She extracted a bud from one ear and cocked her head. "Say that again?"

Callie mimicked the head-cock and pitched her growly voice to its sweetest range. "Here in the valley, darlin', we use 'please' and 'thank you.' Care to give that a try?"

"You aren't my mother," the girl bit off, but then shrugged. "*Please* say that again."

Callie, caught mid-thought in *Good thing I ain't your mother,* then blushed. "Well, shoot, honey. With all that negotiatin', I plumb forgot what I asked you."

The girl smirked. "My mom forgets shit all the time. I say it's because she drinks so much."

"I wouldn't know about your mom. But you, you sure got a mouth on you." She saw the sudden hurt look in the girl's eyes. "Shoot, never mind that. What *did* I ask you?"

"Do *you* drink too much too?" Now those mascara-blackened eyes showed amusement.

Callie's pause-and-stare was exactly long enough to warn the girl about the coming reply. "Child, when me and you know each other long enough to borrow a tampon and you've given me cause to like you more'n to want to whip your smart little ass, I just might answer that. Till then, how much I drink ain't your business. And by the way, I recall you askin' if we're the cops, but those earplugs or whatever kept you from hearin', so it ain't me fallin' behind in this conversation." She pulled up to her full dignity. "I am Mrs. Callie Martin, receptionist and dispatcher for this office, which is the Adams County Sheriff's Department." She took the briefest breath. "And your name is?"

Grace was tough, or wanted people to think so, but she was only fourteen.

"My name's Grace Ellonson, Miss Martin. I'm from Minnesota."

"Really?" Callie said, more kindly. She pointed across the hallway. "Our Ed Northrup over there, he's from Minnesota too. A long time ago, anyway."

"Yeah, I know. My mom's talking to him."

What Callie called her mental *Curious Meter* clicked on and emitted a low hum. "What're they talkin' about?"

"Me." The girl had relaxed a little and leaned against the counter, which came up to her chest. She folded her arms atop it. "She thinks I'm fucked up."

The obscenity drew Callie's frown. "Well, your mouth could use some work. You know, you oughta lay off them swearwords till you're of age."

The kid giggled. Callie thought how young she really was. "You mean, like I can drink and say fuck when I'm twenty-one?"

Recalling her own youthful snap, Callie sighed. "Yeah, somethin' along those lines."

"Did you know it's legal for me to, like, *actually* fuck somebody when I'm like seventeen? Or even now, with my mother's permission."

Callie blushed to the roots of her red hair, then shook her head. "Shoot, let's change the subject. Why's your mom think you're fu... screwed up?"

The girl was having fun now. "So 'screwed' is better than 'fucked'?"

"Stop that," Callie said, exasperated now. "Just tell me. Ain't Minnesota got any psychologists?"

The girl shrugged. "Yeah, they do, but I don't listen. They go, like, 'tell your mother your feelings' and shit like that. But she's, like, too busy fucking – oh, I'm sorry – screwing her boyfriends to care how I feel."

Callie was quiet. She felt a stab of sympathy, but she couldn't get past the language. "Grace Ellonson, I gotta say that mouth of yours is hurtin' my ears. Think we could ease up on the language a bit?"

Grace looked surprised. "I guess. You're kind of old fashioned, aren't you?"

Callie chewed on that. "Well, I reckon I am, if old fashioned means your edges got wore off. You think these 'fucks''n such are better?"

A frown, but a thoughtful one, crossed Grace's face. "I think the body's good, so body words have to be good."

"I heard that someplace too. You might jus' be right." She squinted at the girl. "Okay. So humor an old-fashioned lady. Let's hold off on the body words, shall we?"

"Can I say 'intercourse'?"

"If it comes up appropriate. But, honey, it ain't gonna come up appropriate talking to me." Callie tried to smile, but there was a tinge of sadness behind it. "Okay," the girl said, friendly now. Callie saw, past the studs and the dirt, her young healthy skin and the freshness in her eyes. The big wall clock said thirty minutes past quitting time, but something about this child held her. "So tell me, honey. They ain't any good psychologists in Minnesota? Why'd your mom drag you out *here*? We're Noplace!"

"I'm not your honey," said the girl sharply, then shrugged. "She brought me here because she was married to Dr. Northrup once."

Callie's curious meter redlined. The math wasn't hard: The girl looked to be thirteen, fourteen. So she couldn't be Ed's daughter, unless... The curious meter surged into *ORANGE ALERT*. Maybe he snuck back to Minnesota one time fourteen years ago. Here was that perennial question that kept working its way around the valley's networks of story and rumor and speculation: Who was Ed Northrup before he came to Monastery Valley? Right there across the hall was the answer! Callie almost wanted to go over and knock on the door.

"So you know Dr. Northrup, then?" she asked, hopefully.

The girl shook her head. Just then her phone beeped twice. She pulled it out of her hoodie pocket, and, holding it in both hands, studied it for a moment, and then began tapping it with her thumbs. Practically shivering with the itch for news of Ed, Callie waited impatiently. The girl was absorbed in her tapping.

"Whatcha got there?" Callie asked, nodding at the phone, wanting to get back to Ed.

"Amanda. My friend."

"You gonna answer it?"

"No, silly. We're texting. We don't *talk* if we don't have to."

"What's *texting?*"

Grace tapped a few more times, then looked up at Callie. Disbelief blended with curiosity in her voice. "You don't text?"

Callie shook her head. "Ain't never done what *you're* doin,' tappin' on my phone, except to call somebody. What is it?"

Without warning, the girl folded her arms again on the counter, lowered her face into them, and began sobbing quietly.

"I miss Amanda *so* much," she gasped between sobs.

Callie had just swept around her counter and gathered the sobbing child into her arms when Ed came through the door, followed by a gaunt and withered woman with an angry, tormented face.

*   *   *

As Ed pulled open the heavy glass door and saw Callie enfolding Grace, Mara pushed past him and abruptly pulled Grace from Callie's arms. Callie said, "You got a lonely little girl, there, ma'am."

"Did you hurt her? Why is she crying?"

Grace pulled away from her mother. "She didn't hurt me. She was being nice to me." She sniffled. "I miss Amanda. I hate it here."

Callie deliberately ignored Mara's insult. She stuck out her hand. "Callie Martin, ma'am. You must be Grace's mother."

Mara's hand brushed Callie's for the briefest second. "Mara Hertz."

When Mara turned back to Grace, Callie rolled her eyes at Ed. "Stayin' in the valley for a while?" she asked.

"We'll have to see," Mara replied. "Ed may be helping Gracie with some things."

Grace looked away. "I didn't ask him to."

"We'll discuss it another time."

"Bullshit. You've already fucking decided." But she looked quickly at Callie.

"There's that mouth, honey. I'm thinkin' you'll be wantin' to say you're sorry to your mom." Callie smiled, but her voice was iron.

Grace shook her head, but then said, "Mom, Callie here is real old-fashioned, not like you. She says I don't get to say 'fuck' till I'm old enough to drink."

Mara seemed non-plussed. "I never said you could say that word."

Grace moved in for the kill. "No, you just say it all – " but Callie headed her off. "Never mind that now, Grace. It's *your* mouth we're talkin' about, not your mother's."

Grace, inexplicably, smiled. "Yeah. Sorry, Miss Martin." And as an afterthought, "Sorry, mom."

Behind their backs, Ed winked at Callie, then said, "Let me show you the way to the motel. After you're settled, I've got some leftover stew for dinner." He didn't need the gossip that would swirl across the valley if he had dinner at the Angler with a second woman this week.

At the Jefferson House motel, he parked beside their rental car outside the office. When Mara came back from the office and unlocked the door to Number 7, he carried in their bags. Grace had a small carry-on – Ed figured it contained more black clothes – and Mara had three large and heavy suitcases. As he was unloading the last bag, a sheriff's black-and-tan SUV drove slowly past the motel.

Ed straightened and peered at it. Andi Pelton was driving. He couldn't tell if she had seen him, but he waved. The SUV slowed a bit as it passed the parking lot, but didn't stop.

*   *   *

"This is so cute," exclaimed Mara as Ed let them into his cabin. "It's so, ah, cowboyish." She turned to Grace. "Don't you think Ed's cabin is just the sweetest, Gracie?"

Grace shrugged. "It's okay. And my name is Grace."

He'd built it himself, of logs he'd cut from a stand of wildfire-dead

Ponderosa pines up on the mountain, and he was proud of the place. The deep and welcoming front porch offered cool shade in the hot months, a place to sit and watch the warm spring rains. The front room stretched the width of the cabin, one end the sitting room with its wood stove, the dining area and open kitchen on the other. Behind them were two bedrooms and the bath, and above the sleeping rooms a loft, reached by a handmade ladder of small logs. Mara glanced suspiciously at the two bedroom doors.

He loved the place. It wasn't *cute*. And Mara would not be sleeping in it.

Ed lit a fire in the wood stove, and put the leftover stew in a Dutch oven to heat. He set the long oak dining table for three. When they sat down, Mara picked at the stew, as if her plate held something suspect. Grace, darting glances at her mother, tasted nothing. Ed cut thick slices of the bread, but Grace only looked at them.

"You baked this, Eddie?" Mara asked, taking a small bite.

"Ed. And no, I bought it in town."

Mara inspected her slice. "Such a little homebody you've turned into. Bread, beef stew." She placed the bread on her plate, only the smallest bite gone.

Grace watched them warily.

"You're not eating much," he said to Mara.

She winced. "I'm afraid my appetite's gone, Eddie."

Ed filled his mouth with stew to keep himself from saying anything. *She can play her name-game alone.*

Grace said, "His name is Ed, Mom."

"I *know* that, Gracie."

Grace pulled the black hood up and disappeared into it, then abruptly stood and went to the couch and fell onto it.

Mara shrugged, and then asked, "Do you have any vodka, Eddie? Ed?"

He looked at the girl sitting silently on the couch, then nodded. "Sure, Mara. Still use a dash of dry Vermouth? On the rocks?" He was determined to get the evening done without reacting to her.

"Yes, exactly. You have a good memory. And two olives."

"No olives, sorry."

From inside the hood came Grace's voice, "Have you ever gotten drunk without olives, Mother?" she asked, her voice all innocence.

Mara ignored her. "No problem, Ed. Skip the olives."

When he handed Mara her drink, Grace pulled back the hood and said, "Can I smoke here, Northrup?" She looked defiantly at her mother.

"Goddamnit, Gracie! You are not old enough to smoke, especially in other people's houses. You know that as well as I do."

"I'm old enough to smoke at our house!"

He interrupted them. "Only outside on the porch, Grace. You'll need a coat." She had only the threadbare sweatshirt. He tossed her his parka.

The girl jumped up and swung it around her shoulders like a cape, grabbed her backpack, and went out. As she closed the door, Mara hissed, "You allow a child to smoke? Is this what I can expect from your psychology?"

Ed stood up and cleared away the dishes. The fire was low, so he went into the living room to pile on two logs. Mara watched him from the table. He came back and sat down across from her. She glanced at his stomach.

"You've gained weight," she said.

Payback for the office interrogation, he thought, ignoring it. *Probably deserved.* "Why are you really here, Mara? You know I can't help Grace over a weekend, and I know you have no intention of staying in a place like this."

"You don't know any such thing. I intend to do whatever it takes to help her. And I don't appreciate your letting her smoke."

"Let's get this straight: If I am going to work with her, I pick the battles. Kids smoke. I haven't got any credibility with your daughter and I need to find some fast, because tomorrow morning I'm going to ask her if she wants my help. If she says yes, I'll need it."

"And if she says no?"

"If she says no, that's it. But tell me. I still want to know why you came out here. There are fine psychologists in Minneapolis."

"I thought maybe you and I..."

Just then, his phone rang. He excused himself.

It was Andi Pelton. Her voice was police-formal. "Sheriff Stewart requested I keep you informed about the investigation into the flyers."

"Oh, sure. Thanks for – "

Without waiting, she continued, "One of the waitresses at the Valley Inn, a young woman named Henny, saw Victor Sobstak stapling something to a power pole when she came into work a little before five this morning. She states that she didn't know what it was, though, or remember which pole it had been. She also states that she hadn't given it any thought until I asked about it."

Ed sighed. "Do you think it could be Vic?"

"That's who she reported seeing. I'll pay a visit to Mr. Sobstak's ranch in the morning. That's about all I have at this time. Was there anything else you wanted to know? About the investigation?"

Ed was puzzled by the uncomfortable rigidity of her speech. He asked, "You all right, Andi? You sound kind of upset."

She was quiet a moment. "Well, I guess I was annoyed when Ben told me to keep you informed. He wants us to start dating, you know."

He laughed. "Yeah, I know. Don't worry. We're on to him."

"I guess. I just don't want any complications." That was it.

He went to the kitchen to pour himself a glass of wine.

"Who was *that*?" Mara asked.

"Work. A case. Deputy Pelton with information for me."

Mara smiled bitterly. "He a friend?"

He shook his head. "She. No, just a professional associate, I suppose."

"Not a girlfriend?"

"Drop it, Mara. What were you saying?"

She took a mouthful of her martini, waited, swallowed. "I was hoping maybe you and I could, I don't know, see if – "

He snapped it off. "No, Mara, never. You're not welcome here."

The bluntness of it jarred her and her face paled past its unhealthy gray. "As if I would want to stay in your god-forsaken wilderness." It came out as a hiss.

The front door opened and Grace came in, smoke-smell surrounding her. "Well, at least I'm not busting in on another make out party. You two having a fight already?"

Ed frowned. "No, just getting the ground rules straight." He turned to Mara.

"Tomorrow morning, then? Nine o'clock at my office?" Mara nodded curtly.

Ed said to the girl, "Grace, tomorrow morning I'm going to ask you if you want to talk to me about whatever's bothering you." She started a protest, but he put up his hand. "Don't answer now. Sleep on it. It'll mean staying with your mom here in the valley for a while, so give it some thought. If you say no, I'm fine with that. But if you say yes, I'll do everything I can to help you out."

Grace was quiet for a moment. "Don't bother. I'm going to say no, so you might as well forget tomorrow." She turned toward the door, then back. "Oh. Thanks for letting me smoke." She dropped his parka on the chair.

He picked it up, wincing a little from the cigarette smell. "No answer yet. Think it over." He pulled his keys from the pocket and started to put on the parka.

To Mara he said, "I'll show you the way to the motel."

Mara's voice was liquid ice: "We can find it."

"Okay, then," he said, taking off his jacket. "There's a good breakfast place, the Valley Inn, about four blocks south of the motel. I'll see you at my office at nine, and we'll talk about what's next." He looked at Mara. "For Grace."

Mara pushed the girl, who'd again pulled up her black hood, out the door ahead of her. "Fine. For Grace."

From under the hood came a subdued mutter, "Don't do me any fucking favors."

Ed closed the door. *I won't, sweetheart,* he thought. *I won't.*

NINE

Friday, January 27

ED AWOKE FEELING calm and restored. Last evening's cruelty toward Mara had dissipated, leaving in its wake a touch of pity. *She looks like hell,* he thought, something Mara would despise. And a kid like Grace no doubt was a burden. Sleeping as well as he had surprised him, as did this morning's calm. Running in the new snow, sounds muffled by the soft powder, he actually enjoyed himself. Instead of the dread he'd expected to feel about meeting with Mara and Grace, he felt a tranquil curiosity. Not for a minute did he think Grace would ask him for help, so Mara would fly her back to Minnesota in a fury. How would their story eventually play out? Probably not well.

His cruelty to Mara left no regrets. He'd rejected the mother but left room for the daughter, though he knew she would not choose to stay. What fourteen-year-old would? It was Mara's stupid, reckless idea to drag her out here. He did have one regret, though: the big gut that Mara kept glancing at. As he ran, he resolved to really lose it. Starting now. He pushed his run a half-mile longer.

*   *   *

A Cheerios breakfast later, it was nine o'clock when he went into the building. Opening the waiting room door, he muttered to himself, *Showtime!*

The room was empty. He puttered a while, watering plants, making coffee, straightening magazines. At 9:20, just as he was thinking of calling the motel or the Valley Inn, the door opened hesitantly. Grace peered around it, then came in all the way. Ed watched the door for Mara, but it closed behind the girl.

"Sorry I'm late," Grace said in a subdued voice. There was none of last night's sullenness and anger. "I couldn't remember where your office was."

"Didn't your mother..."

"She said she'll meet us here in a while."

"Where is she?" he asked, as nonchalantly as he could.

Grace shrugged. "She went out in the middle of the night. She said she'd meet me here." Grace pulled an envelope from her backpack. "She said to give you this."

The sealed envelope contained a single handwritten sheet, and ten one-hundred dollar bills.

Eddie, I was called back to the Twin Cities to handle some business arrangements. Something came up unexpectedly that needs my attention. The enclosed is for Gracie's room and expenses until I can free myself to return. It shouldn't be more than a few days, a week at the most. If longer, I'll try to notify you.
Mara

He put the letter on his desk, battling his anger. *I'll try to notify you?* He coughed to settle his voice. "What's your mom's cell phone number, Grace?"

"I already tried. She's not answering."

"Maybe when she sees it's me calling she will." Grace dictated the number, and Ed dialed, but Mara's phone went directly to voice mail. Careful not to alarm the girl, he kept the anger out of his voice as he left a request for her to call.

"How about your home number?" he asked Grace, whose eyes were wide. He dialed it and heard three rising tones, then the standard female voice: "We're sorry. The number you have dialed has been disconnected. No further information is available at this time."

Grace must've seen his scowl. "What's wrong?" she asked.

He covered. "Wrong number. Why don't you give it to me again." Grace rolled her eyes and dictated it one slow number at a time, as if helping an old man across memory's street. Ed dialed again and pretended to leave a message, asking Mara to call him when she arrived.

Grace's eyes were wide, moist as a young doe's. "Where do you think she is?"

Ed considered shielding her, but instead handed her the letter. As she read, she looked up at him, shock on her face. She teetered, and he guided her down into a chair. She pulled up her black hoodie.

Some minutes later, Grace was crying in a chair across from Ed, who sat on the edge of his desk. When his cell phone buzzed, they both looked sharply at it, and Grace wiped her eyes.

He looked at the caller ID: *Magnus Anderssen.* "I'll take it later," he said to Grace, who was looking at him with wet red eyes. Outside, the sky was the gray of dying skin.

"Is it my mom?"

He shook his head. "A friend."

After a few moments, she said, "What's your name again?"

"Ed Northrup."

"Northrup, do I have to stay in that fucking motel by myself?"

*   *   *

Ed drove Grace back to the Jefferson House to collect her bag. She'd been uncommunicative until they pulled into the lot, a drive of four blocks. She said, "This town is, like, too small."

He looked over at her, eyebrows raised.

She sniffled. "I hate this fucking place."

Handling her fear by being angry, he thought. He looked at her quizzically.

"Do I have to watch my mouth with you too?" she asked.

He considered it. "No, not when we're alone, but if we're with other people, yeah. Out of respect."

"Nobody respects *me*. Why should I?"

"Because you need us, at least till your mother comes back."

"I don't need you people."

Ed nodded and pulled the truck into the slot in front of Number 7 and put it in neutral. "Okay. Out you go."

Grace opened her door and climbed down from the cab. Ed shifted to reverse.

"Hey! What the shit?" she barked.

"Close the door, Grace." He looked ahead. "You don't need us." When she didn't move, he reached across and pulled shut the door and locked it. He began backing out.

"Fuck this, Northrup!" She pounded on the window. He continued slowly rolling back. Grace yelled something else, then deflated, her fury draining out like water from a torn bag. She walked to the door of Number 7, and began twisting the handle viciously.

Ed continued his retreat, but more slowly, watching her. At last, she turned toward him, her eyes streaming, and sank down on the cold sidewalk in front of the door. He slowly pulled back in, got out, and sat down beside her.

"She didn't leave me a key," Grace sobbed.

He said nothing.

She sat still on the sidewalk. After a few moments, she said, "Northrup?"

"What?"

"Fuck it. I could use a little help."

He nodded. *Couldn't we all,* he thought. "I'll get another key. We'll get your stuff." he said, and felt the smallest pressure against his shoulder, as if she'd leaned into him. He almost put his arm around her, but instead just waited, sitting beside her on the cold cement.

PART TWO

TEN

Later

B ACK IN THE office, Ed was trying to decide what to do. Grace sat, hood up, texting, no doubt to Amanda, no doubt about her mother. She sniffled now and then. He needed to talk to Ben, but the sheriff hadn't called back. *What's next?* That was the second question. The first was, where the hell was Mara?

Grace pulled her hood back and said, abruptly, "What do you do, anyway?"

Odd question, he thought. Was the girl fending off her fear by making small talk until her mother walked through the door? Pretending this was normal?

"I'm a psychologist."

"I didn't ask what you are. I asked what the fuck you do."

Ed looked at her, considering whether to respond to the question or the obscenity. He said, "I've been wondering about that lately myself."

"Wondering what?"

Absurdly, he thought about telling her about his Sunday on the Coliseum, about his depression. *Sure, tell a suicidal fourteen-year-old about your own flirtation with suicide!* Still, she *was* fourteen, and now her mother had abandoned her to the mercy of strangers. Would it hurt so much to start things out with some honesty?

She pushed. "Wondering about what?"

He decided to skip the depression talk. He told her about Oliver Tweedy's death, and then, without thinking, he told her something he hadn't yet admitted to himself. "I'm not sure I want to be a psychologist any more."

"Then why don't you quit and do what you want?"

He chuckled. *Out of the mouths of babes.*

He started to explain that his patients needed him, but wasn't that the point? If he was tired of being needed, why not do something that no one needed him to do? His mother once had reprimanded him for wanting to play college basketball instead of entering the seminary. "God wants you to be a priest, Eddie, so stop your selfishness and get to work!" *In other words, the hell with your wants, do what others need you to do.* He liked Grace's advice better.

So he chuckled, but Grace looked hurt and pulled her hood up. Ed explained about his mother and why he'd laughed. She pushed back the hood. "You mother was a bitch too?"

The word didn't offend him, but applying it to his mother was troubling, stirring a vague memory, something his father had once said. He couldn't recall it. "Yeah, I suppose so," he said.

"I'm right?"

"Yeah, I think you are."

"Maybe *I* should be the fucking shrink here." She sounded pleased with herself, but when he gave a small frown at her language, she asked, "Are you like that Callie lady?"

"In what way?"

"About swearing? Are all you adults around here tight asses?" Before he answered, she changed the subject. "I'm starved. Let's go to McDonald's."

"Sorry, no McDonald's. I'll bet you *are* hungry – you didn't touch the stew last night. Let's get you breakfast." He set his office phone to forward calls to his cell, in case Mara called.

Grace frowned. "No McDonald's? This place is, like, Death Valley."

As they went past the sheriff's department, he changed his mind.

"Look, I gotta get the sheriff looking for your mom, just in case she's run into trouble. I called, but he hasn't called me back. Why don't you run down to the Valley Inn – it's just a block down the street – and I'll come over in a half-hour or so." He pulled a twenty out of his wallet and started to hand it to her.

Grace's face blotched red. "Don't make me go alone." She looked very young.

"I'm sorry." He thought it over. "Let's go back to the office and order you a pizza."

She sniffed. "For, like, breakfast? Awesome."

When they got back, Ed called Alice Lansing at the Valley Inn and asked her to send over a pizza. He cupped the receiver: "You want everything on it?"

"I hate pepperoni."

To Alice, he said, "No pepperoni. Otherwise the works." He listened a moment. "Yes, for breakfast. Somebody here needs a pizza."

Then he said to Grace, "I'm going to go over to the sheriff's office. You wait here for the pizza."

When she got teary again and pulled her hood back up, he realized he'd done it again, so he walked over to her and touched her head as if knocking lightly on a door. "You don't want to be alone, do you?" The hood shook vigorously.

"Willing to stay here with a friend of mine while I get them looking for your mother? My friend's a nice lady." A tentative nod.

He dialed Oliver Tweedy's number, explained the situation, and Ardyss came directly over. Ed introduced them, and Ardyss made the perfect amount of comment on how nicely the color black suited Grace's complexion and how fashionable the studs were. The girl's eyes rolled, but she smiled. Then she stuck her hand out to Ed, palm up. "Me 'n Miss Conley'll be needing that twenty."

*   *   *

When Ed pushed through the department's big door, Ben Stewart was leaning on Callie's reception counter, giving some instructions. He turned and saw Ed. "Well, now, look who's droppin' in for a little law'n'order. Mornin', Ed," the sheriff grinned.

Ed nodded at them both. "Morning, Ben, Callie. Ben, got a minute?"

Callie turned to her computer screen. "I got me some work to do. You boys do your talkin' someplace else."

Following Ben into his office, he closed the office door. Ben said, "This by any chance be about your lady friend and her little girl over at Jeff House?"

"It would." Ed seldom bothered asking Ben how he knew these things. Callie probably told him.

"I'd have called sooner, but we got other stuff goin' on. What's the story?" While Ben poured a cup of coffee, Ed summarized what had happened.

Ben frowned. "She just showed up without asking?" He handed the cup to Ed and went around his desk, sat, and rested his boots on the desktop.

"Oh, she asked all right. I told her not to come. Turns out she was already in Missoula."

"Ain't that ballsy! And now she's flown the coop and left the kid here?" Ed handed him Mara's letter.

Ben scanned it silently, then muttered, "What kind of mother leaves her little girl with a bunch of strangers?" He sucked in a long breath. "So where's this lady friend of yours going?"

"She's no friend, Ben. She's my ex-wife, and the letter says Minneapolis."

"Describe the lady."

Ed did. He was struck again by how gray and withered she had looked.

Ben lowered his feet from the desk and flipped open his Rolodex and dialed a number. "Let me ask Missoula to check the airport." He waited a moment. "Sheriff Marks, please. This is Ben Stewart over in Adams County.... Sure, I'll hold." He held out his dirty cup with *Best Damn Sheriff in Montana* printed on it to Ed and nodded at the coffee pot. "Fill 'er up..." and then spoke into the phone, "Hey, Johnny. Ben Stewart here... Just fine, just fine... Marlene's good. How's your Jo?..."

Well, that's real good news. No chemotherapy, then?... Great news. Look, John, I got me a situation I could use a hand on."

After describing Mara, he said, "Got me a matter I need to chat with her about." He made no mention of Grace. Sheriff Marks asked something.

"No, don't arrest her, but you might kinda firmly suggest that she sit her butt down in Missoula till I can get over there." He listened. "Yeah, I'll drive with a friend of mine, soon as you get to her." He nodded to Ed, listening. "Will do, partner. Thanks for the help." He hung up.

"What about the little girl's daddy," he asked Ed. "Where's he?"

"I don't know. Apparently he's not in her life, but I'll find out."

"Do that – and the other relatives too. If we don't find the mother quick, we gotta get some family out here to pick the girl up. What's her name again?"

"Grace."

Sighing, Ben rubbed his eyes. "Pretty name." He opened his eyes and stood up. "Get me that family information. Soon as I hear back from Missoula, I'll give you a ring and we'll head over."

On his way out, Ed paused at Callie's counter. She asked about Mara and Grace, and was outraged when Ed told her what had happened. "That poor little kid! A mother like that, I guess I can see why she's testy. Where's she stayin'?"

"They were at the Jeff House. But I suppose she'll stay at my place."

Callie pondered this. "I'm thinkin' not. Nope, that won't do, her bein' a little girl and you a single man and all."

"Callie! You can't be thinking – "

"It ain't what *I'm* thinkin', Ed. You'd never lay a hand on her, I know that. It's what the talk would be. You know."

Ed knew. People talked. Over the generations, the Anderssen Ranch and the Monastery of St. Brendan on the mountain had exerted parallel moral forces in the valley's life, but there was a third force as well. Early snows, late blizzards, wildfires, relentless summer heat – all ravaged the people's plans and dreams the way mountain ice scoured rock. A rancher's cattle and his hopes could both die in an April blizzard. July's heat, slicking the young folks with sweat and lust, could melt their caution until, in a single moist moment of desire under the burning stars, their lives changed forever. These stories of life or love or loss would be told and retold, exchanged like currency back and forth between the mountains.

Was the gossip true? Sometimes, but always it *might* be true, and so the stories carried the cautions by which people survived. If the storm of '56 did not entirely ruin Charley Wright's hay crop, it could well have, so get your hay in early. Was Lucy Moran *really* raped that hot August night under the ballpark stands? No, but had it been one of those boys from another valley, who knows? Cinch up your jeans, darlin'. A story's truth lay not so much in its facts, as in its warning. And so the valley's talk itself generated a morality, a kind of truth that philosophers cannot parse: A web of stories, a living wisdom that only the eventual turning out of things can verify. Anything that was told might turn out true, because once upon a time in the valley, it was.

So yes, Ed knew, people would talk.

Ben stuck his head through the door. "I'm thinkin' we maybe got us a child neglect situation here. I'm gonna call Rosemary in."

Ed glanced at Callie, who lifted her eyebrows. Rosemary Rasmussen, the valley's social worker, contracted with Child Protection Services up in Helena to handle the occasional child abuse problem. If Ed could spare Grace that, he wanted to. He said, "Let's see if we can locate the mother or somebody in the family first. If we can't get her back with family by Monday, we can talk to Rosemary then."

Ben frowned. "We ain't supposed to fool around with a CPS issue."

Callie chimed in. "Aw, Ben, you know what'll happen. They'll ship that little girl up to the Children's Home up to Helena. We can take better care of her right here."

Ben rubbed his chin. "You two got a plan where she can stay?"

It came to Ed like a gift. "Ardyss Conley was just telling me she doesn't have enough income to stay in the valley." He pulled out the envelope and counted the money again. "Mara left a thousand dollars, so we could use that to pay Ardyss to take Grace in, at least till we find the mother."

"Perfect," declared Callie, her glare at Ben daring him to object.

"Ardyss'll take good care of her – and she'll clean up that girl's mouth while she's at it."

The sheriff raised his hands, palms out. "Okay, you win. Monday then. But if we ain't found somebody from the family by Monday nine a.m., we call Rosemary."

* * *

Before returning to his own office and Grace, Ed sat in Oliver's office chair thinking about the girl. If she *was* suicidal, would this push her too far? Suppose they failed to find Mara today? How would Grace, alone and afraid, handle that? It wasn't fair to leave Ardyss to manage that risk alone, so tomorrow's climb up the Coliseum trail would have to wait. He had to stay here, close to Grace. He felt the *black dog* stir. Another self-sacrifice. *So much for doing what I want.*

Or maybe Grace could go with him? Some stretches of the trail were hard, but generally not too strenuous, and she looked healthy. Why not? After all, *do what you want* came from her, didn't it? He chuckled and closed Oliver's door on the way to his own office. Grace's voice squealed inside. "You never did!" She was giggling. Perhaps she hadn't yet tipped to the gravity of her situation. In the office, a large pizza box, four pieces gone, rested on his desk.

"Northrup! Ardyss says one time she slept with, like, five cowboys on the same night. I'm like, she's full of shit, right?" Grace's eyes were dancing. Ed thought of her mother's eyes, thirty-five years ago, eyes he'd thought he loved.

Ardyss, holding a piece of pizza as if it were a hand of cards, gave Ed a broad wink.

He could hardly imagine it, knowing her devotion to her husband, Price, but he went along with the joke. "If Ardyss says it, she did it." Then, of course, he understood.

Ardyss tapped Grace's frail shoulder. "There. Now, young lady, I don't talk 'shit.' What did we agree about your language?"

Grace mock-rolled her eyes. "You people and your sensitive ears!" She adopted a fake-serious tone. "We agreed I don't need to swear, there's other ways to *emphasize my points.*" Then her face clouded and she asked Ed, "Did my mom call?"

"No, sweetheart, nothing yet. The sheriff's trying to locate her."

"I'm not your *sweetheart.* I'm called Grace." Her voice was assertive, but her face looked shattered.

Ardyss, who was almost exactly as tall as Grace – the younger woman growing, the older woman diminishing – put her old arm around the girl's bony shoulders. "You tell him, girl. These men'll say anything to sweet talk you." She gave Ed another wink.

"To get in our pants, you mean," Grace said, half angrily.

Ardyss mock-hit her on the shoulder. "Language again?" Grace asked.

"Language."

"But it's true."

"Sure it is," agreed Ardyss. "But you aren't supposed to know it for three, four years yet."

"Not where I'm from."

"Child, at the moment, you aren't where you're from."

Grace's shoulders crumbled, and she turned to Ardyss, who enfolded her, quietly stroking her hair, until Grace abruptly pulled away and savagely wiped her face. "Forget it. And I'm not a child."

ELEVEN

The same day

MAGGIE SOBSTAK ABSENT- mindedly rinsed the pan she had now washed twice, gazing out the kitchen window at the long rolling hills rising east to the mountains. Was she done with Vic? Did she still love him? Or was something else going on that she couldn't yet see? Twenty-three years ago, her marriage had been a volcano, all fiery eruptions, joy and lust and anger. Had it gone dormant these last years, only to roar alive with explosions of her corrosive jealousy and Vic's boiling defensiveness?

Maggie, for all her simplicity, was not simple. She'd read how, three billion years ago, colliding tectonic plates had lifted these same mountains she watched from her kitchen window, forcing volcanic eruptions all along the impact zone. Were married people like tectonic plates, unstoppable pressures grinding against one another, one implacably subsuming the other amid volcanic fury and the explosion of emotion?

Should I leave him? she wondered, rewashing the pan. *Or fight for him?*

A black Cadillac Escalade crunched slowly into the yard outside her kitchen window. Nosing in against the weathered wooden fence surrounding her snow-buried garden, the car pushed the fence back a few inches. Maggie snorted at the discourtesy. The two men sitting in the front seat wore sunglasses. The driver got out, a short man, with wide shoulders and arms that bulged the sleeves of his suit jacket. He wore a big Stetson. Maggie thought, *He ain't no cowboy.* The man approached the back porch door and knocked.

Maggie dried her hands on her apron and opened the door. She was momentarily startled when the door didn't squeak, then remembered oiling it.

"Mrs. Sobstak?"

"That's me. Your truck's on my fence."

"Is your husband at home?"

"You fixin' to back your vehicle off my fence?"

He held very still a long moment, then said, "Yes, ma'am. After you tell me if your husband's at home."

Maggie laughed a humorless laugh. "Well, it bein' ten in the mornin' on a workin' ranch in Montana, I figure the answer to that one is no."

His taut thin lips did not smile. Maggie could not see his eyes behind the sunglasses. "Where might I find him, then, ma'am?" His politeness was sharp as a filet knife. He annoyed her.

"You mind takin' off them shades, sir?" Maggie countered. She didn't like this guy. "I don't often talk to a person I can't see his eyes."

The man waited another ominous moment, then slowly removed the sunglasses.

He had ice-blue eyes, killer eyes. She shuddered. "Victor's in the workshop, there." She nodded toward the shed, then nodded at the Escalade. "Let's get that vehicle backed up a piece."

The man tapped his hat brim twice and nodded. "Thank you, ma'am," and stalked slowly back to the Escalade, got in, said something to the other man, and backed it up six inches. The other man got out, never glancing at Maggie in the doorway, and together they crunched across the dry snow toward Vic's workshop.

*   *   *

Vic aligned the grinder precisely and turned it on. When he pressed the steel mower blade against it, orange and yellow sparks erupted, blasting against the guard and scattering across the cement floor. The grinder's shriek covered the sound of the shop door opening. When Vic pulled back the blade to inspect its sheen, the Reverend Crane's voice startled him.

"Victor. Working in the fields of the Lord, are we?" Crane had to shout over the grinder's whine.

Vic turned, annoyed at the interruption, then cowed when he saw who it was. "Well, no sir," he shouted back. "Just sharpenin' some mower cutting bars for spring." He switched off the machine.

"'And He shall beat their swords into plowshares,'" Reverend Crane intoned, genially.

Vic, recovering from his surprise, nodded. "I'm real flattered you're here, Reverend."

"Well, as I recall, you agreed to this meeting, Victor."

Vic felt abashed. "Oh, yessir. Yes. I did that, for sure. I'm jus' tryin' to say, well, I'm honored."

Reverend Crane looked pleased. "Well, then, Victor, I believe we can get down to business."

There followed a string of flattering sentences that Vic, used to the bullshitting of cowboys, enjoyed but knew for what they were. Finally, he said, "So what is it that I can help you with, Reverend?"

"Well, Vic – I may call you Vic?" At Vic's nod, he continued. "It's really quite straightforward." There followed another passage of talk about tax laws, too-big government, and the patriotic duty to "stand our ground."

Vic picked up another mower blade, a fifteen-inch shank not unlike a short sword, and waved it at the stack of blades awaiting their date with the grinder. "Reverend, all due respect, but I got me a pile a work to get to this mornin'. Think maybe we can move along to what I actually can do to help you all?"

Stetson moved forward. "When Reverend Crane has a point to make, he makes it in his good time, friend." His voice was a rattlesnake's buzz.

Reverend Crane waved Stetson off. "Thank you, Michael." He turned to Vic. "You've got yourself a well-appointed shop here, Vic." He looked around at the neatly hung tools, at the clean workbench. "I admire a man who keeps his tools sharp and clean and ready to use."

"And you're wantin' me to be one of your tools."

Reverend Crane clapped his hands softly. "Perceptive, Vic! Indeed I do. I have a mutually beneficial proposition for you. A way, let us say, to sharpen the tool."

"And that would be what, exactly, Reverend?"

Crane nodded to Stetson. "Michael will provide the details."

"All due respect, I'd rather hear 'em from yourself, Reverend," said Vic. Stetson unsettled him.

Crane's smile disappeared. "Michael will provide the details, Victor." Vic caught the formal name. He looked at Stetson.

Stetson looked directly at Vic without removing his shades. "*You* have a tax problem. If you pay your taxes, you will probably lose the ranch, because the bank won't front you the money for a tax loan *and* next year's operating loan. *We* want a tax refusal case in every Montana county and you can be the one here in Adams County. You refuse to pay your federal taxes, and we'll provide you a good tax lawyer at no expense to you. You won't lose a penny. You save your ranch, we get our Supreme Court case." He leaned back against the workbench, arms folded.

Vic narrowed his eyes and looked at him a long moment, then said, "I ain't never told you about no tax problem."

Stetson shrugged. Reverend Crane said, "Victor, men come to our meetings for two reasons: They hate the federal guv'mint and want to do something about it, or they have tax problems. You don't hate the guv'mint, so you have tax problems. Am I wrong?"

Vic shook his head.

"Then it doesn't matter how we know."

Vic picked up another blade and wiped off its dirt. He flipped on the grinder and put on his safety glasses and ground one side of the blade. Over the screech of the grinder, he shouted, "I refuse to file my taxes and you'll pay for my legal defense?" Stetson nodded a yes.

Vic shut off the grinder. "Reverend?"

"Yes, Vic, that's what you get."

"And if I lose? Who pays the taxes and the penalties and such?"

"We do, Vic. Everything. But you won't lose."

He turned over the mower blade in his hand, inspecting its unfinished side. "And why would you do this?"

"As Michael told you, Victor, we get our day in the court system. We believe you might have a good chance to make it to the Supreme Court."

"I reckon I ain't too interested in makin' it into any goddamn court."

The Reverend's voice darkened. "Such as bankruptcy court?"

Vic roughly flipped on the grinder and began sharpening the other side of the blade. Stetson, who had been leaning against the bench, reached across and jerked the grinder's power cord from the outlet. "The Reverend's asking you a question," he snarled.

Vic glared at him, making his calculations. He stood six inches taller than Stetson, but they were six lean inches. The shorter man was stocky, his arms and shoulders were strong, and Vic had no doubt he knew how to use his weight. On the other hand, Vic was holding a sharpened steel blade. Stetson probably outweighed him, and the thin straight lips showed a meanness that Vic had never seen in the usual barroom brawler. He took a deep breath, plugged his machine back in, and then switched it off.

He said to Stetson, "How about we do this like grown-ups?" Stetson folded his arms and leaned against the workbench. Vic turned to Reverend Crane. "So tell me again exactly what I gotta do for you."

Crane smiled coldly. "The first thing, you don't file your income taxes this April. Simple as that. When they send you the letter, you let us know and we'll take care of everything."

Vic lifted his ball cap off his head and scratched his scalp. "You said 'first thing.' What's the rest?"

"Well, the next thing is you pass along to us, that is, to Michael here, the names of everybody you know who supports the Negro for governor here in the valley."

Vic turned to the grinder and flicked on the switch. Stetson stood up from the workbench and reached for the power cord. Vic flipped off the switch, glaring at him. "And if I do, what happens then?"

Stetson growled. "Not for you to know, brother."

Vic bristled. "I ain't your brother. And you touch my equipment one more time, *brother,* me and you will do this the hard way." He hefted one of the mower blades.

But he was already mentally reckoning. How would losing the CW Ranch balance against this game Crane was proposing? Setting the blade on the bench, he picked up another and wiped it down with the rag. Could he live without Maggie's respect, much less her love? If he lost the ranch, how could she respect him? The ranch meant every goddamn thing they'd dreamed of together, and if he lost it, would he lose Maggie too? He felt a cold draft, and looked at the shop door, which Crane and Stetson had left ajar. Through it, he saw the long fields, his fields, rolling in snow-blue waves up to the foothills below the eastern mountains. He knew every coulee and rise of that land, every copse where his cattle shaded from the summer sun. He saw Maggie's silhouette in the kitchen window, and felt a rush of emotion. He dropped the wiped blade beside the shiny one on the bench.

"I don't file, you provide the lawyer?"

Reverend Crane nodded, irritably. "As I said, Victor."

"Provided I name names."

Crane glanced at Stetson, who said, "Whatever. You tell us who supports the Negro. It isn't 'naming names.'"

Vic flipped on the switch and pressed the wiped blade against the spinning grinder. When it was shiny, he turned the machine off and said, "If I say no?"

Stetson folded his arms, a mean grin playing on his lips. "You say no, good citizens that we are, we inform the IRS you're threatening to refuse to file your taxes. That you're maybe a Posse Comitatus member. They'll watch you, and if you don't pay, they'll nail you to the cross. If you pay, you go bankrupt." Stetson paused. "Figure *that* math, cowboy."

Vic slowly picked up and inspected another dirty mower blade. "Looks like you boys got me cornered." He glanced at the rat rifle hanging fifteen feet away on the workshop wall; Stetson followed his look and calmly walked over to the rifle, took it down, and disarmed it.

Vic gripped the blade hard, but held still.

Reverend Crane said, "Cornered? That would be one way to say it, Victor. You can see it as you're joining forces with Jesus Christ and his promises for America. And Jesus isn't a bad side to be on."

Vic carefully wiped the dirt off the blade in his hand. Siding with Jesus wasn't an itch he needed to scratch. Maggie's opinion of him was something else again. What Charley Wright would think mattered too. The closest man to a real father he'd ever had, Charlie would say, "Tell 'em to go to hell, Vic. Just protect Maggie." Even his own Daddy, that goddamn poor excuse for a cowboy, not to mention a father, would say, "Take care of your woman, boy," even if that was the last thing the old buzzard did. Vic felt himself losing his footing. How could he take care of Maggie if he lost the goddamn ranch? He turned on the grinder, relaxing into its whine, holding the dull blade at the perfect angle. Sparks scattered across the floor. Reverend Crane stepped away from them.

Still, even if his daddy hadn't done it, Vic tried to live his daddy's one rule: "Take care of your woman." No, two rules. "And do the right thing." But what if taking care of Maggie meant doing something that wasn't right? He bent over, pressing the dull blade harder against the grinder and watched the spray of red blue orange sparks scattering off the metal. He glanced angrily at Stetson, daring him to pull the plug again. Sinking the blade into the asshole's skull would be real goddamn satisfying.

Then, the blade sharp and shining, he switched off the grinder and straightened up. "Reverend, you need to let me think this over."

Stetson growled, "This ain't a negotiation."

Reverend Crane waved him silent. "I guess I'll be needing your answer by, say, Monday morning? You good with that, Victor?"

Vic heard the formality and the threat. "Yes, sir. Monday will do just fine."

"Good," said Reverend Crane. "From here on, you contact Michael. Not me." He handed Vic a business card. "Michael's my personal representative in this." Reverend Crane reached out and shook Vic's unsettled hand. Stetson, still hostile, reached into his briefcase and pulled out a sheaf of flyers.

"Put these up in town," he said.

Vic bristled. "I ain't agreed to do that again."

Reverend Crane laid a conciliatory hand on Vic's arm. "Victor, Victor. You are either with us or against us. And against us, you will lose your ranch." The hand squeezed hard. "We *will* have your answer on Monday?"

Vic withdrew his arm. "Monday."

Through the open door, the crunching sound of another vehicle drew their attention. They all looked out. A police SUV was pulling into the yard.

"Well, hell," muttered Stetson.

*   *   *

Driving slowly into the yard, Andi noticed the big Cadillac Escalade with its Idaho plates. After parking beside it, she jotted the plate number on her note pad. She sat a moment, collecting her thoughts. Although Maggie's stonewalling had annoyed her, she hoped today would be different. She tried to conjure some sympathy. *People hide things because they're scared of something. Or somebody.*

Andi paused and looked briefly up across the rolling rises toward the mountains. *So beautiful. I can be happy here.* Against the yard, in the pasture, two cows lifted their heads from the hay berm to stare at her.

*   *   *

In the shop, Reverend Crane whispered harshly, "If she comes in here, we're preaching the gospel of our Lord Jesus. Nothin' else. You clear on that, Victor?"

Stetson quickly pulled a pamphlet out of his briefcase and thrust it at Vic. It read, "Jesus is Our Promise!" in blood-red letters.

Vic chuckled, although the sheriff's vehicle made him nervous too. "What you fellas afraid of? You got them hot-shot lawyers, right?"

Stetson pressed close to Vic and his voice was even more menacing than before, and his breath was rank. "We're preaching the *gospel*," he growled. "You say anything different, there'll be shit landing on you and on your wife you can't even imagine."

Vic glanced at Reverend Crane, who nodded.

But the woman deputy went up to the house instead.

*   *   *

Maggie met her at the door, standing in the doorframe.

"Mrs. Sobstak? I don't know if you remember me, I'm Deputy Sheriff Andrea Pelton from – "

"I know who you are, and I ain't got no more to say today than I did last week."

Andi's heart sank. "I'm glad you're feeling better, Maggie. I – "

"You don't know how I'm feeling, Deputy, and my name ain't Maggie to you."

The hostility swept her breath away, but Andi tried again. She decided on politeness first. "My apologies, Mrs. Sobstak. I thought maybe we might have a chat about – "

Maggie interrupted again. "Well, you thought wrong, then. We ain't havin' us no chat."

Andi hardened her face. *All right then*, she thought. *We'll do 'er the hard way.* "Mrs. Sobstak, we believe that someone, possibly your husband, might be abusing you."

Andi saw the flinch, but Maggie's face recovered quickly. she said, "I ain't somebody who gets abused, honey." Her voice had an edge like sharpened steel.

Andi looked straight into Maggie's eyes. "You made *yourself* that drunk last week? I'm told you don't use alcohol."

Maggie held her eyes for a moment, then looked over Andi's shoulder – she stood in the mudroom door, two steps higher than Andi – toward the mountains.

Looking up at her, Andi could see hesitation in her face, and decided to ease off for the moment. She turned and gazed out to the mountains. "You have a beautiful place here."

"That's so."

"Nothing like this where I'm from. No mountains, no animals, except maybe some of the men." She tried a smile, but Maggie didn't respond. Andi added, "The men who abuse women."

Maggie's scowl deepened. She said, "Deputy, this ain't where you're from. You ain't got mountains there and you ain't got nobody who trusts you here. You want information? Maybe you oughta go back where they know you. You're an outsider and people here don't talk to outsiders."

Andi's eyes narrowed. She said, "I'm told you used to like meeting newcomers with the Welcome Wagon."

Maggie recoiled a moment, then leaned forward. "Who told you that?"

"Is it wrong?"

Maggie stared down at her. After a long moment, she wiped her hands on her apron and said, "We done here, Deputy? I could offer you a go-cup of coffee for the ride back to town."

Andi, stunned, covered it quickly. "Very kind of you, Mrs. Sobstak, but no thank you. I suspect you've given me what I need." She walked back to her vehicle.

* * *

After the sheriff's vehicle and, minutes later, the black Escalade rolled out the driveway, Vic rushed into the kitchen, stomping two rights, one left before he slammed the door. "What'd that deputy want?" he demanded.

"Who were those men talkin' to you in the shop?"

"Answer my question, Maggie. We got us a goddamn problem here?"

"You're damn right we got a problem, Vic. That sheriff thinks somebody's abusin' me, meanin' *you*. Now tell me who those men were."

"How'd you give her that idea? I ain't abusin' nobody!" He roughly grabbed a coffee cup out of the drainer and poured it full, too fast. Coffee splashed on the floor.

"Damn it, Vic!" she said, grabbing a paper towel, leaning down to wipe the floor.

"Answer me! How'd you give her the idea that I'm abusin' you, goddamn it! I ain't never laid a hand on you 'cept in love, and damn little of that lately, I'd say."

She stood up. "Oh for God's sake, Vic, listen to yourself! Why the hell would you think I want sex with somebody who's hangin' out with strange men and won't talk to his own wife?" She dropped the paper in the trashcan. "You think I just turn on and off like some switch?"

"No, ma'am, I'm thinkin' you're permanently off, far as I can see. And I ain't *hangin' out*, I'm working on a deal to save this goddamn ranch, if you want to know. Not that I get the feelin' you give a rat's ass."

"Vic! Stop it! I care as much about this place as you do. But you don't tell me nothin'! And now the sheriff thinks you're abusin' me 'cause of that drunk day." Maggie could feel herself swelling up toward anger, or grief, or toward some emotion she didn't want him to see, not now.

But Vic could not see or hear past the word *abuse*. He slammed the coffee cup on the counter and spilled the rest of it, then savagely threw it against the refrigerator door, shattering it.

"Vic!" Maggie screamed. "Stop this! Stop it now!"

He whirled on her, his rage with Stetson and the tax burden and all of it focusing on Maggie, like sun's heat through a lens. He rushed at her, his calloused hand fisted, raised. She cringed, arms up around her head. He pulled up, and she looked up at him, her eyes flaring, then rose up before him. "Don't you never raise your hand to me again, Victor Sobstak."

Slamming the mudroom door, he stalked back out to his grinder and the blades.

*   *   *

Rolling pastures, quilted in white, lined the highway. Small herds of Red Angus grazed the long berms of hay laid out in the fields. Some raised their heads to watch Andi's vehicle. She looked down toward where the river took its westward swing, running under the brown canopy of cottonwoods along the base of the Monastery Range. On her drive out to the Sobstaks' place, she'd enjoyed the beauty of the mountains. She'd thought she could be happy here. She'd been wrong.

Andi told herself Maggie's rebuke wasn't real, but it had stung. She drove slowly, ignoring the hills and the cattle and the far-off cottonwoods. Was the happiness that twenty minutes ago had seemed possible now out of reach? Maggie was right: *I am an outsider here.* But Chicago? Trade this quiet place for the bullets and the danger? Swap the loneliness for long numbing hours in a busy place where she could forget? Loneliness. She hadn't used the word to herself before. She *was* lonely, though, not just alone.

Her knuckles whitened on the wheel. Why were these people so damn unwelcoming? She snorted. *They're not, not most of them. Maggie's trying to push me away from something. I'm just...* What? A mile later, she knew the answer. She was lonely, and Maggie's rejection only made it worse.

Should she go back to Chicago? Didn't she have people there? Her captain had been clear: "Have fun, Andi. When you get it out of your system, come on back. You've always got a job here." A job, sure, but *people* were what she needed, not a job. "But I've got people in Chicago," she said aloud. *Who, exactly?* Two girlfriends who hated their jobs, their husbands, and their lives; a bunch of deputies who drank too much or had sex on the brain; one college roommate who had four kids and no time for dinner with a friend; and her aunt with Alzheimer's. Oh, and Andrew, her ex-, already remarried to the slut in Andi's bed. What kind of *people* is that?

The loneliness came again. Maybe she'd gotten the fun out of her system, and it was time to go back.

Some fun.

*   *   *

Same Day

Ed's cell phone buzzed as he was explaining the plan to Ardyss and Grace.

Ardyss looked thrilled to have Grace stay with her, but the girl was somber. Ben Stewart spoke. "Found 'er," he said.

"Where?"

"In the air. Johnny Marks pulled some strings at the airport. Your ex – left at 6:30 a.m."

Ed frowned. "I don't recall a 6:30 flight to Minneapolis."

"You don't recall it because there ain't one. She went to Las Vegas."

"Damn."

Grace looked at Ed with alarm. "What?" she demanded. Ed held up his finger and mouthed, "In a minute." He stepped outside so Grace wouldn't hear, and passed on to Ben what Grace had told him, and what he remembered, about family members: She hadn't seen her father since she was five, and she knew only his name, Lawrence Ellonson, not where he was or how to reach him. The only living grandmother, Ellonson's mother, was in a nursing home for Alzheimer's patients in Wisconsin. Grace didn't know where. She'd never met any aunts or uncles or cousins, and she thinks her father was an only child. To Grace's information, Ed added, "Mara was an only child too. Both her parents died in an auto accident in 1973. I never met any relatives."

"So there ain't no family other than the father, and we don't know where he's at – that what you're tellin' me?" Ben asked.

"Looks that way."

"Well, looks like I better call Rosemary."

"That'll mean taking her up to the Children's Home in Helena."

"Afraid so."

"Give me the weekend, Ben, like we talked about. Ardyss Conley's willing to take Grace in. Maybe I can work something out that'll be all right with Rosemary. And maybe we can find the mother."

"In Vegas." Ben's voice dripped doubt.

"Right."

"Where people go who don't want to be found."

"The weekend?"

Ben waited a moment before agreeing. "First thing Monday, if she ain't back."

TWELVE

Sunday, January 29

THE BITTER WIND snatched Ed's cap as he walked up the path to Ardyss Conley's small house to pick up Grace. Yesterday had been tough: the girl had complained about everything he'd tried to do with her. When he'd proposed hiking up the Coliseum on snowshoes, she'd snorted.

"I don't hike, Northrup. That's for jocks."

But when he'd brought it up again last evening, she'd surprised him by agreeing, although her tone said, *If I have to*.

He grabbed his hat, which had landed in the snow, and mounted the steps. A vigilant old lady, Ardyss opened the door before he knocked, and nodded curiously at the hat hanging in his hand.

"Most men wear those on their heads."

He stepped inside. "True, but my hand was cold. Grace ready?"

"She won't come out of her room."

"Why?"

"I haven't a clue." Ardyss shut the door against the wind. "Ask her yourself." She pointed at the closed bedroom door.

Ed knocked on Grace's door. "Hey, Grace. It's Ed. Breakfast, remember? Then the hike?"

No answer. He knocked again, louder.

From behind the door: "Go away."

"Hey, Grace. We've got a plan."

Muffled, but clear enough, "Fuck your plan."

Ed put his hands in his pockets and sighed. This was turning into work. "Grace? Can I come in?"

"No."

Elizabeth Murphy had been found behind such a locked door. He stayed calm, tried the handle. Locked. He felt a touch of fear. "Come on, Grace. It's time for breakfast."

"I told you, fuck breakfast."

Ardyss had come up behind him and whispered, "This girl ain't been foul-mouthed since she's been here with me. Something's wrong."

Ed nodded. He raised his voice. "Damn it, Grace, come out here – or let me come in. You're scaring us."

Nothing. Then, after a long wait, the click of the lock. The door opened slowly. "Ardyss only." Grace half-hid behind the door, her face red and angry, tears in her eyes. A dark stain on her jeans spread across the half of her groin that he could see. She did not look up. "Satisfied?"

Ardyss clucked and pushed Ed aside. "You just leave us girls to handle this. Go make yourself some coffee or something." She shut the bedroom door, but quickly opened it again. "Ed, run over to Art's and pick up a box of sanitaries." The door shut again.

Ed started to ask what sanitaries were, then shut up and left.

*   *   *

Ten minutes after he had passed two boxes through the barely opened door – "I didn't know tampons or napkins" – Ardyss came into the kitchen. "She'll be out presently." She started roughly scrubbing some plates in the sink, annoyed. "That darn woman never left her any tampons. Poor kid, she was embarrassed to tell me about it, so she gets her period this morning all over her jeans." She let out a loud sigh. "What kind of mother would do something like that?"

She looked accusingly at Ed, but before he could say anything, Grace came into the kitchen wearing black sweatpants that said "Pink" across her rear. She looked defiant. "All right. Screw it. You said breakfast."

Ed nodded. "Breakfast it is. Grab your coats. Or your sweatshirts."

*   *   *

At the Valley Inn, Grace glowered at the menu. Ardyss and Ed knew their orders, but waited for her. Henny brought coffee. She brushed a hair out of her eyes and took their orders. When Grace ordered a cheeseburger and fries, Henny tilted her head in sympathy. "I'm sorry, but it ain't lunch for a couple hours yet. How about that sausage 'n egg wrap? It's *real* popular."

Grace never looked up. "I don't want a fucking sausage and egg wrap, I want a goddamn cheeseburger and fries. Is this a restaurant or what?"

Henny's eyes widened, and she looked at Ed. He said to Grace, "Either you fix the language – remember what we agreed? – or stay hungry."

Grace glared, then shrugged and muttered, "Oh, sorry. I didn't mean I don't want a *fucking* sausage and egg wrap, I meant I don't want a *plain* sausage and egg wrap."

Henny suppressed a smile.

"I want a burger. And fries." She glanced at Ed. "Please."

"Sorry," Henny said. "We don't serve lunch till 11." Her pencil hovered above the pad.

"Christ," muttered Grace. "This is fucking ridiculous."

Ardyss leaned conspiratorially across the table until her face was inches from Grace's. In her old lady's whisper, she said, "Grace, dear, your language is starting to fucking piss me off."

Grace's eyes widened, then she and Ardyss started giggling. When they finished, Henny said, "I think you'd really like the wrap."

Grace looked up at her, still laughing. She said, "Well, thank you, ma'am. I'll do the wrap." She glanced at Ardyss.

The old lady nodded approval.

Just then, Ben Stewart walked in and, on his way to another table, he stopped to chat. He extended his big hand to Grace, who tentatively shook it, her small hand vanishing inside the beef of his. "Miss Grace, I'm Sheriff Ben Stewart. Mrs. Conley takin' good enough care of you?"

"Have you heard from my mother?"

Ben cocked his head, but answered, "Well, no, ma'am, I haven't. We missed her at the Las Vegas airport, so the Clark County Sheriff's office down in Nevada is looking for her. We'll let you know soon as we find her. And we'll find her."

"Why did she go to Las Vegas?" Grace asked. Friday, when Ed had told her Mara had flown there, she'd asked the same thing; he'd said, "I have no idea. Do you?"

Ben Stewart grimaced. "I ain't got no idea. Do you?"

"No," she said sullenly.

"Well, darlin', we'll find her." He turned to Ed, but Grace interrupted him. "Don't call me darling. I'm not a darling."

He smiled. "Good enough." He said to Ed, "You folks up to something today?"

"After breakfast, Grace and I are going to climb the Coliseum."

Ben beamed. "Now that's real good." He rubbed his hands together. "Miss Grace, you enjoy your hike. It's one of the high spots of life here in the valley."

Ed laughed. "High spot. That's good, Ben."

Grace frowned. "I don't plan to stay here in the valley," she said. She turned and looked out the window.

Ben frowned, then looked at Ed. "Best of luck," he said, then clapped Ed's shoulder and left for his table across the room.

Henny brought their food. Ed had ordered his usual: the eggs Benedict, hashbrowns, and toast. Grace looked from his plate to his stomach. "Keep eating like that and you're gonna get fatter," she smirked, and bit into her wrap.

*   *   *

At Anderssen's Outfitters, Todd Olson geared Grace for the climb. Her black sweatshirt was thin, frayed, and unzippable. She needed a real coat, and real boots and the socks to fill them, snow pants, the works. Like most kids, she had left her gloves at home. With her hat and scarf. Ed emerged from the outfitters' three hundred dollars wiser – that for girls like Grace, color ranked above function, and brands trumped bargains. He'd put his foot down when the only jacket Grace would try on was the most expensive model from North Face. "They're on TV," she said, as if that explained something.

"I can't afford that much for a jacket, and it's not as warm as this one," he said. He handed her a jacket better suited for the Montana winter.

"It's brown," she said.

"It's warm," he answered.

Her wrinkled nose spoke a volume of distaste, but when he frowned, she tried on the jacket.

*   *   *

They said little on the hour-long drive down the valley and up the winding road toward the Coliseum and St. Mary's Lake, the source of the Monastery River. Beside the road, the newborn river cascaded down to the valley floor. As they climbed, Grace said, "Northrup?"

"Yeah?"

"Why'd you come out here from Minnesota?"

His gut tightened. "It's a long story. I'll tell you sometime."

She snorted. "Fuck *sometime*. I'm out of here as soon as my mom comes back."

"Uh-huh."

The road came to an end at the lake, in the shadow of the soaring Coliseum, and they rumbled across a wooden bridge into the trailhead parking area. On the far shore of the lake, St. Brendan's Monastery was visible under the pines, but Grace didn't appear to notice it. Climbing out of the cab, she looked up at the great granite amphitheater looming thirteen hundred feet above them.

"You want me to climb up *that*?"

"Not straight up the face. There's a good trail up the side." He pointed toward the gap in the trees.

"I can't do this," she said, her eyes clouding.

"Let's give it a try, Grace. If it's too hard, we'll stop."

He opened the tailgate and Grace sat sullenly on it while he strapped on her snowshoes. Ed wondered how she'd do, and if they reached the summit, how she'd react to the view from the top. He felt uneasy, remembering his last hike up the mountain and his near-fatal mistake. If it had been a mistake.

The first few hundred yards of the trail wove on the level through thick pines. Grace grumbled about the straps being loose, and Ed, tightening them, noticed that one was frayed. His tightening didn't stop her grumbling, but when the trail steepened, hard walking and heavy breathing did. They switched back and forth up the flank of the mountain, the trail winding among tall pines. Occasionally, they paused to catch their breaths and to look through the trees to the massive granite rampart. Ed ignored his uneasiness. Gradually, the white lake shrank as they climbed. At one rest point, they looked down on the monastery, looking like toy buildings at the edge of the lake. Looming over them, the sheer wall of the Coliseum reddened in the late morning sun. Grace was silent.

The day glowed. The snow shone almost blue under the green elegance of the pines, and the rugged cirque brooded over the lake, an eminence of enormous power. Ed led them slowly, lying to himself that it was to make it easier for Grace; his paunch set the pace.

Even so, Grace lagged behind.

At first, he let her drift back, assuming she wanted to be alone. After a while, when he turned up the next switchback and looked down to check on her, she hadn't appeared around the lower bend. Ed waited a moment, then turned back.

She was sitting on a rock looking out over the vast spaces. He felt a chill. *If she had jumped...*

"I can't do this. It's too hard."

"Do what, Grace?"

"This." Her hand swept around, indicating the mountain, the trail, the snow, the forest.

"Why not? Is it too steep?"

"It's just stupid. This sucks. I want to go back to Ardyss's. It's warm there." Ed studied her new jacket. "You're cold?" he asked.

"No, why would I possibly be, like, cold? Christ! It's only fifty below zero and I'm stuck on the side of a fucking – " She amended herself. " – on the side of a ridiculous mountain with somebody who'd rather just leave me behind." She sobbed.

Ed sat down on the rock beside her and put his arm around her. The girl pushed it away. Neither said anything for a while.

Then he said, "Grace, I blew it. I thought maybe you wanted to be alone, so I didn't stick with you. Won't happen again."

"You're sick of me."

Ed tried to keep it light. "No, not yet. I'll let you know when I am, okay?"

Grace sat up straight. "Yeah, fine. You do that. But don't, like, leave me behind any more, even when you're sick of me."

They continued climbing; Ed let her lead. When the switchbacks ended, they climbed through sloping meadows, wide smooth carpets of utterly white snow bordered by soaring trees. Grace, inexplicably exuberant, said, "I've never seen snow like this before. I want to break it up!" She plowed off, foot-printing the untouched snowfield in circles and arcs. Ed enjoyed watching her running in her snowshoes, until, exhausted, she came back toward him and plopped down in a drift, breathing heavily. After she'd rested a few minutes, they trudged into the trees edging the meadow, and when they emerged, they were approaching the rim. Ed steered them away from where he'd stood on the cornice.

They turned at the top and went to the edge – Ed kept them well back, explaining about snow cornices, trying not to sound as spooked as he felt – and stood gazing down into the river canyon and out across the long valley. Far below, the dime-sized frozen lake shone sun-yellowed, and the small red roofs of the monastery buildings gleamed on its western shore. To the west, waves of mountains stretched into a blue haze. Grace stood quietly, breathing hard. After a few moments of quiet, Ed rested his hand on her shoulder. "What?" the girl said, startled, pulling away.

"They don't have this where we come from, do they?"

Grace shook her head. After another moment, she said, "What if I jumped?"

Ed stiffened, flooded with the same fear he'd felt when he'd been out on the cornice.

Grace grunted and peered down. "I'd go, like, splat."

"Let's back up a bit," Ed said nervously. He turned from the rim and walked back a few paces. Grace looked at him queerly, but didn't move. "Did I scare you, Northrup?"

He made light of it. "No, but your mom would kill me if anything happened to you."

Grace snorted. "Like she cares." She turned for a brief moment out toward the valley. Then moved back closer to him. They stood looking out over the long valley for a few more minutes, then turned from the rim and retraced their trail, Grace going slowly in the lead.

*   *   *

As they started down the switchbacks, Ed thought about Mara's claim that Grace was using meth. He reviewed the day, and saw no evidence for it. Even the mention of jumping seemed teenage and provocative, not desperate. Nothing like the desolation he'd felt on that terrible Sunday.

Suddenly, Grace stumbled and fell, rolling down the deep snow toward the edge of the cliff. Ed threw himself forward and grabbed her coat. When he pulled her back on the trail, she was trembling. Her right snowshoe had broken loose. While he examined it, she covered her fright – her face was white – with sputtering anger about his stupid idea and this ridiculous mountain. He didn't answer. The strap had broken at the frayed spot. He tried to use the longer of the broken pieces, but it was too short, so he reached into his pack for his knife and cut a piece of his belt to size. To tighten it enough, he worked a new hole in the leather. Grace had stopped her grousing and studied him as he worked.

When the belt-piece was tight around her boot, she said, "None of my mother's husbands or boyfriends could fix that. They'd, like, pay some Mexican to do it."

"I don't see any Mexicans up here," he said, smiling.

"I guess not," Grace looked at him. "You walk right behind me the rest of the way."

"I've got your back." Saying it felt good. Grace never smiled.

*   *   *

Monday, January 30

Next morning, after his run to Milk Creek and back, Ed allowed himself one piece of unbuttered toast and one egg. Grace's comment at breakfast yesterday had rankled, and she'd made another snide remark about his weight at dinner. After the entirely unsatisfying breakfast, he stopped at the sheriff's department on the way to his office. "Ben in?" he asked Callie.

"Not yet. You here about that little girl?"

"Yep. Do you know if there's any news from the other sheriffs?"

"Nothing I know of."

"Has Deputy Pelton, uh, Andi found anything new about the flyers?"

Callie stiffened. "I reckon the deputy ain't keepin' me in her confidence."

Ed looked at her. "You and Andi not getting along?"

Callie blushed. "We've had words. But we started to patch 'er up. Got interrupted by a loose cow." Ed looked puzzled.

"Don't worry. We'll straighten 'er out." Callie peered at her computer screen, still blushing. "Kinda puzzles me, to tell the truth. I had us down as girlfriends here in the department." She brushed a hair out of her face. "We'll see if I got that one right or wrong."

Ben pushed through the big glass door. "Well, just the man I need to see," he said. "You hear from Miss Grace's mother?"

"No. Did you?"

Ben shook his head. "The silence of the scrammed."

"So we call Rosemary?"

Ben nodded. "We call Rosemary," picking up the phone.

They set the meeting for ten-thirty that morning. Ed went across the hall to see a patient, and after the session, returned to Ben's office. Ten-thirty came and went. Ben called, but got no response. Twenty minutes later, Rosemary Rasmussen swept in, resplendent in an elegant lavender and gold shawl draped over her shoulders, brilliant against her azure dress and accented by a huge multi-colored shoulder bag and cascades of carefully color-matched beads.

"Such short notice, Ben. I could barely put my thoughts together, not to mention my outfit." She chuckled. Ed thought, *favorable sign*. She asked Ben, "So what's the story? Who's the child?"

Ben briefed her. From her voluminous bag, Rosemary extracted a leopard-skin notebook and a Waterford pen, and made careful notes in a tight, neat hand that belied her bulk. At selected moments, her eyebrows lifted quizzically. At one point, she tapped her pen against the notebook and looked at Ed. "Your ex-wife? This child is your daughter?"

"No, she isn't my daughter. She's no relation to me."

"Yet your wife left her with you. Of all the people in all the places on earth, she left her in *your* gin joint?"

"Not my wife, Rosemary, my *ex*-wife. She's been married five times, I think, since me. She claims Grace needs my help. As a psychologist."

"What's the matter with the girl?"

"From what I can tell so far, nothing more than being fourteen and unwanted by her mother. Mara says Grace is suicidal and may be using meth, but I haven't seen any sign of either. Angry and defiant, but wouldn't you be?"

Rosemary arched her eyebrows. "And the mother wants *you* to help her."

"That's what she said."

Rosemary's enormous brows lifted again, even higher, in an unmistakable gesture of doubt. Some years ago, Rosemary had asked him to work with a thirteen-year-old, and he'd told her that he didn't work with kids. "And *can* you?"

Ed hesitated, thinking of Elizabeth Murphy. He'd believed he could help her, hadn't he? He brushed that aside and nodded. "Yes, Rosemary,

I can." To himself, he thought, *Maybe*.

"You told me you couldn't work with kids," Rosemary said.

Ed said, attempting levity, "No, I said I didn't, not that I couldn't. Anyway, it's moot. I'm not going to be her therapist."

Rosemary nodded to Ben to continue. When the sheriff arrived at the delicate matter of Grace staying with Ardyss, he hemmed a bit, a sailor yawing near a reef. But Rosemary erupted. "Are you out of your minds?! Ardyss Conley's in her seventies, and childless! What does she know about fourteen-year-old girls?"

Ed started to defend Ardyss with the pizza story and the way she handled Grace's menstrual accident, but Ben cut him off.

"You got a better alternative, Rosemary?" Ben's voice carried the flat and neutral tone that signaled he was done playing nice.

Rosemary, momentarily defensive, started to describe the Helena Children's Home.

Ben merely shook his head. "Come on. This kid don't need that place. We'll find her mother and get them back together in no time. Let's keep it simple."

Rosemary started to object, but he talked over her. "And the mother left money to pay Ardyss."

That calculation took only a few seconds. Rosemary nodded. "We can keep the girl here without costing Montana Child Protection a penny?"

Ben smiled, nodding. "Yep. That's the nut."

Rosemary shot back, "I supervise everything."

Ben nodded again. "Exactly." Ed objected, but Ben shushed him. "Rosemary, I'll inspect Ardyss's place every ten days and report to you. Ed here'll, uh, visit with the girl every day, kind of watch over her." He looked at Ed, lifting one brow as if to say, *help me out here*. Ben was making it up as they went along.

Ed frowned. Another unwelcome chore. "Uh, sure. She'll probably be gone in a week."

Ben looked expectantly at Rosemary, who also frowned. She said nothing for a moment, and Ben said, a bit impatiently, "Look, Rosie, we ain't negotiatin' world peace here. Ed here can check in with you every, what? Every week?" He darted a look at Ed that said, *Just go along!* "Hell, I'm givin' you a report every ten damn days." He emphasized the *damn* skillfully. "And like Ed says, the mom said she'd be back in a week or so."

Rosemary glared. "The name is Rosemary, Sheriff. Note that I'm not insisting on Ms. Rasmussen."

Ben smiled graciously. "My apologies, Miz Rasmussen."

She nodded. "Very well. I'm charged with ensuring that the child is not harmed, and with you two watching over her – under my supervision – I suppose there are advantages to having her stay in the valley." She capped her pen and said to Ed, "Let's say a ten-minute visit every day. And call me each week. If she's here that long."

She continued. "If I get your report, Sheriff, every ten days, that will allow me to document that we're protecting this child." She turned back to Ed. "I want you to normalize her life with us, as much as possible. To start, let's get her in school."

Ed shook his head. "For a few days? It's not worth the trouble."

She just looked at him. "Children in Montana go to school."

Ed thought about the alternative in Helena. "Okay, then. School it is."

Ben rubbed his hands together. "So we have us a plan, then?"

Rosemary uncapped her Waterford pen and jotted a note about her decision. She handed it to Ben. "Sheriff, will you please make two copies, for yourself and Ed? Yes, we have a plan. You'll keep me informed of any changes?"

"Rosie, you'll be the first to know."

"Rose*mary*, Sheriff." Her tone could tighten piano strings.

Everyone shook hands. Rosemary gathered all the papers into her bag, deliberately adjusted her shawl, and made her exit.

Ben clapped Ed on the shoulder. "That worked out all right, I'd say."

"School's a bit much, but we'll work it out. I doubt Grace will like the news."

"Ain't our call."

"Yeah, we're pretty much playing catch-up all around."

*   *   *

Wednesday, February 1

Ed ushered Maggie into his office. "Can I get you a cup of coffee?" he asked.

"You make it?" To his nod, she said, "No thanks." Maggie thought Ed's coffee was weak.

Uncharacteristically, as soon as they sat down, Maggie began talking.

She told him about the quarrel on Friday, how the deputy had upset her and Vic's visitors had obviously upset him in the shop and how, after nearly hitting her, he'd had spent the weekend with the boys in the bunkhouse. Ed was half-listening, his mind wandering, wondering how Grace was doing at school. He dragged his attention back to Maggie, who was describing Vic slinking home late Monday night. "I didn't say a word when he came in the bedroom," she said. "Jus' lay there, hopin' he'd say somethin', but he just nodded at me, turned over, and fell asleep." She shook her head.

"I was in a daze all mornin' yesterday," she said. "I barely got the chores done and almost didn't make Vic's lunch. When he come in, he ate without makin' a peep." She paused. "He sure jolted me awake right before he went out again, though. He said, 'I got somethin' to tell you after dinner.'

"I went nuts, Ed. One minute, I was sure he was leavin' me and I started plottin' ways to leave him first. Maybe I'd drive to Missoula, or Great Falls, jus' walk out on him, let him stew in his own juices for a day or two. But soon's I thought that, I'd just start cryin' and blamin' myself, tellin' myself I should apologize for bein' jealous and not givin' him enough sex, figurin' ways to do him so good he'd never leave." She stopped, mortified.

Ed put an encouraging look on his face, and said, "It's fine. Keep talking."

"Well, then I'd get mad all over again and think, I ain't cookin' no dinner for him when he comes home from wherever the hell he is. I'll put him on notice I can fight too."

"Did you?"

She looked down. "Naw. I cooked his favorite spaghetti and meat sauce. My mother only ever gave me one piece of marriage advice: 'If you kids have a fight, fry up a big ol' onion just before he comes home. That smell'll make a man forgive jus' about anything'."

Ed laughed. "Your mother was a wise woman."

"My mother was a tramp. But she knew her way around men. Anyway, I started fryin' that onion. Vic didn't even take his hat off when he come into the kitchen, he just sniffed the air, and come over and wrapped his arms around me. 'Damn, that does smell hearty!' He held me a minute and said, real sincere like, 'I sure feel bad about how I been actin' and some of them things I said, darlin'. When I heard that, I figured, that don't have divorce written all over it, but all I said was, 'You *was* a bit rough on me.' I put a little hurt sound in my voice – I ain't proud of that – and I unwrapped his arms and started stirrin' the sauce, like I was still mad. He's lookin' over my shoulder, askin' 'What's cookin there, sweetheart?' and when he sees, he says, 'Oh my, my, spaghetti and meat sauce!' Next thing I know, he's leanin' his butt on the counter, foldin' his arms, lookin' smug and pleased with hisself, and then he says, 'You're fixin' to make up to me, ain't that so? You ain't cooked me spaghetti and meat sauce in months, ever since you got on that jealous streak.' He had that self-satisfied look he gets when he wins at poker, like he's outsmarted everybody. I kept stirring my sauce, but I felt like dumpin' it on his cocky head."

She took a sip of water. Ed waited. She went on, "Well, I made him wait a spell before I said, 'Maybe I'm fixin' to make up, maybe I ain't. But if I ain't got cause to feel jealous of you out gallivantin' at night, then I need to know what you *are* doin' out there.' He was smiling real big now. For Vic, that meat sauce proved he was forgiven. Then he says, 'Well, Maggie, that's what I was aimin' to tell you about tonight, after we have this awful good dinner you're stirring up there.'"

Ed said, "Ah."

She nodded. "I says, 'You gonna tell me where you been goin' these nights you're out till all hours?' Vic says, 'Uh-huh.' So I says back, "Tell me now,' but he says, 'Nope, let's enjoy some of your good home cookin' first. Then we'll have us that talk. I think I'll get me a beer.'"

Ed asked, "Did he talk to you after dinner?"

Maggie snorted and shook her head. "Naw, he was all, 'now you jus' trust me, Maggie, I'll get 'er all straightened out.' I couldn't weasel nothin' outa him."

"You sound mad."

"Why ain't he talking' to me? We used to be partners. If it ain't a woman, why ain't he talking'? Darn right, I'm mad."

"Uh-huh."

"Here's what else I'm mad about. That morning, while them visitors was in the shop? That woman deputy comes snooping around and gives me this cockamamie story about somebody's abusin' me! She figures it's Vic, and she's tryin' to get him. You bet your last dollar I'm mad. I'm mad at him and I'm mad at her."

Uncomfortable because he'd talked probably too much to Andi about Maggie and Vic, Ed asked, "So what do you want to do?"

Non-plussed, Maggie put her water down too hard on the side table. She grabbed a Kleenex from her purse to wipe up the spill. "Well, you tell the deputy next time she talks to you, I can take care of myself jus' fine and I don't need her creepin' around my place unless she's got serious business there."

"If she thinks you're being abused, that's pretty serious."

"Don't *you* start on me, Ed."

"You're mad at *me*."

"Don't you be talkin' about me to that deputy."

"I never said anything about what we've talked about, Maggie." He cringed at how defensive he sounded.

Maggie got out of her chair and faced the window. After a few moments, she turned and stood facing him, her arms hanging limply at her sides. "Oh, hell... I'm mad, but... I'm mostly scared. What'm I gonna do?"

Ed waited until Maggie returned to her chair, and when she was composed, said, "I think for starters you have to get Vic to talk to you."

"Hell, Ed, I been tryin'."

"Well, try again. And if he won't talk, bring him in and I'll try to get him to open up."

"I could easier get a cow to fly than bring Victor Sobstak in here."

Ed laughed. She looked abashed. He said, "Sorry, that just struck me funny. Well, keep trying. And if you get that cow flying, teach me your trick." She smiled a weak smile.

*   *   *

The phone was ringing. Ed had just sat down to his dinner, and he looked regretfully at the pork chop, mashed potatoes, and gravy he'd warmed in the oven after the quick drive home. It should have been his Wednesday on the corner with Ben, but the sheriff had gotten tied up at a domestic and couldn't make it; Ed had brought home to-go food from the Angler's kitchen. Maybe he wouldn't answer? The food smelled unbearably good. He sighed and walked over to the phone, expecting to hear a patient's voice.

"Hi," Andi Pelton said. "Just an update on the flyer investigation."

"Oh. What's new?" He liked how firm her voice sounded.

"Well, we followed up on this church in Idaho – it's in Twin Falls, the Church of Jesus Christ of the American Promise. It calls itself a patriot's church, which usually puts them pretty far out on the wingnut spectrum."

Ed cradled the phone on his shoulder and slid his plate back into the still-warm oven. He said, "That flyer's way beyond *patriotic*. And what does being a patriot have to do with being a church?"

"Uh, that's above my pay grade, theologically," Andi said.

He chuckled. "So, we don't know who actually *posted* these flyers, just that they come from this church in Idaho."

"Well, so far Vic Sobstak looks good for the guy who hung them, but maybe not. The church is apparently run by someone named Loyd

Crane."

"Who is he?"

"Don't know yet. The Google machine doesn't have anything on him, and not too much on this church. I've got some calls out to the county sheriff's office, so we'll know more tomorrow."

They were about to hang up when Andi said, "Say, how's the little girl? What's her name again?"

"Grace Ellonson." Ed's stomach growled and he looked toward the oven. "When I called, Ardyss said she was taking a nap, but they'd gone girl shopping and Grace is fine. We got her started at the high school yesterday afternoon."

"Bet she loves that."

"Last night she told Ardyss that the other kids are, in her words, a bunch of hicks. Ardyss pretended she didn't know what the word meant, and they apparently had a pretty good talk about city kids and country kids."

"Good for Ardyss."

"I took her up the Coliseum on Sunday. She did pretty well, her first time on snowshoes." He left out the part about her falling. Andi was quiet a long moment. "Sounds like, uh, fun."

"It was." Ed wondered what her hesitation meant.

They finished the call. He pulled the plate out of the oven, not feeling quite so hungry. Talking about the flyers brought up that horrible image of Landon Burke – a fine man, one Ed respected. Recalling the hate-filled words sickened him.

And pork chops won't help the weight, he thought.

His stomach growled. He could get serious about the weight, tomorrow. No, Friday. He'd start a diet on Friday. Just now, though, the Angler had cooked some delicious pork chops.

* * *

Thursday, February 2

After Grace had come to his office after school for their daily visit, Ed suggested that they pick up Ardyss and have dinner at the Angler. When he called, Ardyss said she wasn't feeling well, a touch of the flu. So Grace and Ed locked up his office and crossed Division Street through a gauze of powdery snow materializing out of the dark sky. They took a table in the bar, which was cozier on snowy evenings. Ted came over and introduced himself to Grace.

She said, "Can you give me a beer?"

Ted chuckled. "I can, if you stay here long enough to turn twenty-one. Meanwhile, what *can* I bring you?"

"A beer," she snapped. Ed started to say something, but Ted gave him a look.

"I'm thinking I could bring you a Coke," he said to Grace.

Grace said. "Then I don't want anything." She pulled her hood up and started thumbing her cell phone. Ed rolled his eyes as he ordered a Fat Tire, and Ted went to pour it. Grace continued staring at her phone.

Ben Stewart and Deputy Andi Pelton came into the bar. Grace looked up.

The sheriff came over to their table. "How's it goin', Miss Grace?"

"It's stupid I can't have a beer if I want one."

Ben's eyebrows lifted. "May be stupid, but it's the law, darlin'." He smiled.

"Well, it's stupid. And I'm not your darling."

Ed interrupted. "Would you two care to join us for dinner?"

Ben shook his head. "I'm on the corner with Jerry Francis in ten minutes. Deputy Pelton here could, though."

Andi said to Ed, "I was just briefing Ben on the Church of Jesus Christ of the American Promise. Quite an outfit, it turns out. But I don't want to intrude." She looked at Grace. "I'm Andi, Grace. We haven't met before."

Ed was surprised that Grace reached out to shake her hand. "Eat with us."

Andi smiled and pulled out a chair. "Sounds good."

Ben went over to the corner of the bar and settled on a stool. Grace looked at him a moment, then asked, "Is he your boss?"

"He is," Andi said. "I've worked for him about nine months now."

"What did you do before?"

"I was a Chicago cop. Cook County Sheriff's Department."

Ed saw Grace narrow her eyes. "I've been to Chicago before. My mom calls cops 'pigs.'"

Andi looked back at her evenly. "Yeah. A lot of people do. It's actually a pretty good word for us."

"It is? I thought it, like, pissed you guys off."

"Naw," Andi said, firmly shaking her head. Ed glanced at her, curious what was coming next. "Pigs clean up all the shit in the farmyard. And you know what?"

Grace shook her head.

"When they have to, they eat human flesh." Andi kept a very straight face.

"Gross!" said Grace, but she was quiet until they ordered.

*   *   *

After they'd ordered, Ed asked Grace how school had been.

"It sucked."

Andi restrained a smile. Ed tried another tack. "What sucked?"

"School."

"You in a bad mood?" he asked.

"I'm not in any mood. You went, how was school, so I went, it, like, sucked."

Ed sipped his beer, then said, "You're right." He turned to Andi. "And how was *your* day?"

"It sucked," she said, and then she and Grace burst out laughing.

Ed frowned, annoyed. "Is this a girl thing?"

Andi shook her head. "No, but you're easy to gang up on."

Grace grinned at her, then said to Ed, "Yeah, Northrup," she said. "Don't you, like, know to never ask a teenager how school was? School just sucks."

Then Andi said, "I heard you two hiked up on the Coliseum last weekend. Are you going again on Saturday?"

Grace said, "I can't." She hesitated before going on, "Some kids invited me to help decorate the gym for the dance Saturday night."

"Grace, that's great!" Andi said, touching her on the arm. "What time do you decorate the gym?"

She looked uncomfortable. "In the morning sometime. I can't go."

Ed asked, "How about later in the day?"

"Uh, me and Ardyss have plans."

When Ed asked, Grace wouldn't tell them what her plans with Ardyss involved. Andi wondered aloud if the older woman might be taking her shopping for clothes for the dance. Grace didn't answer.

While they were eating, Ted stopped back at their table. "Put Friday evening two weeks from now on your calendars! We'll be introducing the new spring menu. You're all welcome."

Grace said, "I won't be coming. I won't be here then."

Ed was astonished. "Grace! Has your mother contacted you?"

She shook her head. "I'm going home. Amanda's father said he'd buy me a ticket, and I can live with them till my mother shows up."

Ed's reaction surprised him. He would have expected to feel relief at such news, but instead, it was disappointment. Andi watched Grace for a long moment, a hint of respect in her eyes. After a moment, she looked up at Ted. "Could we have a minute, Ted?" The bartender excused himself. Andi turned back to Grace.

"I'm afraid that isn't going to happen, honey. Shall I spell it out for you?"

"Don't, like, call me *honey*. Spell *what* out?"

"Your exact situation here."

"I know my *exact* situation." Her voice was surly. "I'm out of here next week."

Andi leaned across the table in her direction, and she spoke very slowly. "You are a minor whose parent has abandoned you, we hope temporarily." She glanced at Ed, then continued. "Until either your father or your mother can be found, the state of Montana has assumed legal responsibility for you. Let me be really, really clear here, Grace." She stopped.

"You're being, like, *fucking* clear." Grace glanced at Ed, who lifted his eyebrows but said nothing. He was still trying to figure out why news of Grace's leaving should disappoint him.

Grace glared at Andi. "You're clear. I'm a prisoner. No options."

Andi leaned back. "Actually, you have two options. You can stay here or you can stay in the Children's Home in Helena, until we locate your mother or your father. Child Protection wanted to put you there, but Ed talked them into letting you stay with us."

"Oh, so my options are, like, Juvie Hall or the armpit of Montana? That's *options*?"

"I'm not sure either one is quite as bad as that, but yeah, those are your options."

"I could run away."

Ed swallowed a mouthful of ale and said, "Yep. You can go north; it's a thirty-five mile walk to the next town. You can go south, but the road ends up at the monastery."

"Yeah, and I could hike up that fucking mountain and jump off." She folded her arms angrily.

Andi touched her arm. "Come on, kid. Put on your big girl panties and deal with it. We can make this work, and when your mom comes back, it'll be all over."

Ed was grateful for Andi's direct talk and her manner with Grace. For one thing, it spared him the task.

Grace stared at Andi as if she were speaking Urdu. Her face registered something between surprise and sorrow. "No, it won't be over." She sighed. "When *she* comes back, it's just another kind of bad." Then she stared up at the ceiling fan circling slowly in the shadows above.

The adults ate in silence for a few minutes. Then Grace began to giggle. She looked at Andi. "Did you really say 'big girl panties'?"

Ed chuckled. "I believe she did."

Grace picked a French fry off Andi's plate and nibbled it. "Okay, then. If I have to put on *big girl panties* – " she smiled broadly now – "then I get to drink a big girl's drink." Without pausing, she reached over and picked up Ed's ale, nearly empty now, and drained it in a swallow, looking triumphant.

Ed started to object, and Grace looked directly at him, daring him to react.

After a quick glance at Andi, he forced a smile. "Did you like the beer?" he asked. Grace shivered and shook her head. "Beer sucks."

THIRTEEN

Friday, February 3

ANOTHER "CATCH-UP" FRIDAY.

Before he tackled the week's leftover chores, Ed checked his messages. The only one was from a very upset Maggie Sobstak. Ed called her back. "He hit me!" Her voice was ragged, raw.

"Maggie, that's terrible." His mind raced to the crucial points. "Are you safe? Is he still there?" Vic was escalating. How dangerous would this become?

"Yeah... no, uh, he's outside somewhere... I don't know. Somewhere." Her agitation, to Ed, sounded more like suppressed fury than fear.

They talked through the first shock, then he asked her to come in. He started opening his appointment book, noticing the cookie crumbs mashed in the pages. Today was supposed to be the first day of the diet, wasn't it?

"Not today," she said.

He hesitated. "Why not? Let's not take this lightly."

Her silence stretched out. Finally, she said, "Ain't nothin' light about this, Ed."

He heard the rebuke. "Well, do you have someone you can stay with for a while?"

"I ain't goin' no place. This is my home."

"It's dangerous now, Maggie. If Vic hit you once, he'll likely hit you again."

Maggie said nothing.

"Listen, the research is crystal clear – "

"I ain't interested in research, Ed. Maybe Vic hit me once, but he ain't never hittin' me again." Her voice had the tight grain of oak.

"I'm worried about your safety, Maggie."

"I've got the .22."

"Maggie! Think about that. If you shoot Vic, it'll be you who gets arrested."

"He ain't gonna hit me again, I promise you that."

Ed sighed. The *black dog* was stirring again. "Okay, then. Can you and Vic come in and see me?"

"Me and Vic? You're kiddin', right?"

"No, Maggie. I'm not."

"Why him? Vic ain't your patient. I am."

"I can make it safe for you guys to talk about this. A third party can defuse things." He paused, then asked, "How about tomorrow?" Maggie remained silent.

"Maggie, you there?"

"I'm here."

"Will you bring him in?"

"When?"

"Tomorrow. Nine o'clock. No, make it ten."

"On Saturday?"

"Maggie, please."

"I'll try."

It was the most he was going to get from her. "Okay, Maggie. Ten tomorrow."

When she hung up, he absently grabbed a cookie from his briefcase stash. As he finished it, he remembered the diet. *Damn. Okay. Tomorrow. Really.*

*   *   *

After school, Grace showed up in a mood blacker than his. Ed had spent the day with paperwork and errands – and munching on cookies – and feeling dread about how the Sobstak's situation could deteriorate. Grace plopped down and looked directly at him and said, "Don't, like, therapize me, Northrup."

"Bad day?"

"Don't even fucking start."

"All right, then. What do *you* feel like talking about, then?"

"For a shrink, you sure don't listen. I don't fucking *feel* like talking about anything. You guys can hold me prisoner and force me to come in for these stupid meetings, but you can't make me talk."

Ed nodded. "True enough." He looked at his watch and lied. "CPS says we do this for thirty minutes every day after school. I don't care if we just sit here."

"Me and you aren't going to fucking 'just sit here.'" She snatched her cell phone out of her bag.

"Texting Amanda?" No answer.

"Right, then," he answered, and started typing his notes. Grace glanced up from her phone and watched him for a moment, her eyes narrow. Her phone beeped. Amanda, he assumed. The girls texted back and forth for a long while. Ed kept his back to her and continued typing. When Grace's little beeps stopped, Ed knew Amanda, or whoever, must have signed off. He kept working.

After a few minutes of silence, Grace said, "Why don't you, like, invite me to do something with you tomorrow?"

Ed swiveled to face her. "You're not decorating the gym?"

She shrugged. "I lied. Nobody asked me to help." She looked forlorn.

Ed felt a surge of sympathy. "Uh, sure, how about a movie?"

"Yeah, pity the fucking orphan. Like I should bother to ask."

He waited a moment, startled by the sudden mood shift. "Could we maybe declare a truce? I know you feel like a prisoner, but I don't like this arrangement either."

"What you mean is you don't like me."

He nodded. "Sometimes I don't."

"So don't, like, do me any favors."

"And sometimes I think I do like you."

She looked at him, her eyes dark, then looked away and spoke to the wall. "Wow, am I grateful. He sometimes *thinks* he likes me." She snorted. "What's there to like, anyway?" Wash out the sarcasm, it might have been an honest question.

He took it that way. "You're funny. You catch on fast. You're honest, mostly. And your bullshit detector works."

She considered him for a moment. "And what about the things you *don't* like?"

"Oh, it's not that I don't like – "

"Bullshit alert."

That brought him up short. "Right. Okay, then." He thought for a minute. "I really hate it when you act like a snotty little bitch who can't admit that we hicks could care about what happens to you." His feeling about it surprised him.

She looked hurt. "Nobody gives a shit about me. Just Amanda."

"I'm not asking you to believe it, just meet us halfway."

"That's adult bullshit for when you have to do what they want."

What a life this kid must've had, he thought. "You're not the only one your mother fucked over." Her eyes widened. "Back in the day, she did the same thing to me she's doing to you, and she's screwing with both of us now. Not your fault and not mine. So how about we suck it up and help each other get through a seriously ugly situation?" He couldn't make out how she was taking that, but her head was tilted, like she'd heard something new.

After a moment, she said, "I should, like, put on my 'big girl panties' and deal with it."

He laughed.

"I can have a say?"

"Big girls do. Snotty little girls don't."

"Snotty little bitches, you mean."

He shrugged. "What's your say?"

"No therapy bullshit. I've had all the therapy I need."

"Agreed. You've had all you need. What else?"

She lowered her head. When she looked up at him again, her lips and chin quivered. "Will you try to like me?"

Ed thought of Elizabeth Murphy, and how she'd so slowly come to trust him, before the end. He felt a rush of warmth. This kid was no meth addict. She craved love, not dope. His breath caught as he made the connection: *Just like me: I need love, not food.*

He made his voice as embracing as he wished his arms could be. "Yes, I will. And maybe you can try to like me just a little too?"

FOURTEEN

Saturday, February 4

NEW SNOW GLISTENED on tree branches and fence wires strung along roadside fields under the morning's cobalt sky. Red Angus cattle wore white blankets, steaming. Ed had lumbered heavily through his sunrise run, oblivious to the beauty of the morning. Today, well, yesterday, he'd promised to start the damn diet, and dreaded it. After the run, stepping on the scale and sucking in the belly that obscured his view, he'd seen that since New Year's, he'd lost exactly zero pounds, which made him hungry. The carefully shopped Mexican-grown vegetables and greens in his refrigerator couldn't compete with his favorite Saturday breakfast at the Valley Inn. Before grim resolve took over, he dressed quickly and drove into town.

After downing the eggs Benedict, hash browns, and jellied toast, he got to the office thirty minutes before the Sobstaks. *Cookies all day yesterday, Benedict today – no wonder I feel lousy.* Yesterday had been a disaster for Vic and Maggie, and this session probably would be a calamity. The thing with Grace had ended well, though, and he replayed their talk for a moment to cheer himself up. He hoped she could live up to the bargain.

For that matter, he hoped *he* could. He hadn't been so good at sticking with things lately. He rubbed his stomach.

What to do for the Sobstaks? The first violent act in a marriage ruptures more than skin or bone, and restoring trust would be like raising a grounded ship. He rubbed his face vigorously to get the blood flowing. The eggs Benedict were a bad start to what would likely be a tough session.

The waiting room door clicked open. *Showtime.* He went out to greet them, but Maggie stood alone, holding her large bag against her chest with both hands, like ballast. Thick makeup barely hid the bruise below her left eye.

"Vic wouldn't come," she said nervously. "Will you see me anyway?"

"Of course, c'mon in. Oh, how about some coffee?" She gave an apologetic smile and shook her head, pulling a thermos from her bag. "I figured you'd make it, bein' Saturday and all. Brought my own, if you don't mind?"

He smiled and they went into his office. As he closed the door, he asked, "What did Vic say?" With Vic missing, it seemed futile, but he had to start somewhere.

"He said he was sorry. Said it'll never happen again. Said we don't need no marriage counseling, we can work it out ourself."

"How do you feel about that?" This felt even more futile.

Maggie just looked at him, her head tilting. Finally, she said, "You know, Ed, I figure with all your schoolin' and all these years listenin' to people like me, you probably know how I'm feelin' as good as I do. I got me a pile of better questions than how am I feelin', and I reckon you probably have a few good ones of your own."

Ed bristled, but he asked calmly, "Maybe you're sending my way some of your anger at Vic?"

"Ya think? Well, you're right." In the waiting room, her bag clutched to her chest, she had seemed subdued, nervous, but not now. "Ask some questions that'll do me some good, or answer mine."

His sense of futility, unaccountably, departed; this unexpected duel generated an energy he hadn't felt in months. "All right, then, how do you want this to turn out?"

She nodded. "Now there's a good one." She opened her thermos and poured coffee into the mug. Steam billowed up around her face. "Want some?" He shook his head. She sat back and took a sip. "I make pretty good coffee."

He waited.

"I'm a good cook, a real good cook. I keep a clean house." She sipped again. "You know, Ed, I can castrate hogs and pull a calf out of a cow's belly and –" she seemed to wrestle with something for a moment – "and I can damn well satisfy a man. I keep the books good and I can drive any tractor we got. And I ain't stupid."

"Uh-huh." *No, you're not,* he thought.

"So he ain't got no cause to treat me like he's been doin'."

"Treating you badly is one thing. Hitting you is something else again."

Maggie nodded, and took another sip. "Yeah, that set me back some. All day yesterday, that's what stuck in my mind."

"And today?"

"Don't get me wrong, it still needs figurin' out. I been turnin' it and turnin' it all night long."

"And?"

She waved her hand at him. "Give me a minute here. I'm workin' my way to your question."

Ed nodded and sat back.

Her jaw was set hard. "Let's say he never hits me again, let's say he treats me like a queen, opens doors when I walk through, tells me every mornin' he loves me, and never forgets the toilet seat. But suppose he still don't treat me like his partner? Suppose he don't let me in on whatever the hell's botherin' him, makin' him crazy enough to hit me? That ain't the kinda marriage me and him had before, and it ain't the kinda marriage I want. So how do I want this to turn out? I want my partner back." Her eyes flashed, though they were moist.

Ed nodded, but he doubted Maggie was going to get her partner back.

She dabbed her eyes with a cloth. "You think I'm crazy?"

"No, you're not crazy, but it's a tough row to hoe, once things turn violent. How are you going to talk it through if Vic won't come in?"

Maggie looked puzzled for a moment, and then she relaxed, chuckling softly.

"It's not funny, is it?"

She shook her head. "No, no. What you're thinkin' just broke through the fog, is all. Yesterday, you said you could make it safe for me and him to talk, now you're sayin' we can't talk if Vic won't come in here. What you mean is you don't think we can talk to each other any more now that he hit me, right?"

"I don't know that I thought of it that way."

She leaned toward him. "Ed, there's worse things in a marriage than a slap here and there. Hell, I slapped Vic once, a long time ago. He had it comin' and he knew it."

There are worse things in a marriage than a slap here and there. The night Mara had moved out, after Elizabeth and all the trouble, she'd stopped at the door and snarled, "You're as shitty a psychologist as you are a lover." She hadn't needed to slap him.

He said, "You've got a point, Maggie."

"What you gotta do is help me figure out how to talk Vic back into bein' my partner again. You up to that?"

"Absolutely," he said, with a confidence he wasn't sure he felt. "Let's get to work."

"Good. No more of that feelings crap."

He laughed. Now and then he forgot how the grit of these valley people improved the odds. He said, "Why don't you pour me a cup of your good coffee now?" They went to work.

*   *   *

After Maggie left, Ed drove to Ardyss's to pick up Grace for the movie. She met him at the door. "Ardy's real sick," she whispered, then turned back into the living room.

Ardyss lay on the couch in the dim light, looking gray and frail, her eyes closed. When she opened them, her head didn't move. Then she closed them again. Her whisper was almost inaudible. "You kids go to the movies. I'll be fine."

Ed went down on a knee and felt her hand, then her forehead. "You're burning up, Ardyss."

He looked at Grace, "How long has she been sick?"

"I guess all day yesterday. When I got home from your office, she was right there." Grace nodded at the couch. "She threw up a lot. I cleaned her up."

Ardyss grimaced and shushed her weakly. "Hush, child."

Ed pulled out his cell phone and tapped 9-1-1. Callie answered. "Callie, it's Ed Northrup. Ardyss Conley is very sick. Can we get Doc Keeley over here?" He gave the address.

"I'm on it."

Ardyss was feebly shaking her head. "Too much fuss."

Ed touched her arm gently. "Not too much for you." Then to Grace, he said, "Would you go get a few wet washcloths? And how about a glass of water. She's probably dehydrated."

While Grace went to the kitchen, he knelt beside the couch, softly brushing Ardyss's brittle gray hair from her clammy forehead.

Grace came back with the water, then left for the washcloths. Ardyss was murmuring something when Ed's cell phone interrupted. "Northrup." He listened a moment, said, "Thanks, Callie," then hung up. "Doc Keeley's on his way." Ed gently eased Ardyss upright and held the glass to her lips. Grace came in with the washcloths, and when she saw Ardyss trying to sip, she went back into the kitchen and returned carrying a large stockpot, setting it down beside Ardyss on the floor. "She'll puke the water up," she said.

Ed bathed the old woman's forehead with the washcloth, and after a few moments, Ardyss moaned and turned toward the pot and vomited.

When she rolled back, Grace picked up the pot, but Ed stopped her. "Let's leave it. Doc Keeley may be able to learn something from it."

"Gross." But Grace replaced the pot, looking scared.

Ed saw Doc Keeley's pickup outside the window, and he opened the front door. The rush of cool air felt good and he realized he still wore his coat. Doc Keeley came in quickly and nodded to Ed and Grace before kneeling beside Ardyss. While he was examining her, Andi

Pelton came in.

To Ed's questioning look, the deputy said, "Ben's rule: A deputy checks on emergency calls."

Ardyss was too weak to talk, so Grace answered the doctor's questions calmly, giving meaningful details. Andi and Ed glanced at each other more than once, impressed.

Finally, Keeley stood up and lifted the pot and inspected the contents. When he sniffed the liquid, Grace looked away. Keeley said, "I'll have to ask you folks to step into the kitchen while I examine her."

Grace stepped forward. "Why can't I stay?"

The doctor started to say no when Ardyss's frail hand brushed his pant leg. He looked down at her. "Let the girl stay, John," she whispered. "She's a comfort."

Keeley shrugged. "Very well, young lady." He gestured to Andi and Ed, who left for the kitchen.

After his examination, he said to Grace, "I doubt that it's serious, probably just flu. But in an older person like Mrs. Conley, even the flu can turn bad in a hurry. So I think we probably ought to take her to the hospital. We can keep her comfortable, slow down the vomiting, and rehydrate her easier there." He took out his cell phone.

From the couch, the whispery voice said, "I don't have insurance, John."

The doctor frowned and said, "Well, let's not worry about that at this point. We'll work something out."

Grace raised her hand. "I'll take care of her. I can do it."

The doctor looked squarely at her. "How old are you, young lady?" Ed stepped back into the room, followed by Andi.

"Fifteen," said Grace.

"Fourteen," said Ed, instantly earning Grace's glare.

Ardyss whispered, "All I need is pills, water, and rest?"

Doc Keeley said, "Well, I'd rather run an IV to keep you hydrated, but yes, basically."

"And I'm not dying?"

"I think you've got a bad case of the flu, Ardyss, but no, at the moment you're not dying."

"Then I'll stay here and Grace can take care of me."

Doc Keeley looked at Ed and Andi. "What do you folks think?"

"I think Grace can handle it," Ed said. Grace looked surprised.

Andi interjected, "I hate to ask, but what about school?"

The doctor said, "That's not till Monday. If Ardyss," he turned directly to her, "if the vomiting doesn't stop by tomorrow or if your temp goes up, I'll want you in the hospital anyway." He turned back to Andi. "So school shouldn't be an issue."

"We got ourselves a deal," said Grace, clapping her hands once. Everyone laughed, except Ardyss, who vomited again.

*   *   *

When Ed returned with the prescriptions Doc Keeley had written, Andi and Grace had gotten Ardyss into a clean nightgown and into her own bed. Andi and Doc had left. Ed started to explain the medications to Grace.

"The doctor already told me all that, Northrup. He said to call him if her temp hits 103."

"Let me look up his number for you."

"He gave it to me. I already put it in my phone."

"All right, then." He was impressed with her organization. She'd already put a piece of paper and a pencil by the bed, and had written Ardyss's temperature on it. 102.

Grace said, "Sorry Northrup, I can't go to the movie with you. I gotta stay here with Ardy."

Ed smiled and patted her on the shoulder. "Are you sure you're okay staying alone?"

"Yeah. She'd, like, do it for me. We live together."

"Do you want me to stick around with you?

She squinted at him. "You don't think I can do it?"

"No, I just didn't want you to stay alone if you don't want to. You'll call me, though, if anything comes up or you need something?"

"Jeez, Northrup. I'm not a little kid. I can handle it."

"Got it," he said. He grabbed his coat and left. Grace opened the door behind him and yelled, "Northrup! The deputy told me to ask you to call her."

"Okay, thanks."

When they connected, Deputy Pelton said, "Oh, thanks for calling, Doctor, uh, Ed. Could you meet me at the station for a few minutes? I'm in a meeting right now, but I've got some news about this Loyd Crane guy you might be interested in."

"Sure. How about a half hour?"

*   *   *

When he came into the reception area, Callie said, "How's Ardy?"

"Sick. Grace is taking care of her."

"Is that smart?"

He said, "It'll be all right. I'll check on her every couple of hours, and she agreed to call if anything goes wrong."

Just then Andi came in and added, "I've got midnight shift tonight, so I'll keep an eye on them too." She gestured Ed back to a small conference room.

Ed said, "So what's the scoop?"

"Loyd Crane is the reverend at this church. My contact in Kootenai County, over in Idaho, tell me he's on the edge of some shady stuff, but nothing they can prove."

"Shady stuff?"

"Tax resistance schemes. His sermons sometimes edge over into anti-government tirades. Apparently, he's one of those sovereign citizen types, you know, the guys who don't accept any governmental authority. Kooks."

"That would fit with the flyers, I guess. But how do they get from Idaho to here?"

"We can't make that link yet. They say he's gone on trips a lot of the time, two, three days at a time."

"Nobody knows him around here?"

"I think maybe Vic Sobstak might be the contact. But how he knows Crane I haven't put together, and Maggie won't let me near him."

"I just finished seeing – " But Andi's face lit up and she interrupted him. "The motel! If Crane comes here, he probably stays at the motel." She reached for a phone, dialed. "Callie? Could you patch me through to the Jefferson House motel? Thanks." In a moment, her phone rang. She identified herself, then asked her question. After a moment, she thanked the caller and hung up.

"Somebody named Michael Smith – I doubt that's the real name – rents a room for 'meetings' every two weeks or so. The motel guy doesn't know what these meetings are about, but the name Crane rings a bell. And this Michael drives a Cadillac Escalade with Idaho plates."

"Good hunch," he said. "So this meeting could be where Vic connects with Loyd Crane – or Michael Smith, if that's his name."

"Could be. Of course, we don't have proof Victor was the one doing the flyers, but it's the one concrete report we've heard. Have you learned anything new from Maggie?"

Ed tightened. Maggie had been explicit that he shouldn't talk about her with Andi. "Well, I don't know that I can say much. Confidentiality, you know."

"Okay. How about hypotheticals? I'll speculate, you tell me when I'm off track."

Ed was used to this with Ben. "Sure. Go for it."

"To start, Crane's into tax resistance. So hypothetically, anybody attending his meetings has tax problems. Or maybe hates the government, since that comes up in his sermons."

"Makes sense."

"If Vic was hanging Crane's flyers, he maybe got them at one of the meetings, which would suggest either he hates the government or he's got tax problems." She looked at him expectantly.

"I don't know about taxes, but that's the direction I'd go. I don't think the Sobstaks hate the government. They're good people." He felt uncomfortable skirting Vic's attack on Maggie. *There're worse things in a marriage than a slap.* Then he remembered Maggie's Jeff House Motel matchbook. "You're on the right track with the Jeff House meeting."

"You know something?"

"Nothing I can tell you."

She looked annoyed. "Well, we know that Vic got Maggie drunk, then dumped her at the Angler. Why?"

"Can't say. This is your hypothetical, not mine."

The annoyed look didn't go away. "Okay. Why does a man get his wife drunk?" She narrowed her eyes, thinking. "Sex."

"Been known to happen." He enjoyed her thought process.

"But why leave her at the bar? He sure didn't get lucky that way." She scrunched her nose, concentrating. "He *didn't* dump her. He went to get cigarettes, or condoms, or something. When he came back, my vehicle scared him away." She raised her eyebrows. "Plausible?"

"Plausible. Fits with what I know. Except for this: Vic's sex needs don't play into the tax scheme idea, do they?"

She frowned, nodding. "Nope. So I'm either wrong, or we got two things going on. Abuse in the marriage and a tax thing. And we know that financial problems often lead to domestic abuse."

He nodded, feeling cautious. Maggie had downplayed Vic's slap, but Andi's using the word *abuse* inclined Ed toward skepticism. He spoke carefully. "I think you're getting warm."

"Thanks for that," she said. "I'm about run out, though. Sure wish I could subpoena your notes about Maggie." She laughed. "In my dreams."

He nodded. "Well, keep looking at Vic. Your hypotheticals seem on target to me."

Andi checked her watch. "I caught midnights tonight," she said. "Gotta get home for a nap."

Ed had been trying not to stare at the notch in her right earlobe, and he knew she'd caught him looking at it. As he was leaving, he thought, *What the hell?*

He turned back to her and asked, "What happened to your ear?"

She self-consciously touched the notch, her face reddening. "A boyfriend bit too hard," she said.

FIFTEEN

Sunday, February 5, 1:30 a.m.

VIC SLIPPED SILENTLY out of bed and prowled to the bathroom. His mind was boiling after yet another argument with Maggie, who'd come back from the psychologist's all hot to talk. Why didn't she just trust him? He hadn't given her a single goddamn reason not to. Well, maybe the Jim Beam thing, but that was one goddamn mistake. Okay, hitting her, that's two; but she made him so goddamn frustrated. When he finished, he didn't flush, hoping he wouldn't wake her. He dressed silently and went outside, closing the mudroom storm door quietly as he could. Something seemed missing as he closed it, but he couldn't place it. In his shop, he retrieved the new stack of flyers from their hideout, and climbed into the truck.

As he pulled out, the drifted snow muffled the tires. That's good. He looked back; no lights on. She maybe won't wake up. He hated deceiving Maggie like this, but he kept the lights off until he went over the rise and then down toward the highway, out of sight from the house. Goddamn, hiding this Reverend Crane business, that's a mistake too. So that's three. The falling snow, lit in his high beams, stretched in front of him, a gray curtain. He drove slowly into town.

Them flyers, they maybe ain't too good an idea either. They're pretty raw, and if Maggie caught him with them, the shit'd really hit the fan. Tell the truth, though, the Reverend had him over a barrel. Not just the tax thing, worse. Vic gripped the wheel hard. That first round of flyers, that was the goddamn barrel.

Friday night, after he'd slapped Maggie, he'd felt so miserable that he had called Stetson to pull out of the deal. Stetson's voice had been matter of fact at first, as if he were reading the beef futures.

"You're in, Sobstak, and you're staying in."

"Look, Mike," Vic had said, "I'll sort out my tax problem. Don't get me wrong, I appreciate what you and the Reverend are tryin' to do for me, but – "

Stetson interrupted, no longer neutral. "Shut up. It isn't about your taxes now. You hung up the posters I gave you, right?"

"Yeah, and I was thinkin' that maybe that ain't such a great – "

"I said shut up. Let me spell this out for your miserable country ass. Hanging those flyers is a federal offense. So either you're still in with us, or the next visitor you'll be getting at that sorry dirt farm of yours will be the FBI."

Replaying the conversation as he drove, Vic's eyes misted. Tears combined with the heavy snow slashing into his headlights blinded him; roughly, he brushed his eyes dry and slowed the truck. Goddamn, if Maggie'd leave him over the tax thing, she'd be gone faster'n you can say Jack Robinson over them flyers. Even if it wasn't a FBI offense, it sure as hell would be a Maggie offense.

Stetson's parting words had chilled him. "You're in, Victor, and if you don't keep hanging those flyers and doing what we tell you, I'll be having a meeting with your wife."

When Vic had exploded at that, yelling that nobody threatens Maggie, the line had clicked dead.

The snow seemed lighter. Ahead, he made out the faint glow of Jefferson's streetlights. Sonny Carter hadn't come out with the county plow yet. Vic worked his way around town, tacking up the flyers on the old wooden poles and trees, working in the snow. The picture of Landon

Burke was sick. Goddamn, the words was sick too. Probably *is* a federal offense, just for the goddamn picture. The more flyers he tacked up, the sicker he felt.

He longed to drive home and crawl in next to Maggie and forget this whole goddamn deal. Or tell her the whole lousy story. He decided to hang one last flyer on a telephone pole just past the Jefferson House motel, then hightail it. Maybe it'd all be a bad dream in the morning. In case somebody came along, he parked his pickup in the motel lot, behind the line of trees.

*   *   *

Andi yawned at her desk. She looked at her watch: Two in the morning. She hated working midnights. She was always dragging, especially in the long middle hours. Maybe a cruise around town would wake her up.

The night dispatcher was dozing at the switchboard.

"Bertie?"

The woman stirred. "Sorry, Andi. Sleepy night."

"Got that right. I'm going to drive around for a while, check out what's happening."

"Ain't nothing happening at this hour."

Andi sighed. "Tell me about it."

*   *   *

She cruised slowly down Division Street. Toward the edge of town, she saw something on a pole. Another flyer? She pulled over and ripped it down. It was foul, worse than the first one. She tossed it onto the passenger seat and drove up and down the streets on the west side. She didn't see any more flyers on that side, so she crossed Division. She found a dozen tacked up along the east-side streets.

She pulled them all down, wide awake now, and angry.

She pulled back onto Division near the Jeff House motel.

*   *   *

Vic was stapling a flyer to the pole when headlights swept across him from behind. He stiffened. The vehicle had turned onto Division and caught him square in its lights. *Must be a couple a' drunks slidin' home from the Angler or the Dew Drop*, he told himself. but the vehicle had turned onto the highway from the wrong side. He averted his face so the driver couldn't ID him. The lights passed, but then the vehicle made a fast u-turn and aimed back directly at him. *Goddamn! That female deputy.* Vic glanced at his own truck; it was invisible to the sheriff from where her vehicle was. If he ran directly to it, though, she'd have plenty of time to drive in and corner him in the goddamn lot. He ducked into the trees where the snow wasn't so deep, and stayed under their cover until he came to a brush field along the river. Using the brush as cover, he worked along the river's edge, then groped his way in the snow-filled darkness behind the motel. At the corner, he peered carefully across the parking lot. The woman cop had ripped down the flyer and was shining a flashlight on it. Goddamn. He never thought about fingerprints.

Settle yourself, Victor. You ain't never been fingerprinted.

Vic waited, panting. She scanned the snow around the pole with her light; finding his tracks, she followed them into the trees. As soon as she disappeared, he dashed to his truck and climbed in. The *click* of the doorlatch sounded thunderous. As soon as the engine turned over, he roared out of the lot, fishtailing north onto the highway. As he sped past the sheriff's vehicle, she came running out of the woods, flashlight swinging toward his front license, but he was far enough past her. *The snow's falling thick enough*, he hoped, *she'll never get the rear plate*. By the time she'd jumped in her vehicle and made the U-ball, Vic figured he'd be doin' ninety into the night, lights out. She'd never see him.

After a moment's relief, Vic stiffened again: He was leaving tracks in the new snow. Goddamn! His heart pounded. Her lights appeared in his rear-view, snow-dimmed, maybe a half-mile back. He pushed it to 100, but he started to fishtail and backed off. At 80, she didn't seem to gain on him. He inched it up to 85 and felt stable enough. *She must be drivin' careful*, he thought. Her lights seemed smaller.

But all she needed was to follow his goddamn tracks.

The driveway to his ranch flashed past. No use leadin' her right smack home.

Another mile, and he saw flashing lights far ahead, coming fast toward him. *Goddamn!* He started to panic, but they were yellow, not blue and red. Snowplow! Sonny Carter coming down from his place up north. As they approached each other, Vic switched on his headlights and flicked on the high beams, hoping Sonny, blinded, wouldn't recognize the truck. Sonny's round face shone like a moon up in his high cab, glowing a luminous green from his dash lights, and then they swept past each other. Exultant, Vic swerved into the clean lane the plow had left behind, and killed his lights again. No tracks! He was driving 85 now, by instinct more than anything. The turnoff to Nate Wilken's ranch would be coming up soon and he waited till he just could make it out and then he stood on the brakes, swerving down into the driveway, skidding sideways till he got the truck under control. *Hope she didn't see the goddamn brake lights.* He drove slowly down into a grove of trees along the river and switched everything off. Now it was just a matter of waiting – and hoping Nate didn't wake up and come out to investigate.

Eight or ten minutes passed. Then, up on the highway, the sheriff's SUV flew past, light bar flashing. He wondered why it had taken her so long, then considered that maybe she'd stopped Sonny to ask if he'd seen anybody. Vic felt queasy. Sonny, though, was a notorious drunk, even on the job, and with the goddamn high beams, maybe there'd be a chance he hadn't recognized the truck. Goddamn better hope so.

He waited another ten minutes, and finally the sheriff's vehicle drove slowly back toward town, light bar dark. She shone her searchlight down Nate's driveway, but he was well hidden and she didn't stop. After another ten, he drove cautiously out to the highway and turned south toward his own place, watching nervously in the rear view in case someone was coming up on him from behind. Driving lights-out on a snowy night was nuts. The whole goddamn thing was nuts. He had a last worry – what if she had decided to check in on Maggie and him? At his drive, though, there were only the two tracks he'd made coming out, and those had almost filled with snow. Vic relaxed. He was wrong about it being his last worry.

At the end of the drive, all the house lights blazed, and the yellow light streaming out the kitchen window framed Maggie's head and shoulders. After all the furor of the night, Vic's body tensed as if he'd been struck. Exhaustion swept through him, even though his heart was still pounding.

He stomped the snow off his boots, two stomps right, one left, and let the mudroom door slam behind him. Maggie was dressed in her housecoat, holding a cup of coffee, leaning back against the kitchen counter, examining him.

"So I wake up at, oh, maybe a quarter of two in the mornin' and my husband ain't in bed beside me. I look around and his truck is gone. And then an hour or so later – and let me tell you, Vic, a woman can go from scared to pissed in a lot less than an hour! – I hear a siren out on the highway and see flashers goin' past, and then twenty minutes later, my husband comes drivin' into the yard with his lights out in the middle of a snowstorm! And you know what, Vic?"

Vic reckoned he oughta go on the offense, but goddamn, he was bushed. "Can we talk this one to death in the morning, darlin'? I'm *real* tired."

"Oh, I'll bet you're real tired. You been out doin' somethin' real tirin' in the middle of the night. But hell, fucking some whore at the Jefferson House don't usually rouse the sheriff's office. What're we talkin' about now, with them sirens and all?"

"Come on, Maggie. You got me cold." He rubbed his eyes. "Ain't nothing I can say. But why don't we get some shut-eye now and have this fight in the mornin'?" Vic couldn't remember being so tired.

"No, Vic, we ain't doin' that. Because if you don't give me somethin' to make me stay, I'm leavin' now. You hear that?"

They were both astonished when Vic's head and shoulders slumped forward, and he quietly began to cry.

*   *   *

Bertie looked up, alert, when Andi came into the department. "You catch him?"

Andi shook her head. "Uh-uh. Bastard pulled over into the plowed lane and I lost his tracks."

"So you don't know who it was."

"I waved Sonny Carter down, but he said the guy had his high beams on so he didn't see his face. Thought it was probably a Chevy or a Ford pickup. I think it was a Ford."

"Hell, that narrows it to maybe 200 people, don't it? Anyway, Sonny's probably drunk, this hour of the night."

Andi nodded. "Yeah, he smelled of it. I wondered if I shouldn't DUI him, but I wanted to get flyer man." She waved the sheaf of flyers. "I gotta go write this up."

*   *   *

Next morning

A few minutes after nine in the morning, Ed knocked on Ardyss's front door.

Grace opened, looking exhausted. Ed touched her shoulder. "You all right, kid?"

"She's, like, not getting any better," Grace said, her voice quivering. "Am I doing it wrong?"

"You're keeping up with the medicine?"

"Yeah, but she just barfs it up. Same with the water. I'm really trying. I *am!*" She began to cry.

Ed pulled her into his arms, and she didn't resist. A hum began in his throat. He swayed softly side to side and she leaned into him, until a moment arrived and they parted as if a signal had been given. He handed her his handkerchief. She inspected it.

"Is this clean?" she asked.

"Unblown by human nose."

"That's stupid," she said, dabbing her nose and eyes. "Thanks," she held it out to him.

"Keep it."

She stuffed it in her jeans pocket. "Thanks for the, uh, you know." Her shrug implied the embrace.

"Let's see Ardyss." Following Grace into her room, he thought about where that humming had come from. And how good it felt.

Ardyss was gray, her moisture boiled away to ash. He touched her forehead. She was burning up. "What was her last temperature, Grace?" he whispered.

"102.6. That was..." she looked down at a sheet of paper on the bed table, neatly ruled in columns. "That was at eight-thirty."

He checked his watch. "So, 40 minutes ago. Let's take it again," Ed said and picked up the thermometer resting beside the paper.

Grace removed it from his hand. "I do it." She dipped it into a glass of water and slipped it gently between Ardyss's colorless lips. The old woman twisted her head feebly aside, pressing her lips together. Her brow furrowed.

"It's just me, Ardy. Grace." Her voice was tender. "One minute's all you need to keep it in."

Hearing the girl, the old face relaxed. Grace inserted the thermometer slowly, murmuring comfort. The old frail hand fluttered, blindly seeking something in the air. Grace held it in her left hand and probed the scrawny wrist for a pulse with her right, staring intently at the clock across the bed. After a moment, she laid Ardyss's hand on the bed and stroked it, while carefully working the thermometer free. The instrument stuck momentarily to Ardyss's dry tongue and lips; Grace gave it the gentlest turn and withdrew it.

"102.8," she whispered, her eyes frightened. She leaned over and kissed Ardyss's forehead, then jotted the number onto the paper and took the thermometer into the bathroom to wash it. Ed picked up the sheet of paper. It was a chart listing Ardyss's temperature, pulse, dose of medicine, and number of times she vomited for every hour since yesterday at three p.m. The pulse entries varied all over the place; the medicine had been delivered promptly every three hours as ordered. The vomiting had not stopped, and the fever had slowly risen over the past six hours.

The girl stayed up all night, Ed thought, looking at the hourly notes. Grace returned and tidied the table.

"Where'd you learn to do this, Grace?" He waved the paper.

She shrugged. "My grandma, my dad's mom, stayed with us once. She was real sick and old, and Mara didn't like her. Grandma was always nice to me, so I took care of her." She took the paper out of his hand. "Guess Ardy, like, kinda reminds me of her."

Ed started to ask more, but a sound whispered up from the bed. Grace snatched the stockpot and helped Ardyss, almost too weak to roll onto her side, spit a thready thin line of liquid into the pot. After she was settled again, shrunken and pale under the covers, Ed whispered to Grace, "I'm thinking we need to get her to the hospital."

Ardyss's eyes moved slowly beneath their lids, and she rasped a whisper, "I'm sick, not deaf. Speak up."

Grace giggled, then sobered. "He says we need to go to the hospital, Ardy."

Ardyss's hand lifted an inch off the bed and moved faintly side to side. "What do you say, child," she whispered.

Grace glanced at Ed, who nodded. Grace lifted Ardyss's gnarled hand in her own. "I think we should go."

The old eyes opened slightly and Ardyss turned weakly to see Grace. "Stay with me, dear," she whispered.

*　　*　　*

Melissa Hanson, working against desiccated skin and collapsing veins, needed four tries before lodging the IV needle in the back of Ardyss's bruised hand. At each attempt, Grace had flinched, intent as a bodyguard, and when Melissa hung the two bags on the chrome pole, Ed had given Grace's shoulder a gentle squeeze. He felt his cell phone vibrate in his pocket, so he stepped out of the room to answer.

Andi Pelton said, "Ed? Got a minute?"

"I'm at the hospital. Ardyss Conley's sicker."

"I'm sorry to hear that. What are you going to do with the girl?"

"Damn." He grimaced. "I haven't thought about that yet. She stayed up all night taking care of Ardyss. She's did a great job, everything's organized, but she's scared."

"I imagine. Well, let me know if I can do anything to help." Ed heard her yawn.

"Did you want something?"

"Yeah." She yawned again. "Sorry. Busy night and I'm still a bit wired. Had a car chase in that snowstorm last night." She told him about it, then asked, "Do you know what kind of truck Vic Sobstak drives?"

"An F-150, I think. Yeah."

"F-150. Thanks. Well, I'll let you go back to Ardyss. Call me if I can help." The last word was cut off by a huge yawn. "Get some sleep," Ed said.

*   *   *

In her room, Ardyss was sleeping, and Grace was watching Doc Keeley listen to her lungs and abdomen. He stood up and turned as Ed came in. "Not good, I'm afraid," he said, pitching his voice low. "She's getting a ton of antibiotics, but they're all coming back up. I started IV meds and we're pushing lots of fluid." He gestured at the hanging bags. "But I don't know what's wrong. I still suspect the flu, but the lab folks are on it and we'll see what they find out. My plan is to keep her sedated and medicated until the fever comes down. She probably won't vomit much with the stuff I've got her on."

Grace keyed on every word. "Is she dying?"

Keeley looked at her kindly. "I don't know how to answer that, Grace. People her age don't bounce back easily from something this harsh. We'll do the best we can to help her, and then see what she can do on her side."

Grace looked stricken. "I wanted you to say no," she said, and sat down in the chair beside Ardyss's bed.

"Why don't you folks get something to eat? Ardyss'll be sleeping all day."

Grace shook her head. "She told me to stay with her and I am."

Ed said, "Look, Grace, I know this is hard for you, but – "

She waved him silent. "No therapy. Our deal was no therapy. I'm not leaving her."

Ed nodded. "Got it. Can I bring you something back from the Village Inn?"

"You're leaving? Now?" Grace obviously disapproved.

He nodded. "Yeah, the food's better there than in the cafeteria. But I'll be back in an hour or so. Want a burger or something?"

"Two. And two orders of fries. And a strawberry shake. I didn't eat anything since yesterday morning."

Doc Keeley frowned. "In that case, I'll call our cafeteria and hustle up that order for you."

As he walked to the restaurant for breakfast, Ed worried. With Ardyss in hospital, what would Rosemary do? How could he keep Grace from being sent away?

*   *   *

The late morning sun streamed in Vic's shop window, laying squares of yellow light in the center of the concrete floor. The snow had stopped around nine. He paced, tracing a triangle from his workbench opposite the door, to the table and cabinets of power tools on the side wall, to the tall gun locker beside the door, and back to the workbench, again and again, some of the circuits quick and agitated, some slow and thoughtful. It was a spacious shop, eight-hundred feet square, and each leg of his triangle was eighteen or twenty feet. In the back corner, where his triangle-pace didn't take him, old Charley Wright's ancient grandfather clock chimed one bell. Vic looked. Eleven-fifteen. Goddamn, the whole morning gone, pacing. Vic felt like an animal unreconciled to its cage.

Last night – well, this morning, really – Maggie had relented when Vic had burst into tears and they'd gone to sleep, him in their bed, Maggie on the couch. As bushed as he'd felt, he hadn't slept more than a couple hours, and when gray light tinged the eastern sky, he'd brought a pot of coffee out to the shop and started pacing. He hadn't stopped. No way could he tell Maggie the goddamn truth.

He paced around and around. For long periods, his mind was a bare room. For other stretches, it buzzed and chattered, unable to untangle what to do. At the end of each leg, his fingers would delicately caress the workbench or the tool chests or the gun locker. Occasionally, he paused to lay his whole hand on one of the tools or machines or on the old wrought iron latch of the gun locker, as if they were the shoulders of friends. Vic felt fond of these tools. Keeping a ranch alive, sooner or later you need every one of these goddamn things in here – his dad's old hand tools, Charley Wright's power tools, the table saw and the miter saw, the grinder he'd been working when Crane and Stetson barged in. The air compressor, the guns. He was fond of the rusty snowplow parked outside the shop door. Fond of the cabinets and shelves of chemicals and paints and stain, the brushes, the pans, the rollers and extension poles. Of the electrical stuff, in boxes and bushel baskets, wire and old outlets and screws and nails of every size. Even of the rhythmic tick of Charley Wright's old clock. Charley's great-granddad, so the story went, had carried the clock over from England all the way to Monastery Valley in 1867. The longer Vic paced around and around, the more convinced he grew that the ranch old Grandad Wright had started, the second oldest spread in the valley after Magnus Anderssen's Double-A, was about to go under, thanks to goddamn Vic Sobstak.

He paced and brooded.

Goddamn. If old Charley'd just got hisself a kid, the kid would know how to save the place, but no, Charley didn't and you buy the goddamn place and think you'll have the good life now, and what's it take? Eleven years, and you're over a goddamn barrel. You try to wiggle outa this tax deal and Stetson shoves the goddamn FBI up your ass. You play it out and you end up in federal prison someplace like Minnesota where they say it's just as goddamn cold but they ain't any mountains to look at. You try to do what your daddy raised you to do – work hard, do a good job, and take care of your family – and before you can say Jack Robinson, you're up to your ears in shit and you can either keep your mouth shut and suffocate or scream till you choke to death.

As he made the turn at the gun locker, he slapped it hard. At the workbench, he ripped a hammer down from the pegboard and slammed it hard on the bench, again and again, faster and faster until his arm faltered. He tossed the hammer onto the workbench, disgusted at his weakness. He paced.

And it ain't just the farm, now you're fixin' to lose Maggie! You try to jump Reverend Crane's ship so you can hold on to her, you lose the ranch and maybe go to prison any-goddamn-way. Or you stick with Crane and Stetson and some goddamn miracle happens and you save the ranch, but Maggie ain't on it with you. So any goddamn way you play this out, you lose Maggie or the ranch — the only two things you care about in the whole goddamn world.

Vic had arrived again at the heavy oaken gun locker, and struck it again, this time with his fist. The pain jolted up his arm, and felt crazily good. He slammed his fist into the oak again, then again, the pain a firestorm now, slamming and slamming until his hand was bloodied and broke.

He'd been injured before, in bar fights or ranch accidents. One time, during weaning season, when he'd separated a calf from its mother, the cow's kick had broken his arm and three ribs. No matter what happened, though, he could always come crawling in the kitchen door and Maggie'd tend to him. Vic's eyes welled up. He wanted to walk across the yard holding his broken hand and come in through the mudroom to show Maggie, to let her bandage him gently and put on a fresh pot of coffee. But she was fuming in the house, working her way from pissed to whatever's after pissed, waiting for his explanations. Which would only make everything go straight to goddamn hell.

There ain't no lie that'll make it okay to sneak out at midnight in a goddamn Saturday night snowstorm.

Then he stopped his pacing, cradling his bleeding hand. *Why not tell her the* truth?

He leaned back against the old gun locker, cradling his bloody hand, working it out.

You just lay out the whole mess, A to Z. Tell her about the taxes and about Crane and Stetson and the FBI. You tell it all and you tell her you need her help to figure it out. Let her help you, like it's always been.

Seeing at last a way out, Vic clapped his hands, but the pain staggered him, shocking him back to reality.

A goddamn pipe dream. Like that time you was sixteen and got drunk and wrecked Daddy's truck and thought if you told Ma the truth she'd fix it so Daddy wouldn't beat the crap outa you? Instead, Ma beat the daylights outa you herself, and later, Daddy did too. Get real. You tell Maggie the truth and it's adios, *Victor Sobstak.*

Why not? Why couldn't he tell his own goddamn wife the truth? Victor paced, chewing on it, holding his hand up. Maggie would help, wouldn't she? Tell her! He stopped near the gun locker getting it, finally. *My goddamn pride. I can't tell her because I can't bear her knowing I've lost the ranch. It's that goddamn pride daddy was always trying to beat out of me.*

His hand was throbbing. *Where's that first aid kit?* In the gun locker. Holding up the broken hand, he fumbled with his other hand in his jeans – *damn awkward gettin' your off hand into the right-hand pocket.* He was sweating now, his bad hand throbbing something fierce. He got the locker open and pulled the first aid kit down from the upper shelf beside the shells. As he did, the shop lights gleamed on the barrel of his elk rifle, and froze him still.

Never in fifty-four years, never, in a lifetime of troubles that had came at him like pissed-off cowboys in a bar fight, never once had Vic Sobstak pictured placing the barrel of a rifle in his mouth. Dazed by the sheen of light off the cold blue steel, he pictured it now.

Shaken, he shut the locker door. "Don't you think like that," he said half-aloud. "Your old Daddy never taught you that way." *Funny, though,* Vic thought. His daddy'd died in a hunting accident. Aloud, he said, "Ain't I the only one who thinks Daddy's death was surely an accident?"

But what if they was all right? What if Daddy killed hisself that morning on the mountain, why, that puts the barrel of this here elk rifle in a different light, don't it?

He made his circuit again. Over his shoulder, the gun locker seemed alive, as if it was willing him back. It seemed to make its own gravity, pulling him in like a meteor. For a time, Vic steeled himself against it. The barrel's sheen gleamed in his mind. For long minutes he resisted, but then, watching himself from a distance, he opened the locker and lifted out the gun. The shop went dead silent. He noticed, absently, that his hand no longer hurt, although he could see blood seeping from the swollen ravaged skin. He didn't care. With his good hand, he carried the rifle to the workbench.

Like the hush when the jury foreman unfolds the verdict, the clamor in Vic's head had stilled when he lifted the rifle out. He moved in a zone of numbed silence, as if the air had thinned out. The cold of the blue steel barrel signaled a decision he had no choice but to accept.

He laid the rifle on the workbench, more alert than he could ever remember being, noticing the hammer he had earlier dropped there. On the pegboard, he saw a naked space shaped like the hammer and calmly hung the tool in it, satisfied. Sawdust crowded around the table saw. He brushed it with his left hand into the waste barrel. He watched dust rising into the sunbeam, his mind as quiet as a monk's.

A draft brushed the side of his face, from an unnoticed crack at the door he must have left ajar hours ago. *No matter.* From the gun locker, he lifted down a box of shells. He glanced, curious, at his broken right hand. The bleeding continued, but he did not feel pain. Clamping the box of shells under his right arm, he carefully closed the gun locker and latched it, replacing the key in his pocket.

At the bench, he worked the box open with his left hand. For some reason he could not recall, his right no longer worked. *No matter.* He had great difficulty trying to put the shell into the rifle, but felt no frustration, only a detached calm. He stopped trying for a moment, resting.

He looked serenely at his tools, at the sunbeam, at the steel of the elk rifle. *This is the way,* he thought, and started again, trying to chamber the shell. He would only need the one.

PART THREE

SIXTEEN

Just Then

THE SHOP DOOR jerked open, flooding the room with daylight and cold air. Maggie's dark form was silhouetted against the outside light. Vic couldn't make out her features, but he could smell her familiar fragrance, lavender soap and bread flour. He felt her eyes fall on the rifle shell in his hand, on the open rifle on the bench in front of him.

"That shell for me or you?" she asked.

As if the mute button had been suddenly switched off, the silent intensity of the past few minutes vanished and the clamor and agitation and pain crashed into Vic again. "Maggie!" was all he could force out for a moment, then "You ain't got no business out here." That had been their rule forever: Maggie did not come into Vic's shop.

Maggie let the door close behind her and walked directly to him and took the shell out of his hand. She rolled it around in her palm a moment, then put it in her apron pocket. "I came out 'cause you ain't comin' in, and we gotta talk, Victor."

Vic inhaled a long, shaky breath, the pain in his hand almost too fiery to bear. He was facing the bench, his head turned toward Maggie, and then he looked away from her, down at the open box of shells. Maggie reached around him and grabbed and threw the box across the shop – shells scattered everywhere. "Me and you, Vic, we talk. We always have."

"Ain't nothin' left to talk about," he said in a defeated voice.

Maggie looked at the rifle, then back at Vic. "Then let's start up this way," and she turned his body toward her and held his face between her hands and kissed him.

Vic sagged back against the bench, clutching his broken hand. "I ain't sure I can tell you, Maggie."

Maggie ignored what he'd said. "That kiss, that's how I pretty much feel about you, 'cept for bein' pissed about whatever you're not tellin' me. And by the way, me bein' pissed will be temporary once you start actin' like we're in this together. The kiss, that'll be permanent."

Goddamn. What a girl you married! He forced a smile, but he could feel it came out twisty.

Maggie's stiff index finger jabbed his chest. "That is, permanent *if you talk*, cowboy." She pushed him hard.

Vic steadied himself with his right hand on the bench. It caused a surge of pain. His eyes watered.

He held the broken hand out to her: new blood and mangled skin. Maggie's head tilted softly and she made a small sound. Resting the bloody hand in both of hers, she studied the damage. She looked up into his eyes. "You come up to the house and let me tend this. We'll talk after."

Vic nodded. "I need to lock up the rifle."

Maggie had not let go of his hand. "Give me the key. I'll do it." She let go his hand.

Vic nodded and fished out the key, and she locked the gun and dropped the locker key in her apron with the shell. As they closed the shop door, Charley Wright's grandfather clock chimed noon. Vic followed Maggie up to the house.

*   *   *

Gone beyond words, perched on a kitchen chair with a towel over his lap, Vic held his broken hand in front of his chest and watched Maggie work. She laid out a basin and towels on the counter, and pulled a tube of antibiotic cream and a spool of tape and gauze from their first-aid kit. She put a nearly full Jack Daniels bottle on the counter, and set a glass beside it. Setting the basin on his lap, and lifting his hand gently over it, she flushed the wound with warm water. He flinched. Maggie reached behind for the whiskey and filled the glass. "Drink it down," she said softly. "I'll wait a minute." The Jack warmed him and after a few moments, he held out the broken hand. "Go ahead. I've had worse."

He sagged in the chair as she cleaned the torn skin, then felt for breaks. He winced, but held still.

"Lucky man," she said. "I don't think nothin's broke too bad." She softly dried the skin and salved it with antibiotic and wrapped his hand in gauze and tape. Sweat had broken on his forehead. "Sorry, Vic, but-"

"I know," he said weakly, pain-smacked. "I believe I need to sit down."

"You are sitting down." She took the basin and dumped the bloodied water in the sink.

"In my chair. Maybe catch some of the Super Bowl."

"No, we gotta have us that talk, Vic."

"I can't talk now. Hell, I can't hardly keep from tippin' over. Let's just watch us some of the Super Bowl pre-game, then we'll talk." He went into the living room and flopped heavily into his chair. With his left hand fumbling the remote, he turned on the TV and found the game.

"Victor, you don't even like football."

"Hell, Maggie, give me a goddamn break, eh? It's Super Bowl." But he barely looked at the screen, staring vacantly, sitting immobile except to pour more Jack Daniels into his glass each time it drained. He could feel the numbness spreading, thank God, although images of the elk rifle penetrated the haze. *Goddamn it.* Wasn't he caught in the goddamn grinder on this? He swallowed another big mouthful of whiskey.

"That's about enough, Vic."

He grunted and lifted himself on his good hand out of the chair, pivoting a bit tipsily before righting himself. He felt his sloppy gait, so he stepped deliberately, toeing a straight path to his study, proving to her he wasn't drunk. He closed the door and cradled the phone with his shoulder while dialing Stetson with the good hand. Goddamn inconvenient. As he fell back into his chair, the door opened and Maggie glared in. "Who you callin'?"

He shook his head. "Jus' give me a minute. I gotta straighten this out."

"What, Vic? Straighten what out?"

He glared at her. "Give me room, Maggie. We'll talk when I'm done." Vic listened to the ringing as Maggie, her look angry, frightened, moved fast across to the desk and lifted his revolver from the top drawer. He started to object, but Stetson had picked up and growled at the other end. Vic waved Maggie out. When she closed the door, he told Stetson he had to talk to Reverend Crane, that he needed out.

Stetson cut him off. "We told you, you help us, or we will fuck with you and your wife."

Vic slurred a protest, but Stetson shut him off. "You're warned, pussy," and hung up.

Vic slumped over his desk, ignoring the pain as he cradled his face in both hands.

Maggie wasn't holding the revolver when he shuffled into the living room. He ignored her and stood looking out the long view to the eastern mountains. He heard her voice. "You got it straightened out?"

He slumped. "I need a drink."

"You've had plenty."

He considered that. "Yes, ma'am," he slurred. "I've had plenty. Jus' ain't had *enough*." He offered her a weak smile as he fell back into his chair and refilled his glass.

"Vic, we're talkin' now."

He nodded sluggishly. "'Solutely. Le's just finish up the game here," he nodded at the Super Bowl. "Then, we talk."

By kickoff time, Vic was snoring softly in his chair.

*   *   *

At the same time

In Ardyss's room, Grace, in the chair beside the bed, was lightly snoring, head tilted back, mouth gaping. A schoolbook lay open on her lap. Ardyss too was asleep. Ed, after checking on them, stepped out into the hallway and closed the door quietly. He frowned, dialing his phone.

Jim Hamilton answered. "Father Hamilton. How can I help you?"

"It's Ed. Are you free for a couple of hours?"

"No baptisms today, so yeah. Planned to watch the Super Bowl, but that isn't till four. Why?"

"How about keeping me company at the hospital?"

"Hell. Who's sick?"

"Ardyss Conley. Real sick. And Grace's got it in her head that she has to stay with her, so I feel a little trapped."

"Tell Grace you're coming over here. It's just across the street."

"She doesn't like being left alone."

"She's with Ardy, you said. So she's not alone. Tell her and come over."

Ed hung up. He was surprised by his passivity. Why should he feel trapped by Grace's decisions? For a minute, he thought about it. *It's not her.* What then? *I feel responsible for her.* Then he knew why: The Helena Children's Home.

He opened Ardyss's door. "Grace," he whispered. The girl stirred, then woke suddenly.

"What's wrong?" she whispered, sharply.

"Nothing. I'm going across the street to St. Bernie's for a little while. Call my cell phone if you need me."

She frowned and closed her eyes. "You didn't need to wake me up." But as he stepped into the hall, his cell phone buzzed.

It was Ben Stewart. "Trouble in paradise, pal. Rosemary heard about Ardyss bein' sick, and she's on a tear to take that little girl up to Helena. Come up with a plan and call me back in five."

"Damn," Ed muttered. He called Jim back, explaining the situation. "I'm going to make some calls, Jim. Maybe I'll drop by when this gets straightened out." When he hung up, he called Andi Pelton's number.

She didn't answer. *Damn.*

He called Jim back, and the priest offered to call some of the families in the parish to see if any could take Grace in. Before they'd finished talking, Ed's cell vibrated. He looked at the ID: Pelton. "Another call, Jim. Gotta go."

She sounded sleepy. "I couldn't wake up quick enough to answer. What's up?"

"I'm sorry, Andi. I didn't mean to wake you." He'd forgotten her midnight shift.

"Well, I'm awake, so what's going on?"

Impressed again with her quick wake-up, he told her about Rosemary.

After a moment's pause, she said, "Look, the girl can stay with me. Ben'll let me work days or you can hang out with her here if I have a different shift. It's only till we find the mother or Ardyss gets better."

"Our deal is that Grace comes over to my office every day after school, so you could pick her up after she talks with me, say, four-fifteen or four-thirty every day. That work?"

"Perfect. Shift's over at four."

Ed sighed, relieved. "I really appreciate this, Andi."

Grace, sleepy-eyed, stumbled out of Ardyss's room just as he clicked off.

"Ardy's asleep," she said, yawning.

"She'll probably sleep all night now. How about we head home? You'll be staying with Andi till Ardy is better."

Grace shook her head. "I'm staying here. Ardy told me, 'Stay with me.'"

Ed started with "No, I think... ," then stopped. He said, "Go back in with Ardy, Grace. I'll be out here. I've got a phone call to make." Grace looked crookedly at him, then went back inside the room.

He dialed Ben Stewart, who picked up in the first ring. "I heard," Ben growled. "Andi called. You all right with this?"

"With Grace staying with Andi? Sure. Andi said you would put her on days for the duration. That work for you?"

"No can do. We'll make it work over here best we can, but she'll get some evenings. I can keep her off midnights."

"Well, when that happens, I can stay with Grace."

"Don't say that to Rosemary. This could go south real fast."

*　　*　　*

Not long after he hung up with Ben, Andi Pelton came into the hospital and waved.

Ed smiled. "Sorry I woke you."

"No problem. Ben went for our plan."

"Yeah, I just talked to him. He says you'll still have to work some evenings. I said I could stay with Grace till you get home. I can rest on your couch."

Andi frowned. "Not sure that's a good idea. I don't really know you well enough to have you sleeping in my house."

"Well, I have another problem before we get to that. Grace refuses to leave Ardyss. I don't understand why she's so loyal, but she's fierce about it."

Andi said, "Let's get some air."

Outside, Andi looked up at the freshening sky. After a long silence, she said, "When I was sixteen, I wanted to be a cop so bad it hurt. My dad – did I tell you he was a cop? – loved the idea. My junior year, the year before my mother died, I won this summer internship to do ride-alongs with the town police, and that summer, instead of kissing boys, I rode in the back seat of a squad, drinking it in like a baby sucks tit." Ed laughed.

Andi smiled, "Sorry, cop talk. Anyway, one afternoon, we were patrolling and they spotted a body in the ditch. She was a little girl, maybe 12, bruised and dirty but alive. She had leaves in her hair, but no blood. The EMTs got her to the hospital, but the cops kept saying things like 'She sure fucked herself up,' like it was her fault. I got mad. I said, 'No little kid lies in a ditch because she wants to. Give her some respect.' The cops laughed at me a little, and now, I know that laugh."

"What does it mean?"

"It means, 'You're right, but *so what*.' You see too many kids thrown in ditches, you get hard."

"And that story applies to Grace how?"

"Seems to me she's trying to hang on to something that matters to her, and in her situation, I'd say that's a good thing. Let's not go, 'So what?'"

Ed looked at her. "That's wise, Andi. Thanks. But if Rosemary finds out I'm leaving her here, it's all over."

"You can cross that bridge when you get there. But Grace needs people on her side for a change."

"I like what you're saying, Andi, but I just – "

He stopped himself, ran his fingers through his hair, torn. Why was he letting fear drive everything? He felt the *black dog* stir. *Hell, all it'll take is a couple nights sleeping in a hospital chair.* "You're right. I'll let her stay, at least tonight."

Andi smiled and mock-punched his shoulder. "Good for you."

Ed caught a movement inside the lobby door. When he looked, Grace was watching them, arms crossed, a fierce frown on her face.

SEVENTEEN

Monday, February 6, early

THE PHONE RANG through Vic's hungover haze, and Maggie's muffled voice came from beyond the bedroom wall. He groaned and rolled over to check the clock; the room spun when he moved his head. 6:40 a.m. The bedroom door opened and Maggie tossed the phone on the bed beside him, then slammed the door.

"What?" Vic snapped into the phone.

"Boss, we got trouble in the near pasture." It was Bud Alsop, Vic's foreman.

"What kinda trouble?"

"Rather you just come out here and take your own look."

"Shit," Vic muttered, "give me a few minutes." He climbed into his clothes, balancing himself against the dresser. His hand was throbbing and he had trouble buttoning up. He walked straight enough, though, into the kitchen. "You got a pot on?" he asked Maggie.

"What'd Bud want?"

"Says we got trouble and I need to come look. We got coffee?"

Instead of pouring him a cup, she pointed at the pot. "Pour your own."

He glared at her, but grabbed a cup and filled it, then went into the mudroom and put on his coat and stepped into his boots.

"I'm comin' with you."

Vic stood up to his height. "No, Maggie, you ain't." He caught her hesitation. "Don't worry. I ain't goin' anywhere to shoot myself. This is some other goddamn thing." Vic didn't know that after he'd passed out yesterday, Maggie had scoured the house and his shop, hiding all the ammunition and locking the weapons in the gun locker and concealing the key.

She studied him. "All right, but when you come back, we're talkin' about what the hell is goin' on, and what you were fixin' to do with that shotgun shell."

Vic squirmed into his coat. "You don't need to know that."

She closed her eyes slowly and nodded. "Yeah, I need to know that. All of it."

His shoulders slumped. "Goddamn, Maggie. When I come in, you'll get it all."

*   *   *

In the near pasture, Vic snarled at Bud, "What you got that needs me out here?"

Bud chuckled. "You hung over, or just feelin' like a sonofabitch?"

"Don't start in. I already got me too much to deal with this morning. What's this trouble?"

Bud pointed through the pasture gate: Two black mounds lay on the snow in the dim light. "Well, boss, you just got yourself a little more to deal with." They walked out into the field toward the dark shapes, two downed cows; below their necks, the snow was stained dark red.

"What the hell?" Vic snapped.

Bud grabbed the muzzle of the nearer animal and pulled up its head. A long bloody gash crossed its throat.

Vic put his coffee cup on the snow and stooped to inspect the wound. "Goddamn," he whispered, his mind snapping crystal clear – and frightened. *What time did I call Stetson?*

Alsop let the head drop. "Yeah." He lit a cigarette. "Want me to call Ben Stewart?"

Vic jerked upright. "Naw, I don't think so."

"Hell, Vic, we got tracks from a pickup – " he pointed them out, snaking from the gate to within fifteen feet of the carcasses. "And them boot prints are probably theirs, if me and you ain't messed 'em up already. Whatever made these cuts was big, like a disk blade maybe, or a sickle. Ain't your average cowboy's knife, tell you that. Ben maybe can catch this bastard."

Just maybe, thought Vic. *And when he does, he catches me too.* To Bud, he said, "Forgot my smokes," and reached out his hand.

"What'd you do there, boss?" Alsop asked, nodding at the bandages, which were rusty with dried blood. He shook another Camel from the pack and lit it for Vic.

Vic took a deep drag on the cigarette to calm down. "Ain't nothin'. I got pissed off doin' taxes and had a little conversation with the gun locker. Maggie fixed 'er up."

Bud drew on his own Camel, nodding at the bandages. "That increase your refund?" he asked, chuckling. When Vic growled, Bud said, "So, you want me to call Ben?"

"Naw, I oughta be the one. I'll call him from the house." He bent to pick up the cup.

"Here. Use my cell."

Vic snapped at him. "We in some goddamn rush here?"

Alsop pulled back his phone, an eyebrow cocked. "Well..." He leaned over and laid his bare hand on the first cow's neck. "These girls is still warm, Vic. Whoever done it wasn't here too long ago. I'm just thinkin', Ben'll want the evidence quick as he can get it, no?"

Vic shrugged, forcing himself calm. "Sure, good point. I guess I *am* a little hung over, thinkin' a little slower'n usual. Go ahead. Give Ben a call."

*   *   *

Ed came in breathing heavily – his run had felt good, despite the night on a plastic hospital chair. The air wasn't so cold and Saturday night's snow had settled enough for comfortable footing, like running on grass. Snow had piled in tiny hummocks on the rocks in Milk Creek. Ed listened, hearing some kind of music, until it struck him that he was humming with the water. Such a new feeling!

Coming in the door, he was pulling off his jacket when the phone rang.

"It's Ed," he answered.

"You alone?" Ben Stewart growled.

"What? When aren't I alone?"

"Damnation! It's too damn early in the mornin' for problems like I got."

"What's this about?"

"Can you be here in twenty minutes?"

"No, Ben, I can't be there in twenty minutes. I have to shower, get ready for the day, and eat something. And I have a patient at eight-thirty." It struck him. "Shit! I have to get Grace to school!"

"Okay, then. Get your ass here in thirty." Ben said, and hung up.

*   *   *

Grace wasn't in Ardyss's room. Ardyss was still sleeping. Ed ran out to the nurse's desk. Melissa Anderson said, "She said to tell you, 'Thanks for forgetting me, Northrup.'" Melissa's eyes twinkled. "She walked across the parking lot to school. I kept an eye on her til she went in the building."

"Thanks, Mel," he'd managed, embarrassed. "I'm not exactly parent material."

She laughed. "Who is?"

Ed smiled and went on to Ardyss's room.

Ardyss was half-awake and weak. She narrowed her eyes when he came in, confused. He said, "It's Ed, Ardyss."

She whispered, her voice crackly and dry, "Where's the girl?"

"At school. She'll be back around four-thirty or so."

"How long is that?"

"About seven hours."

She sighed and looked up to the ceiling. "She was here all night," she whispered. "She's a good girl. Taking care of me." A tear ran down the side of her face. "It's not good for her."

Ed patted her hand. "You're *very* good for her, Ardyss. Staying with you is important to her."

The old head did not move.

He waited a moment. Her voice was fainter. "I think I'm dying. *That's* not good for her."

"Doc thinks it's a flu, but he says your age is the wild card."

She strained a smile and turned her face toward him. "About the only thing left of me that's wild." Her eyes closed, but she whispered again, "It's funny. Before this, Grace was making me feel more alive. Guess not."

Ed patted her hand again, and she grasped his. "Tell Grace," she stopped for a breath. "Tell Grace I'm trying."

*   *   *

Behind his desk, Ben was steaming, evidenced by the pink in his cheeks. Andi Pelton was already sitting in front of him, and he was reading a page of notes, ignoring her. Ed smiled at Andi.

"Sit your butt down," Ben barked. He looked down again at the page. "It's what, not even eight o'clock Monday morning and already I got me three problems involving you two." He looked up at them.

Ed smiled. "That's a bunch of problems for one morning."

"Your sweet ass it is, and it ain't funny. Here's number 1." He glared again at the page, then continued, "You two let that little girl Grace stay at the hospital overnight after we agreed she'd stay with you." He glared at his deputy.

"Yes sir, we worked it out. Ed stayed – "

"Did you see my lips asking you to speak, Deputy?"

Startled, Andi stammered, "No, no sir. No lips."

Ed said, "I stayed with her, Ben."

"Then how the hell did you answer your damn home phone when I called you at a quarter to seven?" The humor had disappeared.

Ed started to explain he'd come home at five to have his run, but the sheriff cut him off.

"Right. Here's problem Number 1. Rosemary Rasmussen already tore me a new asshole 'cause of your stunt and she's making noises – real loud noises – that she's gonna pick up Grace Ellonson. Unless you two scofflaws do better'n last night, that little girl's on her way to Helena. She said, and it ain't my words, 'One more chance. One.'"

"Here's what I think, Ben," Ed began.

"When I'm ready to hear what you think, I'll ask," the sheriff said. "Here's Number 2."

Ed shook his head, a little exasperated. "Wait up, Ben. I don't know what you were doing all weekend, but I've been at the hospital a good share of the time with Ardyss Conley. She's pretty sick, and we're – "

Ben waved him off. "Yeah, yeah, which brings me to Number 2. Can anybody explain to me why my only female deputy is out on the highway chasin' somebody at two o'clock on a Sunday morning in a goddamn Montana snowstorm?"

Beside him, Ed felt Andi bristle. "I wrote 'er up," she began. "The flyer guy..."

"Sonny Carter calls me at three in the morning to ask who Deputy Pelton was red-lighting at that hour. This makes me real curious, I'll tell you. And do I get a phone call or a visit? Nothin', not a damn word all day Sunday."

Andi sat still. "You want me to explain?" Then added, "Sir?"

"Later. Number 3 first." He shuffled the papers on his desk until he found a pink message slip. "At exactly seven-twelve this mornin', we got a call from Buddy Alsop out at Vic Sobstak's place, asking for a sheriff to come out and investigate the murder – he called it that – of two heifers. Says their throats were cut." He looked back and forth between them.

After a moment, Ed asked, "And that involves me how?"

Ben pounced. "Maggie Sobstak's your patient. She got drunk bad enough to be hospitalized and Deputy Pelton, here, thinks maybe

Victor's abusin' her. According to her report of last Friday – " He held up another paper on his desk and looked at it a moment, then glanced at Andi. " – the deputy observed some odd goings-on out at the CW when she went out to talk to Maggie, including that Maggie wouldn't say boo and there was an Idaho-plated Cadillac Escalade in the yard. Idaho's where these flyers are out of, you'll recall, and the plates are licensed to the church of Jesus Christ of the American Promise, which takes credit for the damn things. And now we got throat-slashed cows and I'm damned tired of getting phone calls I don't know nothing about."

He looked angrily past them at the photo, on the back wall where he could see it at moments like this, of the 30-pound lake trout he caught up on Lake Pend Oreille. His shoulders sagged, and his tone changed. "My job is to know what's going on around here, and all of a sudden I don't know squat."

Ed waited a moment as Ben's wrath subsided. After a moment, he said, "Which problem do you want to start with?"

*   *   *

Twenty minutes later, out in Reception, Callie Martin grinned as Ed emerged from Ben's office. "I reckon those teeth marks on your ass match the ones on Deputy Pelton's."

"Callie! Gross," Ed said, pretending shock.

"Yep, but Ben chewed your fanny pretty good."

"You could hear him out here?"

"These walls ain't *that* thick, darlin'." She laughed a small laugh. "I thought him callin' you – " She consulted a scribbled note. "– a 'damn double-dog droopy-dick do-gooder' had a real ring to it." She smiled slyly.

"So you probably also know why Ben's so pissed off."

She nodded solemnly. "You let little Grace stay with Ardy last night, and he's gotta cover your sweet ass – which I'm guessin' he now owns – with Rosemary."

"You know everything, don't you?"

Callie's smile faded. "No. I can't for the life of me figure why that woman left that little girl here in the valley."

*   *   *

The sheriff's department SUV rolled slowly up to the pasture gate where Vic waited, its big tires crunching in the snow. Ben Stewart opened the passenger side window, and Vic pointed to where Bud Alsop stood beside the dead animals and said, "Best to walk from here, Ben." He pointed out the suspicious tracks, which came across the field from the far gate. Ben jumped out before Andi brought the vehicle to a full stop.

"Anything been moved or touched here, Bud?" he yelled as he crossed the remaining twenty yards of snow.

The foreman shook his head. "Not since I called. I been watchin', Ben. Me and Vic lifted her head for a look-see – " He pointed to the near heifer. "Ain't nothin' else been moved. Them tire tracks was fresh when we found 'em." He pointed behind the animals to the tracks six inches deep in the fresh snow. Ben leaned over, hands on knees, studying them.

"Good," he said, standing up. He turned toward Andi, who'd walked up behind him. "Call Callie and tell her to get the state mobile crime lab out here a.s.a.p."

Maggie, wearing a heavy sweater, was walking into the pasture as Ben gave the order. Her arms were folded against the cold. She frowned as she passed Andi Pelton going back to the vehicle. Vic, his throat tight, asked, "You think they'll bother over a couple heifers?"

Ben studied him. "That all this is, Vic? A couple heifers?"

Vic hesitated, his mouth dry. "You think it's somethin' else?"

"Let's do this like on TV. I ask, you answer. So, this just about the cows?"

Vic forced a grin, hoping it didn't look goofy. "Well, if it ain't, I got no goddamn idea what it could be. Looks like some shit-ass kids out screwin' around. To me."

"Is there anybody upset with you? Fired anybody lately? Any problems around the ranch?"

Maggie was watching Vic, who was hoping he looked thoughtful. "Nope, pretty much business as usual around here. Anything come to mind, Bud?"

Alsop shrugged. "Ain't been no problems I can think of, Sheriff." Maggie glanced at him.

Ben caught the glance. "You got anything you want to add, Miz Sobstak?"

She looked quickly at Vic, then shook her head. "No, nothin' to add, Ben."

Andi called from the vehicle. "Callie says they want to know why you need a crime scene for animal deaths."

Ben lifted his cap and rubbed his head. "Crap on toast," he muttered. Louder, he said, "Tell them I'm thinkin' terrorist activity here." He turned his head and spit politely. "Assholes." He looked at Maggie. "Pardon my French."

Maggie nodded. "I've heard worse, Sheriff. You really think it's terrorists?"

"No, and neither will the crime lab guys. They'll piss and moan, but they'll come. I sure as hell want to find out whose truck drove in here last night."

Vic glanced apprehensively at the woman deputy walking back from the SUV. *That's the one thinks I'm abusin' Maggie.* She joined them. "The mobile can't get here for two or three hours," she said.

Ben nodded, then said to Vic, "Deputy Pelton was tellin' me about a black Caddie SUV she saw out here around noon Friday. Can you tell me who that was?"

Vic's heart raced and he felt his face blush. He swallowed. "They was preachers, Ben. I been..." He swallowed again. "I been thinkin' about givin' my life to Jesus." He looked a quick "keep quiet" at Maggie, who registered shock, then made her face blank.

Ben, catching Maggie's surprised look, said, "That so? We ran those plates. Turns out they're owned by a church over in Post Falls, Idaho, same church as puts out some posters we been trackin'." He gave Vic a moment to sweat. "You can't find Jesus a little closer to home?"

Vic shrugged, trying to keep his face friendly, though his heart pounded. "I guess none of the local preachers turn my crank."

The sheriff looked a bullet at him, then shrugged. "Whatever turns your crank, I guess. Anything else come to mind, Vic?"

Vic felt his heart pounding, knew his face was giving him away. He forced a laugh. "You'll be first to hear, Ben."

Stewart snorted and turned to Andi. "Deputy, let's get this scene secured." He told the Sobstaks and Bud Alsop to hang around to talk to the crime scene technicians. "I'll have to ask you to move out of the pasture now, if you don't mind." As they walked back to the house, Andi backed the SUV out of the field and she and Ben secured the gate with yellow crime tape.

As they did, he said, keeping his voice low, "Thought I'd give Vic a little scare, lettin' him know we're onto the flyers. Preachers! Up to now, Vic's seemed a decent guy, and he sure as hell ain't religious. And that Caddie belongs to those wingnuts in Idaho. Gettin' Jesus, my ass!"

Andi said nothing.

"Go on around the pasture fence and tape that outer gate." He pointed to the distant gate where the tracks came in. "I gotta haul my butt back to town, so I'll take the vehicle and send somebody out to pick you up after the state bozos get here. Use the time to see what you can squeeze outa Vic."

Andi gestured toward the truck parked in the yard, and said, "Ben, that's the pickup I chased Saturday night."

The sheriff frowned. "That's Victor's. You sure?"

"Ninety-nine percent. I'd say it's the one."

He rubbed his chin. "Well, that's the coffin nail, then. Victor's our man for the flyers. Get some more on those 'preachers,' then we'll visit him again."

"You want me to wait out here? It's cold."

"Hell's hot. You just stand there and contemplate your sins."

Andi laughed. "Recent or ancient?"

Ben mock-punched her shoulder. "Last forty-eight hours." He slid behind the wheel of the SUV, and Andi said, as she pushed his door shut, "No sins the last forty-eight."

He smiled. "You need a life," he said, and drove out the long drive to the highway.

*   *   *

A couple of minutes after Ben left, Vic came out of the house, got in his truck, and moved it over to the pasture gate where Andi was leaning. He climbed out. "Deputy, you climb in here and stay warm. The heater's pretty good once she warms up. No use standin' out here in the goddamn cold." After politely showing her the music stations on the radio, Vic rejoined Maggie and Bud in the house.

"Coffee?" he asked.

Bud said, "Gimme a to-go cup, Vic. I got work to do."

Vic said, "Hey! Stick around. Ben said we should wait to answer questions."

Maggie snorted. "You go ahead, Bud. Victor and me got a problem to sort out. We'll call your cell when they get here." She rummaged in a cupboard and produced an insulated cup and poured Bud a cupful.

After Bud left, Vic said, "Why don't you take a cup of your good coffee out to the deputy, darlin'?"

"I ain't talkin' to that woman, Victor, but you're about to start talkin' to me."

"Now, Maggie, that ain't like you. You're the one who coffees everybody."

"Talk to me, Victor."

Vic grunted. Hard to tell which throbbed more, his hangover headache or his broken hand. "Well, she's a guest on my ranch and I'm takin' her a goddamn cup of coffee on a cold morning." He poured a cup and went out the mudroom. He turned back. "And she thinks I'm abusin' you, so I'm showin' her some gentlemanly behavior."

*   *   *

"Thank you, Mr. Sobstak," Andi said when he knocked on her window and gave her the cup. Vic leaned his forearms on the lowered window, trying to make a friendly impression.

"Who'd do a goddamn thing like that?" He gestured toward the dead cattle.

"I don't know, Mr. Sobstak." She smiled. "Tell me about the religious interest you've developed."

He felt blank for a moment, then nervous. "Oh, the preachers." He stood up straight, his thoughts racing. "Well, it's a kind of Christian church, or somewhat. They talk to me about the Bible and such." He tried to look philosophical. "They tell me I gotta quit swearin' and drinkin', which gives me second thoughts, I'll admit." He tried another smile, and knew it didn't work.

Maggie stood on the porch and called him. He frowned, annoyed, then changed it to a smile for Andi. "Well, duty calls."

Back in the kitchen, he went on the offense. "It ain't right, you tellin' the world about our problems, Maggie. Thanks for the goddamn support in front of Bud."

Maggie poured two mugs of coffee and handed one to Vic. "Drop it. We talk now, Victor. Sit down at the table and tell me what in the good Lord's name is goin' on. And don't give me that baloney about gettin' Jesus."

"Now, Maggie, let's just get the crime lab people behind us, then we can talk."

"Try this on for size, Vic. You don't talk to me right now, right here, I'm goin' to town and tell Ben Stewart what I've been watchin' around here lately. All of it. I'm your wife and your partner, for God's sake! If you don't trust me, why then, hell's bells, we're done."

Vic felt a chill: She maybe meant it.

"Whoa up, there." Vic sat down at the table, trying to figure out a way to escape. "We'll do all the goddamn talkin' you please, but just give me a little time to straighten things out."

Maggie put down her mug and walked into the mudroom. She started to put on her coat. She said, "You've had time. Talk to me now, Vic, or I'm leavin'."

Vic looked at her. "You're for real? You'd leave? You'd tell Ben?"

"Everything." Vic heard a quiver in her voice. He took a long swallow of coffee, thinking fast.

"Maggie, Maggie, Maggie." He ran his uninjured hand through his hair. "Let's just sort this out. I'll – "

"The only sorting I'm interested in is you talkin'. You talk, or I walk."

"I talk or you walk? You're suddenly Montana's poet lariat?" Maybe an attack would throw her off.

"It's *laureate*. You never know. Maybe I'll make a living as a divorced lady writin' poetry in some coffee shop over in Missoula."

"Goddamn, woman." Vic held out his mug, giving up. "Top this up, and sit your sweet ass back down. I'm fixin' to talk."

*　　*　　*

At his office after his two o'clock patient, Ed took two messages off his voice machine. The first was from Maggie Sobstak, the other was Grace's: "I'm at the hospital and I'm staying. If you want to see me, you come here." *Payback for running out on her this morning.* He called her back.

She answered quickly. "Northrup, I'm staying with Ardy. You come here."

"No, Grace, our deal is you come *here* after school."

There was a long silence. Then, "Fine," and an abruptly dead line.

Maggie's message interested him. "Me and Vic talked. We need to see you. Call me." A pause. Then, "Please."

He looked at the clock: twenty to four. He'd promised to fix Jim Hamilton's toilet and have a drink around five. He could squeeze the Sobstaks in after talking to Grace. He called Maggie and she agreed they could be there a little after four.

Ten minutes later, Grace stormed into the waiting room and slammed the door.

"All right, I'm here," she snapped. "What?"

"Like we agreed, you and I talk until Andi picks you up for dinner."

"I'll eat at the hospital." She stood at the door, as if about to bolt.

"That's fine. Take it up with Andi. How's Ardyss."

"Her fever's lower and she's not vomiting."

"Good. She wanted me to tell you she's trying to get better. She doesn't want you to be disappointed in her." Ed pondered the bond between Ardyss and Grace. Whatever its meaning, it grounded Grace.

Grace shook her head impatiently. "I *know* she's trying, and I should be there to help her. Come on, Northrup. Let me go back. Andi can meet me there and we can eat in the cafeteria."

Opening his mouth to refuse, Ed saw the fierce loyalty in her eyes. "Why's this so important to you, Grace? You don't really know Ardyss."

"How should *I* know why it's important? You're the shrink, so, like, *analyze* it. It just is, okay?" But almost immediately, her eyes pleaded. "Fuck it, Northrup, *you* know. Ardy was willing to take care of me. I can't let her, like, be all alone when she's sick. Besides..."

He waited a moment. "Besides?"

She blushed. "I don't know anybody at school. I need somebody to be with. You're busy."

Ed's heart went out to her. "Okay, Grace. Go on back. I'll ask Andi if she can have dinner with you, and I'll come over around eight to pick you up."

Grace whirled into the waiting room, trailing a loud "Thanks, Northrup!" behind her, and slammed the door.

Ed laughed and called Andi. He relayed Ardyss's improvement and the change of plan. "So can you check on Grace after your shift? Maybe have dinner with her? I've got to go over to Jim Hamilton's after I see my last patient. I should get to the hospital around eight. That work for you?"

"Sure, although we have a training at seven I have to be at." Andi paused. "You've *got to* visit your friend?"

"Well, if you put it that way, no. Of course not."

"With friends, it's what you want to do, not what you've got to do." That annoyed him, but he said nothing.

Andi said, "Okay, I'll drop it. How's Grace?"

"Crabby about something. And lonely. She said one reason she stays with Ardyss is she doesn't know anybody at school."

Andi said, "That won't last. Crabby, though, that's about us pulling her away from Ardyss – go to school, come home overnight."

Ed smiled. "Good analysis, Doctor Pelton. Not to mention getting abandoned by mom. Well, that's her problem."

"Not hers alone," Andi said. "When you're fourteen, adult demands are a threat, and you're the available adult, so expect crabby. Anyway, dinner's fine."

Ed started to say something about liking Andi's take on things, but changed his mind.

Andi said, "Hey, before we hang up, about those cows at the Sobstak's ranch?"

He stiffened. Whatever had happened, it might be the reason Vic and Maggie were coming in. "Ben said they were killed. Problem number 3. What happened?"

"The techs thought it was a machete, but they don't think the tire prints will tell us much."

He decided not to tell Andi the Sobstaks were coming in. Maybe Vic had confessed an affair and they wanted marriage help, which wasn't police business. If this cow incident was bringing them in, he'd loop her in later, if he could. He glanced at his watch. They'd be here momentarily.

"Earth to Ed?"

"Sorry. Just thinking about Vic and Maggie."

"Well, clue me in if you learn anything. See you around eight."

"Count on it." He wished he could mean it wholeheartedly.

*   *   *

As soon as they sat down in Ed's office, Vic went on offense. "I ain't here for no East Coast crap, I'm here for Maggie." His fists bumped a little on the arms of the chair. Ed noted the crusty bandage on his right hand.

"That's fine, Mr. Sobstak. What *can* I do for you both?"

"Like I said, this is for her." He wagged his head toward Maggie. "Talk to her."

Maggie shook her head, but spoke gently. "Vic? We're partners, remember?"

Vic grunted. He arched an eyebrow and confided to Ed, man-to-man, "*Partners*, meanin' I do like she wants."

This time, her voice sharpened. "Vic! We're got us some bad trouble and we're in it together, so just get over yourself and let's get this fixed."

Ed watched Vic sit back and fold his arms across his chest. He winked at Ed. "Feisty, ain't she? It's why I married her."

"That she is, Vic. You made a good choice there." Then he turned to Maggie. "Your husband's just making sure I know he's really the boss." He turned back to Vic. "I get that right?"

"Hit the nail on the goddamn head," Vic said. His broken hand unfisted stiffly and rested on the arm of the chair.

Ed said, "All right, Vic, you want to tell me what's going on?"

Vic looked at him. "Nope, but I guess that's what I'm goin' to do, eh?"

Vic, helped by Maggie, his elbows leaning on his knees, told it all, then fell back in his chair. "Goddamn! All this confessin' wearies a fella." Maggie patted his arm.

"Your turn, Doc," Vic said. "What do we do about this mess?"

"Well, unless I missed something, I think we've got three or four messes. One, your tax situation. Two, this Reverend Crane business – and that's really two messes, this guy Stetson's threats and the 'federal offense' for hanging the posters." Ed wondered how he could tell Andi about that. "And three, or I guess four, you lied to Ben Stewart this morning about the cows."

"Yeah, that could be trouble," Vic muttered.

"Right," Ed agreed. "Well, these messes really aren't in my arena. For the tax problems, I think you need to talk to Ms. MacArdell next door. She can help you with that. The legal stuff, I think we should get the sheriff's office involved."

Maggie looked aghast. "The sheriff's? You mean that deputy?"

"No. I'll talk to Ben Stewart. He'll know how to handle it." He smiled. "And I think maybe there's mess number five."

"Hell," Vic said. "We come in with one, then it's four, and now we got five? How's this helpin'?"

Ed chuckled. He realized he hadn't enjoyed a session like this for a very long time. "Well, you had it when you came in, you just didn't talk about it. It's the damage done to your marriage, broken trust." He waited a moment. "Am I wrong?"

Maggie was nodding. "I s'pose," Vic said. He scratched his scrubbly chin. "Yeah, that's fair enough."

Maggie said, "That ain't the hard one, Vic, we'll work that out. Mess number six, though, is this sex thing, and she's a tough one. We ain't plowin' with the same team there."

Vic swung around to face her directly. "Maggie! What're you sayin'?"

"What I'm sayin' is I want my partner back, but I want my *man* back too, not jus' to dip your dick and roll over. I need you to make my body feel like it's a place you like to spend time in, not jus' a place to bury your stress." Her face was beet-red – it had cost her to say these things in front of two men. A feisty woman indeed.

Vic swallowed, and looked nervously at Ed. "This okay to talk about?" Ed nodded.

Vic turned to Maggie. "At home, Maggie. We'll talk about 'er there. If that don't do the trick, we'll rope in the doc."

Ed waited, and after a moment, Maggie nodded. "We'll see. I ain't been myself the last few weeks, worryin' about you, where you're goin' out to and all. I ain't been hospitable to nobody, fearful, testy. I been mean to that deputy, and I know she's only thinkin' about me. I want you back, but I want me back too."

Vic nodded, but when he didn't answer, they both looked at Ed. He said, "Well, let's get to work on one through five. If you need me for six, let me know."

Vic blushed, then blurted, "How 'bout tossin' out a couple ideas for number six? Just for a warmup?"

*   *   *

They tackled the tax problem first, and Vic and Maggie agreed to let him make them an appointment with Leese MacArdell to work a solution. Vic was astounded to learn that the IRS would help them work out a plan. "That ain't what Reverend Crane says."

Ed nodded. "I imagine not. No money in that line of thinking."

Ed dialed Leese's number, suddenly remembering that he'd contemplated having an affair with her. He sighed. That was pre-Grace. When she answered, he said, "Leese, it's Ed. Say, do you have any time to see Vic and Maggie Sobstak this week? I know it's a busy time."

He grabbed his pen – his Connie Fuller pen that Leese said he should use to write her a note if he "got interested" – and jotted a time. He said to Vic, "Can you see her tomorrow at nine?" Vic looked at Maggie, who nodded.

Ed thanked Leese and hung up. "Now, about Crane and the flyers, we need to get Ben Stewart involved." Maggie looked alarmed, and Vic jerked up straight.

"I'm thinkin' that ain't such a great idea." Vic stood up and paced a turn around the office. "Stetson made it real clear if I tell anybody, Maggie here's in danger and the FBI or the IRS gets called. Don't forget that!"

Ed calmed him. "Easy, Vic. Ben and I have a way to talk about things without naming names. We just talk about the situation and he gives an opinion. He's not obliged to do anything because he doesn't know who I'm talking about."

"You wouldn't tell him it's us?" Vic sat down again.

"Exactly."

Vic looked doubtful, but asked Maggie. "What do you think?"

Nervous as she looked, Maggie said, "I'm thinkin' we can't handle Crane alone."

Vic crossed his arms and lowered his chin, staring at the floor. Finally, he looked up at Ed. "Goddamn." He rubbed his red eyes. "Okay, call the sheriff. But no names."

Ed dialed, putting the phone on speaker so the Sobstaks could hear everything. As he did, he glanced at his watch. Five-twenty. *Hell, I'm supposed to be over at Jim's. Well, he'll understand.*

*   *   *

Ben picked up immediately. "Stewart. Speak."

"Ben, it's Ed. Look, I've got a juicy hypothetical for you."

"I'm off the clock. Let's say we do this tomorrow."

"No. It's important."

"Some porno about you and my deputy, I hope? You two getting it on yet?"

"Drop it." Vic and Maggie's eyebrows lifted, and Ed regretted using the speakerphone. "No, listen." He detailed what he'd learned about the Sobstak's problem with Crane.

"Hold on a sec. Let me get to a more private place." There was a long silence on the speaker, then rustling sounds. Ben came back. "So, hypothetically, we talkin' Victor Sobstak here?"

The Sobstaks flinched, and Ed grimaced, *really* regretting the speakerphone. "*Ben.*" It was the best he could do.

"Okay, okay. So this hypothetical person hangs the flyers and then wants to back out and gets him and his wife threatened?"

"Yes." Ed watched Vic's tense face. Would Ben connect the "threat" with the cows?

"And then this guy agrees to hang more flyers in return for help with his tax problem?"

"That's right. And he confirms the flyers come from that Reverend Crane over in Idaho."

"Loyd Crane. Yeah, we know him. From that Idaho church." Vic and Maggie glanced at each other, faces grim.

"Right. So it's *quid pro quo*, flyers for tax advice."

"All right. So your question is hypothetically what?"

"Is hanging those flyers a federal offense? Or any kind of offense for that matter?"

Ben's sigh rumbled on the speaker. "You know, pal? We got us two choices."

"Which are?"

"My idea, or we call the county attorney."

"Let's hear your idea."

Ben coughed into the phone, startling everyone. "Sorry about that, Ed. Look, you got me at happy hour. I'm drinking some fine Scotch."

"You're on the corner?"

"Nope, not today. I'm over at Connie Fuller's. We're tyin' some trout flies."

"And tying one on?" Ed added, making Vic smile, and Maggie frown.

Ben cleared his throat, thunder on the speaker. "Anyway, about those flyers. My opinion, it ain't no federal offense. This here's still a free country. Man can hang any crap he wants on a telephone pole, so long as it don't incite to riot, cause discrimination against a protected group, or directly violate a protected group's speech or status."

"Well, you've seen the flyers. Do they do any of that?"

"A politician runnin' for governor ain't a protected group. He's fair game for any asshole with half a brain stem."

"So no federal offense."

"Not that I see."

"Hypothetically, then, if the person posting the flyers has a compelling justification for doing it – "

"You sure we ain't discussing Victor here?"

Ed tried to reassure the Sobstaks with his eyes, and said, "Ben, just work with me."

"Hell, whatever. You and your confidentiality! Give me this 'compelling justification.'"

"One, he could be bankrupted if he can't pay his taxes. Two, his wife could be, and I quote, 'visited' by Reverend Crane's sidekick."

Ben was silent. "Interesting. Sounds like intimidation, maybe conspiracy of some kind. I'd have to ask the county attorney on that. But yeah, if those threats are real, I think the flyers don't mean squat, especially if your guy helps us out."

Maggie visibly relaxed back into her chair, but Vic leaned forward, urgently swiping his finger across his throat. He mouthed, *the cows, the cows*. Ed nodded and said, "Ben, the threats are real."

"People always think they are, but they're usually just hot air."

"Not this time."

"What do you mean?"

"Give me a minute, Ben." Ed looked questioningly at Vic. He jotted a note and held it up: *Should I tell him? Will you help him?*

Vic looked at Maggie, then back at Ed. His eyes registered fear, but he nodded.

Ed said, "Ben, still hypothetically, say our guy's a, uh, a goldfish dealer. Suppose that during the night, two of his goldfish were pulled out of the water and suffocated. Let's say this guy got so scared he lied to the sheriff about who did it. Would the sheriff – "

Ben's voice broke in. "Would the sheriff be pissed and charge him with obstruction? You can bet your sweet hypothetical ass the sheriff would!" He paused, then finished, "If suffocating goldfish was a crime, which it ain't."

Ed hesitated for a moment, then asked, "Is slashing a cow's throat a crime?"

Ben said, "You hit a deer with your truck, and it's crippled but it ain't dead, the right thing's to shoot it or cut its throat. But cows in a field? That's animal cruelty, and whoever did that, I want his ass. Your guy was scared, I get that. Your goldfish dealer maybe even told his sheriff he's thinkin' of givin' his life to Jesus. So I'm hopin' Jesus warns him not to let the the trail get too cold before he figures out I can help."

"Do you think you can protect my guy? And his wife?"

"Good God, Ed, I'm the sheriff of this county! Talk to them. Get them to talk to me. The sooner the better."

"I'll call you back." He reached for the *Off* button.

Vic blocked his hand. "No need to wait, Sheriff. This here's Victor Sobstak. Me and Maggie are sittin' here in Doctor Ed's office, and I can tell you whatever you need. What you want us to do?"

Ben was quiet for a moment, then said, "You feel safe out there overnight?"

"We're armed, Sheriff. And we ain't afraid to shoot."

Maggie looked alarmed and laid her hand on Vic's arm. He brushed it off.

The sheriff's voice said, "Well, let's not make this worse'n it is already. You go on home and lock your doors. Tomorrow, you and Mrs. Sobstak come in to my office at 10:00 a.m. and we'll take it from there."

"We're here, Sheriff, right in town. We could meet you now."

Ben laughed, more thunder on the phone. "Victor, I'm sitting in Connie Fuller's trout fly shop. There's a real nice oak fire burning in his fireplace, and we're drinking 12-year-old single malt Scotch. If you think I'm tradin' that to talk about asshole tax resisters and cow-killers on a cold Monday evening, Mr. Crane ain't your only problem."

Maggie laughed, and Vic smiled a full smile, his first. "You put 'er that way, Sheriff, we'll see you tomorrow mornin' at ten."

Hanging up, Ed said, "Well, you got yourselves two meetings tomorrow morning. Back to back." After the Sobstaks left, Ed realized how tired he was. The long night on the plastic chair in the hospital was taking its toll, but he'd promised to fix Jim's toilet. He sighed and locked up the office.

EIGHTEEN

Fifteen minutes later

BEFORE ST. BERNIE'S, he stopped at the hospital. Ardyss was sleeping. Her nurse told him there was no real improvement, although the fever had come down two points, and the vomiting had stopped.

"That sounds like improvement to me," he said, smiling. The nurse smiled back. "I guess Doc's worried about how slow it's going. Her age, you know." He nodded and went to the room. Grace was watching television.

Ardyss was sleeping, so Ed whispered, "Hey, Grace. How's she doing?"

"She's not puking so much, I guess. All she does is sleep."

He took a breath. "Looks like we've got a problem."

She looked alarmed. "What problem?"

He ran his fingers through his hair. "We caught a load of grief from the social worker for letting you stay here last night. Either you stay the night at Andi's, or you go up to Helena."

"Fuck that. Ardy told me to stay with her and I'm staying."

"I want to say yes, honey – "

"My fucking name's *Grace*. Why can't you people remember that?"

He felt sorry for her, but damn. "Well look, whatever your name is, you're not staying tonight."

Grace huffed and threw herself into the chair. "Then you're going to have to drag me. And don't you dare touch me, or I'll file a complaint."

Ed's laugh stirred Ardyss awake. She looked confused. "What's the matter, child?"

"They won't let me stay with you, Ardy." She had tears in her eyes again. Ed felt rotten, but the thought of Grace going away felt worse.

Ardyss extended her arms and wiggled her fingers, pulling the girl to her bed. Grace sat down next to her.

Ardyss pulled her head down close, and whispered in her ear. Then kissed her forehead. Grace sat up, looking tearfully toward Ed.

He steeled himself. "Not tonight. You're going to stay with Andi."

"You're not the boss of me."

Ardyss chimed in, weakly. "Go home, child. Come see me tomorrow after school."

Touched by the girl's devotion, Ed thought of a compromise, said, "Grace, I'm going to help my friend Jim fix his toilet. Andi's coming here for dinner with you, and you can stay with Ardyss till I'm done, around eight o'clock." Grace glared at him, but said nothing.

With some misgiving, he said to her as firmly as he could, "At eight. Be ready."

"Don't tell me what to do, Northrup."

A weak cough from Ardyss's bed: "Stay with me till Ed comes back, dear."

She slumped in the chair. "Only 'cause you say so, Ardy."

*   *   *

"Ah, the late Doctor Ed," Jim Hamilton said as he opened his front door. "Don't stand there letting in the cold."

Ed looked back out at the sky. Snow had been falling all afternoon, now illuminated by the street lights.

"Sorry I'm late, Jim. Busy day. But I think we've solved the Maggie

Sobstak mystery." He yawned.

"Really?" Jim closed the door. "Really? What's the story?"

Ed hung his coat on the rack and said, "She'll tell you about it."

"You tease. Well, then, how about we solve *my* problem?"

"Your unflushable toilet."

"The same. Want a drink while we work?"

"Sure. While *we* work?"

The priest poured two glasses, handing one to Ed, saying, "While *you* work.

The laborer is worthy of his hire."

Ed pointed at the second glass. "So what's yours for, Father Non-laborer?"

Jim held his glass in toast position. "I myself cannot watch a man working without proper fortification in my hand. When you work and I don't, I feel guilty. This – " He held up the glass. " – eases my pain."

Ed snorted. "Show me the toilet."

While he drained the water and began to dismantle the broken mechanism inside the old tank, he brought Jim up to date about Ardyss and Grace. He mentioned how they'd stayed the night at the hospital.

"Letting her stay is playing with fire, Rosemary-wise."

Ed grunted. The locking nut below the tank was rusted stuck. He leaned his weight into the wrench and was just about to give up when the nut jerked, then began to loosen. "I know. But I think Grace is trying to prove she's more loyal to Ardyss than any adult has been to her."

"A sound psychological analysis, Doctor." Jim was grinning.

Ed, already tired from sleeping last night in a chair, flashed him a sour look. He finished unscrewing the nut and lifted the broken mechanism out of the tank.

"Where's the new one?"

"It's in the tub. Jackie said it should fit."

"Did you measure it?"

"No, I just asked her. She runs the hardware store, after all."

Ed held the old guts against against the new one. "Should fit," he grumbled, and started to assemble it.

"You sound grumpy."

Ed tightened the valve and let the water into the tank. No leaks. He flushed it twice, watching it silently. Finally, he turned toward Jim. "I'm sorry. I'm tired and I can't help but worry about Grace. But damn, she's a pill."

Jim picked up the old mechanism and inspected it, then tossed it into the wastebasket. "Let's go sit down. I'm tired from all this work."

After they'd refreshed their glasses and Jim sat in his fireplace chair, Ed stood at the front window, watching bursts of snow eddy in the street light. He rubbed his eyes. "Man, I'm bushed," he said, as he sank into the other chair in front of the fire. "I'm afraid Grace won't cooperate tonight, and she'll end up in Helena. She was pretty explicit that if I dragged her out of her chair, she'd file a complaint."

"That's your beef with the girl?"

"I don't have a beef with her. She's, uh, fourteen, and she's smart enough to protect herself. I doubt I'd be any sweeter if I were in her shoes." He remembered his own anger in the weeks after Mara left him.

They sipped quietly for a while.

Jim broke the silence. "May I say something?"

"Could I prevent it?"

The priest chuckled. "I'm worried about you. You're depressed."

"They teach psychiatric diagnosis in seminary?"

"Hey, I'm your friend, and it doesn't take a PhD to see you're hurting."

Ed swirled the Scotch in his glass, steadied himself. "You're right. But tonight it's about Grace." After a long silence, Ed gave up. "I almost committed suicide back in December. Accidently."

Jim looked at him hard. "Accidental *suicide*? Come on."

"I wasn't paying attention and hiked too far out onto a snow cornice. I wasn't consciously thinking about dying, but obviously..." His voice trailed off. Ed found himself quietly weeping.

Jim said, "That's some serious shit, buddy. What are we going to do about it?"

As he was savoring Jim's *we*, Ed's cell phone buzzed. He looked at it. Andi Pelton. He quickly blew his nose, opened the phone, and said hello.

"Look, Ed, Grace just called. Ardyss apparently crashed again. I'm on my way to the hospital. Can you meet us there?"

Ed agreed, and shut down the call, still reverberating from weeping. He rubbed his eyes. Jim looked sadly at him. "No time for you, eh?"

Ed shook his head. He hadn't felt this tired in years, and from the surprising tears, he knew the weariness wasn't all from sleeping in a chair. He sighed and explained to Jim what was happening. The priest stood. "People die inconveniently, don't they?" He studied Ed, then put his arms out, Ed stood, and the two men hugged. "Call me. Let's keep talking about this."

Ed nodded, hoping that he would. Outside, he had to brush four inches of snow off his truck.

*   *   *

Ardyss's hospital room was vacant. He hurried to the nurses' station. Melissa Hanson looked up.

"Where's Ardyss?"

"We moved her to ICU. Her temp spiked again and her blood pressure's off the charts. Doctor Keeley is with her." She looked concerned. "You feel all right, Ed?"

"Yeah, Mel, thanks. Just tired." His eyes must've been red.

He hurried to the far side of the hospital, to the ICU wing. Andi and Grace were sitting in the relatives' waiting room. Grace's face was blotchy from crying. Ed sat down beside her. "What's going on?" he asked Andi, above Grace's head.

But Grace answered first, her voice flat. "She's dying." She started to cry, but when Andi reached over to her, she brushed her hand away. Andi's eyebrows lifted at Ed.

Ed opened his mouth, but Doc Keeley was coming into the waiting area.

"How is she, John?" Ed said.

He shrugged. "We're using ice to cool her down, and she's sedated. I called a geriatric medicine guy I know in Great Falls, and he's coming down tomorrow morning."

Grace was peering intently at him. "Can I be with her now?" Keeley shook his head. "Only for two minutes, just to say goodnight – but don't talk to her, say it in your mind. We want her to sleep."

Keeley escorted her into the cubicle, and Ed stood beside Andi, watching through the glass. The girl approached the bed, and stood there, arms wrapped around herself. She leaned toward the bed and seemed to be speaking, silently, to Ardyss's sleeping face. Then, fluidly, she leaned down and kissed the old lady's forehead. Ardyss's eyelids fluttered without opening, and it seemed to Ed her dry lips smiled faintly, but she remained asleep.

When she came back out, Grace announced that she would sleep in the waiting area tonight.

Ed's weariness fueled his annoyance. "Grace, damn it, you're going to Andi's. Now."

She whispered, almost violently, "Fuck you, Northrup."

Andi touched Ed's arm, and said, "Grace, Ed and I are going to have a cup of coffee. You can stay here till we're done, then we'll go home."

"Don't do me any favors."

Ed held his tongue.

*   *   *

They found a conference room and Andi closed the door. She looked into his eyes. "You're mad."

Outside the window, the snow was falling straighter now. The flakes were bigger, billowing in the light. He nodded. "She's pissing me off." Andi grunted.

He sighed. "Doesn't she annoy you?"

"Sure, but I was a fourteen-year-old girl once. She's in love with Ardyss, and we get in her way."

"I know all that." It came out sharper than he meant it.

Andi frowned. "Look, I'm not the enemy here. Let's be the adults and figure this out."

"Yeah, you're right." He felt stretched, over-tired. "Andi, I really appreciate your help with this."

She smiled. "Like I said, I was a fourteen-year-old bitch once. Least I can do for the universe."

Ed touched her arm. "Well, thanks anyway. What say I let her stay another couple of hours, then I'll drive her out to your place?"

"Sounds okay to me. But I'm out of here. I've got that training at seven and then I have to get her bedroom ready."

They went back to the waiting room. Grace was sullen. Ed said, "We've got an idea, Grace."

"Fuck you guys," she answered.

"Andi's going home to get your room ready, and I'll stay here with you until..." He glanced at the clock on the wall. "Until ten. That's three hours. Then I'll drive you out to Andi's."

Grace said nothing, then walked over to the window and stared into Ardyss's room. Andi rolled her eyes faintly, touched Ed's arm, and left.

Three hours later, Ed handed Grace her back pack. "Time to go. I'll drive you home."

Grace said nothing. She followed him silently to his pickup; the snow was already seven inches deep. *What'll set off the explosion?* he wondered.

In the pickup, Grace scrunched angrily against her door. After a moment, he said, "What's going on, Grace?"

"You won't let me stay with Ardy."

"To make sure Child Protection doesn't take you away."

"Fuck them."

He put his hands on the wheel and looked out into the night. The snow was already drifting across the highway. "Grace, I'm really tired, so it's possible I'll get irritated about stuff I usually can ignore, but give me a break, would you? 'Fuck them' doesn't really help. What else is bothering you?" Silence.

Ed cranked up the heat; no use sitting in the cold. He waited.

"You're, like, taking me to that sheriff's house. You don't care how I feel." *She wants me to get angry, to hurt her, push her away.* He relaxed.

"Actually, I do care how you feel, and you'd feel a lot worse if you got taken up to Helena."

She shrunk further into herself, arms folded. "Bullshit."

"Come on, kid. Give us a break."

"Don't call me 'kid.' Who's giving *me* a break?"

He glanced over; her eyes were full. "I'm sorry, Grace. This all must be pretty hard on you."

She glared at him. "No *therapy*, Northrup. Don't try your 'oh, tell me more' crap."

"I'm not doing therapy, and I don't want to make you unhappy. I'd like to figure out how to fix that."

"I don't need fixing."

"Did I say that?" He was getting mad; the idea of the Children's Home was taking on a new allure.

Grace said nothing for a moment. Finally, she shook her head. "No *therapy*."

"No therapy, it's our deal. What can I do to make this easier?"

"Northrup!" she shouted. "That's *therapy!*"

"*No it is not!*" he shouted back, his restraint weakening. His hands banged the steering wheel. "It's me asking you how I can help. It's one fucking friend wanting to figure out how to be a better fucking friend!"

She looked shocked for a second, then tittered. "Northrup, your language!"

He caught his breath. "Well, I'm mad."

Grace cocked one eyebrow up. "Yeah, you are." She sniffed. "I guess you, like, scare me or whatever. My mom always forgets me. She's never home and if I call her cell phone, she gets all pissed, like I'm spoiling her fun. I'm scared you'll forget me too, like this morning. I'm nobody to you, but you – and Ardy – are all I've got out here. And to Ardy, I matter."

Ed waited quietly. He should have pointed out that Andi was being very generous in allowing her to stay there. Andi's story of the little girl in the roadside ditch came to mind. He said, "I'm sorry."

It must have caught her off guard. Her arms unfolded. "No you're not." She sat still, staring out the window at the darkness. Finally, she said, "Well? Aren't you going to give me the lecture? About how I don't understand adults and how hard their lives are?"

He shook his head, weary of the argument. "No."

She looked surprised. "Why not?"

"Because you're right."

She looked surprised. "I'm right?"

"Yeah. This is a lot harder for you than it is for me."

She looked away. "Sorry is easy, but it doesn't change anything. If you're really sorry, you'd let me stay with Ardy."

He started to answer, but Grace pulled farther into the corner. "Fuck you, Northrup. Fuck all of you."

*   *   *

Grace didn't relent on the drive to Andi's. When they'd stopped at Ardyss's, she had stormed in angrily to get her clothes and toiletries. When they got to Andi's, Andi had made up the bed in her guest room. She showed Grace around – the bathroom, the refrigerator – but Grace was sullen. After staying in the bathroom for a long time, she went into her room and slammed the door. She'd hardly said three words, none of which remotely related to "thanks."

"She'll get over it," Andi whispered. "A glass of wine?" She was already pouring two glasses. Ed thought about it. He wanted to think about his tears at Jim's, but maybe getting to know Andi a little more would be nice. "Sure, wine would be good."

This was Ed's first visit to her house. She'd been in the valley nine months or so, and she'd made the place comfortable and warm, with soft chairs and a plump couch facing a fireplace: cozier than he'd expected from a cop. He wondered when the last time his cabin had been so clean.

"Do you use the fireplace?" he asked.

"It works, I'm told, but I haven't figured out the flue."

"Do you have wood?" Ed asked, as he reached up inside the firebox, found the gritty handle, and pulled the damper cable. A little shower of ash fell onto the fireplace apron. "It's open," he said, standing up and brushing his hands on his jeans. "Can I use this paper to start it?" He gestured toward the newspaper on the couch.

"Sure," she said, and went out the front door. Snow billowed in before she closed it. The storm was heavier.

Ed crumpled the newspaper and put it in the hearth, then looked in the old woodbox beside the fireplace for kindling. When Andi brought in an armload of wood, he said, "Any kindling out there? Or a hand ax?"

The wood, dropping into the box, clattered loudly, and Grace called from the guest room, "Can you two shut up, *please*."

Andi lifted her eyebrows and whispered, "the princess and the pea." He chuckled and went out to the woodpile, where he found a pile of kindling at the end. He shook the snow off and brought it in and laid the sticks atop the crumbled paper. Andi struck a match and lit it. Cold as the kindling was, it took two or three minutes to catch fire, but it caught and Ed laid on a few split logs.

Andi handed him a wineglass and sank onto the couch; Ed started toward a chair, but Andi said, "The couch is more comfortable." He sank down beside her.

"Yep. Comfy," he murmured. They put their glasses on the table and talked about Ardyss's condition. After a time, he added another log to the fire. When he sat down, the couch bumped the wall, and Grace yelled again: "Be *quiet!*" He started to tell Andi about the girl's fear of being forgotten.

He hadn't gotten far into the story when Grace's bedroom door opened and she came out.

Seeing them sitting together, Grace stopped, made a little gasping sound, then turned and slammed her door.

Andi frowned. "What was that all about?"

He shrugged. "As you're fond of saying, being fourteen, I'd guess."

Andi yawned and looked at her clock, and Ed stood up, yawning too. "Whew. Midnight. I have to get home."

She touched his arm and pointed through the window. Heavy snow blew almost horizontally, swirling in billows. "Drive safe." The wind rattled a window.

"Damn," he said, going to the window and looking out. "There's a good eight or nine inches already." He turned back toward Andi. "Welcome to Montana."

"Just be careful," she said, yawning again.

*   *   *

Despite his fatigue, Ed drove alertly, cautious in the blowing snow, worrying how the Grace problem would end. As he was passing the Jefferson House Motel, his cell phone buzzed.

"It's me," Andi said. "Grace just ran off! I was in the bathroom when the front door slammed. She left a note. It said, *Fuck you guys. I'm going to see Ardy. She cares about me.*"

"Christ!" Ed slowed and turned the truck around. "I'll be back in ten minutes."

Andi said, "No, don't come all the way back. I'm going after her now. I've got snowshoes. You come slow and watch for her along the road. I'll track her if she leaves the road. I don't want to wait till you get here."

"Uh-uh. Don't go out in this alone. Wait for me."

"Don't argue. We're wasting time. Besides, I'm ten years younger than you and I'm not carrying an extra fifty pounds."

"Thirty," he muttered. "Okay, but use your phone and stay in touch. Storms here aren't like Chicago."

"Let's go. She's out there."

NINETEEN

Tuesday, February 7

S NOW SWIRLED IN the headlights.

The dashboard clock read 12:28 a.m. He drove slowly, flashers on, hoping that Grace had stayed on the road. On the chance she was in a ditch, he pulled out his big flashlight and carefully swung it back and forth, lighting the right, then the left side. Unlikely she could have come this far yet, but he searched diligently anyway. Spotting a shadow on the west side, he pulled over and waded through the drifts. A road-kill doe, already partly crow-eaten.

*　　*　　*

Andi prayed the black pockets in the deep snow were Grace's tracks. They led down the drive and along the road for a hundred yards, then veered off into the field where the fence was broken down. Andi followed, her hat pulled down against the wind-whipped snow stinging her eyes. They had to be Grace's tracks – there were no other similar pockets, and they followed one another in a line, if a crooked one.

Despite the powerful flashlight, thickly blowing snow blinded her. When engulfed in a swirl, she had to wait for the gust to die. The dark footprints, sunk deep in the snow and already filling in, trailed across the field ahead of her. *Grace's been out here fifteen minutes*, she thought. *Shit.* Andi found the going barely passable, even with snowshoes. The snow was deepening, the wind buffeting her. She kept her fear in check. If this was hard with snowshoes and a flashlight, how could Grace make it? Andi forced her pace. At least the footprints were still there, black-shadowed in the light.

*   *   *

Back in his truck, Ed inched along the shoulder of the highway. Nothing. She couldn't have gotten this far in the time they'd been searching. His cell phone buzzed.

"Anything?" Andi said, huffing.

"Nothing. Where are you?" he asked.

"No damned idea." She peered into the blowing snow. "The field south of my place. Maybe a half-mile from home. Hold on." There was a long silence, then she said, "I'm maybe five hundred yards east of the highway, maybe a mile or so from the edge of town."

"How do you figure that?"

"GPS on my phone. Police issue. Surprised it works in this blizzard. Keep searching the ditches. I'll stay on her tracks. If they're hers."

"Jesus." If they weren't Grace's... Ed shook his head to clear it. "Andi, are you all right?"

"Better than Grace is. Look, I'm going to move along. I'll call if I need help."

"No! Call every few minutes. Stay in touch."

He spotted another hump in the ditch – no, a shadow cast by an oddly shaped pile of snow. Ed jerked the truck into park, and jumped out. *Damn!* How long can a person survive half-buried in snow?

He ran around the side of the truck, but couldn't find the hump or the shadow. Everything looked different out in the storm. He swept the light back and forth, moving along the highway. After a hundred yards, he turned and retraced his steps, even more slowly, light-headed with fear. *Slow down! Breathe.*

Still no hump. Picturing Grace under the drift, dying, he got back in the truck and very slowly backed along the highway, scanning the ditch in the light of his headlights. There, the shadow! Halfway down toward the fenceline, ten feet ahead of his truck. He parked where the headlights still cast the shadow, jumped out, and couldn't see the shadow! On the ground, his sightline was much lower than up in the cab. He climbed back inside. There it was! He fixed the shadow in his mind, jumped down, and plowed through drifts to the pile. He dug into it with his hands. Another deer, frozen solid. *Shit!* He climbed up to the truck.

*   *   *

Not good, Andi thought. Even with the snowshoes, she struggled, felt herself tiring. Grace couldn't have made it through here, could she? Had she missed the girl somewhere back? The tracks were still visible, and she'd followed them carefully all the way, so she dismissed the thought. *Trust your method,* she reminded herself. Still, her fear was draining her; the cold and wind were taking their toll. She checked her phone's GPS screen: Drifting east, away from the highway. Away from Ed. If these footprints were Grace's, the girl was disoriented. Andi called Ed.

*   *   *

"Find her?" he answered sharply.

"I'm worried. The tracks are going *away* from the highway. Can you tell where you are?"

Ed pulled his cell phone out of his jacket and hit the GPS app, praying there'd be signal. "Give me a minute," he said, waiting for his location to come up. It felt forever. When they lit up, he gave her his coordinates.

From her own screen, Andi read him her own. "Get as close to these as you can and wait for me. She isn't along the highway."

"How do we know that?"

Andi waited before she answered. "We don't. But you haven't found tracks, right?"

"I didn't see any, no."

"So we go with the evidence we've got. We've got to hope she's ahead of me."

"It's a risky bet," he said.

"It's the only one we've got, Ed." After a silent moment, she added, "I'll call again."

He made a last search along the highway, peering now for footprints or tracks close to the road. When he reached the broken fence line, he saw two sets of tracks. So Grace was in the field. Andi was right. He turned around and found the rendezvous point and waited. It wasn't just Grace alone in the snow – he set aside his anger with her – it was Andi too.

Powerless, he slammed both hands against the steering wheel. His phone buzzed.

*   *   *

"I found her... alive." Andi was breathing almost too heavily to speak.

"Where are you? I'll come."

"No," Andi said. "We'd likely... miss each other... I know where you are." Her transmission stopped. Ed almost panicked. He heard static, then: "I'm bringing her in. Keep your cab warm."

As he started to object, she hung up.

Ed checked his GPS again: He was exactly where Andi expected him to be.

*   *   *

The wind and being on snowshoes made lifting Grace into the fireman's carry awkward. When she got the girl up, Andi took a step and swore softly, lowering her gently onto the snow. Her left snowshoe had worked loose. She shone the light on it and saw – *Thank God* – it was only the strap coming unclipped. She tightened it, then stooped to pick up Grace again.

"Let me sleep," the girl murmured.

She weighed that. Sleep meant hypothermia, but a struggling burden would be harder to manage than dead weight. She said to Grace, "Go to sleep, Grace. Just sleep." After a moment, she gasped as she lifted the unconscious girl onto her shoulder.

Staggering, she checked her GPS, turned herself around, and started plodding. After twenty steps, she rechecked the GPS and felt a surge of relief. She was heading true.

Snow boiled and the wind gusts staggered her – once hard, then again, then again. Andi nearly fell. She lowered the girl to the ground. After catching her breath, she half-lifted Grace, but the wind knocked them both down again. She was too tired, and Grace, now half awake, was struggling. Andi let her rest in the snow.

*   *   *

Ed's phone buzzed. "I'm here," he answered.

"I can't make it."

"Where are you?"

"I think I'm about two-hundred yards east-south-by-southeast of your position." She read off her GPS coordinates. "I can maybe carry her a little further, but can you come part way?"

"I'm on the way. I'll find you, Andi." Fear, mingled with relief, swamped him.

He checked the gas gauge. *Plenty of fuel.* He left the truck idling at the side of the highway so it would be warm when they returned. If they returned. *Think!* He grabbed his phone and studied the GPS. On the note pad from the console, he scribbled a note directing anyone who checked the cab toward Andi's coordinates. He rummaged behind the seat and pulled on boots he found there – though his socks were already soaked from his first two forays into the snow in the ditches – then grabbed blankets, and set out, climbing over the highway fence and heading into the darkness.

Each step sank two feet into the snow, and his boots filled with snow. A wind gust knocked him down. As he worked across the field, he checked his GPS every few paces and repeatedly corrected his direction. After five minutes, he was cursing his weight. He fell again when his foot plunged deep into a drift. The falling snow was so thick he couldn't see five feet, even with the light. He called Andi.

"Where are you?" she answered.

He read off his position.

Her silence frightened him. "Andi? Andi! Talk to me!"

"I'm thinking. We're maybe – how far's a geographic second?" She was quiet again. "We're between thirty and fifty yards apart. Stay where you are. I'll come to you."

Ed said, "No. You're carrying Grace. Tell me how to get to you."

Andi directed him and in four minutes, he found them. Twenty-five minutes later, they were driving fast up to the hospital emergency door. Grace was admitted for hypothermia and put in a warming bed. Andi was examined and released.

"I have to call Ben," she said. "Any hospital visit by a deputy, Ben gets called."

"And if Grace is involved, Rosemary Rasmussen gets called."

How close the girl had come to dying hit him just then, and Ed sank into a chair. Andi looked at him sympathetically. Ed murmured, "I was terrified I'd lose you out there."

"Me?" She looked surprised.

Ed felt his blush. "Freudian slip. I meant you *both*."

Andi sat down beside him. "I got pretty scared a couple of times myself. But I figured we'd get her."

Ed said, "We're a good team." As he said it, he realized he meant it. And that he *had* been terrified that he'd lose Grace, irritating as the little shit could be.

TWENTY

Wednesday, February 8

ANOTHER DAMN NIGHT in a hospital chair. His cell phone was buzzing in his pocket. He answered.

"You sound half asleep," Andi said.

"What time is it?" He thought back to the night. "Did last night really happen?"

"Seven in the morning, and yeah, it happened. We're lucky."

"Where are you?" he asked, still disoriented. When he'd fallen asleep in the waiting room, she'd been beside him.

"At work. I took your truck to get my uniform and my vehicle. Had to leave your pickup at home, but I can swing by the hospital and we can get it. Twenty minutes?"

"I'll meet you at the front door." He looked at his watch.

While waiting, he checked on Grace. She was sleeping, although the nurse said she looked stable. He also looked in on Ardyss, who also slept.

A few minutes later, Andi pulled into the hospital lot and Ed climbed in the sheriff's SUV. She smiled at him. "How's Grace? Should I go in and see her?"

He shook his head. "She's sleeping. The nurse says she's doing all right, considering. They don't see any signs of frostbite or serious hypothermia. You saved her life, Andi."

She didn't reply.

Ed looked at the newly plowed mountains of snow around the parking lot. "Is it a mistake? My trying so hard to keep her here? Maybe I should let Rosemary take her to Helena."

Andi shrugged. "Well, it sure complicates our life."

"*Our* life? Oh, yeah, her staying with you."

"No, I meant, neither of us was planning on a midnight hike in the snow."

He chuckled. "I wonder why she did it. Do you think it was her being so pissed at me?"

"Look, Ed, I'm sure you're a good psychologist, but don't blame yourself for her insecurities. Whoever fucked her up did it before you came along."

Ed nodded. "You're right. I guess it's just that I'm feeling responsible for her." He paused. "Whatever, let's go get my truck."

She pulled the vehicle around in a U-turn, but before she could exit the lot, Ben Stewart pulled in front of them. The radio crackled. Ben's voice barked, "Back in the hospital. Rosie Rasmussen's on her way, and she's pissed. Get inside. Over."

Andi looked at Ed and said, "Guess your truck just got postponed."

*   *   *

Rosemary came into the waiting area. Despite the early hour, she fairly radiated energy and color. A spring-green shawl draped over her azure tunic, accented by a turban the color of sunshine on hillsides. Contrary to her colorful clothes, her scowl was fiery. "I think our little plan has just come to an end," she announced.

Andi said, "Ben, I'm on patrol this morning, so I'll catch you guys later."

Ben said, "Go."

She stepped around Rosemary, looked back at Ed, and mouthed *Call me*. Ben pointed at the conference room and said, "Let's take 'er in there."

In the conference room, Ed told Rosemary what had happened.

Rosemary's Waterford pen paused, poised above her notepad. "You were at Deputy Pelton's home until *what* hour in the morning?"

Outside her line of vision, Ben shook his head and rolled his eyes. Ed read, *Bad move.*

Feeling defensive, he said, "I drove Grace out there after we left the hospital, Rosemary. We had to stop to pick up her things at Ardyss's apartment. Andi and I had a glass or two of wine, and talked. Apparently Grace ran off about ten minutes after I left. Andi was in the bathroom."

Rosemary interrupted him. "Obviously, this child's a runaway risk. You're not adequately safeguarding her. Drinking wine while you should be protecting her hardly seems sufficient to me."

Ed bristled, and despite Ben's vigorous head-shake, he snapped, "Give it a rest, Rosemary! My personal life isn't the issue here. This is an unhappy kid and I'm doing the best I can in a lousy situation. My having a glass of wine with Deputy Pelton is none of the state's damn business. How about a little support here?"

She looked startled, but recovered quickly. "The girl's welfare *is* the state's business, Ed." She looked down at her notepad, then back at him. "You're right, perhaps I'm a little upset. She's ultimately my responsibility, you'll remember. If something worse had happened..." A tear gathered in her eye. She dabbed it away quickly.

Ed, surprised at the tear, softened his tone. "Yeah, me too." He reached and touched her arm. "Shall we start over?" Rosemary nodded.

"Here's how I see this. Real parents of fourteen-year-old girls can't predict their moods and behavior. I've known Grace for, what, not even two weeks. Obviously, she's got rotten judgment and she's impulsive, but I still think we're better for her than the Children's Home."

Rosemary frowned. "If what happened last night displays *that*, it's hard for me to agree."

Ben interrupted. "Rosie, tell me somethin'. If the girl ran away into a blizzard up in Helena, what would the Children's Home do?"

Rosemary looked at him, then gave a wry smile. "Point well taken. They might not even notice she was gone till breakfast, if she was smart about it." She jotted a note, then looked up at Ben. "And my name is

Rosemary, Benjamin."

"Mine's Ben, Rosemary."

She grunted. "So what can we do to ensure this doesn't happen again?"

Ed started to answer, but Ben interrupted. "I think Ed here oughta sleep on Deputy Pelton's couch till we find the mama." His grin widened. "And move the damn couch against the front door."

Ed started to protest. Rosemary said, "Perhaps. I'll admit I'm skeptical. But let's give it a try. Do you think Deputy Pelton will mind Ed sleeping there?"

Ben shook his head. "Naw. I'll make it an order."

*   *   *

Ed left the conference room to see how Grace was; Doc Keeley met him outside her door.

"She's going to be fine," he said. "Kids recover fast. She's complaining about the breakfast." He chuckled.

Ed smiled. "She lets you know what's on her mind, doesn't she?"

"Hypothermia is tricky, though. Let me keep her here till dinner time, just to be on the safe side."

Ed started to open Grace's door, then paused. "Ardyss?"

Keeley shrugged. "About the same. The geriatric guy's coming down as we speak. Maybe he'll know what's going on."

When he came into her room, Grace's eyelids flickered. *Pretending sleep.* Ed noticed something different about her. He leaned closer: Her studs were gone. None of the metal she'd been wearing yesterday was visible. Ed stepped out and called Andi, hoping she hadn't left on patrol.

"Rosemary agreed I should stay at your place," he said, "so two adults are monitoring Grace."

Andi was quiet for a moment. "We make a good search-and-rescue team, Ed," she said. "But moving in? Not such a good idea."

"It won't be for long."

"I don't know. It's one thing taking Grace in."

"But?"

"But I haven't had a man living with me since..." She didn't finish.

"Look, I won't be living with you. Don't make this harder than it has to be." He stopped himself. Andi was being very generous here. "I'm sorry. I shouldn't have agreed with Ben without checking with you."

"This is *Ben's* idea?" she snapped.

"Yeah."

"God, he'll do anything to get us together. That sneak!"

Ed sighed. "I know. But look, for Grace?"

She was quiet for a moment, then said, "For Grace. Okay. But let's meet and lay out the ground rules."

"I need my truck, too. What ground rules?"

"We're not dating, Ed."

"It never occurred to me that we were."

Her silence surprised him. Not as much, though, as her reply. "Well, that's a little disappointing to hear."

He was grinning as he stepped back into Grace's room.

*   *   *

He made some noise as he settled in the chair – which was more comfortable than the waiting room chair he'd slept in. After Grace finally stirred, acting surprised that he was in her room, attempts at small talk sputtered out. She was hostile and close-mouthed. *Defensive*, he figured. Finally, he said, "Are you angry about something?"

She glared at the wall. "Fuck you."

Ed clenched his jaw. This wasn't any longer a troubled kid he could feel detached about. She'd turned into his problem, and she was pissing him off. He briefly wondered what was going on with Mara – had she been found yet? If Grace continued to be so hard to get along with, Mara could have her.

"Why'd you run away last night?" he demanded. She looked startled at his tone.

"What syllable of *fuck you* did you, like, miss?" She swung around angrily toward him. "And I didn't *run away*. I decided to go see Ardy." Another moment passed, and then she exploded. "I saw you guys on that couch last night! Even after I asked you to be quiet, you're out there talking and making noise. Probably making out. You forgot what *I* wanted, even after I *told* you I'm scared you'll forget me, which thank you very fucking much means shit to you."

Ed kept his calm. "You ran out into that storm because you thought we forgot you? We were talking *about* you, if you want to know. And Deputy Pelton and I aren't dating. We don't make out."

Grace scooted away a few inches farther across the bed, away from him.

He pushed it. "What about trusting me instead of almost killing yourself?"

"I didn't almost kill myself."

It was so absurd, he laughed out loud.

She glared at the wall, folding her arms tightly against her chest.

The same vertigo and trembling fear he'd felt above the Coliseum drenched him, only this time for Grace. He intuited the terror she must have felt in the storm. This wasn't about him. He took a long breath. "Grace, if Andi hadn't used all her police training and her GPS to search for you, you'd be dead now and she'd probably be dead too." His voice cracked at the end.

Grace went still. He could see she was barely breathing. "Why should I care?"

But her words were just sounds filling space. Her eyes were watering up, and he saw she was straining not to cry. He said, "This morning, the state wanted to take you to Helena, to the Children's Home. I argued that I wanted to take care of you."

"Ardy can take care of me. Thanks, but no thanks." But her voice quivered, fear sounding brave.

The old resentment, his *black dog,* brushed against him, but he pushed it aside. Somehow this kid had started to matter to him. Perhaps the search in the blizzard, or his terror that they'd lose her, had switched on some odd affection. Who knows? Whatever, she'd gotten inside him.

"Grace, any more shit like last night, and I won't be able to keep you. In the Children's Home, you'll be surrounded by drug addicts and dealers, girls who cut and burn themselves and boys who rape their sisters – and anybody else they get their hands on." She flinched. "You'll eat crap every day and go to a lousy school inside the walls and you'll be allowed outside an hour a day, and you'll never see Ardy or any of us again." He paused. "Not, I guess, that you care about that." She said nothing, but the wall of anger in her eyes was collapsing.

He went on. "And when your mom finally comes back, they might not even let you go with her, because she abandoned you."

After a long pause, she muttered, "Why should you, like, give a shit?" He thought about that. Finally, he said, "I have no damn idea." She looked stonily at the blank TV screen.

He said, "But I do."

She looked away from him, but her shoulders slumped. Her voice came quiet, tentative, as if only now she'd learned the words. "I know."

*　　*　　*

Same day, ten a.m.

When Vic felt out of his league, he played offense. His daddy'd always said, "Show the assholes who's boss." He banged open the door to the sheriff's department and barged across to Callie's counter, leaving Maggie to fend with the heavy door herself. Callie frowned.

Without waiting for Maggie to catch up, he said, "I'm here to see Sheriff Stewart."

Callie slowly raised her eyes to his. "Got an appointment?"

It threw him off. "Uh, Callie, Ben told me to come at ten."

Callie peered through her reading glasses at the computer screen, tapping a few keys. "No appointment here, Mr. Sobstak." She knew Vic perfectly well, and she also knew how to slow down pushy civilians.

Maggie came around behind him. "Callie, nice to see you. Ain't it been an age? Could you kindly check and see if Sheriff Stewart's got a minute for us?"

Callie smiled. "Mornin', Maggie. You been keepin' well?" She knew exactly how Maggie'd been keeping, and Maggie knew she knew.

Maggie blushed. "Up 'n down. Found out I got me an allergy to Jim

Beam."

"Well, that club's got a lot of members, love." Callie tapped a few keys. "You folks just go on back. Last door on the left."

After they had settled nervously in the sheriff's office, Vic tried taking the offensive again. "Sheriff, I'm here under protest. Ed Northrup talked me into this, and I want it on the record I can goddamn well handle this problem myself." Maggie looked sharply at him.

Ben waved him quiet. "Look, Victor, from where I sit, it looks like I'm pretty much your best friend at the moment. What say we dispense with the bullshit and talk business? That work for you?"

Vic deflated fast; he nodded, then tried sweet talk. "Reverend Crane says the county sheriff's the only legitimate political power."

Ben leaned back in his chair and steepled his fingers. "You know, I'd be flattered, but frankly, this guy Crane's flyers have pissed me off enough that I don't give a good godd – " He looked at Maggie. " – a fig about his political philosophy. Besides, he's wrong as a Republican in a union hall. We got us a Constitution that lays it all out nice and clear."

Chastened, Vic nodded. "Got it, Sheriff. So what do you want me to do?"

"For starters, call me Ben."

"All due respect, Sheriff, my daddy taught me to – "

" – and all due respect to your daddy, Vic, he's been dead a long time and you and me got us a serious problem, and I don't need a partner who's more worried about whether my ass is properly kissed than about whether our plan has a Chinaman's chance of working."

Vic was silent. Maggie raised her hand.

Ben looked at her. "Yes, Miz Sobstak? You got an edgewise word?"

Maggie nodded. "I reckon I got a few."

"Say 'em."

"Well, one, 'Chinaman's chance' is sorta racist, so maybe you oughta try 'a slim chance' or somethin' along that line."

Vic groaned, "Jesus, Maggie," but Ben said, "Noted."

"And, Ben, you're right we're in this together. Me and Vic, we had the same talk the other mornin'."

Ben smiled. "Thank you, ma'am."

"And third, I ain't jus' Vic's wife, I'm his partner, so stop talkin' between yourselves as though I ain't here."

Ben smiled and gave Maggie a small salute. "Yes, ma'am. Got 'er loud and clear."

Maggie saluted back. "And Ben," she said, "If your name's Ben, my name ain't 'ma'am.'"

Ben guffawed. When he caught his breath, he said to Vic, "Well, buddy, all we gotta do about this Crane fellow is send your, ah, partner here after him!" After they finished laughing, Ben outlined his plan.

Vic was to stay engaged with Reverend Crane, apologize for his lack of faith, and recommit to the full package. Flyers and all. Then, Ben proposed, "Once you're back in, we'll send you into one of their meetings wearin' a wire."

Maggie interrupted. "What's a wire?"

"A hidden microphone. I want Crane to incriminate himself about this tax refusal bullsh – business."

Vic felt jittery. The plan sounded risky. He ventured, "The other thing I'm supposed to do is tell them who here in the valley supports that guy Burke."

"Why?"

"Don't know. I'm guessin' they want to scare 'em off. I figure Reverend Crane ain't no Democrat."

Ben thought about it for a few moments. Maggie interrupted his thoughts. "I'm still worryin' about this hidden microphone plan. Ain't that dangerous?"

Ben nodded. "It could be, but we'll do it right, so they won't know. And my deputies and I will be right next door."

Vic was secretly relieved Maggie had raised the danger question. Putting a bold face on it, he said to her, "Ben's givin' me a chance to help, darlin', not just snitch. That's real important for me, Maggie." What surprised him was, he actually meant it.

They went back and forth about it, and Ben watched. Finally, Maggie gestured defeat. "You'll keep him safe?" she demanded of Ben.

Ben nodded. "You bet, Maggie. We know about Crane, but he don't know about us. He'll figure killing the cows scared Vic back in line."

Vic's own doubts were fading, and having something active to do to stop the nightmare pleased him. Goddamn, he wasn't a man to sit back.

So they had a plan. The next meeting with the Reverence Crane was Friday night, Vic said. "Do I wear the wire then?"

"No, we wait on that till Crane and this Stetson guy really believe you're back in. Then you wear it."

*　　*　　*

Ed, coming to the department during a break to check on the search for Mara, met Vic and Maggie as they came out the door.

"How'd it go?" he asked Vic.

"It went," Vic said. Maggie said, "We got us a plan."

"Good to hear. And the meeting with Leese?"

"Went good too. Got us a plan there."

From his office, Ben's voice boomed. "Ed! A minute of your time back here!"

Vic said, "Obliged," and stuck out his hand. They shook and Ed went inside.

In his office, Ben said, "Me and the Sobstaks got a plan. I'll spell out the details on the corner tonight." Ben shuffled some papers until he found one and lifted it up. "Your little girl's runaway mother checked into some flea-bag motel in Vegas. Wait." He peered at the paper in his hand. "In Henderson. But it appears she moved on before the sheriff's department could catch up with her."

"Flea-bag? That's not like Mara. No more information than that?"

'Nope. Now you see her, now you don't."

"What do you think she's up to?"

Ben shrugged. "Who knows? From the motel and her behavior, I'd think drugs or maybe gambling. Was she a user?"

Ed shook his head. "Not when I knew her. But she looked haggard when she was here."

"Well, could be drugs, then. Or could be she stiffed a loan shark. We'll find out soon enough."

*   *   *

Ed walked the corridor to Andi's cubicle, and found her in.

He started to fill her in about the Sobstaks.

"Ben told me. Why didn't you call me with your hypothetical last night? It's my case." She sounded irritated.

It hadn't occurred to him. "I'm sorry, Andi. I thought you guys – "

"Us *guys* take our job seriously – when I'm working a case, it's mine, not Ben's."

"I didn't realize – "

"Uh-huh. So future reference? Call me on my cases." Then she softened. "How's Grace?"

He thought about their conversation in the hospital. He shrugged. "She blames us for her running away last night. Says she thought we forgot about her when we made noise."

Andi snorted. "I was fourteen, but that sounds more like five." She sighed. "Well, I guess I'm involved now. I want ground rules."

"What do you have in mind?"

"Like I said, I'm not real keen on you moving in – even for a while. I want ground rules."

"Absolutely. How about meeting for lunch to set them up? Afterward, we can get my truck."

"How long's Grace staying in the hospital?"

"She's getting discharged before dinner, so we're all staying at your place tonight."

Andi hesitated. "Makes me uncomfortable, Ed. I won't lie to you."

*   *   *

Maggie watched Vic pacing in his study, holding his broken hand upright.

"What if the Reverend don't buy it?"

Maggie waited him out. He didn't need an answer; it was just his nerves settling themselves.

He stopped and grunted. "You dial," he said. "I'm goddamn one-handed." It wasn't true – he'd been able to use the hand for little things for a couple of days. She smiled to herself as she tapped the number into the touchpad and handed him the phone. He tilted his head to the left, toward the phone.

"Reverend Crane, please." He paused. "Victor Sobstak, from Monastery Valley." He paused again. "Montana."

He whispered to her, "He's comin'." In a moment, he said, "Reverend Crane? It's Victor. Victor Sobstak. How are you, sir?" He spoke loudly.

Maggie put her finger to her lips, warning him to soften his tone. He nodded. In a quieter voice, he said, "Well, sir, I guess I owe you an apology." Listened. "Yes, sir. I know we need to stay strong... in the faith, yes sir." The top of Vic's ears turned red, the first sign he was getting angry. She shook her head sharply, mouthing the words, *Stay calm*. He nodded as if to say, *yeah, yeah*. "Yes, sir, I was way off base doubtin' you, I got that now. I guess I got some sense knocked into me." He rolled his eyes at her as he listened. "Yes, sir? That's passed now, sir, I reckon." His entire right ear, the one she could see, reddened now. "Yes, sir, I know you don't care what I reckon." He held the phone away from his ear a moment, but Maggie shook her head sternly, mouthing *follow the plan!* The ear flamed red. "Yes, sir, sure as hell, sorry, I'm back in line now. I just had to sort myself out some. But I'm in line now, all the way."

He sat back against the desk, his eyes flaming. Maggie put her hand on his shoulder and smiled softly. Reverend Crane was going on at some length. Vic groveled. "Yes, sir, I know you can't. I won't give you no concern about my, uh, my loyalty. Not no more, sir. You can count on me." Another pause. "That too, sir. I'll report to Michael like you want. But I wanted to apologize directly to you." He stood upright again, his forehead now going beet red. "I said I will, and I will. Soon as I find out if anybody's supporting Burke, I will." A moment. "The nigger, yessir." He inhaled a long breath; Maggie, though puzzled and a little shocked at the word, encouraged him with her eyes. "No, sir. I'm in line now. You can trust me."

He nodded back at Maggie and gave a dark smile. "Friday? Yes, sir. I'll be there."

He slammed the phone in its cradle and sat back against his desk, breathing heavily. "Damned if I can stomach that man any more." He rubbed his face roughly, then smiled. "But I did it, didn't I?"

Maggie said, "You did it. You sounded like a whupped dog."

"Felt like one. I hope the sheriff's plan works. Eatin' crow's goddamn hard on a man."

*   *   *

Before retrieving his truck, Ed and Andi ordered lunch at the Village Inn.

When the waitress left, Ed said, "Okay, then. Ground rules."

"First rule, you stay on the couch. Period."

When his eyes widened, she added, "As in, not in my bed."

That told him something, although he wasn't entirely clear what. He said, "I think of you as a friend, Andi. Let's keep it there. What are the other rules?"

She shrugged. "I guess that's the big one."

Ed nodded. "I share food costs and I pay for everything Grace needs." A moment later, he added another. "I drive her to school every morning."

She nodded. "I can bring her home after work, though."

"How about we decide who drives home day by day? I generally work later than you do, and Grace'll want to stay at the hospital. No reason for you to stay in town when you're done."

"Sounds like a plan."

"I've got another ground rule: if we eat at your place, I'll cook."

Andi smiled. "Good, I hate to cook. I have one more."

"Shoot."

"We put a bell on the front door."

*   *   *

When their food came, Andi asked, "What brought you to the valley?" Just a friendly, let's-get-acquainted question, but it aroused his old anxiety. The *Black dog* growled.

At first, his mind scrambled to change the subject. But after a moment, he gave it up. *I can't hide from this forever.* He put down his fork and rubbed his fingers through his hair. "Well, it's a tough story."

*   *   *

Elizabeth Murphy had been fourteen years old when she'd first stepped into his Minneapolis office. She'd been skinny and scruffy, her wrists scarred, her face splotched with acne. Thick black mascara outlined her eyes; her hair hung in dirty brown strings. A bandage had wrapped her left wrist, and she wore thumb rings. Black fingernails. She'd torn her jeans in back to reveal skin just below her underwear, and wore a wrinkled Grateful Dead T-shirt. To his "You like the Dead?" gambit she'd turned her head silently and stared out the window.

She wanted to be called Elizabeth. She wanted not to talk. Her mother had barked, "Liz, you *will* talk to Dr. Northrup. I insist." So Elizabeth had given one-word answers, daring Ed to frame questions that forced a sentence out of her. It became their game, and Elizabeth was good at it. When he'd occasionally asked something that trapped her into speech, she would smile crookedly at him. Once she said, "Good one."

That game faded, of course, and after a few weeks they settled into real work. She was depressed, yes, but underneath her surly resistance, she delighted him. His "good one" questions elicited reflective answers, answers a fifteen year old should not be able to frame so maturely. He'd asked her, "Why do you think your mom wants rid of you?"

"She's lonely. My dad works all the time, and she waits for him to come home. I watch. When he comes in, she smiles and gives him a drink, but he won't talk to her. She blames me. One time, she yelled at me, 'Since you came, he's been gone to me!' Last summer, I saw her kissing our neighbor, and she knows I did. She wants me out of the way."

She'd brought him dark death-drenched poems: Their words were steel, but their lines wove together like lace. When Ed had praised them, she looked away. When she turned back, he saw a tear at the corner of her eye. "Mother says they're bizarre."

One day, he asked about the wrist.

"I cut it."

He asked her if she wanted to talk about why.

"Why would I *want* to?"

He shrugged and waited. She knew her own answer, and he knew she would talk when she decided to.

Finally, "I did it for her."

"Your mother?"

A nod. Ed waited again.

"She wanted rid of me. Wants rid of me."

He spoke before he'd censored himself. "I don't want rid of you, Elizabeth."

Elizabeth had simply stared at him for a long moment, then looked out the window in her usual way. They hadn't said another word that day. Elizabeth appeared for her next session dressed as closely to normal as she ever got.

That was the turning point. A few sessions later, he'd asked point-blank that Elizabeth agree not to kill herself. She'd thought long before nodding her head.

"You agree?" he'd asked.

"If I do, *quid pro quo?*"

What a bright kid. "Yes. Quid pro quo."

Again a long silence, then finally, "My mother doesn't hear anything I say?"

"That's been our deal."

"And one other thing. I want to pay you. I don't want her paying you any more."

"I'm expensive, Elizabeth."

"How much?"

"Seventy-five dollars a time."

She was silent. "I can pay ten dollars a time. And when we're done, I'll keep paying until it's done." She handed him a gold coin. "I got a bunch of these from my grandpa when he died. They're ten dollar coins." Ed had been touched. He fondled the coin a moment, then put it in his pocket. He had always kept it there, protecting him, perhaps. Or reminding him of his guilt. Until that December Sunday on the Coliseum when he threw it away.

*   *   *

He stopped. Andi said, "She reminds me a little of Grace."

He nodded. "This next part gets harder. It was May 12, 1984."

"You remember the date?"

"I doubt I'll ever forget it. Elizabeth's mother called, very pissed. 'She's done it again! She says she'll keep doing it until she gives me what I want. What in god's name does she mean by that?' I asked what she'd done. 'Cut her goddamn wrist again. Why? Tell me why.'" He grimaced. "I trusted Elizabeth's agreement not to kill herself, so I decided this was a cry for help. I asked Mrs. Murphy if I could talk to Elizabeth."

"What did she say?"

"She said no. She told me to explain why Elizabeth did, these are her words, 'such hateful things.' She said Elizabeth was locked in her room, being disciplined for cutting herself. Her next words chilled me. She said, 'She will call you when I release her.'"

"Child abuse?"

He shrugged. "Maybe. Elizabeth never mentioned any actual physical harm. Anyway, the mother demanded that I tell her what Elizabeth talked about. I reminded her that we'd all agreed I wouldn't do that. She blew up. Said she didn't give a good goddamn what the agreement had been, and that unless I told her why Elizabeth did such horrid things, she was terminating the therapy."

Ed's voice caught. He took a drink of water. Andi looked concerned. "Your eyes are teary. What happened?"

"Elizabeth never called. That night, when Mrs. Murphy unlocked the bedroom door, she found her hanging from the ceiling fan. It hadn't pulled down. She only weighed ninety-seven pounds." His eyes spilled over.

Andi's eyes reflected his sorrow. "Ed, I'm so sorry."

He dabbed his eyes, caught his breath. "That was the start. The Murphys sued me for malpractice. Elizabeth's mother lied on the witness stand about our phone conversation, claiming she *begged* me to come to the house but that I refused."

"What did you say?"

He looked down, finding it hard to continue. "I told the truth, but the jury didn't buy it." He took another sip of water.

Andi said, "So you lost?"

He wrestled with his answer. "The lawsuit, yeah, and my license – the Murphys filed a complaint with the psychology Board, who suspended me for two years." He paused, unsure how to go on. *Might as well get it out.* "I felt huge guilt about Elizabeth. If I'd insisted on talking with her, maybe gone over there..." His voice faltered and his eyes filled again. "Sorry."

Andi simply touched his hand across the table. He took a ragged breath.

"Mara served divorce papers one year to the day after Elizabeth died."

"The bitch! She dumped you after all you'd gone through?"

"I thought so at the time. Turns out she was having an affair with somebody."

"Who?"

Ed picked up a French fry and studied it for a moment before putting it in his mouth. After chewing a moment, he said, "So that's why I came to the valley. Twenty-seven years ago." He swallowed the potato. "How about you? What brings you out here?"

"Come on: Who?"

He grimaced. *What the hell.* "Boy, you're pushy. It was my business partner, Paul Carlen, my best friend from grad school. Or so I thought."

"That sucks."

He put up his hand. "That's enough, I don't want to talk about it."

"It's, what, twenty-plus years, isn't it? You can't *still* be that upset about it."

For a moment he was surprised, then annoyed. "That wasn't called for."

Andi shrugged. "Maybe not. But we're going to have to trust each other when we talk about Grace, and if we're going to be friends beyond that, I don't want to fight your ex-wife's ghost every step."

"Huh," he grunted. "You're right, but the news about Paul isn't twenty-some years old. It's only a few days. Mara spilled these particular beans when she dropped Grace into my lap."

"Oh, damn. I'm sorry for my remark."

"That's okay, so, yeah, I'm still angry." Suddenly he resolved to finish it all.

"There's something else."

Her look spoke of readiness to hear it all.

"Thursday, when I talked with Mara, I was terrible to her. I rubbed her nose in every sordid affair she'd had, or at least in the ones she'd admit to. It was cruel, totally unnecessary."

"She had it coming. Look what she was planning to do to you."

He cleared his throat. "That's the problem: I'm not sure she was planning to leave Grace. I think she left Grace because I treated her so roughly."

Andi shook her head gently. "You catch guilt like most people catch cold, Ed."

You think? Ed suddenly wanted to confess about climbing the Coliseum in December. That went too far, though. He could talk about it with Jim. Maybe. They were long friends. When he picked up his coffee cup, his hand shook slightly, so he held it with both hands. "Okay, let's rummage around in *your* closet."

She squinted at him and started to shake her head, then stopped herself. "Why not?" She told him about her divorce.

"You caught him screwing somebody else a *month* after you got married? What a jerk."

"Who, him or me?"

"Why would I mean *you?*"

She wrinkled her nose as if detecting an odor. "Because I *was* one. I don't think I loved Andy – that was his name too, Andy. Our friends thought that was cute. *The two Andies.* I was forty-four and thinking it was getting late, although I was happy enough being single." She grimaced. "Well, sort of happy. Anyway, Andy pushed and pushed to get married, but he needed somebody who *really* wanted him, and I didn't, not enough. The truth is, when I caught them doing the nasty, I was relieved, like it was my ticket out. Out of the marriage, out of Chicago, out of getting shot at by assholes."

"You prefer being single?"

She looked at him strangely. "Did I say that?"

He shook his head. "No, but you said you were relieved."

She waited a moment, then said, "I guess I wanted to be with somebody, but at the same time, it was too weird. I'd been single since mom died when I was sixteen."

After they talked a little about her mom's death, Ed abruptly said, "Tell me about getting shot."

"Nope, that's not something I talk about."

"Hey! You forced me to talk about Paul."

"Forced?"

Ed smiled. "Touché. So you left Chicago to get away from getting shot and from the jerk who forced you to get married."

"Hey! Nobody *forced* me. And it wasn't *shot*. Shot *at*. Big difference."

"*Talked* you into getting married. Like you talked me into talking about Paul."

She looked thoughtful. "You're right. Sorry. But I don't talk about getting shot at."

Ed thought about that. "You defend what you want and don't want better than I do."

She laughed softly. "After I caught Andy and his slut in my bed, I vowed nobody's talking me into something I really don't want – or out of what I do want." She hesitated, absently touching her notched earlobe. "That sound too hard-ass?"

He'd bit into a French fry, so he shook his head, chewed quickly, and sipped some water before answering. "No, I need more of what you've got. I've spent too many years pretending I don't have wants, while telling my patients to say what they want."

"Well, you oughta get over that."

He smiled. "All right, let me start with this: I want to know what *really* happened to your ear."

Her hand went again to her earlobe. At first she looked like she wouldn't say, then she grinned. "I told you already. An old boyfriend bit too hard."

*　　*　　*

After lunch, when Ed turned into the corridor leading to Grace's room, she was running toward him, arms up, waving. "She's better! She's better!" She launched herself into his arms, giddy, sobbing through the words. "They said... her fever... broke... during the night." Her small body was heaving with emotion. "She's not going to die, Northrup!" He held her close as she wept. She seemed to have decided to let him back in.

"Let's find out if they'll let us see her," he said. Grace broke from his embrace, dashing down the hallway like a colt. When Ed got to the ICU nurses' station, the nurse was saying ". . . very weak and still very sick. Letting her rest is the best idea right now."

Grace said, "She wants me near her. Can't I at least show her I'm here?"

The nurse looked at Ed. "It's true," he said. "Ardyss asked that Grace stay with her. Maybe two minutes? Just enough time to say hello?"

Grace started to protest, but Ed put his hand up. Grace clamped her mouth shut. Maybe her ordeal last night had earned him some capital. The nurse stood up. "Let me just take a quick look and see if she's up to it."

Ardyss was awake, lying on her back, eyes closed. Ed could not avoid thinking that her skull resembled a death-mask and hoped Grace didn't notice. Grace went directly to the bed and touched Ardyss's hand. "I'm here," she whispered.

Ardyss opened her eyes and turned her head toward the girl. She gave a thin smile. "Yes, child. You're here." The old lady lifted Grace's hand to her lips and kissed it, then sank back into the pillow. Her eyes closed.

Ardent, Grace said, "I'm staying with you, Ardy."

Ardyss, without opening her eyes, said, "Who's taking care of you?"

Grace looked startled. She glanced uncomfortably at Ed. Then she said, in a small voice he could barely hear, "Northrup is. And I guess the deputy, Andi."

Ardyss gathered her breath. "Go home with them now. That's where... I want you." The effort depleted her. "Come after school every day." She closed her eyes. "I'm getting better, child, but I want to sleep."

Ed touched Grace's shoulder, nodding toward the door when Grace looked back at him. *Time to go*, he mouthed. She frowned deeply, but left a kiss on Ardy's hand and followed him out.

Later that afternoon

Ben hadn't arrived when Ed came into the Angler to sit with him on the corner. Ted, who was leaning over his crossword puzzle on the bar, stood. "The usual, Edward?"

"No, pour me something new, Ted."

"What? A change? Are you ill?"

Ed smiled. "Nope. Pour me a different beer. An IPA."

Ted turned to his taps, looking back over his shoulder. "Turning over a new leaf?"

"No, just a new beer." But Ed smiled. His talk with Andi about ground rules had been more than interesting. Sobering. He felt relief – surprise! – about telling Elizabeth's story.

Ted coastered the beer in front of him. "Bitterroot Brewery's Single Hop IPA. They're over in Hamilton."

Ed sipped. "Tasty."

"Always good to make a change, Edward."

Just then, Ben barged into the bar, bellowing, "Ted! I need a beer more'n a priest needs a prayer book." He plunked himself on his corner stool.

"So tell me about your plan with Vic and Maggie," Ed said.

"Whew! Give me a minute! I just sat my ass down and already you're talkin' business."

"Take your time."

While he waited for his beer, Ben asked, "How's the girl?"

"She's doing all right; came home last night without a peep. She's made a new friend at school, a girl in her class named Jen something."

"You and her have your regular afternoon chitchat?"

Ed nodded. "Yep. She seems to have learned something since the runaway." He sipped the new beer. "Andi's a little annoyed with you."

Ben nodded. "Uh-huh. She thinks I overstepped by suggestin' you sleep with her."

Ed coughed up some ale. "Not 'sleep with her,' Ben! Geez. You suggested I sleep *on her couch*."

Ben sipped his beer. "Step 1, boy. Step 1."

"Jesus, you're devious."

"Name's Ben. Devious? Roger that." He took another sip. "So then, about Vic."

He told Ed about the plan. "Vic called this Reverend in Idaho and groveled, and the guy invited him to their meeting Friday night. That goes down all right, next time we'll send him in with a wire."

Ed said, "Is that safe?" He felt suddenly uneasy.

The sheriff grunted. "We're professionals, Ed. Don't worry your civilian head."

"Well, you know best."

Ben saluted. "I do. Look, conspiracy to evade taxes ain't no small crime. I want this asshole. And those flyers ain't givin' me tender feelings toward him."

"If these are the guys who killed Vic's cattle, what about their threatening him and Maggie?"

"We'll be right there."

"Who's *we*?"

"Me and my deputies." Ben turned and looked him in the eye. "So tell me. Why not take Andi out? She's a nice kid."

Ed laughed. "Andi's forty-six years old. We're friends, not kids. Don't be pushy."

"Am I being pushy, Ted?"

Ted, at the sink, looked over his shoulder. "What's the right answer, Benjamin?"

"Screw you, Ted."

"I'd love to, but my heart belongs to Lane."

Ben laughed.

Ed said, "Yes, you're being pushy. Tell me why you're so keen to get us together."

Ben sipped his beer and put it down slowly. "Ain't never had a female deputy before. She's tough – hell, her captain back in Chicago said he'd take her back in a heartbeat. But, you know..." He stopped, uncomfortably.

"If you didn't love Marlene so much, you'd go after Andi yourself."

Ben snorted. "Hell no, that ain't it."

Ed waited. If Ben wanted to talk, he would. If not, he was granite against wind.

After a few moments, Ben said, "Marlene and me couldn't have kids, you know. Your basic sperm insufficiency."

"I didn't know that."

"Yeah. I been past it a long time, but it's why Marlene ain't so much in love with me anymore."

"I never knew that. I'm sorry, Ben."

The sheriff drained his beer and held up the glass to get Ted's attention. "I'm over it." While Ted poured him a fresh pint, Ben continued, "But when I hired Andi, I had this feeling like, I don't know, like she's a daughter. That's crazy. My god, she shoots straighter than I can and beats me on every measure except shoulder strength. And I'm only eight years older than her." He paused as Ted coastered his pint.

Ed leaned his elbows on the bar. "I like her. She's smart, and she's good with Grace."

"Kind of like a wife, eh?" Ben grinned.

"Stop it." Ed frowned. "You're kidding, right?"

"I am the soul of wit, bucko. But listen, I don't think I *could* make a play for her, not really. That's what I mean she feels maybe like a daughter, one I couldn't have. I just want to keep her happy. It's selfish – if she's happy, she stays. If she's unhappy, maybe I lose a good deputy." Ben's voice caught at the end.

Ed waited.

"Anyway, if you and her were to cook something up, my money says she'll be happier than bein' alone." He looked hard at Ed. "And you would be too."

Ed shook his head. "She's not interested in a relationship." As he said it, though, he wondered if that were true.

Ben looked at him. "You're an expert on Andi Pelton even before your first night on her couch?"

"Well, from some things she's said," Ed said.

Ben snorted. "Seems to me you ain't exactly been droppin' your line in her water."

Annoyed now, Ed said, "Drop it, Ben. She and I just talked about this. We're starting a friend thing here, so we're not dating. Period."

Ben pushed his glass an inch away, stood up, and stretched. "Can't fault a man for tryin'." He picked up his glass and drained it. "Marlene and dinner await," he said, and pulled on his coat, looking out the window, where new snow was falling. "By the way, just so you know. Vic's supposed to tell this Reverend Crane about Burke supporters in the valley. I told him to deliver your name. Figured you wouldn't mind." Before Ed could protest, he pushed through the door and was gone into the snow.

TWENTY-ONE

Friday, February 10, evening

HEAVY WET SNOW splashed on his windshield as Ed drove to the hospital to pick up Grace from her evening visit with Ardyss. The wipers were swiping wet flakes flopping on the cold glass. As Grace climbed into the passenger seat, his cell phone buzzed. It was Ben Stewart.

"Got news about the little girl's relatives. Seems the mother's the only one left. The father and the mother had no sibs, far as we know, the grandparents are dead, except the one with Alzheimer's, and there's evidence the father died in South Carolina."

"Evidence?"

"A death certificate. Listed as no known address, so they ain't certain it was him, but the name, Lawrence Ellonson, and the birthday are right. The sheriff's office is checking the social to be sure."

"What did he die of?" Ed asked.

"Cocaine overdose."

Ed nodded. "Mara mentioned he had a drug habit."

"Well, I got me one more piece of news. As we speak, Victor's meetin' with the reverend. All goes well, next time we'll wire him up."

As Ed ended the call, Grace looked across at him. "You were talking about my mother."

He told her what they'd learned. Her eyes filled with tears, although she said nothing, staring through the windshield.

He started the truck. "Sad?"

She said nothing. He looked over at her. "I'm sorry about your father."

"Fuck it, Northrup. I didn't really know him."

The windshield wipers clicked, back and forth.

*   *   *

Parked in the shadows at the end of the Jefferson House lot, Vic Sobstak absently watched the windshield wipers losing ground against the accumulating snow. Seeing the Idaho plates on the big Caddie outside Number 18 had weakened his resolve. Crow was not his dish, and the sheriff's plan had him eating platefuls of it. Now that it was time, he had a hundred reasons to back out. He conjured an image of the dead heifers to buck himself up.

That woman knows me, goddamn it, he thought. When he'd left home, Maggie had squeezed his good hand. "If you get nervous, think what they did to those cows, Vic." Sitting in his truck, Vic appreciated her conviction, but goddamn, she wasn't the one facin' the music. He rehearsed his lines. *Go in, be sorry, kiss their goddamn asses. This ain't no time for bein' self-righteous.* He fortified himself with another thought about the cows, switched off the wipers and the truck, and stepped out into the storm. *Goddamn, this here's a hard plan.*

He knocked on the door and Stetson opened. "Found some balls, Roy Rogers?" he sneered.

Vic pretended a smile. "Somethin' along those lines," he said, and then, couldn't help himself. "If I find me another pair, I'll pass 'em along, Mike." Stetson glared at him, his lips a hard thin line.

The other men in the room looked confused by the exchange. Vic sat in his usual spot on the side of the bed opposite Stetson. When Reverend Crane looked hard at him, Vic could get no clue to the feelings in those cold blue eyes. "You're back in our little fold, then, Victor?" The Reverend's voice was very flat.

Vic met those eyes. "I am, Reverend. Got my questions answered, so I'm good."

Franky Concini, the logging foreman up on the Double-A, asked, "What questions, Vic?"

Reverend Crane answered. "Victor here needed some reassurance that our cause is just, didn't you, my friend?"

Vic felt venom in that voice, and not trusting his own, nodded.

Franky persisted. "Fill in the blanks for me, Reverend. What questions exactly? Vic's usually got a pretty good question or two, maybe we all need to hear the answers." He looked at Jackie Moen, squatted in his usual spot against the wall. Jackie's hat was pulled low over his face. It bobbed once.

Stetson straightened on his side of the bed and growled, "You pussies can shove your questions where it don't shine. Let's get to work."

Franky rubbed his stubbled chin and nodded once before slowly putting on his hat. "Let's not and say we did," he said, and stood out of his squat and started toward the door.

Vic snatched off his hat and waved Concini to a stop. "Whoa, there, Franky. It wasn't nothin' to be worried about. Just had some thinkin' to do about what's best for the CW – and I reckon what's best is workin' with the Reverend here."

Stetson looked angry, but Crane broke the tension with an arm around Concini's shoulder. "There's really nothing to be concerned about, Franky. You know Vic with all his questions." He laughed. Franky smiled weakly, but resumed his squat next to Jackie Moen, and Vic put his hat back on.

Thirty minutes or so later, as the others left, Vic hung back, and took off his hat again.

"Yeah?" Stetson said.

"I'm thinkin' I'll be gettin' some of that information you folks wanted."

"Information?"

"Burke supporters. I'm hearin' that Doctor Northrup is a supporter."

"Who's Doctor Northrup?"

"He's the psychologist in town, Ed Northrup. Everybody respects him."

"You fuck with us, we'll fuck with you," Stetson whispered. "And your wife."

Reverend Crane put a hand on Stetson's arm. "Michael, let it go. Victor's learned his lesson."

Vic nodded. "Got that right, Reverend." When he put on his hat again, his hand trembled; he brushed past Stetson into the wet snow.

* * *

Andi's vehicle was in the yard when they pulled in. Ed started to get out.

Grace didn't move.

"Coming in?" he asked.

She didn't answer for a moment. "What did my father die from?"

Ed considered what to say, decided on the truth. "Drug overdose. I guess he had a habit, from what your mom said."

"A mom who doesn't want me and a drug addict father." She sounded bitter.

I'd be bitter too, he thought.

Then she surprised him. "Northrup, can we go up that mountain again?"

"Sure. How about Sunday?"

TWENTY-TWO

Sunday, February 12, mid-day

ATOP THE COLISEUM, resting from their hike up the snowpacked trail, Grace sat on a drift beside Ed, gazing quietly out over the long valley. The long line of the highway cut north through snow-bleached fields glowing in the westering sun. Ed looked at the snow cornice, aware that something was changing in his life: He no longer felt anything like he had that day, and he didn't like the reminder. Shadows lengthened on the fields down in the valley, and the Monastery River in its westward arc across the valley reddened in the sun. Ed felt, more than heard, quiet sobs beside him.

He shifted closer, put an arm around her shoulder. The girl pulled away. "I'm fine," she muttered. "I just wish my mom could see how, like, beautiful this place is. Maybe she'll be back when we go down." She fell silent, wiping her eyes.

They gazed across the tree-carpeted mountains, up to the granitic peaks sharply edged against the cobalt sky. Grace shook her head and muttered, "She wouldn't care. She never liked this kind of beautiful stuff, only clothes and shoes and rich boyfriends."

After a moment, Grace's voice sounded very small, "Is she coming back?" She continued staring out into the immensity of the valley.

Ed put a hand on her shoulder and said, "We haven't found her yet, but we will."

Grace shook off the hand. "She won't come back, even if you find her."

They got up, Ed stiffly, Grace quickly, and stood a long moment, gazing out. Just as Ed was about to turn and lead them back down the trail, Grace said, "I wonder what it'd be like to just step off the edge?"

Next morning, Monday, February 13

Ed woke in a wash of grief. In his dream, Grace had leaped into the void, and he could not catch her. He lay awake for an hour, puzzling out why she'd said that about stepping off the edge. In her time in the valley, she'd showed no clinical signs of being suicidal, and she had seemed as cheerful as she ever was on the trek down. She only growled at him a couple of times. The dream's afterwash of grief told him something, but what? Was it about her? Or him?

After the sleepless hour, he left Andi's before dawn, moving quietly so as not to wake her or Grace. At his cabin, he changed into running clothes; the chill in the house told him the furnace had broken down again. When he checked, though, the pilot light glowed; he dialed up the thermostat.

The workout began, uncomfortable as usual, but he ran a half-mile beyond his usual turnaround at Milk Creek, enjoying the light powder drifting down and the quiet crunch underfoot. On the way back, he stopped on the bridge and listened. Something in the burbling of the creek reawoke his dream, and his chest tightened at the thought of Grace's falling from the Coliseum's rim. But when he resumed running, his mood rose as he ran past trees sugared with new snow. Dawn pinked the mountains. Even with the added mile, his last stretch was almost pleasant. He wondered what he weighed now.

*   *   *

At the office, Ed knocked on Leese MacArdell's office door. She was watering her plants.

"Howdy, stranger. What brings you to the outer reaches of our building?"

He laughed; his office door was twenty feet from hers. "I thought I'd follow up on Vic and Maggie Sobstak. They're – "

"Ed, you've been avoiding me."

Taken by surprise, he stammered, "No, I haven't."

"Baloney," she said. "Ever since I made a pass. If you're not interested, that's not a problem. What *is* a problem for me is you not talking to me."

He blushed. "Maybe I have been a little ambivalent." He paused. "Well, honestly, I'd intended to take you up on your offer."

Her eyebrows arched. "Really? What happened?"

"I stopped in to console Ardyss about Oliver, and one thing led to another and I got side-tracked."

"I'm flattered," she said, her face skeptical.

"Then Grace showed up and, well, with her here, it's not the time for an affair."

"Baloney. Everybody knows you're sleeping with the deputy, so don't hedge. I told you I wanted to stay friends, however it went, and I mean it."

"I'm not sleeping with her, Leese. We're not dating. Rosemary wanted me to stay at Andi's till we find the mother, to keep Grace safer. You heard about her episode during the storm?"

Leese nodded. "You're not even dating?"

"Uh-uh. So maybe when Grace leaves – " He stopped, feeling discomfort at the thought of Grace leaving. He shook that off. " – who knows. About you and me."

She shrugged. "Whatever, Ed. Look, I took my shot and if I missed, that's fine. It's not the first time. But don't treat me like the plague."

He was embarrassed and a bit surprised that his friendship mattered that much to her. He said, "I won't keep my distance."

She nodded. "Good. Now what about the Sobstaks?"

"They said you have a plan. You can help them?"

"No problem we can't solve. He owes a pile of tax, but Marty Bayley at the bank agreed to refinance the loans on the ranch. The interest they'll save will be enough each month to keep the IRS happy. We're meeting with them over in Missoula next week to work out the payment plan."

"Great, Leese. I knew you'd figure it out."

As he was leaving, Leese said, "Don't forget your tax numbers. Seventeen days."

"This weekend," he said. He wondered if he meant it.

*   *   *

After the day's last patient left, Ed walked to the hospital to look in on Ardyss. Grace was sitting in Ardy's room, doing homework. The old woman looked asleep.

He whispered hello, then told Grace that Andi was working the evening shift. "I'm eating with my friend Jim. You want to come?"

Grace shook her head. "I'll stay with Ardy and eat dinner here."

Ardyss was weak, but wearily and slowly, she was improving. At the sound of their voices, she opened her eyes. Ed asked how she was feeling, but she waved that question away. She said, "You're keeping company, I'm told."

Ed at first didn't catch her meaning. "Keeping company?"

The old lady smiled. "Now don't be shy. Your deputy friend. Grace here tells me you're staying at her place."

He mistook Ardyss's tone for disapproval. "Well, not really, Ardyss. In fact, we're just friends. I'm staying there on orders from Rosemary." Grace grunted.

Ardyss smiled. "Oh. Grace here made it sound a little more juicy. I kind of was enjoyin' the idea that maybe you and the deputy had a thing going." Her filmy old eyes misted more and she sighed. "Can't help thinking of my Price, more than fifty years we loved each other. There's nothing sweeter." For a long moment, she drifted away; then she roused herself. "Just don't you lose sight of this little girl, you hear?"

Grace looked up. "I'm no little girl, Ardy. I can, like, take care of myself. You just keep getting better so me and you can be together again."

But Ardyss, tired as she was, brushed a strand of grey hair away from her face and said, with a sternness that surprised Ed, "And young lady, you stop this nonsense, running around in snowstorms! The nurse told me what happened. It's a wonder you didn't catch your death of foolishness."

Grace looked stunned. Her arms folded across her chest in a gesture Ed was starting to recognize. He intervened. "It's fine, Ardy. Grace and I have it all worked out now. Won't happen again. Right, sweetheart?"

"My name's *Grace*," she snapped, but quickly added, "Not again."

* * *

Ed spent a couple of pleasant hours with Jim, who only brought up his depression once. Around eight, Ed picked Grace up and they drove out to Andi's.

"Look, I'm going back to my place for my running gear and some clean clothes. Are you all right being alone here for a half hour or so?"

Although her eyes widened quickly, she shook her head. "I'm not a wuss, Northrup."

* * *

As he came in the front door, the red eye of the message machine was blinking. He checked his watch, and half-decided to ignore it. He was drowsy after the wine with dinner at Jim's – and a pre-steak Scotch – and he wanted to get back and crash on Andi's couch.

He picked up the phone. Might be a patient. Or Grace.

One message. He sighed and punched the "Listen" button.

The voice snapped him awake. "You can stay alive and be happy in the valley, or you can support the nigger politician and be real sorry. Your choice. We're watching you." It was a gruff male voice, unrecognizable. The dead sound when the message ended chilled him, as if someone were still on the line, listening.

He went to fix the morning coffee, but his hand trembled and he spilled grounds on the counter. Then he remembered he wouldn't be here in the morning. He leaned against the counter a moment, calming down, then put away the coffee and dialed Andi.

When she came on the line, he told her about the phone message.

She was crisp. "What time was it left?"

"Well, before I came in." He checked the time stamp. "Seven forty-six. I came in about eight-thirty."

"It was a male, right?"

"Yeah."

"Who knows you're supporting Burke?" Full-dress cop mode.

"Rosemary. Leese MacArdell. Jim. Ardyss. A few others. And anybody they happened to tell. And remember, Ben told Vic Sobstak to name me as a contributor, part of his scheme to trap Crane."

"Right. I don't know Rosemary or Leese very well. Do you think either of them – ?"

"Hell, no. Neither one would ever do a thing like that. But if they told anybody, it could be all over the valley."

"So it could be anybody," she said. "But my money's on Crane." She was quiet a moment. "Has anybody been in your cabin?"

Ed stiffened. He hadn't checked. "Let me look around, hold on."

There was no one in the cabin, although the bedroom window was open an inch; did someone break in and then partially lower it on their way out? There was no damage to the sash. He swung around to look in the closet. No one.

Ah. He'd opened the window himself, to freshen the air. *Must've forgot to close it.* That's why the house was cold this morning.

When he came back on the line, Andi said, "He called when you could easily have been there. He might be interested in a confrontation." She paused. "What *are* you doing there? Shouldn't you be with Grace?"

"Yeah. I just stopped by to pick up my things for the morning."

"Got it. Well, I'll be home around eleven. We can talk about the threat then."

When they ended the call, Ed grimaced. He'd hoped to be sound asleep by eleven.

*   *   *

Tuesday, February 14

After running and then taking Grace to school, he slid into the two-top booth at the Valley Inn. Henny poured his coffee. He grumped, "What kinds of cereal do you have?" She listed them.

"I'm on a diet," he said, as if he were confiding a dire, perhaps fatal, diagnosis.

Henny's eyes flicked to his midriff, then snapped back to his face. "Good for you, Dr. Ed. Mind a suggestion?" She patted her ample hip. "I've got loads of diet experience."

He didn't want a suggestion, but said, "Go ahead."

"Don't make yourself miserable. Eat what you want, but eat less of it."

His mood lifted. "Good advice." He ordered a poached egg on toast and a single bacon slice. *She's got a good head on those shoulders,* he thought. *But a little too much weight on those hips.* His lack of charity chagrined him. *Listen to the fat man criticizing Henny's weight.*

Ben Stewart came in, and dropped onto the bench across from Ed. "A word?" He sat silently for a moment, glowering. "When exactly were you planning to fill me in on this threat?"

"I talked with Andi."

"Christ in a sidecar, Ed! Some asshole threatens your life and you don't call me?!"

"She was on duty, you weren't. I didn't want to disturb you."

"That ain't your decision." Ben's fingers were drumming on the table.

"Sure it is. Andi and I talked it over last night – "

"It ain't her decision either, damn it. Terroristic threats are crimes in this state and crimes are *my* decision. Your damn safety is *my* business."

"You're angry."

"Damn straight I'm angry."

"Come on, Ben, it was probably some drunk cowboy having his fun." It was as improbable as it sounded.

Ben scowled. "We got us tax conspiracy meetings at the Jeff House, racist hate flyers on our telephone poles, two cows with their throats slashed, I told Vic Sobstak to feed 'em your name, and now this. You tell me how that adds up to a drunk cowboy havin' fun."

"Well, when you put it like that." Ed nervously ran his fingers through his hair.

"That's exactly how we're puttin' it. So here's what's gonna happen. First, your answering machine tape is on my desk by noon today. Second, you've already been switched to the phone company's voice message system, so hustle your ass home and turn off your machine." He pulled a folder from his briefcase and handed it across to Ed. "Here's your instructions for setting up your voice mail account. Third – "

"Hold on, Ben! I didn't sign up for voice mail. My old machine is just fine."

"No, sir, *you* didn't sign up, I had Callie sign you up first thing after I saw Andi's report. When all this gets solved, if you want to go back to the last century, be my guest. But as long as we got phone threats goin' on, I need call-tracing capability, so you're on the system till I say so."

"Patients call me on that phone, Ben. I can't let – "

"You can and you will. We ain't violating nobody's privacy – unless it's your drunk cowboy." Ben nodded toward Ed's drumming fingers. "Now *you're* mad."

"I think we're overreacting here."

"You think *I'm* overreacting here."

"Right." He stopped drumming.

Ben sighed. He waved at Henny to bring him coffee. "I hope to the good God you're right. If anything happened to Andi's future boyfriend, I ain't sure I'd forgive myself."

"Hey! Andi and I are just friends, damn it. No boyfriend about it."

Ben snorted.

TWENTY-THREE

Wednesday, February 15

ED RAN ON the slushy shoulders of the highway. Overnight, the thermometer hadn't dropped past freezing for the first time all winter. Snow had started melting, little puddles and rivulets along the highway. As he ran, he thought about last evening. Andi, after her third shift in two days and with only six hours' sleep the night before, had suggested they eat at the Angler; Grace had surprised them with her pleasant conversation.

"Me and my girls did something awesome today."

"Whoa," Ed had said. "Who are your *girls?*"

She shrugged. "I got two new friends at school, Jen and Dana. I don't know their last names."

Andi said, "Good for you, Grace! Are they freshmen too?"

She looked at Andi as if she were asking a bee if it made honey. "Why would I even know somebody who's not a freshman?"

He laughed. "So what did you and your girls do that was awesome?"

The girl blushed. "We joined, like, Junior Search and Rescue. Did you know they take you on helicopter training if you earn enough training points? That's going to be so rad."

"Rad?"

"Northrup, you're so old."

Replaying the banter, Ed smiled as he ran through damp air, splashing in the puddles of snow melt along the side of the highway. Past the spot where he'd waited in his truck for Andi to find Grace, he ran on another half-mile before turning back. His muscles flowed more smoothly than they had in weeks. No, months. The sweat under his clothes was almost sensuous. Maybe Henny's diet advice was working. He laughed at himself. One day!

He picked up his pace. A little more sweat, a little more speed, a little less belly. He pushed hard the last half-mile to Andi's place, enjoying the burn in his thighs, then walked in circles around the yard a few times, panting, cooling down. On the porch steps, as his breathing slowed, he stood and looked at the late stars over the mountains, dim in the last dark.

Grace and Andi were eating breakfast when he finished his shower, and while he ate – cereal and a banana – they left for their days. Before he drove to town, he called his new voice mail system to see if patients had cancelled. There *was* a message. Palms moist – another threat? – he punched the number to retrieve it.

It was the voice of Jerry Francis, now, since Oliver's death, the only lawyer in Jefferson. "Ed, Jerry Francis here. I've had an urgent call from an attorney representing your ex-wife, Mara Ellonson Hertz. He wants me to convey a very important message from her. Can we meet this morning? Call me."

Mara's coming back. His bitterness surprised him. Wasn't Grace a trial? Sure, but...

As he punched in Jerry's number, he knew there was something else in his resentment. He cared what happened to Grace, and Mara wasn't good for the girl. The stove clock read seven-ten. *Good.* Jerry wouldn't be at work yet. He could just leave a message, and put off whatever was about to happen. *On second thought, I could just call later.* He was about to hang up when Jerry answered. "Francis here."

"You're working early," Ed said, wondering about his reaction. He understood it – Mara would bring no good to any of them.

"Yeah. This lawyer called me at nine o'clock last night – that's ten back in Minneapolis, if you can believe that. They must be real go-getters."

"Mara's back in Minneapolis?"

"No, but her lawyer is. Can you come over?"

"What's the message, Jerry?"

"Not on the phone. Believe me, you need to hear it in person. Can you come?"

"I'm booked till eleven this morning. How about eleven-fifteen?"

"Well, that'll have to do. I'm free all morning, so if you can shake loose sooner, come over."

"There's a rush?"

Francis hesitated before answering. "Oh yeah, a big rush."

*　　*　　*

Before his first patient arrived, Ed dropped into the sheriff's department. Ben and two deputies, Andi and Pete Peterson, leaned over Callie's shoulder, peering at her computer screen. Andi looked up and smiled, then turned back to the screen, the smile immediately gone. Ed waited, wondering about the urgency of Mara's message. The deputies were pitching their voices low, so he heard only occasional phrases from Ben.

". . . Number 17... next door... all feeds come here to you, Callie... Make a list – all the tech stuff, vests, the works... Peter here goes in first." Abruptly, Andi straightened and said, loud enough for Ed to hear, "Ben! I've got more experience with entries like this than the whole rest of the department. You –"

Ben shushed her. "Let's take that offline, Deputy."

Callie flickered an alarmed glance toward Ed, then rejoined the huddle.

Ben noticed Ed for the first time after he'd quieted Andi, and he straightened up and frowned. To the others, he said, "We'll re-convene in my office at – " He looked at his watch. "Nine sharp. Callie, get the IT guy here for the meeting, please."

Callie shook her head. "Me and Bill saw him and his girlfriend at the Dew Drop last night, tryin' to dance. Looked like exercise class at the stroke unit."

Ben frowned. "Meanin'?"

"Meanin', he was wasted, Sheriff. His poor girlfriend was proppin' him up. I doubt he's up and about enough to get in here by nine o'clock."

"Then I'd suggest you get on the horn and *get* him up and about, and if Pete's gotta pick him up with full siren and light bar, well, so be it."

Pete Peterson grinned. "My pleasure, Sheriff."

Ben grunted something, then waved Ed back. "Come with me, Ed. I got news."

*　　*　　*

In the office, Ed said, "My news'll trump yours."

Ben scowled. "Damn! *Another* threat?"

Ed shook his head. "No, not a threat. It's wilder, if you can believe it. Grace's mother's lawyer called Jerry Francis, and Jerry's got a message from her to me. I suspect she's coming back."

Ben poured two coffees. "Hell, that *is* news. What's the message?"

"Jerry wouldn't say over the phone. We're meeting later this morning."

"Hmmm." Ben steepled his fingers against his lips. Ed asked about his news.

"You remember that coke addict who died in South Carolina, Larry Ellonson? Turns out, he's Grace's daddy. His social matches the divorce decree. Looks pretty much like there ain't any living relatives left. You said the girl told you the mother's parents are deceased and there ain't no aunts or uncles on that side, right?"

"I don't think there are any on the father's side either."

"We thought so too, but Ellonson had two brothers. One died in Vietnam, and the other one is doin' life in Folsom prison in California."

"Wow. Murder?"

"Nope. Third-strike conviction for dealing heroin. Dumb shit. Should've moved to Oregon." Ben stuffed a couple of sheets of paper into a folder and looked up at Ed.

"So there's nobody but Mara."

"Seems to be," Ben said. "Another topic, on this threat you got. Dickie Flure signed me a court order allowing us to get your phone messages, and I got that underway now. But I got some other news."

Ed sighed. "Hit me."

"I'm cancelling our meeting on the corner tonight. The – "

Ed finished for him. "You gave Marlene a nice Valentine's Day present so she wants you home early?"

Ben went to the credenza and refilled his coffee cup. "And Mary Poppins gives good head. Hell, it ain't Marlene, though she did allow as the helicoptered roses was a nice touch."

"*Helicoptered* roses?"

Ben blushed, which Ed had never seen him do. Ever. "Had my buddy in Missoula fly his chopper over and drop five dozen red roses in the snow in our back yard just after I cooked her favorite dinner." He blushed again, then coughed and took on a business air. "Anyway, my news is this Reverend Crane bastard's comin' into town for another meeting Friday night. Vic's goin' in with a wire, so we'll record the meeting and hope to get some real evidence. That's what we were planning out there—" He gestured toward Reception, "—when you poked your nose in. Anyway, got too much to do to sit around Ted's bar tonight."

When Ed nodded, Ben grinned. "And you'll probably be entertainin' the little girl's mom tonight anyway."

In the office, after his nine o'clock patient was gone, Ed checked his voice mail, touched by another burst of anxiety when he heard the stutter tone. But it was Maggie Sobstak. He glanced at his clock: Vic and Maggie were scheduled right now, at ten. Trouble? He called her back.

"Ed, me and Vic, we can't come in this mornin'. We got another meetin' with the accountant – "

"Leese?"

"Yeah, she's real nice. Anyway, we gotta go see the IRS in Missoula next Monday. Ben wants us in town tomorrow and again Friday on that wire business, and I gotta come in later this afternoon to talk with Father

Jim about the organist job. We got chores that can't wait, so another trip into town just ain't gonna fit. No offense intended."

"None taken. Shall we keep the session for next Wednesday?"

"Sure. Maybe all this tax worry will be past and we can work on problem number 6."

"Number 6?" He remembered what number 6 was just as Maggie said, "You know."

They said goodbye. He was free to talk to Jerry.

As he was getting his coat on, Andi knocked. "Ben told me you got a message from Grace's mother. What does she want?" Her voice was neutral.

Ed wondered if she was angry. Did she consider Mara her case too?

"I have no clue what she wants. I'm on my way to find out. My guess is Mara's coming back." He looked at her. "Should I have told you instead of Ben?"

"No, that's okay; Ben's on this one too. Lawyering-up usually means something bad. She's setting you up for something."

He nodded. "Knowing Mara, I'm about to get fucked again."

Andi tilted her head. "Fucked in a bad way, you mean."

Odd thing to say, he thought. "Yeah."

She smiled. "Well, call me when you find out."

Ed nodded. "Will do." He finished putting on his coat, then stopped. "It's nice outside. It's supposed to snow, but if it stays like this, how about we all go out to my place for steaks tonight? Pretend it's spring."

She shook her head. "Can't. I caught a second shift today. We're getting ready for Vic's deal on Friday, so I'm going to be tied up the next couple of days. You'll have to cover Grace."

He nodded. "Sure, that'll work. What time will you be home?"

"Late. Oh, by the way, this morning, while you were running, Grace was talking on her phone."

"*Talking* on her phone? Not texting?"

"Yeah. I'm a little embarrassed to admit it, but I eavesdropped. I think it was a *boy*."

"Not Amanda?"

"Hard to say, but tell me what you think – I heard her say, *If I can shake free, how about we, like, hook up?"*

He winced. "*Hook up* is teen for having sex, isn't it?"

"It could mean just get together."

"Good."

"Or have sex together."

"Damn."

"Exactly."

*   *   *

Jerry Francis's law office might have passed for a ski resort. Darkened beams and river rock columns graced the entryway. Ed glanced up. The sky was clouding over from the west, gray with coming snow. *Forget spring grilling tonight,* Ed thought as he opened the massive oak door.

Jerry, chatting with his paralegal in the lobby, heard Ed come in and turned, extending his hand. "Thanks for coming over." He led Ed into his big office. One wall, behind the desk, was cherry-wood panels, stained dark, on which hung a gallery of photographs. Two walls were lined with law books, the bookcases of one surrounding a massive fireplace, in which a fire crackled. The fourth wall was floor-to-ceiling windows facing the Monastery Range. Jerry gestured toward two overstuffed leather chairs fronting the fire. Ed sank into one and said, "So you have a message?"

Jerry chuckled as he settled into the opposite chair. "Cut to the chase, shall we?"

"You said there was a rush."

"I did, yes." He looked apologetic. "I'm sorry. Can I offer you something? A Coke? Coffee? A drink?"

Ed shook his head. "No, thanks. The message?"

"Right, the message. I've been retained by an attorney in Minneapolis who represents your ex-wife. He has instructed me to convey to you some information and a proposal."

"You've been retained? So you work for Mara?"

"Indirectly. And only to convey the message. If you accept the proposal, I have been asked to represent you in the subsequent negotiations, at no expense to you."

"Negotiations?" Ed thought, *Shit, Andi's right: Something bad's coming.*

"I'll get there, Ed. With me so far?"

"There's a proposal involving me. If I accept the proposal, there will be negotiations. And you come with the package."

Jerry blushed. "I was unclear. I *could* represent you, or you can find someone else. In either case, all expenses would be paid."

"Paid by whom?"

"By your ex-wife."

"I don't get it. But maybe I could use a cup of coffee after all."

Jerry picked up his phone and asked the paralegal to bring in two cups of coffee.

"You'll understand in a moment," he said. He went to his desk and lifted a page of notes. "Let me review. I want to be an honest broker here," he murmured as he scanned the notes, reading as he slowly moved back and sat down. He dropped the notes on the coffee table. There came a discreet knock on the door. Ann, the paralegal, carried in a tray of coffee. She poured two cups, and set cream and sugar on the table beside the notes. Ed seethed with impatience.

Jerry thanked her and held out a cup to Ed. He took it, started to reach for cream, decided to take it black.

"Thank you, Ann," Jerry said. When she closed the door behind herself, he spoke in a level, neutral tone. "Grace Ellonson's mother Mara is dying in a hospital in the southwest. She is expected to live between two and ten days, although her physicians say that these are very gross estimates and could err either way. They insist that she will die soon."

Shocked, Ed recalled Mara's appearance when she'd come to his office – wasted, stiff, gray, her face gaunt. But dying? Had she been dying then? He felt something well up – anger? fear? He calmed his breathing. "What's she dying of, Jerry?"

The lawyer looked apologetic. "I'm not at liberty to say."

Ed nodded. How like Mara, to cling to control to the end. His dread increased: Mara's control usually spelled trouble for him.

"So what's the proposal?"

The attorney nodded. "Mrs. Hertz is willing to sign over to you parental rights to Grace Ellonson, on the condition that you agree to raise Grace to adulthood. If you agree, her will makes you her sole heir and beneficiary, with Grace secondary if something should happen to you during probate."

Ed sat stunned. Impossible. Utterly impossible. He jumped up from the soft chair, splashing coffee on the broad smooth expanse of coffee table. Momentarily distracted, he mumbled an apology.

"Ed, forget the coffee. This is huge. You've a right to be upset."

Ed strode to the glass wall and gazed out at the rugged mountains. Billows of blackening cloud prowled the sky over the Monasteries, and long fingers of gray smeared eastward, dimming what sun there was. He turned toward the lawyer. "Signing parental rights to me?! What the hell, Jerry? Did I ask for them? She wants *me* to raise Grace? Why?"

Jerry spread his hands, and said calmly, "I have no idea. My understanding from her attorney is that there is no living relative."

He ran his hand through his hair. "Yeah, I learned that this morning. But why *me*? She hated me." Ed tried to think, turning back to gaze out at the mountains.

Below the windows, the river flowed through town, clogged with broken ice floes.

"I suspect that her feelings about you are more complicated than that."

Ed sighed. "Which I should know, I suppose."

"None of us can be objective about our own, uh, situations."

"So, what do I do, Jerry? How can I decide this?"

"Talk to the people you trust. Let them help you."

Ed laughed darkly. "That's not something I'm very good at." He came back and sat down in the chair. He was trembling, as he had on the Coliseum after almost falling. How could he possibly make a decision like this? *Concentrate*! "So what are the next steps?"

Jerry said, "If you decide to accept the proposal – "

"If I decide to be Grace's step-father."

"Actually, legally speaking, you'd be her father. Adoptive."

"God." He looked again out at the mountains.

The attorney waited a moment, letting it sink in. "Anyway, if you accept, we meet to sign the adoption documents, and that's it. Mrs. Hertz has already signed a new will. Her lawyer has power of attorney to decide which will to use."

"Which will? What's that mean?"

"There are two wills, one if you say yes, one if you say no."

Ed thought that was odd. "And if I say no?"

"I'll relay your answer back to Minneapolis, but my understanding is there's no backup plan. If you say no, I call Rosemary Rasmussen and Montana takes charge of the child when the mother dies. Whoever she ends up with will be quite rich."

Ed grimaced, imagining how it would be to watch Grace be put in a car and driven away. "Nobody takes charge of Grace."

"Either Montana will or Minnesota will, and whichever does will try to find adoptive parents. But..."

"All right, I take your meaning." He looked again at the mountains. The snow clouds boiled closer. "Jerry, I need time."

The attorney's face clouded. "The paperwork is all ready to go, but filing and recording everything could take a couple days. Maybe longer. I need your decision tomorrow. Friday latest."

Ed closed his eyes and laid his head back against the soft leather. "Mara strikes again," he whispered.

"Pardon me?"

"Nothing," Ed said. He stood up and moved unseeing toward the beautiful pine door. "I'm sorry about the mess, Jerry," he said, gesturing at the spilled coffee on the table. "I'll decide."

*   *   *

Ed had never cancelled an afternoon of patients before, but he was too dazed to see anyone. He called people in a fog, making vague apologies. *This must be what it's like finding out you've got cancer.* Like the roiling sky, his mind was full of clouds. He felt numb as a slapped face.

"Talk to the people you trust," Jerry had said.

He called Jim, but got no answer. At the beep, he muttered a quick "call me" and hung up. Ben was in a meeting. Magnus Anderssen was up in Helena, conferring with legislators about something. Luisa said she'd have him call Ed when he returned. He started to dial Leese's number, instead called Andi's cell phone, and when it rolled to voice mail he simply asked her to call, unable to say more. Then he did something he had never done in Montana. He went home for a second run.

*   *   *

Mara's dying. He didn't feel sad, or glad. Puzzled, perhaps. Had she dropped Grace on him for the girl's sake, left her here where someone might love her – or, at least, take care of her? Selflessness wasn't like Mara. If care was being dished out, Mara would be the recipient. He pictured Grace standing atop the Coliseum, wishing her mother were with her to see the beauty of the valley. Teenage bravado aside, the girl loved her mother. But the mother was dying. Could the abandonment have been a twisted final act of generosity?

His footing in the melting snow was solid, and running in daylight, seeing the trees and mountains and fences, made things more interesting. None of this registered very deeply. He kept imagining Mara dying.

He stopped in the road, breathing hard. *Suppose she wasn't dying? Suppose this was her scheme to be rid of Grace?* He stood on the shoulder, suddenly enraged.

His fury goaded him to run. *Fuck her!* At one point, he screamed it aloud, and ran harder. How like Mara to fake her death so she could dump her 'something to do'! He had to talk with the doctors!

And then, a few moments later, he thought, *Suppose she's trying to dump the girl and I catch her out and refuse to take Grace. Would Mara let her go to the state? How's that better for Grace? Damn!* He pounded faster still, enraged at the inexorable choice, almost sprinting, until the extra poundage trumped his rage. He pulled up, breaths heaving beside the snowplow drifts, hands on knees, expecting to vomit. Didn't.

When he felt better, he walked. Hadn't Jerry said the other attorney had talked with the doctors? Would a lawyer go along with a scam? He resumed jogging, slowly now, thumping raggedly over the Milk Creek bridge, going farther along the road. As he ran, the last feeble sunlight went out. Glowering clouds towered over the valley. To the west, veils of steel-gray snow draped the mountainsides. Big storm coming.

He wondered what Ben would say.

Jim's advice would be, *Follow your heart*. Even running and short of breath, he laughed aloud. Since when had he ever followed his heart?

He turned back and jogged again, heading home.

The first wet sloppy snowflakes slapped his face as he approached Milk Creek again. He hadn't run so far in years, and he was tiring. He stopped on the bridge, as he always did, and listened to the water. He thought about Grace's contempt for him. No, not contempt. She was afraid of him, afraid of what was happening to her. She was a little girl abandoned in a strange world. Could he make her a home in it? Could she let him?

He'd seldom seen the creek at midday. It was beautiful. A momentary rift in the clouds allowed sunlight to burst through, illuminating cascades of falling snow and casting his shadow onto the ice and rolling water below. He studied the shape of his head, his shoulders. *What do I want?* Not a question he'd much considered. The sonorities of water under the bridge played their counterpoint to his breathing, the sounds blending, water and air. *Love whom you love.*

Behind him, an air horn blasted. Thundering toward the narrow bridge, the semi's driver warned him. He ran off the bridge onto the wider shoulder, waving as the trucker blasted by. *I want to love whom I love.* He resumed jogging, slower now. The snow fell, fat soft flakes that melted on his warm cheeks. What did he want? Whom did he love?

Walking the last curve up to his cabin on the ridge, he knew he wanted the impossible. That was why he'd trained himself not to ask what he wanted – it was always something beyond him.

But, he wanted Grace. He wanted to learn whether he could love her, and whether she could find a way to love him. *I'm crazy*, he thought as he walked on sore legs up the final yards. He couldn't say he'd begun to love the girl. *You can't just* decide *you're going to love someone someday*. On the cabin steps, he paused to look up at the sky, from which long sheets of snow hung down, gray with wet and cold, almost splashing around him.

Inside, he called Jim again. *I'm nuts. I want to be Grace's father,* he thought, listening to the ringtone.

"Father Jim. How can I help you?"

"No Scotch, no BS, just talk. Can I come by?"

"Ed?"

"Yeah. I'm going crazy. I need to talk."

"You've always been crazy, so you're waking up. Good sign. I have a meeting with Maggie Sobstak in the church in five minutes. Meet me there."

He dialed Andi's cell. It went to voice mail again, and he clenched his jaw. Where was she? He left her a second message, telling her to call. He left a different message for Grace – that she should skip their "visit" at his office and go directly to the hospital. He'd pick her up there. He chuckled. His own father had never been so directive. So bossy. It was always, *It's up to you, son,* which, as any child knows, means, *Don't bother me.*

*   *   *

When Ed yanked open the church door, Maggie Sobstak stumbled on the other side. Ed caught her arm. "Excuse me, Maggie," he said.

"Sorry, Ed. Startled me. I just met with Father Jim."

"Ah," he said.

"Can I ask a favor?"

He stifled a sigh. Taking on Maggie's problems was the last thing he wanted just now. But he said, "Sure," trying not to sound insincere.

"Vic's doing this wire thing on Friday. Could you be there? I'm nervous." As if she hadn't explained enough, she added, "I could use a friendly face who knows what's goin' on." She looked into his eyes, then above him, out into the sky and snow falling more heavily now.

Ed shivered; snow had fallen under his collar. "Of course," he said, pretending charity. *Pretend will have to do.* "What time?"

"Three, three-thirty I think."

"I'll be there. I'll double-check the time with Ben."

Maggie leaned over and kissed his cheek. "Thanks, Ed. You're a friend."

It took him aback. What a one-sided friendship it was – he couldn't tell her about the only thing he cared about right now.

Inside, Jim greeted him from near the altar. "She'll be playing the organ Sunday," he said. "I'm glad."

"You're sick of singing *a capella*?"

Jim chuckled. "No. I'm glad Maggie's over her rough patch."

Ed thought about Vic's meeting with Crane. "Let's hope so." He looked at his friend. "I need to talk, Jim."

Jim looked at him kindly and ushered him into the cloister walk between church and rectory. "So, you're crazy. That's no news. What's up?"

"You'll never guess." As they walked through the covered passageway, he described Mara's proposal.

"Wow," the priest said. "From dickhead to dadhood!"

"Clever," Ed muttered. "And totally insensitive."

They sat at the kitchen table with a cup of coffee, talking around what he really wanted to get to. *Say it*, he ordered himself. *Words!* Finally, he did. "I'm afraid I'll fuck the kid up. Do you think I should do this?"

Jim stood up and said, "Follow me." He led them to the bathroom whose toilet Ed had fixed.

"Flush it," he ordered.

Ed pushed the handle, annoyed at Jim's ignoring his question. The toilet flushed smoothly. "This tells me what?"

Jim looked exasperated. "Let's see." He held up fingers, counting off. "One. You can counsel difficult patients. Two. You're smart and compassionate, and three, almost everybody who knows you likes you, even if you don't notice it. And four, you can fix almost anything. You built your own house and you hunt your own meat. So pardon my French, pal, but I'll be damned if I can see how you think you can't do God's own job with Grace what's-her-name."

Ed shook his head. "Ellonson. But here's the selfish truth." He looked at his watch. "What time is it?"

The priest glanced at Ed's watch. "Being crazy keeps you from telling time?"

"Funny. It's two-thirty. Is it too early for a Scotch?"

"You said no Scotch and no BS."

"So I did. Let's amend it no BS. This requires serious thinking."

They went into the living room. "So, you were about to confess a selfish truth."

"Yes, I was. The selfish truth is I've been seriously depressed, and it's partly because I let a little girl die twenty five years ago. I don't want to hurt Grace."

"Of course you don't." The priest rubbed his chin. "You're correct. Such confessions require divine sustenance." He went to the liquor cabinet, poured, and handed a tumbler to Ed.

"So you don't want to hurt Grace, which is perfectly reasonable. But how *do* you feel toward her?"

The purl of the water in Milk Creek came to Ed's mind. *Love whom you love.* "I think I'm starting to care about her, as much as you can care about a bratty kid who belongs to someone else. And I'm afraid of her."

Expecting Jim to ask him why he was afraid of Grace, the next question surprised him. "And her feelings toward you?"

"Jesus! You name it. Hate, contempt, curiosity, fear, anger, tolerates me sometimes, wants my approval. Now and then she laughs at my jokes. She's afraid I'll abandon her."

"Sounds like a normal teenager and her father."

Ed shook his head. "Uh-uh. Normal teens love their fathers."

"And you're not her dad, so you're afraid she can't love you."

Ed started to object, but stopped. It was true. He nodded. "In principle, I know she can. Even hostages can fall in love with their kidnappers."

Jim nodded. "The Oslo Syndrome."

He shook his head. "Stockholm."

Jim rolled his eyes and sipped his Scotch. "But you want the real thing."

"Yeah, and there's another thing. I'm afraid she'll blame me for Mara abandoning her."

"And what else?"

Would adopting Grace atone for Elizabeth? A surge of feeling silenced him, afraid his voice would crack. When he was ready, he said, "That girl I let die? She was fourteen too. I'm afraid to take on that responsibility if I'm going to let her down."

Jim swirled his Scotch. "You know what, pal? I've known you twenty-seven, going on twenty-eight years. And you've never let me or anybody I know down. You won't let this girl down."

The two men sat companionably for a few moments. Finally, Ed sighed and asked, "What should I do?"

The priest chuckled. "I don't tell people what to do. I ask them what they *want* to do."

"Jerry said to talk to the people I trust. I trust you."

"Honored, genuinely; but tell me what you *want* to do.

"Do you think I should say yes?"

"You know me, Ed: I tell people to believe in themselves, and you came here, so that's what you must want to hear."

Ed nodded. "Probably right." He looked at his whiskey. "Follow my heart?" He snorted. "Jim, it's the biggest damn decision I've ever faced, I have to make it in a day, and I haven't followed my heart in fifty years."

Jim looked at him sympathetically. "Bullshit, pal. You just haven't admitted it to yourself."

The truth of it rocked him. Ed sat stock still. Jim was right. *I follow my heart well enough, but I tell myself it's for someone else.*

Finally, Jim said, "Let me ask you. How will you feel the morning after you say No?"

He knew exactly: Like he'd fallen off a cliff amid feathered veils of snow against black granite.

Jim turned to look directly at him. "Ed, I'll say one thing. Whatever you do, do it for love, not out of fear." He tipped up the last of his short drink. "Fear sets a hook. Love casts a net."

Ed swirled the remaining Scotch in his glass, then drained it, its fire warming his chest.

He put on his coat, then turned toward Jim. "You know, I have no idea what that means."

*   *   *

Despite leaving messages, Ed hadn't heard from Andi all day. Andi'd know what to think about this, but she wasn't returning his calls. Irritated, he went to the hospital to find Grace.

Who was unexpectedly happy. "Northrup! I passed the algebra test! I got a 93!"

The algebra test had worried her since the weekend; he'd forgotten. "Good for you," he said, distracted.

"I'm getting all A's so far, except algebra, so this will bring me up to a high B." She was delighted.

"That's great, Grace. Good work." He looked at his watch. Andi should've called by now. Her shift had ended a half-hour ago.

Grace looked puzzled, or perhaps a little hurt. He said, "I'm sorry, Grace. I've got a big problem I'm worrying about, so I guess I'm not very good company." She shrugged. "Whatever." *Great start on fatherhood.*

*   *   *

Andi hadn't joined them at the hospital for dinner. By the time she called, close to eight o'clock, he was very tense. "What happened? Are you all right?"

She apologized, her voice weary. "We caught a raft of problems getting ready for this operation on Friday."

His reply came out more harshly than he'd wanted. "We need to talk about something big." Although he had lowered his voice, Grace, doing her homework in a nearby chair in Ardyss's room, looked curiously at him. Ardyss slept.

"What's the matter?" Andi asked. "You sound mad."

Ed rubbed his eyes, suddenly feeling dramatic, not to mention selfish. They couldn't talk now anyway. He softened his tone. "I'm sorry. It can wait till you get home. What sort of problems did you have?"

She yawned before answering. "Nothing serious, all technical shit. Missing batteries, dead microphones, stuff like that. On top of that, there were two minor accidents, a DUI off the road, and an 11-80."

"What's that?"

"Sorry. Major accident, with injuries. And one of the guys went home with the flu, so we're all stretched. I probably won't get home till ten or ten-thirty. You'll cover Grace?"

Ed had stepped out into the hall to continue the call beyond Grace's hearing.

He lowered his voice again, and said, "Grace is who we need to talk about."

"It'll have to wait, Ed. I'm going to be bushed, and I'm on again at seven in the morning."

"It can't wait, Andi. We have to talk tonight."

She was quiet for a moment. "Is she in trouble?"

"No, not like that, but we still have to talk."

"It better be damn important." Her voice sounded irritated.

"You have no idea."

*   *   *

Riding out to Andi's, Grace talked in the afterglow of her algebra test. "Jen got the same grade as me, and Dana got a hundred. I've got smart friends, Northrup."

"You do," he said, forcing himself to pay attention. "And they have a smart friend too." Out of the corner of his eye, he caught her smile. And noticed that she still wore no studs. The sloppy snow that had started while he was running was heavy now. As soon as they pulled into Andi's yard, Grace jumped out of the truck and splashed through the snow to the door. When he came in, her door was closed. Behind it, he heard her talking happily. Probably on her cell phone. It was almost nine o'clock. He lit a fire and poured himself a glass of wine, and settled down to wait.

*   *   *

When Andi turned into the yard a little before eleven, the lights of her vehicle woke Ed. She came in the door, eyes drawn, shoulders slumped, and glanced toward her bedroom when she saw him waiting. She looked exhausted.

Ed groaned inwardly. Not the condition he needed her in.

She hung her coat and put her gear in the cupboard. "I'm dead, and I go back on duty in eight hours. You sure this can't wait?"

He shook his head. "I got the message from Mara."

She straightened. "Oh, damn, I forgot all about that. I'm sorry. What is it?"

He nodded, looking at Grace's door. "Let's have a glass of wine."

Andi poured herself a half-glass and joined him on the couch. "This going to be a long talk? Only half my brain's on duty."

After Ed told her about Mara's proposal, Andi slumped into the couch and fell silent for a long time. Finally, she said, "So. Suddenly, you've got a kid."

"If I say yes."

"You'll say yes."

The flames danced in the fireplace. Outside, wind buffeted the eaves. "You're right. I'm going to say yes."

She nodded and looked into the flames. "Are you sure Mara's really dying?"

"I wondered about that."

"And you decided it didn't matter."

He nodded. "Adults have failed Grace all her life. I want to stop that." He looked at Andi. "If she's pulling a scam, what good would it do Grace if I say no?"

Rembrandt could not have painted her face more neutral. "Or maybe you want to redeem yourself for, what was her name? Elizabeth?"

He caught his breath. "Thank you, Doctor." Despite his annoyance, he knew she was right. Partly right.

"Well?"

He shrugged. "Maybe. When I first met her, Grace reminded me of Elizabeth. Not so much anymore."

Andi looked at him for a long moment. "But you still want a chance to redeem yourself."

"Would that be so bad?"

Andi sighed and took a long sip of wine. "One of the last talks I had with my mother before she died, she told me I'd had a sister who died the year before I was born. She said something like, 'I loved you better because I blamed myself for her death.' It never left me." She looked at the fire, her eyes wet. "If you do this, Ed, don't tell Grace about Elizabeth. She's a smart kid. She'll wonder the rest of her life if you loved *her*. Even if you did. Don't use her."

"What? I've no intention of using her. What are you talking about?"

She turned and looked at him hard. "Redeem yourself with with your patients. The only relationship you should make with Grace is love her." She stood up. "Love *her*."

Ed wanted to talk more. "You're done?"

She picked up her glass and drained it, still standing. "Unless you have something else to say."

"Have you ever felt something for somebody you couldn't quite name, but it feels real? Something that might turn into love someday?"

She sat down. "Of course I have." She tilted her head as she looked at him. "Adopting her means your whole life changes. Permanently. High school drinking and drugs become your problem. Driving. Sex. College. You don't know with kids. You ready for that?"

He shrugged, athough her list sobered him. "Nobody's ready for all that."

A quiet laugh. "Good answer."

"Do you think I should do it?"

Now her laugh was louder. "I'm no shrink, Ed. I'm a cop. Just do what you think's right."

"And what's right?"

"What your heart tells you."

"Damn. That's what Jim said."

Andi smiled and then yawned. "Look, I have to get to bed."

Ed felt a rush of anxiety. He needed one more thing. "Another minute?"

She frowned, but said, "Okay. But short and sweet."

He thought through what he wanted to say. "Look. I've never had kids and I probably had the phoniest marriage in history. What I know about parenting comes from counseling failed parents or people who can't get over their failed parents. I'm going to need help."

Andi's eyes widened. "I know even less about this than you do."

"You were a fourteen-year-old girl."

She chuckled. "Got me there."

Ed said, "So, are you in?" Catching the sudden cloud in her eyes, he added, "As a friend?"

Andi yawned, then said, "I have to think, Ed. This is new to me. First you move in, now you want me to help raise a kid. I need time."

It was only fair. He'd had all day. "Yeah, I do too. I guess I'm going to do it, whether you're in or not, but please..." He felt the catch in his voice and waited.

When he could, he finished, "Please say you'll help."

When she just looked at him, he lightened it up. "It's only until she's off to college."

She yawned. Wind was pummeling the house and snow was burying the valley again in shrouds of white. Andi yawned again. "God, it's almost midnight."

TWENTY-FOUR

Thursday, February 16

IN THE MORNING, everyone was up at six. Andi yawned over her coffee. While Grace showered, Ed said, "I think we ought to talk to her now."

"What's this *we,* cowboy? I thought you wanted to know whether I'm in on this before you talk to her."

He poured himself a cup. "She has a right to know her mother's dying, at least. Whatever's going to happen after that can wait."

She nodded. "Yeah, you're right." She checked the clock. "After last night's overtime, I can go in late."

He put bread in the toaster and put butter and jam on the table. The smell of toast warmed the air. Grace appeared, wrapped in Andi's bathrobe, a towel around her wet hair, and poured herself a cup of coffee without a word. Then, hesitantly, "You guys were talking about me again last night. Are you getting rid of me?"

Ed shook his head. Andi slid in beside her on the breakfast nook bench; Grace scooted away from her a few inches, looking afraid of the answer. Andi said, "I'm thinking you got that wrong, kiddo."

Grace looked at Ed, who picked it up. "We were talking about taking care of you."

"Ardyss can take care of me. Until my mom comes back. Thanks, but no thanks." Here voice was firm, but her eyes looked anxious.

Andi said, "Grace, listen. We have some bad news and we all have to deal with it – "

The girl's eyes widened, darting wildly from Andi to Ed and back. "About my mother?"

They both nodded.

"Tell me!"

Ed explained Mara's condition. Suddenly, Grace crumbled and fell against Andi, who enfolded her. The two rocked slowly as she wept; her cries broke Ed's heart. After a few moments of rocking, Grace pulled away from Andi and wiped her eyes with the bath towel. Her jaw was set. "I want to see her before she dies. She's my mother." Hiccupped sobs slowed her words, but she continued, "I have a right."

Ed nodded. "You sure do. I'll call the lawyers to set it up."

Grace wiped her face again. "What lawyers?"

Andi stroked her arm and glanced at Ed, who said, "Your mom doesn't want us to find her. She used her lawyer to send me a plan to take care of you. I've got to get the lawyer to tell us where she is so you can see her before the end."

Grace made a bitter half-laugh. "If she's dying, call it dying. I'm not a little kid."

Ed went to the phone and left a message for Jerry Francis. After telling him to start the paperwork, hoping Jerry'd understand he meant the adoption, he relayed Grace's demand, then returned to the table. He hadn't even sat down when the phone rang. He answered, and nodded to Grace and Andi, mouthing *Attorney*. He listened a moment. Then, "No, Jerry, *make* it happen. Grace is her daughter." He listened another moment, then ended the call with "Let's just make it happen. Before it's too late." He hung up and said to the girl, "He's on it."

"Northrup?" Grace's voice pleaded. "Is she really dying?"

"That's what I was told." He watched her head drop, her face closing in, as if something too delicate were sealing over. He touched her shoulder – she did not flinch. "Grace?"

She looked up at him.

"Your mom made arrangements for you to be taken care of. We need to talk about that."

"Not now. After she's gone – " her voice caught and she roughly cleared her throat. "After she's *dead*. Not now."

He shook his head, torn. Compassion urged him to wait, but practicality won. "I'm sorry, but we have to talk now. I need to sign papers to make this thing happen, and you need to know. We can't wait."

She was stone. "I don't care. Sign your papers. Just let me see her."

Andi said, "You didn't ask for any of this, and I'm pissed at your mom for doing this to you, but what we feel about it doesn't matter. You and Ed have a huge decision to make and you have to make it *before* she dies."

Grace turned away. "You two aren't part of this. It's my life and my mother. You're just here for a while. Leave me alone." She looked trapped in the nook, with Andi sitting between her and freedom. She started to push against Andi.

Ed reached across the table and took her hands in his. She tried pulling them away, but he held tight. "Damn it, Grace, shut up for once!" He kept his voice even and warm, but he could see the shock in her eyes. "You're so wrong you might as well be on Mars. Andi and I – " he glanced at Andi, " – or at least I am in this with you, just as far and as deep as you are and we need to talk. Now. So act like the grownup you claim you are."

Grace, looking shocked, waited a long moment, looking at each of them, then saved a little face by saying it to Andi instead of him, but she said it, and they all relaxed. "Another big-girl panties moment?" Andi nodded.

"Okay," Grace said, pulling the towel from around her head and shaking loose her damp hair. "But not now. I need to get dressed and eat before school." She pushed Andi out of the bench and got up and started toward her room, then turned and looked back. "Tell that lawyer to let me see her."

*　　*　　*

Ed had talked Andi into meeting him for lunch. Busy as she was, she made it happen.

After they'd ordered, she said, "I have to get back. We're having a meeting about the operation tomorrow."

Ed felt suddenly anxious. "Do you have to be part of the Sobstak thing?"

She looked quizzical. "It's my job. Besides, there's no real danger. Victor's in, we get the tapes, Victor's out. No problems." She looked at him. "Why the concern?"

Embarrassed, he said, "I don't know. Just... well, I don't want you to get hurt."

"I'm not going to get hurt, Ed. Stop worrying."

"Okay," he said. "Done."

After they'd eaten, he asked her if she could drive with him into the country for a half-hour.

Andi dialed her phone. "Callie? Ben in?" She waited a moment. "Hi, Ben. Say, do you need me at this meeting? Ed wants to talk about the Grace situation." She listened. "Hold on a minute." Cupped the phone. "All right if I tell him?" Ed nodded. She explained briefly, listened again. "Right. Three o'clock's no problem. I'll be there." She hung up and looked at Ed. "Ben got real quiet. He said to remind you about how it feels to have a daughter. What's that mean?"

"Something he told me once." He didn't add, *about you*.

She waited, and when Ed said nothing more, she said, "All right, talk. We have ninety minutes."

"Let's take my truck. I want to show you something."

As they pulled onto the highway, she asked, "So have you figured out why you've decided to adopt Grace?"

He nodded. "You mentioned Elizabeth Murphy, and you're right, it's partly that. Not atonement so much as grabbing a second chance. But that's not the main thing, though. The main thing is really two things. For one, I'm still pissed at Mara, and this gives me a way to be better than she is. That's stupid, but – "

She shrugged. "Not stupid. I get that. What's the other thing?"

Without warning, Ed began to sob. He pulled onto the shoulder. Andi looked sharply at him, then put a hand on his arm. "What's wrong?"

When his throat loosened, he told her about the death of his newborn thirty years ago. "I've always told myself I hadn't bonded with him, so it didn't matter."

"Now *that's* stupid," Andi said, not unkindly. "You know better than that."

Ed wiped his eyes. "You've got quite the bedside manner." He laughed a bit. "But you're right." He pulled back onto the highway and drove a couple of miles farther, then turned onto a newly plowed road leading down to the river. "Let me show you something," he said. They got out. A few feet away from the road, the river rushed black and cold over gleaming rocks. They followed a deer path at the water's edge, slowed by the snow and ice, stepping carefully along the bank for a hundred feet or so toward a huge boulder. Pressing themselves against the cold rock, they inched around into a dark grotto. Water circled slowly. The air was redolent with the tang of lichen and wet earth. Blue ice clung to the rocks.

"Peaceful," Andi whispered.

Ed nodded. "Eighty years ago, a monk up at the monastery jumped off the Coliseum." He shivered, remembering himself poised there. "They trolled the lake, but never found him. I often come here during summers, to swim and think. It's a good place for that. One day, I found the skull."

"After all that time."

He nodded, "Yeah. Things wash up." *Like grief for my son.*

They were quiet for a while. Then he said, "So how about you, Andi? What do you think about Grace?"

She tossed some pebbles into the black water, making a spray of circles. "I don't know, Ed. It's a huge commitment. You and I, if we had a thing and it crashed, we'd be all right. We're grownups. But if I play a role with Grace and then something comes between you and me, what does that do to her?"

He sighed and underhanded a clump of snow onto the black water.

At first, it floated, revolving slowly, then began to crumble, melting into the pool. He sighed again. "You're wise, Andi."

They worked their way back to his truck and climbed in. As he turned the ignition, Andi reached across and put her hand on his arm, as she had when he wept for his little boy. "I'm not saying no, Ed. We just have to see how things work out."

He pulled out onto the road and drove slowly toward the highway. As he turned toward town, he looked across at her. "I wouldn't ask for anything more." He thought about the skull in the grotto. He'd been happy that day, finding it. Today, he was happy again.

*   *   *

Back at the department, Ben was talking with Callie when Ed and Andi came in. He took Ed's arm and ushered him to his office.

"So before I ask you what's the verdict, can you make the three o'clock meeting with the Sobstaks?"

Ed checked the clock, embarrassed. He'd promised Maggie. "No, I've got some things to talk over with the lawyers."

"Not today, numbnuts," Ben said. "Tomorrow. Vic's going in with the wire and Maggie'll need some hand holding."

He felt relief. "Oh, yeah, I already told her I'd be there."

"Good." Ben paused. "So, Grace. You made your decision yet?"

"I did. I'm going to adopt her."

Ben waited, then said, "What's Andi think?"

Ed hesitated. "It's not really about her, Ben. I just wanted her advice."

The sheriff grunted. "My ass. No way in hell you can raise a little girl on your own. You need her help."

Perceptive. Still, Ed was annoyed at Ben's pushing the relationship again.

"What makes you think that?"

"You two would be great together. I'm just connecting the dots."

TWENTY-FIVE

Friday, February 17

A S HE SHRUGGED off his coat for breakfast at the Valley Inn, Ed calculated when he could talk to Grace about the adoption. Last night, she'd stayed late with Ardyss, and had too much homework due this morning, so he put it off. Henny brought coffee to his table. "The usual, Ed?"

"Yep, the usual, thanks." Ed's usual was eggs Benedict, American fries, a side of bacon, toast and jam, coffee with cream and sugar. When she turned to go, he called her back. "Wait, I'll change that. Make it a bowl of All Bran and bananas. I'm on a mission."

"You sure?"

He nodded, and she gave him a thumbs-up. "Good luck with that!"

As he was leaving the restaurant, Andi called. Grace was being insufferable, threatening to refuse to go to school until she could see her mother. Andi said, "I won this round, but she's not easy!"

"Doesn't lean you toward helping, eh?"

She didn't answer for a long moment. "I didn't mean it that way. But yeah, it makes a girl think."

"It's better than getting shot at by gangsters."

She laughed. "Got that right."

Ed leaned against his truck as he talked with her, looking at the soft blue sky above the white peaks, enjoying the unexpected warmth that had come in after Wednesday's snowstorm. "Why don't you and Grace come out to my place for dinner? I'll pick up some steaks and haul out the grill. We can tell her then."

"Uh-uh. Vic Sobstak's going in with the wire tonight, remember? I'm undercover with the entry team."

"Sorry," he muttered. "I keep forgetting that. I'll have to tell Grace afterwards. When does this start?"

"Vic comes in around three-thirty, which is when we go under. I think Crane's meeting is scheduled around five, or whenever the bastard arrives."

"Who is your team?" He kept his voice calm.

"Ben, Pete, and me. I'm the lead."

Ed didn't speak. After a moment, Andi asked, "What's the problem?"

"I don't like Ben's plan. This Crane is bad."

She was quiet a moment, then said, "Ed, let's not do this. We know what we're doing."

"Sorry, point taken. No more second-guessing from the civilian." He tried to mean it.

*   *   *

When Grace came to his office at a little after three, he told her about his commitment at the Sheriff's Department. As she was turning to go, Ed's cell phone buzzed. It was Melissa Hanson at the hospital. "Ed, Ardyss Conley has relapsed. She's unconscious again, and her temp's spiking." When he hung up, he started to tell Grace, but she interrupted.

"When can I see my mother?"

"Grace, the lawyer hasn't called back. The hospital just called. Ardy is sick again."

Grace jerked up. "I'm going over there." She started toward the door.

Ed said, "Wait a second. Let's call the lawyer so we know about your mom, and then we'll take care of Ardy."

She narrowed her eyes. "Call him now, Northrup. I'm going to the john."

When Ed reached him, Jerry Francis said, "The adoption papers are just about ready. The Minneapolis attorney faxed them a half hour ago, and there's a few items I have to insert, but they'll be ready tonight or first thing tomorrow."

"That's good, Jerry, but Grace needs to see her mother."

Jerry stonewalled. "That's not going to happen, Ed. According to Minneapolis, her mother is comatose. That wouldn't be good for a young girl to see."

Ed's stomach growled. He'd skipped lunch, a busy day. "Look, Jerry, if I'm going to be her father, I'll make the decisions about what's good for her, not Mara's lawyer. So represent *my* interests and get the name of the damn hospital." He ended it more sharply than he'd meant to.

Grace came in. "Can I see her?" Her eyes were red.

"I'm trying. Your mother's in a coma and the other lawyer says it wouldn't be good for you to see her like that."

"Fuck him! I know – "

"You know what's good for you and you don't need any adults deciding for you."

Startled, she cocked her head. "Are you, like, dissing me?"

"Dissing? What's *dissing?*"

Exasperated, Grace wiped the tears off her face. "Omigod! Don't you, like, know English?!"

His frustration bubbled up so quickly, he almost yelled. "I know English, and *dissing* has not yet entered my vocabulary. So what the hell does it mean so I can tell you whether I was doing it?"

Her eyes widened. "It's, like, putting me down."

Ed frowned. "Sorry for raising my voice." He rubbed his face. "No, I wasn't dissing you. I was agreeing with you that you know what's good for you."

She paused and thought about that. "So why can't I see her?"

"As soon as we find out where she is, we'll go."

"We? Who's we?"

"You and me."

Grace said nothing for a moment. "What's the thing you have to tell me, besides my mom dying? The thing from this morning?"

He shook his head. *Wrong time.* "You've got to get over to the hospital and I have this meeting. We'll talk tonight when we get home."

Rather than leaving, though, she said, "Northrup?"

"What?"

"What's going to happen to me... after she's dead?" In her voice there was no challenge, only the certainty of loneliness.

Ed's heart ached for her; it *was* time. "I'm going to keep you. Your mom asked me to adopt you. I want to. That's what we have to talk about."

She lifted her backpack onto her narrow shoulders, then stilled herself and looked directly at him. Her hazel eyes, gone serious and calm, were dark with weary insight. A girl's life can go off the rails before it even starts, with only the kindness of strangers to land upon. She said, quietly, "I can't remember anybody who *wanted* to keep me."

He had no idea what to answer, so he just smiled sadly. Grace looked at him intently for a moment, then smiled shyly. And then, as suddenly as the weather had changed, her face brightened. "See you later, masturbator," she sang, and pulled open the door.

* * *

Ed was still chuckling over Grace's parting shot when he locked his office and turned toward the Sheriff's Department door. Leese MacArdell was locking hers. "Hey, Ed. Got my tax numbers for me?" She was cheerful.

"Hey, Leese, I've got a few more days. It's only the seventeenth."

"Eleven days. I hear the sheriff's got an undercover gig going down this afternoon."

Ed's heart stopped. "Where'd you hear that?"

"From Vic Sobstak. I called to arrange Monday's trip to the IRS office and he mentioned it."

"Damn." Anxiety flooded him. "Why'd he tell you? He ought to keep it secret."

"He seemed kind of proud of himself. Said he wanted to make things right, whatever that means."

Ed shook his head. "I sure as hell hope he hasn't told anybody else."

"Yeah, so much for *undercover*, eh? Well, don't forget those numbers."

His cell phone buzzed. Ed looked at the caller ID and nodded a goodbye to Leese, walking slowly toward the Sheriff's Department door as he answered. "Hi, Ed, Jerry here. I've got good news and bad news."

"Bad first."

"The mother's in a coma in Las Vegas, at St. Rose Dominican hospital. Actually, it's in Henderson, a suburb. They say now that she's unlikely to live more than a few hours."

"Should I take Grace down tonight?"

"That's your decision to make, but speed is in order."

Ed sighed. "What's the good news?"

"Our paperwork is ready. Fortunately, her lawyer's got full power of attorney to do the deal with us as long as the mother stays alive. He's flying out here tonight."

"If she dies before then, what... ?"

"We'll make sure she doesn't."

"How will you do that?" Ed felt enormous weariness.

"Leave that to the lawyers. I'll check everything out for you, and we can do the formalities when you get back. Keep your cell phone charged."

Ed made his decision. "Jerry, can you do me a favor?"

The lawyer chuckled. "Ed, my fee for close friends is a hundred dollars an hour."

Ed rolled his eyes. "What is it for guys like me?"

"A hundred dollars an hour. Name the favor."

"Buy me two round-trip tickets, Missoula to Las Vegas, tomorrow any time after nine in the morning, returning... what's tomorrow?" *Damn!* He had no idea what day it was. "Saturday."

"Right. So, returning Sunday morning sometime." He paused. "And book me two rooms at a motel near that hospital – what? St. Rose Dominatrix? Put it on my tab."

"St. Rose Dominican – they're nuns." Ed heard jotting sounds, and then Jerry repeated the instructions. "Anything else?"

"I'll be in touch." He glanced quickly at his watch. Late!

Before opening the sheriff's department door, he made a quick call to Jim Hamilton, but it rolled over to voice mail. *Damn!* He left a message describing everything going on, and pushed through the big door to the department. Bertie, the night receptionist was at the counter, catching some overtime. "They're all in the conference room, waitin' on ya."

In the corridor to the conference room, his phone buzzed. It was Jim. He ducked into a side room.

"My Lord, sounds like the climax of a bad novel!"

"Hello to you too. Yeah, it feels that way. Look, I gotta hold Maggie's hand. Can you do me a favor?" Ed grimaced. Two favors in as many minutes. No, only one. He was paying Jerry.

"Name it."

"Could you check on Ardyss Conley over at the hospital? She's had a relapse, and Grace's going there as we speak. I'd like her not to be facing this alone, and I'm tied up here."

"On my way, dad."

"Don't call me that. And say a prayer for all of us."

"Oh, every day, my friend. Every day."

*   *   *

In the conference room, Callie looked up when he came in. She sat at a computer on a long table against the wall. "I'm communications for this party," she said. "Where you been?" She nodded toward Vic and Maggie on the other side of the room. "We got us some citizens could use a friend." A deputy, whom Ed recognized but whose name he couldn't remember, sat at the table beside Callie, tuning dials on a second console. He nodded at Ed. "Hey, Ed. Nice to see ya." Ed, embarrassed, replied, "The same."

Vic was getting his final instructions from Loren – Loren's last name escaped him. Ed rubbed his eyes again. *Too much going on*, he thought.

He'd known Loren for fifteen years.

Vic stood ramrod stiff in the center of the room, and barely nodded to Ed. Loren fiddled with the microphone taped under Vic's shirt, talking quietly. Behind the permanent outdoor ruddiness of his face, Vic looked pale. Maggie, ashen, her hands folded still on her lap, sat straight on a hard plastic chair to the side. On the table beside her rested two automatic weapons and bulletproof vests. Beside the weapons were a coffee pot on a hotplate, a stack of styrofoam cups, and a large square box of donuts from the Village Inn.

Before walking over to Maggie, Ed asked Callie, "Where are Ben and Andi?"

Callie pointed at the two consoles on the table. "Her and Ben and Pete went under at three-thirty." She glanced up at the clock, which read three-fifty. "We're in good contact with 'em. They're in room 17, next door to Crane's meeting room. Nothin' goin' on yet."

Ed suppressed his anxiety and walked over and rested his hand on Maggie's shoulder. Her shoulder twitched at his touch. "How're you doing?"

"I'm hankerin' for this to be done and over." She nodded at her husband across the room. "Vic's nervous."

Vic glared, but he nodded. "I'm a cowboy. I ain't no goddamn detective. What if I blow this?"

"If it was me, I'd be worried too," said Ed. "You don't have to go through with this."

Maggie looked gratefully at him, and said to Vic, "That's right, Victor. We can just call it off. I'm scared for you."

Callie swiveled in her chair to listen, and Loren, just then buttoning up Vic's shirt, frowned and stepped back. "You getting' cold feet, Vic?"

Vic dropped his head and his jaw muscles worked. When he spoke, his voice reminded Ed of a soft wind in the high pines. "I reckon I'm a bit trepidacious, but I gave Ben my word on this." He straightened up. "I'll do 'er." He smiled weakly. "Goddamn, one time before he passed, me and ol' Charley Wright was elk huntin' and this goddamn griz charged Charley from forty feet. I stood there and shot him through the eye and me and Charley called it in and went on huntin'. A feller who can do that oughta be able to pull the wool over that goddamn Reverend's eyes."

"There you go, Vic," said Callie, approvingly. "Loren, you about done with him?"

Loren inspected Vic's shirt a last time. "Just done."

"Explain the set-up to Ed here."

Loren looked proud. "We got four channels," he said, gesturing toward the console beside Callie's computer. "One for regular traffic, which Bertie's manning out front."

Callie growled. "Bertie ain't mannin' nothin', Deputy. She's *staffin'*."

The deputy rolled his eyes. "The second channel's Victor here." He tapped Vic's chest, where apparently the microphone was. Ed couldn't see anything. "The third one's from Ben and the two deputies, and the last one's the backup team, Chip and Javier. We can all talk to each other, and we all can hear Vic, but Vic can't hear nobody, of course."

Callie pointed to the coffee. "Have a donut. Ed. It could be a long evenin'." She turned to Loren, who had resumed talking quietly to Vic. "Is he all set to go? We should start gettin' ready to move out."

Loren inspected Vic, turning him from front to back and then front again. "Looking real clean. Wired him myself, and I can't even tell." Callie snorted and said to the second deputy beside her, "You double check him, CC." Ed suddenly remembered his name, Chip Coleman. Coleman rolled his eyes, but did as he was ordered, inspecting Vic carefully on all sides. Loren waited until Coleman said, "Can't see a thing. He's good to go."

Loren said to Vic, "You'll be good. Just talk normal, not loud. We'll pick you up."

Vic said, "You boys sure of that?"

"Go on outside and say a couple things, just in your normal tone of voice, then come on in and we'll play 'er back for ya."

After Vic left, Ed asked, "What if Crane has a scanner?"

Coleman had taken his seat at the console and adjusted another dial. "We got secure channels here, Doc. Hats off to Homeland Security." Just then, Vic's voice came over the speaker.

"Well, I'm out front smokin' my cigarette. Hope you all are gettin' this." A pause. "Think I just spotted Crane's Cadillac up the road.

Goddamn. Guess its time to get goin'."

A few minutes later, Vic returned. The recording played back clear and crisp.

"Guess you got me, then," he said.

Loren asked him, "Did Crane spot you?"

"Naw, he was way up at the Jeff House, just turnin' in."

Callie nodded, then thumbed a switch. "Base to Pilot." Ben's voice, pitched low, came back. "Pilot here. We rollin'?"

"We think Crane just pulled in."

"Affirmative, Base. Two men entering Number 18. Vehicle's got the Idaho plates." There was a long pause. "Got us a second vehicle pulling in. Hold on." A long silence. Then, "Two more guys, from the sound of voices.... Huh.... Looks like Franky Concini and Jackie Moen from the Double-A. Let's get movin'."

At his console, Chipper Coleman thumbed the intercom and said, "Time to roll, Javier." He said to Vic and Maggie, "You know the plan. We give them fifteen more minutes, so any latecomers don't see the backup vehicle. Then Javier and me get in place, then Victor, you go in." Javier Ortiz, another deputy, came through the door, all smiles.

"Hey, Chipper. You got the beer and pretzels?"

"I thought you were bringin''em."

Maggie looked petrified.

"Naw," Javier said. "I brought the *Playboys* and the weed."

Callie chuckled. "You boys knock off the crazy talk and get goin'." She head-gestured toward Vic and Maggie.

"No worries, Maggie," laughed Chipper. "Backup's boring. We're just havin' a little laugh."

He and Chipper pulled bulky vests over their shirts and lifted the weapons off the table. Javier grabbed two donuts. As they left, Loren sat down at the console and said to Ed, "Chip and Javier'll be two hundred yards north on the highway, as backup. Just in case. Ain't really no need."

Callie flicked the switch. "Base to Pilot." When Ben gave a quiet affirmative, she told him the backup team had just left. "Eight minutes, Pilot."

Seven minutes later, Javier's voice came from the speakers. "Rider to

Pilot. We're in place, observing your location. You got two vehicles in the lot: One pickup directly outside your door, Subject's Caddy in front of Number 18."

Ben's voice, softly, said, "Roger that, Rider. Base, let's move Partner in."

Loren turned and nodded to Vic. "Showtime, Partner." Maggie gave him a quick kiss, then a long hug, and Ed shook his hand. Vic left. Callie said, "Base to Pilot. Partner's on the way."

Loren adjusted Vic's feed and they heard him whistling softly. Maggie whispered, "He whistles when he's scared."

Loren said, kindly, "No need to whisper, ma'am. Ain't no bad guys can hear us."

Callie said, "He'll be good, Maggie. Ben's right next door." Ed wiped his palms on his pants.

Loren flipped another switch. "Showtime."

*   *   *

Vic's voice (from the speaker): "Hey! Good to see you boys!"

"Too loud," said Loren, shaking his head. "Nerves, I bet."

Another voice: "You sound pretty cheerful for a guy underwater with taxes."

Maggie whispered, "That sounds like the Reverend's guy, the one Vic calls Stetson. He scares me."

Vic's voice (pitched too high): "Mike, Mike, Mike. Let's get off on a new foot. We're helping each other out, right? You help me get out of taxes, I help you get your ideas in court. Right?"

Stetson's voice: "That remains to be seen, cowboy. You turned pussy on us, I recall."

A resonant, deep voice: "Michael, enough. Victor is back in the flock. Correct, Victor?"

Maggie whispered, "That's Crane."

Vic's voice (still pitched up): "I am, sir. And damn happy to be." Loren, in a normal voice, said, "Vic's talking too loud. He's nervous." *Crane's voice (intoning a long prayer)*: Loren jotted notes as he went on.

Ed asked him, "Aren't you recording this?"

"Sure, but I'm flagging the clock times where he says important stuff for analysis later." Occasionally, Loren muttered, "Gotcha, asshole." Crane droned on.

Crane's voice (end of prayer): "Amen. Are there any questions, gentlemen?"

Vic's voice: "Are we still supposed to be puttin' up those Burke flyers, Reverend?"

Stetson's voice: "Shut up, Sobstak."

Loren muttered, "Bad move."

Maggie whispered, her voice tightly strung, "What'd he do wrong?"

"He's pissing this Stetson guy off. No worries."

Ed stepped over closer to Maggie and put his arm around her. He felt her body quivering.

Vic's voice: "Sorry, I was – "

Stetson's voice (interrupting): "Reverend, you were saying?"

Crane's voice: "Other questions?"

Another voice: "So you're tellin' me it's more or less a Christian an' a patriotic duty not to pay taxes. I got that right?"

Crane's voice: "You do, Franky. Some of our friends call it 'starving the Beast.'" Loren nodded. "Franky, eh?" He jotted a note. "That'd be Franky Concini." Maggie's trembling worsened under Ed's arm.

Franky's voice: "Ain't 'the Beast' a name for Satan?"

Crane's voice: "It is. You know your Book of Revelations. We Christians believe our duty – not only as patriots but as believers – is to oppose the kingdom of Satan, even if it means bringing the guvmint to its knees."

As Loren jotted notes, Maggie whispered, "Vic ain't much on that religious talk."

Vic's voice (still pitched high, enthusiastic): "You couldn't be more right there, Reverend. Me, I've always been, uh, a enemy of Satan."

Stetson's voice: "Seems I recall you saying you and your wife don't much take to the religious side of this."

Loren looked over at Maggie. "You think Vic'll ease 'er down a notch?"

Maggie gripped Ed's arm. "Is he doin' it wrong?"

Callie jumped in, fast, "No, no, he's doin' jus' fine. Loren here's just hopin' he'll relax. Everything's goin' great."

Ed gave Maggie a squeeze. "Don't worry."

"Easy to say, Ed. You ain't got your love in harm's way."

*   *   *

A new voice: "So how many people are in on your plan, Reverend Crane?"

Loren grunted in satisfaction. "Good. His name's on tape."

Crane's voice: "Jacky, there's the five of us, of course, and maybe three others in the valley. Across Montana and Idaho, we have... Michael, how many?"

Loren looked again at Ed. "Jacky?"

Ed thought about it, said, "Jack Moen, I would guess."

The speakers were silent for a longish time. Loren said, "Guess they ain't talking."

Stetson's voice: "Probably best not to count out loud, Reverend."

Crane's voice: "We're among friends, Michael."

Stetson's voice: "You certain of that, Reverend?"

Vic's voice (fast): "You can trust *me*, Reverend. Me and my friends here."

Loren muttered, "Shit." Maggie grabbed Ed's hand.

Franky's voice: [Inaudible.]

Crane's voice: "We mustn't reveal our plan to anyone but our fellow patriots. There are forces that hate us and all we stand for."

Vic's voice: "Reverend, I'm assumin' you've got it figured out how you'll cover this up if the sheriff finds out."

Loren groaned, and Maggie grabbed Ed's arm again.

Stetson's voice (angry): "Say *what*?!"

Vic's voice (mumbling): "Well, uh, you know. If we, uh, go ahead with this, uh, conspiracy – " *Vic's voice stops. Then (anxiously) resumes*: "And somehow word gets out..."

Stetson's voice (menacing): "Hold on, pussy. This doesn't get out unless one of you assholes talks."

Loren groaned again.

Maggie whispered, "What's happenin'?"

* * *

Crane's voice: "Michael. Enough, please."

Voices talking over one another. Confused talk. Then, silence.

Maggie said, "Is he doin' okay?"

Loren nodded. "Yeah, now he is."

Crane's voice again: "Victor, you promised some information for us, I believe?" *Vic's voice*: "Information, Reverend?" Loren grunted.

Maggie pressed close to Ed.

Stetson's voice: "Don't weasel, pussy."

Vic's voice (breathing heavily): "Mike, let's drop the gutter talk."

Another silence. Ed tried to imagine what was happening.

Crane's voice: "Victor, you told us you'd bring us new information on the governor's campaign. What is it?" A pause.

Vic's voice (quivering): "Uh, yeah, Reverend. I wanted to say, uh, that psychologist – "

Ed stiffened. Maggie looked at him in alarm.

Vic's voice (continuing, voice shaking): " – supporting Burke. Making a large contribution, I hear. Figured you'd want to know."

Stetson's voice (angry): "What the hell? You told us about him already. This isn't news. What're you – "

Vic's voice: "Well, I'm just sayin' – "

Stetson's voice (cutting in): "Loyd, something isn't right here. This pussy's – "

Vic's voice: "Goddamn, Mike, you quit callin' me that – "

* * *

Loren groans, "No."

He says to Callie, fast, "Get Pilot in there."

Callie thumbs the mic and calls the team. "Base to Pilot. Get in there!" *From the speaker, loud rustling sounds.*

Vic's voice (loud): "Hands off, you goddamn – " and then two heavy grunts, and then Vic's radio goes dead.

*   *   *

Ben's voice (booming): "Go! Go! Go!" Maggie grabs Ed.
Loud pounding sounds.
Andi's voice (big, commanding): "Sheriff! Open this door!"
Andi's voice (again, louder): "Open this door or we are coming in!"
A loud smashing sound and then:
Andi's voice (shouting): "Drop the weapon!" *Shouts, then three loud sounds,* pop, pop, pop.
Ben's voice (screaming): "Officer down! Officer down! Backup now!"

PART FOUR

TWENTY-SIX

Same evening

E D STOOD IN the waiting room, facing double doors marked *Surgery*. Ben, gray-faced, sat behind him, at the end of a row of chairs beside the waiting room entrance. *Officer down.* Ben's scream had stricken Ed. He and Maggie had raced to the hospital, where Andi had already been taken into surgery. Ed looked at the double doors. Dark horizontal scratches ran waist-high across each door; the "r" in "Surgery" had faded. Opaque square windows at eye level glowed yellow from inside. Beside the windows, where hands push, the doors were discolored. He peered through the windows: Another hall, more doors. Harsh ceiling lights. A gurney parked crookedly against one wall, dirty, crumbled bedding piled on its center. He saw rust-colored blotches on the bedding.

A noise behind him. Ben's voice. "Come sit down, bud."

From outside the waiting room came a rush of noise. Grace flooded in, screaming, "Northrup! No! Not Andi!" and fell into him. She clutched him, half-sobbing, half-smothered screaming. He was startled at her reaction; she wasn't close with Andi. Or had another loss breached her already-weakened levees? He looked over Grace's head toward Ben.

Her voice was muffled against his chest; he couldn't hear words. Looking at her scalp, he saw pink-white skin shining beneath her hair, skin so young, so vulnerable, his throat thickened. He tightened his arms around her. From somewhere inside, the hum arose again. For a moment, he swayed with her in his arms. Then, he said her name. It didn't sound like his voice, but it served. *Why am I so emotional?*

She stilled, pressing her face harder against his chest. "She's dead, isn't she?"

Ben, had gotten up and come close, and said, softly, "No, Gracie girl. She ain't dead. They're working on her in there."

"She'll die."

Ben lifted Grace, swathing her in his massive arms. She wrapped her arms around his heavy neck and wept onto his wide shoulder, and tears slid down his broad face. After a time, Ben cleared his throat roughly and said, "No, girl. She ain't dyin' in there. We won't let her."

The double doors thudded open, swung wide, banged into the wall. Doc Keeley was running; he said, "She's going to pull through." Ben gasped, then passed the girl into Ed's arms and Grace put her small arms around his neck and murmured, like a prayer, "She'll be all right, she'll be all right." Ed felt his own tears rise.

*   *   *

Later, they all – Ed, Grace, Ben, Doc Keeley, Maggie, Pete Peterson, who'd been right behind Andi when she was shot – sat in the hospital conference room. Andi lay in the recovery room, Vic in the ER. He'd been shot too, though not seriously.

Ben cleared his throat. "I should really be telling this to the state guys first." He checked his watch. "They'll be here any time now. But let me get this off my chest." He looked off into a distance that only he knew. Ed thought, *He blames himself.* When Ben finally spoke, his voice was low, neutral as a police report. The sheriff's eyes focused on the table. "As you heard, I made the call to do the entry. In my judgment, Vic was in trouble. Deputy Pelton was our lead officer, and she properly announced our presence and demanded admittance. When it was denied, Deputy Peterson opened the door with his foot." He nodded to Pete, who looked stricken.

Ben went on. "Deputy Pelton entered first, followed closely by Deputy Peterson and myself. Our weapons were drawn and ready. One of the men in the room, the one called Stetson I believe, had Victor Sobstak – "Ben glanced at Maggie. " – in his grasp, with a weapon drawn. Deputy Pelton ordered him to drop his weapon. Instead of doing so, he fired. She fell to the left, and as she did so, she discharged her weapon and the shooter fell. He was dead when the EMTs arrived. As Stetson fell, he fired again, but Mr. Sobstak had grasped the shooter's weapon, and the bullet was deflected as it passed though his hand." Ben stopped and looked again at Maggie. "Your husband's a brave man, Maggie. I believe he saved a life."

Maggie, still in shock, managed, "Thank you, Sheriff."

Doc Keeley said, "Maggie, I called a hand surgeon from Missoula. They're sending the chopper, so he'll be here in an hour or so to work on Vic's hand." Maggie nodded. The skin around her eyes was a dull gray.

Ben interrupted his story. "The chopper? For Vic's hand?"

"No, sorry. I asked for the chopper to evacuate Deputy Pelton. They put the surgeon on board."

Grace, her face newly alarmed, asked, "Why do you need to evacuate her?"

"She'll need more surgery, and probably soon."

Grace's alarm seemed to shift to terror. Ed took her hand, and she squeezed his. Hard.

Ben cleared his throat again, then wiped his eyes and resumed his report. "The others in the room had dived to the floor, and Deputy Peterson and I covered them while we waited for backup. Deputy Pelton was conscious. She was bleeding from the right shoulder. At no time did she ask for help. At one juncture, she asked me if Victor was hurt. I reported his hand injury. At that point, the paramedics arrived and Deputy Pelton lost consciousness." He wiped his eyes with a tired hand. "We arrested Loyd Crane and two citizens from Monastery Valley, but

I don't know if we can hold the citizens. That'll be for the county attorney to decide."

No one spoke. After a few moments, Doc Keeley filled the silence. "I can tell you about the deputy's injuries, if you want?"

Ed and Grace both nodded. Ben cleared his throat, roughly. Maggie and Pete Peterson sat silently.

Keeley ran his fingers through his hair. "To tell you the truth, it was a freak. The bullet struck her just below where the clavicle – the collar bone – meets the shoulder and the scapula, less than a quarter-inch from her vest. If it had hit the vest, she'd have nothing worse than a bruise. However, it entered just next to her shoulder and I think it must have ricocheted off her scapula and tore – yes, Grace?"

Grace had raised her free hand, still gripping Ed's with the other. "What's a scapula?"

"Oh, it's the angel's wing bone." Ed reached behind Grace and touched her scapula, and she nodded.

Doc went on. "After it ricocheted off the scapula, I think it ripped through her lung and broke three ribs. Fortunately, the bullet was fully jacketed or she'd have been killed instantly. She probably felt a lot of pain." He looked around. "I think she's going to make it. The next 24 hours should tell us the story."

Ed clenched his fist, thinking of cancelling the trip to Las Vegas tomorrow morning. Then he realized Mara didn't have twenty-four hours left: They had to go.

Maggie was excusing herself. She wanted to sit with Vic. Doc Keeley stood up too, saying, "He's sedated, Maggie. He's not in pain," and they went out together.

There was a small knock on the door. Magnus and Luisa Anderssen came in.

"Are we intruding?"

The big sheriff shook his head. "Mack. Luisa. C'mon in."

Luisa said, "What can we do to help?"

Ben shook his head. "Pray, I suppose. Ain't supposed to happen like this in our valley."

Magnus nodded. "You have that right, my friend." He came over to

Ed. "I understand you knew, uh, know the deputy."

Ed nodded. "I've been sleeping on her couch since Grace here came to town." *Sleeping on her couch, and liking her more and more.*

Magnus turned to Grace, whose eyes were red and puffy. "Grace, I'm Magnus Anderssen. This is my wife, Luisa."

Grace shook his hand. "You're MJ's mom and dad."

Luisa nodded. "I understand my son has taken you under his wing at school."

"MJ's, like, awesome."

Ed thought of Andi's overhearing Grace suggesting she and some boy "hook up." MJ?

Actually, MJ was hanging back at the door. Ed pulled Grace to him softly and whispered to her, "Bring him over. He can sit with you."

A moment later, Maggie came back into the room. "Ed, can I talk to you a minute?"

His resentment flared, but he dampened it and followed Maggie out, gently squeezing Grace's thin shoulder as he passed.

*   *   *

They sat in the waiting room. Maggie said, "Vic's out like a light. I need to talk this out with somebody."

"Look, I'm feeling pretty weird," he said, more brusquely than he intended. The last thing on earth he wanted right now was Maggie asking him to listen to *her* problems. His powerful reaction to Andi's shooting was confusing, upsetting. Sure, she was a friend. But why this intensity?

"We ain't got no insurance," she said. "I ain't askin' for help, but if you could mention it to Doc Keeley before this specialist fellow gets here? With the taxes and all, I ain't real sure we can handle another heavy debt."

"Sure I can, Maggie," he said, curtly. "But let's not worry about it now. We'll figure something out."

Maggie's eyes filmed, and she shook her head. "It ain't the money, really," she said. "I jus' feel so bad. Vic and me, we got our troubles, but in a flash the deputy's hurt real bad and a guy's dead. Our money troubles *caused* all this." She started to cry. "And I treated the deputy so mean."

Ed swallowed his irritation and put his arm around her shoulders. "Maggie, no. Andi was doing her job." He surprised himself, saying that. "You made a mistake with her and you'll fix it later. Everybody makes mistakes. You go back and sit with your husband."

Jim Hamilton had arrived while Ed was talking to Maggie, and was waiting respectfully outside for them to finish. When Maggie went back to the ER, Jim came in and sat down.

"Callie called. What's Andi's condition?" Ed brought him up to date.

Jim said, "You look shell-shocked."

Ed nodded bleakly. "Yeah. I'm a mess. I have no idea why I'm reacting so strongly."

Jim studied him. "No idea?"

Ed felt his throat tightening again. He cleared it. "I think I'm feeling more for Andi than I knew. I don't think I was paying attention."

The priest said nothing. Then, after a moment, he put his hand on Ed's shoulder. "What do you need?"

"Would you go and check on Ardyss Conley? She's in room, uh, 111, I think. She had a relapse and I'm worried about her."

"You asked me that this afternoon, remember? I saw her. They jumped the gun on that 'relapse.' She was already doing better when I visited her this afternoon."

"Could you fill her in about Andi – if she's up to it? So Grace doesn't have to?"

"Of course." He put his hand on Ed's shoulder. "Stay right here."

"I'll be in there." He gestured toward the conference room.

*   *   *

Going back in, he sat beside Grace and MJ Anderssen and rested his hands on the table.

Grace looked torn. "Northrup, should I stay here? I should, like, take care of Ardy."

"Father Hamilton is looking in on her."

"Ardy needs me. But I want to be here for Andi too."

"Go ahead. We'll come get you if anything comes up."

MJ and his parents stood to leave. Ed said, "Magnus, can I have a word with you?" He and the rancher stepped outside and a few steps away from the conference room door.

"Maggie's worried sick about the cost of hand surgery. They don't have insurance." He didn't fill in any gaps about why Vic had been in the meeting in the first place, although he knew Magnus wanted to know: Two of his men had been arrested.

Magnus rubbed his chin, nodding. "I wanted to ask what this is all about, but I assume if you could tell me, you would have." He sighed. "Vic and Maggie are good people. When it's done, find out what it cost and let me know. Luisa and I will take care of it." He extended his hand. "Come out to the ranch one day soon, my friend. I miss you." Then Luisa and MJ joined him, and they left.

*   *   *

When Ed came back into the conference room, Ben stood. "Gotta get back to the office and start dealing with this Crane guy." His eyes had a dark, distant look. Ed started to say something, but Ben cleared his throat, then drew in a ragged breath. "If I ruined that girl's life with my goddamn plan, I ain't forgivin' myself." He held up his hand to stop Ed's reply, turned, and left. Pete Peterson followed. Pete hadn't said a single word.

Ed, as sad for Ben as he was afraid for Andi, made his way to Ardyss's room. He stood quietly behind Grace, listening to Jim telling Ardyss about the shooting. Tears streamed down Grace's cheeks; Ed embraced her from behind, and she leaned back against him. Ardyss's hand covered her mouth. After a moment, she moved over in her bed, gesturing to Grace. "Come in here, child, where I can feel you." Grace climbed into the old woman's bed and arms. Jim pulled the white blanket over them, and he and Ed went back to the waiting room.

Ted Coldry was there. Everyone else had gone. Ted stood.

Ed said, "Grace and I are flying to Las Vegas in the morning to see her mother before she dies."

"The mother's dying? Oh, the poor child. So much sorrow."

"So it seems. There's no other family left to take care of Grace, so Mara dropped her here."

Jim asked, "You're going to Vegas as *who*?"

"Her new father."

Ted Coldry looked back and forth between them. "Come," he waved his hand. "Tell."

Ed filled him in.

"You're adopting Grace?" Ted's hand rose to his lips.

"Don't look so incredulous."

"I'm not incredulous, Edward. I'm on the verge of tears."

* * *

Doc Keeley came to the door of the waiting room and nodded to Ted and Jim. "Ed, a word?"

Outside, he said, "Look, she's holding her own, but the lung damage is serious. There's a top-notch thoracic surgeon in Missoula and she'll be at St. Patrick's Hospital within the hour. Sheila Gramment's her name. When the helicopter gets here, I'm sending Andi over. Dr. Gramment'll do a good job with her."

"You think she won't make it."

Keeley looked down, then said, "I'm not a good enough surgeon for what she needs. She might make it, but she might not. Her better chance is in Missoula."

"Send her."

Keeley put his hand on Ed's shoulder. "Good call. Not that it's yours to make."

"So why did you ask me?"

Doc Keeley smiled. "Didn't ask."

Ed grimaced. "Guess I'm stepping a little bit out of line, eh?" But he felt some of his confusion lifting. He knew what he wanted.

Ed called Ben Stewart and explained the new plan. "I'm taking Grace over in my truck," he said.

"No, you ain't," Ben said. "We'll take my rig. The guys can handle the crap here. Get the little girl and your toothbrushes and meet me at the Department in fifteen minutes. With lights and siren, we'll be there damn near as fast as that helicopter."

TWENTY-SEVEN

Saturday, February 18

T HE SURGERY WAITING room at St. Patrick Hospital offered chairs almost soft enough to doze in. Grace snored. She'd swung between terror and thrill during Ben's wild ride, lights blazing, siren splitting the air whenever he roared past a sleepy driver. The three-hour trip had taken an hour and fifty minutes. Andi was already in surgery when they arrived.

As Grace slept, Ben and Ed had thumbed magazines or stared at the walls. Neither spoke. Ed studied the large tryptich of a mountain scene on the beige wall, trying to stare himself to sleep. Around six in the morning, according to the big clock whose hands never seemed to move, Ed finally dozed. In no time, Ben was shaking him.

"I'm Dr. Gramment," the woman in green scrubs was saying. "Your friend is in recovery." She spoke quietly to allow Grace to sleep. "Her right lung is badly torn up, but she's healthy. I think she'll heal nicely."

"How long, do you think?" Ed asked.

"Lungs are funny," she said. "If they're healthy, they heal pretty quickly. A few weeks, at most two or three months – although she probably won't *fully* recover for a few months, but like I said, the tissue looks healthy and I didn't see any evidence of smoking or earlier damage, so I think her recovery should be reasonably fast."

"She'll be here for two or three months?"

"Oh, my, no," she said, chuckling. "Barring infection, she'll probably be ready to go back to Jefferson in four or five days. She'll stay in your hospital for another couple of weeks, maybe less, then she'll be able to go home. I – " She stopped. "You do have a rehab unit in Jefferson?"

Ben nodded. "Two rooms of the hospital."

"Good," Dr. Gramment nodded, then yawned. "Excuse me!" she said, embarrassed. "It was a long night. Anyway, the bullet passed through her right lung and exited just below her right breast. The scapula itself was damaged, although not as much as we expected, so I asked Dr. Lander – he's an orthopedic surgeon – to scrub in and fix that up, which he did. That shouldn't be a problem, and miraculously, the shoulder joint itself wasn't involved. She has a broken rib where the bullet exited, but other than that, I'm amazed that no major arteries or organs were damaged. Other than the lung."

Ed said, "Doc Keeley said she had three broken ribs."

Gramment nodded. "On X-ray it looks like that, but it turned out to be only one. She's a very lucky woman."

"Except for getting shot," Ben growled.

The surgeon nodded. "Except for that. Anyway, she's in the recovery room, and once she's stable she'll be moved to the surgical ICU so we can keep an eye on her for the first twenty-four hours or so. We'll keep her sedated pretty heavily for the next couple of days."

"Can we see her?" Ed asked.

Dr. Gramment looked at her watch. "Once she's settled in the ICU, you can see her for 5 minutes every hour, but remember, she'll be sleeping. Oh, also, she'll be on a ventilator."

Grace's voice startled them from behind. "What's that?"

Dr. Gramment turned and smiled at her. "Hi, I'm your mom's surgeon."

Grace paled and darted a glance at Ed, who introduced Grace and described the situation.

"Oh, I'm sorry," said the surgeon. She explained the ventilator.

"Is she going to die?" Grace asked.

"No, not at all. But as I was telling your, uh, friends here, she'll be in rough shape for a while. These are tough injuries. But she won't die."

*   *   *

At seven-thirty, a nurse showed them into a narrow, curtained space. Grace gasped. Andi was unconscious, her lower face obscured by white tape holding a tube going into her mouth. Her skin was gray as old snow. Tubes snaked into the backs of both hands, which rested motionless at her sides. Machines on either side of her bed made quiet puffing sounds, rhythmical and regular. The room smelled of bandages and rubbing alcohol. Andi was still. Except for the faint rise and fall of her chest on the same rhythm as the puffing sounds, she might have been dead. Grace gripped Ed's hand.

Ben stood behind them, softly clearing his throat, the only human sound in the room. They stood and watched Andi, until the nurse returned and ushered them out when their five minutes were done.

The three went to the cafeteria, although Ed had no appetite. Apparently Grace wasn't hungry either: She bought a bottle of water. Ed had coffee. Ben looked around at the food service, then grabbed a cup and poured himself a Coke. "I gotta get my ass over to Jeff. Got loads to do there." He yawned again. "What time's your flight to Vegas?"

Ed slapped the table. "Damn! I forgot that. Sometime after 9 o'clock." Fatigue staggered him. He dug in a pocket for the note containing flight information. Grace said, "I'll go by myself, Northrup. You stay here with Andi."

"Honey, it ain't that simple," Ben started, but Grace waved him off.

"I wish everybody'd quit calling me *honey*. I know how to fly, I know how to take a taxi, and I can get to my mom by myself. It *is* simple."

Ed focused. "Let me call Jim before we figure this out." He dialed his cell phone – thank God he had stopped at the office to grab his charger – and the priest answered. "How's Andi?" Ed filled him in.

"What about Las Vegas?"

"We're discussing that right now. Andi's going to be sedated for a day or more. But Ben has to get back to Jeff, and I hate to leave her alone here, so – "

"When's your flight?"

"Nine-twenty-five, I think." He looked at the note. "No, nine-forty-five this morning. Jesus, that's in two hours."

Jim said, "Go. I'll straighten things up here and head over and stay overnight with Andi. What time's your return flight?"

Ed looked at the yellow paper again. "Noon tomorrow. Noon, exactly."

"Okay. I'll have to be back here for Sunday Mass, but I can get to Missoula before noon today."

"Jim, you don't have to do this."

"Shut up. I'm on my way."

*   *   *

After finishing her water, Grace went back to the ICU, while Ed walked Ben to his rig. "Don't drive too fast. You're tired." He clapped the sheriff on his burly back. "Thanks for coming with us, Ben."

He turned to face Ed. "Andi'll pull through." His voice wavered.

Ed felt a flash of irritation. "She came here to get *away* from shooters."

Ben's broad shoulders slumped. "Yeah, and I get her shot." Ed regretted what he'd said. Ben shook his head. "Maybe a guy's too old for this." He put his hand on Ed's shoulder. "She's going to sleep the next day or two. Take the little girl to say goodbye to her momma."

*   *   *

Grace, sitting on the floor in the airport waiting room, was texting.

"How're you feeling?" he asked, looking down from his chair.

She rolled her eyes at him and muttered, "I'm just great, Northrup. Andi's shot and I'm on my way to watch my mom die and yeah, well, I'm, like, just fine and dandy." Her eyes moistened, but she blinked it away.

He grimaced. "Yeah." He nodded toward her cell phone. "How's Amanda?"

"Equally fucked. Her dad just got arrested for, like, embellazing or whatever."

"Embellazing?"

Grace showed him the text. "It's what she wrote."

Ed moved to the floor beside her. "Shit. Poor kid."

She looked at him oddly, then leaned against his shoulder. "Yeah."

His phone buzzed. "Ed, where are you?" It was Jerry Francis.

"We're in the airport waiting for the Vegas flight. Grace's here with me. News?"

The attorney paused. "I'm sorry, Ed. I neglected to ask about the deputy. How is she?"

Ed lowered his voice. "She'll pull through. She's got a lot of injuries." He smiled for Grace's benefit.

"I'm..." The attorney made a long pause. "I'm sorry, Ed."

"Yeah. Me too." Ed was touched by the tone of sympathy in Jerry's voice.

"Anyway, I'm here in the office with Manion Phillips, Mrs. Hertz's attorney." Ed heard a muffled "Hey, Doctor!" in the background. "Nice guy," Jerry continued. "Look, there's a little change of plans. Seems that the doctors don't think Mrs. Hertz will survive the day. Manion has her power of attorney, and it's written in such a way that he can do the deal for her. So, we're nailing everything down here." He paused again. "It turns out, Ed, you're going to be a very wealthy man."

Ed felt a flare of curiosity, but fatigue smothered it. "At the moment, I couldn't care less." Was that true? He stood and walked out of Grace's hearing. "What if Mara dies before you finish?"

"She won't, that's what I'm calling to tell you. We just talked to the hospice doctor and Manion persuaded her to keep Mrs. Hertz on a respirator until you get there. We'll have the papers ready to fax to you when you're in Vegas. Ask for Dr. Anselmo. She's not real happy about what we're doing, but Manny explained the whole story so you won't have to. She agrees it's murky."

Ed sighed again. "Just don't let anything bad happen to Grace, Jerry.

Make it so she gets everything if Mara dies before I can sign the papers. Hey, they're announcing the flight. I'll call you from Las Vegas."

The lawyer said, "Don't worry. Manion and I are going over to Connie Fuller's fly shop. He wants to buy some Montana trout flies."

"Have a ball," Ed answered, annoyed at the lawyers' vacation mindset. "Just be around when I call from Vegas." He ended the call abruptly and walked back to Grace.

"That was rude," she said.

"What was?"

"Walking away."

"You don't want privacy when you make calls?"

She didn't answer. He said, "One more call before we board." He dialed the Adams County General hospital and asked for Doc Keeley, who picked up surprisingly quickly. Ed told him what Dr. Gramment had said, and asked about Vic.

"Vic's surgery went well," Keeley said. "It's probable he'll retain full use of his hand. The hand doc is good. Did you hear what happened?"

Ben's story last night in the conference room was a blur. "Remind me."

"Apparently after the guy shot Deputy Pelton, Vic grabbed the barrel of the gun head on and the second shot went through his hand. There were some small fractures already, so this messed it up completely, but we're thinking when he pulled up the gun he probably saved either Andi's or Pete Peterson's life."

"Really?"

"Yeah, but Vic's going on about being responsible for getting Andi shot, so I'm starting an antidepressant. He thinks it's an antibiotic." He chuckled.

"Good idea. How's Maggie?"

"Like she's seen a ghost. But I heard her calling her foreman, telling him to hire another cowboy for calving season. She's a strong one."

"You got that right," Ed agreed, and they ended the call.

The gate attendant called zone three, and he looked at his boarding pass. Only then did he realize that Jerry Francis had bought them first class seats. He smiled grimly to himself. *At least we'll be comfortable when*

I tell Grace more about the adoption.

*   *   *

"But she's breathing," Grace whispered, standing just inside the door.

The doctor said, "The machine's breathing for her. If we turn it off, your mom will die in a few minutes."

"If you kill her, you mean." Grace looked obstinate.

Dr. Anselmo, a short, salt-and-pepper haired woman in her fifties, heavy from thirty years of lousy hospital cafeteria food, smiled faintly. Ed noticed that she didn't react to Grace's animosity, but only said, "No, dear, your mom was all but dead when we put her on the ventilator. Her lawyers asked me to keep her alive so you could see her before she goes, and so they could arrange for Dr. Northrup here to adopt you."

Grace frowned. To Anselmo, she said, "You can't, like, save her?"

"No, I'm afraid she came to us too late."

"What's wrong with her?"

Dr. Anselmo looked pointedly at Ed. He said, "Is the cause of death known?"

She shrugged. "Ordinarily, we only talk about that with the next of kin."

Grace looked at her. "I'm the next of kin, right?"

"You're young, sweetheart, and we don't usually..."

"I'm not a *sweetheart*." She glanced nervously at Mara's form, turning away and lowering her voice. "I'm a teenage bitch when I want to be, and nothing you can tell me about my mother would surprise me, because she was a grownup bitch who deserved, like, whatever. So just tell me."

Anselmo said, "I need to talk to your father first."

"He's not my father, but talk to him. Then tell me." Grace moved closer to her mother.

Anselmo stepped outside the room. "From what I heard from your lawyer, you haven't formally adopted Grace yet, so I don't know if I should even be explaining this to you." She shrugged. "But the whole situation is unusual, to say the least. Mrs. Hertz is dying – or is already dead, but for the ventilator – of AIDS."

Ed staggered back against the nurse's desk. "AIDS?"

"We believe it probably came from unprotected sex — there are no signs of intravenous drug use." She pulled a chair across the corridor and sat Ed in it. "Are you all right?"

"I'm stunned. And exhausted, I guess." He rubbed his eyes. "Would AIDS explain her looking so, ah, haggard?" He grimaced. "Never mind, I know the answer."

Doctor Anselmo put a hand on his shoulder. "Your lawyer also told me there was a shooting in your town last night. I'm so sorry. This must be very — "

He couldn't think of a word, and resorted to "Yeah."

She patted his arm. "I believe there is some paperwork to complete?"

Thinking of Andi, he was momentarily confused, but then realized she was talking about the adoption. He nodded, getting to his feet. For a moment, he felt dizzy with fatigue, or perhaps sorrow. "Which reminds me, I have to call the lawyers."

"And then we will terminate the ventilator and she will die."

They went back in. Grace was standing beside her mother's bed, holding Mara's limp cool hand. Ed quietly told her about the AIDS.

Her face paled; she put her mother's hand on the bed. "She can't have that. She didn't do drugs."

"They don't know how she got it, but it's what she has."

She looked at her mother's gaunt face, at the spar of a nose. "Take all the tape off. I want to kiss my mom before she dies."

Ed touched her shoulder. "I'm sorry, Grace, but I've got to deal with the lawyers first." He punched Jerry Francis's number into his phone. As it rang, he stepped outside Mara's room. Grace lifted her mother's hand again.

*   *   *

Manion Phillips, Mara's attorney from Minneapolis, introduced himself on the phone. He said, "We need the adoption agreement signed, Dr. Northrup, before we let her go."

"But she can't sign..." Ed, seated at a conference table in a room next to the nurses' station, rubbed his eyes wearily. Dr. Anselmo brought him a cup of coffee and sat down.

"I have power of attorney for that," Phillips said. "*You* need to sign the adoption agreement so we can finalize the correct will on *her* behalf. You do want to sign, don't you?"

"The correct will? Oh, I remember. And yeah, I want to sign."

"Anyway, we need to keep her alive until we get your signed agreement. Of course, Mr. Francis and I are witnesses to your verbal agreement, so if perchance she dies before, we can attest to your intention."

Two wills, attest to his intention? Ed felt a moment's alarm. "Give the phone back to Jerry, please." He waited a moment. "Jerry, is this legal? What's this business with two wills and you guys 'witnessing my intentions'?"

"Don't worry, Ed. Everything's legal. I'll explain when you get back."

"All right." He rubbed his eyes with his forefinger and thumb. "What do I need to do?"

Jerry said, "We'll fax the signature pages to you – there are two of them – so get us the fax number. You don't need to see the remaining pages at this point. Oh, and you'll need to find a notary in the hospital there."

"I'll call right back." He turned to Dr. Anselmo. "I need the number of the nearest fax machine. And a hospital notary."

Ten minutes later, a hospital staff person knocked on the door, and led Ed to an office. She handed him the fax, one page of instructions and two to be signed, and said, "Our notary, Angie, is on the way." He re-dialed the lawyers. "Jerry, you're sure this a good agreement? For Grace?"

"It's a very good agreement, for *both* of you."

"Would you sign it if you were in my shoes?"

The lawyer waited a long moment. "I don't think it's my place to make your decision, Ed."

"Jerry, you trusted me when Colin died." Jerry's son had been lost in an avalanche on spring break a few years back. Ed had helped him through the grief. Ed lowered his voice. "Now, I'm trusting you about, uh, *my* girl."

Jerry Francis cleared his throat. "In my opinion, this is a good agreement, and I would advise you to sign it."

A young woman knocked and came in, and opened her kit.

"I'll call you back," he said to Jerry. "I think the notary just got here." He raised his eyebrows at the young woman, who nodded.

Ed ended his call, and for a moment he held his breath, then signed the papers. Angie – he read her name badge – recorded and stamped them. Ed collected the papers and walked over to the fax machine, inserted them, and pressed *Send*. The machine beeped, but did not start. He stared at it. Angie said, kindly, "You need to put in the fax number. It should be on the first page you got." It was. He punched it in, embarrassed, then watched the pages being pulled through. *What is this going to mean,* he wondered. When the pages fell out of the machine onto the desk, he called Jerry Francis again. "It's done. Can we let Grace kiss her mom goodbye?"

"Wait," the attorney said. "The fax is just starting." There was a long pause, and voices murmuring at the other end. Then, "Don't do anything there until I call you back. Give us ten minutes."

As nervous as he was weary, he returned to Mara's room, and they waited. Grace slumped in a small chair pulled close to the bed, holding her mother's wizened hand. She was silently crying. Ed leaned against the wall, checking his watch every couple of minutes, his own eyes misting as he watched Grace. Five minutes felt like twenty. Ten felt like an hour. After twenty minutes, he tapped Grace lightly on the shoulder.

"Bathroom," he mouthed.

Grace frowned. "Say it out loud."

He forced a smile. "I'm going to the bathroom. Back in a couple of minutes."

Grace's eyes flickered a momentary panic, but she quickly quelled it. "Okay. The lawyers will call your cell phone, right?"

"Right," he said, touching her shoulder again. "Right." Which they did just as he was zipping up. He answered.

"Ed, we're good here. All signed, sealed, and delivered. You're Grace's father now, and Mara's heir. Congratulations."

Pissing and getting pissed on at the same time, he thought, too wrung out to appreciate the joke. He felt only the same weight he'd been feeling, hovering above him, all day. "So we go ahead now? We can let Mara die?"

"You're Grace's father now, Ed. Handle it as you see fit."

The weight came down. He thanked Jerry and hung up, and looked for the longest time into the mirror in the rest room. He saw nothing different.

On his way back to the room, he stopped at the nurses' station and said, "Would you let Dr. Anselmo know we're ready in 403?"

"Ready?"

"To stop Mara Hertz's ventilator."

The nurse's eyebrows lifted. "Oh, yes, of course. I'll send her down."

*   *   *

Ed waited for Dr. Anselmo outside the room, and they went in together. The doctor said, "Grace, your mother's attorney says it's time for us to, uh, let your mom go. Are you ready?"

Grace could not speak. She looked doe-eyed at Ed, who nodded. Grace found her voice. "Will it hurt her?"

Anselmo shook her head. "No, dear, your mother is extremely close to death now and she's only been waiting for our permission to go. It won't hurt her at all. It might take a few minutes, but she'll feel no pain. The body often hangs on after the spirit has left."

"So you'll take off all the tape and stuff, and I can, like, say goodbye?"

"You'll have time, child. I'll get everything ready, and I'll call you in when she's ready."

Grace moved toward the door, her face stern. "Do it." At the door, she turned. "And I'm not a child."

*   *   *

Ten minutes later, Dr. Anselmo emerged. "You can say goodbye now."

Mara lay peacefully, serene, hardly breathing. Grace whispered, "She's so calm."

She approached the bed slowly, as if she might disturb her mother's rest. For a long time, she stood at the side, her right hand softly stroking her mother's pale arm. She studied the gray gaunt face and the sharply hooked nose, the keel of a capsized boat. She tentatively kissed her first two fingers, touched them gingerly to her mother's pale lips, then slowly drew her hand back. She gazed at Mara another moment, and then leaned down slowly and laid her head on Mara's heart, and after a moment's stiffness, relaxed and rested there. Ed looked at Mara's face, almost unrecognizable to him. *So many years*, he thought. *So much pain.*

For a time, Grace lay on her mother's breast, looking up at her face. And then she whispered, "Mommy, I loved you." Mara's shallow breaths slowed, as waves subside when a wind has passed, and then, with Grace's head resting upon her, they stopped. Grace never moved, as still herself as death. Tears wet her cheeks.

Then, after a while that to Ed felt eternal, she raised herself. "My mom's gone," she said.

TWENTY-EIGHT

Sunday, February 19

THE PILOT'S GRUFF voice crackled, startling Ed out of his stupor. They were beginning their descent into Missoula. He ached; every muscle craved sleep, but he'd dozed only fitfully, wasting the free wine and the wide first class seat. Grace had fallen asleep after takeoff and only now stirred herself. She tapped his shoulder. "I decided."

"You decided what?"

"Where I want her buried."

After Mara had died, they'd sat silently in the hospital room, each drifting along a memory-littered shore, leaving her body to the nurses after an hour. In a blur of sorrow and fatigue, they'd sat somewhere on a patio in the warm desert sun and ordered food that neither of them touched, and tried to talk about the decisions facing them, such as where to bury Mara. They had decided nothing. Finally, Grace had turned away. "I can't talk about it anymore. I keep thinking she's going to come back for me."

They'd found the motel, where Jerry'd reserved two rooms, side by side. Grace said, fear in her voice, "Northrup! Don't make me stay alone." Ed cancelled one room, and changed the other to a room with two queen beds. The girl was asleep before he'd even used the bathroom. Tired as he'd been, he'd tossed and turned all night.

Now, the cabin busy with preparations for landing, he looked down at her. "Where do you want her buried?"

"In your cemetery. I want her around me." Her lips quivered, although she quickly pursed them, and he gently put his arm around her. Unresisting, she leaned over the hard console between them. After a moment, she pulled away and simply stared ahead.

Ed thought of the monks of St. Brendan's Monastery, on the mountain beneath the Coliseum. They crafted hand-built caskets. Beautiful objects, almost works of art. He'd take Grace up the mountain to choose one for Mara.

He listened to the sounds of the flight attendant cleaning the galley. They sat quietly for ten minutes or so. Then Grace said, "Northrup?"

"What?"

"How's this going to work?"

"What?"

"You keeping me. Do I call you, like, Dad or something?"

What would the right answer be? "No, I don't think so, unless you want to. I think I'm Northrup and you're Grace. Although, Ed's okay too."

"So what's my last name now?"

"Ellonson, like it's always been." Then he realized he didn't know that for sure. He'd have to ask Jerry.

She was quiet. In a few moments, they felt the rumbling shudder of the landing gear coming down, slowing the plane. Grace tapped him again.

"Yep?"

"Isn't my name Northrup?"

He said, "You know, I'm not really sure. We'll have to check what the adoption papers say. I'll ask the lawyers."

The captain's voice broke in again, crackling with static, telling the flight attendants to secure the cabin for landing. Their attendant came past and motioned to Grace to put her seat upright.

Grace pulled the seat up, then said to him, "Can it be?"

*   *   *

In the taxi, Ed closed his eyes and imagined Andi lying in her bed. He wanted her to be alert, awake, recovering, but when they got to her room, she lay unmoving, unchanged since yesterday. Her pallor and stillness reminded him too much of Mara. Grace must have seen it too, because she gasped and moved behind him. He took her hand, whispering that Andi was just sleeping.

"She looks like my mom did."

"But she's not dying," he whispered. Just then, Dr. Gramment came in.

"Welcome back," she said kindly. "You two have had a real lousy couple of days."

Grace whirled to face her. "Is she all right?"

Gramment nodded. "She had a little setback earlier. Her right lung collapsed – it happens routinely. We re-inflated it easily, and I think it'll be fine."

Grace's eyes widened. Ed squeezed her hand. He turned to the physician. "Should we worry?"

The doctor smiled. "Not at all. She's on a lot of antibiotics and pain meds, so we'll just let her be for the next day or so. I think she'll be well enough to go back down to Jefferson by mid-week, even sooner if all goes well."

"Can we be close to her?" Grace asked.

"Of course. She's sedated, but your being here will be a comfort."

Grace turned back and went to Andi's bedside. Ed moved to the other side, and heard Grace whisper, "I'm staying right here with you, Andi." She shyly cupped Andi's hand in her own. Ed looked at the contrast between her pink flesh and Andi's pallor.

After checking the machine's numbers, and giving the thumbs-up sign to Grace, Dr. Gramment left. Ed gazed steadily at Andi's face, keenly aware that his hand rested on her arm, the first time he'd touched her. After a moment, he looked across at Grace. Was it a lifetime ago that she'd run off into the storm? He watched the girl's gaze falling on Andi's face, saw the same steel in her look that she'd shown with Ardyss. *Where did such a tossed-away girl learn such loyalty?* he wondered.

He wanted things back as they were, and then laughed a little at himself. *There is no back from here.* Hadn't he wanted something to change? Well, something had, all right. His hand still rested on Andi's arm. He didn't move it.

He caught Grace's eye and nodded toward the door. When she shrugged and turned back to Andi, he quietly slipped out and called Vic's room in Jefferson.

Maggie answered. "Vic's doing okay. The hand doctor said he can go home tomorrow. He's supposed to start rehab in a few days. But he's downcast, Ed. He's dark. Blamin' hisself for the deputy 'n' all. He's sayin', even with the IRS deal, he ain't likely to make much of a rancher with a crippled hand."

Wages of sin, Ed thought. He tried to think of something to say, failed. He settled for, "You'll help him through, Maggie." It sounded paltry.

"I'll see to it." She paused, then added, "Well, I guess I'm feelin' guilty myself, 'bout how I treated the deputy. Real guilty."

Ed had no answer for that, either. "You'll have plenty of chances to repair that, Maggie. Andi's going to be all right." They finished the call.

He dialed Ben. The exhaustion in the sheriff's voice matched Ed's. "Good god, I'm thinkin' I'm too old for this job." He cleared his throat. "Tell me about Andi."

Ed filled him in.

"So she's going to be all right?

"What the surgeon says."

"How about the little girl?"

Ed brought him up to date on that as well.

Ben said, "Good. Good. Real good." Ed heard papers rustling. "Well, at this end, turns out that that Stetson asshole was an ex-con, incarcerated in four states for a laundry list from bunco and rackets to assault to grand theft auto and a couple rapes. A real gem. Crane's zipped his lip till his lawyer gets here from Idaho, and he ain't sayin' squat." Ed yawned into the phone.

Ben said, "Go get some sleep."

They hung up. Ed rubbed his eyes and sat in a chair against the wall. He dialed Jim Hamilton.

"Father Hamilton here. How can I help you?"

"Buy me a subscription to 'Drama Quarterly.'"

"Ed. Where are you?"

"St. Pat's. Thanks for staying with Andi overnight."

"No problem. I had to get back to say Mass for the troops." Ed sagged in the chair. Jim was going on, "We had no organist again, Maggie forgot it was Sunday. Poor woman, she felt so guilty when I showed up at the hospital to see Vic. Oh, I dropped in on Ardyss too — they're both looking pretty good, although Vic's depressed, I think. He's blaming himself."

"Yeah, I just talked with Maggie."

"How'd it go in Vegas?"

"Mara died, but Grace was with her."

"Good. Grace handling it? She's an orphan now."

Ed yawned again, then said, "No, she was an orphan *before* Mara died. Now, I'm her... I adopted her yesterday afternoon."

"Wow. Congratulations, buddy."

"I hope." He yawned again.

"Man, you're bushed. Get some sleep, will you?"

He grunted. "Yeah," he said, and hung up. He went back in Andi's room. Grace still held her hand, looking at her steadily, as if her presence could will Andi awake and well. When Ed came in, she said, softly, "Northrup, can I call MJ?"

He handed her his phone, but she looked scornful. "Mine's better."

TWENTY-NINE

Wednesday, February 22

FOUR DAYS LATER, the Missoula morning dawned gentle and almost warm. Ed hadn't run since, when was it, Friday, but each morning he roamed the trails along the Clark Fork River, pondering the changes in his life. Last night, he'd slept well for the first time, although he did not feel caught up. Changes. Adopting Grace was first, of course, but he was discovering new feelings for Andi. Friendship, sure, but something more. Or at least a desire for something more.

Since returning from Vegas, he and Grace had evolved a routine. Mornings, she slept in, while he walked along the river and stopped for coffee at a local shop. Around nine o'clock, he woke her and they went to the hospital for breakfast while the nurses' morning routines occupied Andi. She'd wakened later on Sunday, and was gradually regaining her color. During the day, Grace stayed with Andi, and he spelled her every couple of hours. When he wasn't in Andi's room, he worked the phone with his patients, keeping them steady in his absence.

Andi had been quiet, at times withdrawn. Her smiles, when she smiled, were brief and sad. The breathing tube prevented talking, and she sometimes looked away when Ed talked to her. It had troubled him at first, but no doubt it was normal, considering.

This morning, when they came in, Grace tentatively poked her head around the bed curtain. Andi was awake, and the breathing tube was gone. Grace squealed and rushed to hug her; Andi grunted and waved her away. She croaked, "Ow!" and then lifted the writing pad she'd been using.

She scribbled, *Sore throat, sore ribs, can't talk. Feel a little better. Maybe home today.* She still received oxygen through a nose tube. The plan, she wrote, was to ambulance her to Jefferson Hospital.

Ed touched her arm softly. Her smile was thin; her lips looked sore, chapped.

He said, "You feel *ready* to go home today?"

She made a weak thumbs-up gesture, but she looked away. Ed had asked Dr. Gramment about Andi's distance, which wasn't improving. The doctor had said, "Getting shot takes some starch out of police officers. Not to mention it being only five days since surgery."

She'd gone on, "You're the psychologist, Ed, but in my experience, for police officers, it's not so much getting shot, it's losing control of the situation. Control is paramount. Losing control can sometimes be worse than the wound."

Now, he said to Andi, "You look sad."

Grace said, "Northrup! She's happy to come home."

Andi looked at the girl and made a smile that her eyes did not share. She looked up at Ed, then away.

*   *   *

Two hours later, there was a commotion at the door and the EMTs pushed the gurney into her room. With loud, confident voices they prepared Andi, then counted out the lift firmly: One. Two. Three. They slid her in one smooth motion onto the gurney. Their authoritative voices, their air of competence, seemed to please Andi; her eyes brightened and she grinned. They all went out toward the ER doors, and Ed walked beside her. Just before they loaded her into the ambulance, he surprised them both by leaning down and kissing her cheek. She frowned.

* * *

When the ambulance pulled away – Grace had begged to go with them, but the driver had turned her down – she and Ed returned the rental car to the airport, where Ted was waiting to drive them back to Jeff. Before they got in his car, Ted dropped to one knee, to draw closer to Grace's eye level. "I'm very sorry to hear about your mother, Grace. But I want you to know you'll always be welcome in my restaurant." She thanked him, subdued.

Driving, he and Ed chatted quietly in the front seat, catching up about Andi.

Ed said nothing about his impulsive kiss – or Andi's frown.

From the back seat, Grace said, "I was with her when she died, Mr. Coldry."

Ted nodded and turned partway back to smile sadly at her. "Father Hamilton told me about that, Grace. Was that hard?" He turned back to the highway.

She didn't answer, and in a moment muffled sobs rose from the back seat. Ed extended his arm over the seat and was surprised when she grasped his hand and held it for a few miles, until the sobbing faded. When she let go, he turned and smiled at her, but she was asleep, or at least her eyes were closed. He and Ted continued talking softly. He wanted to talk about the adoption, but not in front of Grace.

After thirty miles, he fell silent. They drove the rest of the way without a word.

The dashboard clock read a quarter past four as Ed drove from the office, where he'd left his truck, to his cabin. Andi was settled, sleeping, and Grace had insisted on staying with her and visiting Ardyss. He needed a nap. At one point on the drive, his eyes drifted closed; he jolted awake at the rumble of the tires on the shoulder. At home, a warm breeze rising from the river brushed his face, so he stood beside the truck, enjoying it. The fields rolling down to the river were patched, snow and open grass. This gentle air smelled of melt, of greening things. He stood beside his truck and savored the view, the ticking of the warm engine, the pale blue twilit sky.

When would Andi breathe delicious air like this again, without coughing, without pain? In a flare of anger, he slapped hard the warm steel of his truck. "Goddamn them!"

Going in the cabin, his mood sour, he picked up the phone and the stutter tone startled him. The week's chaos and emotion had brushed the threats from his mind, and now they flooded back. *Wait. Stetson's dead,* he reminded himself. *The hospital?* His heart pounded. He punched in the numbers roughly.

He heard Magnus Anderssen's clear voice. "Ed, Mack here. I know you've had some rough days, so I just wanted to call and see if there's anything I can do to help. Give me a call, my friend." A pause. "Oh, I've taken care of the Sobstak's hospital bill."

Ed saved the message. He stripped to his skivvies and climbed into bed for a nap. As weary as he was, Magnus's phone call fortified him. *I have good friends.* His eyes closed.

Forty minutes later, he got up, showered quickly, tossed some fresh clothes and his running gear in a bag, and tossed it in the truck. The evening lights of Jefferson twinkled in the middle distance, nestled below the trees astride the river. A few brown roofs were barely visible among the darkening pines. His stomach rumbled, but he was hungrier for this air and this peaceful view.

Damn! It was Wednesday, his day on the corner with Ben. He quickly dialed the Angler. Ted answered.

"Ted, is Ben there?"

"Not yet."

"Look, it's our evening to be on the corner, but I'm exhausted and I want to spend some time with Andi at the hospital. Would you tell him I'd like a rain check. Maybe tomorrow or Friday? Oh, and thanks for bringing us home."

"My pleasure, Edward. And I'll tell Ben. You get some rest." Ed savored a last taste of the breeze and climbed into his truck.

*   *   *

Grace snored lightly in the chair beside Andi's bed, but woke when he came in. For a moment, she looked confused, then her eyes found Andi's sleeping form and she blinked. He smiled at her, and she said, "Potty break." She left the room, and Andi opened her eyes when the door latch clicked; she looked intensely at him. He made the warmest smile he could, but she did not smile back. He came to her side and took her hand, squeezing it lightly. Her return squeeze was weak. She tried a smile, and whispered, "Sore throat. Hard coughing." She pointed to a plastic gizmo, like a large Pyrex measuring jar with a tube off to the side. "Spiro... meter." She wheezed. "You suck air... out... Good for lungs... Makes me cough."

"Good," he whispered back. "The nurses say you have to cough a lot. It helps the healing."

She grimaced.

"Are you in a lot of pain?"

She nodded and whispered, "Meds... help." She gestured toward the IV stand behind her bed. She closed her eyes for a moment.

"You want to sleep?" he asked.

Again she looked intently at him. Shook her head.

He held her hand a while, asking simple questions, did her shoulder hurt, was the sling too tight, was the little blue ball going higher in the plastic tube, did she want some water? After a few nods and shakes of her head, she pulled her hand free and lifted a finger to her lips.

"Stop talking?" he asked.

She shook her head and whispered, "Tell me... about Grace." They had not had an opportunity to talk about Las Vegas.

He told her about the frantic flight and Mara's death. Andi's eyes teared as Ed described Grace's last moments with her mother. He stopped talking, caught in his own emotion, but her impatient look and whispered "Go on" spurred him. He told her about the phone calls with Jerry Francis and the other attorney, and she smiled.

"I want us to share this," he said, tentatively. Meaning what, exactly? He wasn't sure.

She only closed her eyes. A tear came down. He wiped it away. She shook her head slowly.

"What?" he asked, then rephrased it to make it easier for her. "You didn't want me to wipe that tear?" Shook her head.

He was afraid to ask. "You aren't sure about... about helping me with Grace?" She nodded, barely, as if unsure of the answer herself.

His heart was pounding. "Did I hurt you by something I said?" There weren't many straws for grasping.

She shook her head again.

"You don't want us here? Andi. Tell me. What's wrong?"

She looked away from him for a moment, then turned back, giving him the intense look he'd seen before. She placed her hand on her throat as if it would ease the soreness, and whispered, "I'm not... who you... thought... anymore." *Of course she's not,* he thought quickly. *How could she be?* Dr. Grammment had said losing control damaged cops, changed them. *That's what it is, she's misinterpreting it.*

He said, "I like you, Andi. I liked you before, and I like you still." She shook her head. "Need time," she whispered.

Ed gripped the sidebars of the bed, steadying himself. Time. Of all the things Ed knew he had, time was easiest. "All the time you need," he said, forcing a smile. He wanted not to ask the next question – which told him a great deal – but felt around its edges for a moment, then asked it in a soft voice. "Do you want me to stay away?"

Her eyes flared and she shook her head firmly. "Stop!" she whispered fiercely, which caused her to cough. When she recovered, she whispered, "I said... *time...* not *go away.*" He relaxed.

She grabbed the pad and pencil from the table straddling the bed. She scribbled furiously, underlined something, and thrust the paper at him.

I'm shot and I'm changed but I know what I need and <u>*I don't hint*</u>.

For a moment he just looked at the paper, letting it settle in. Thought, *And I'm starting to know what I need too.* He nodded. "Got it." Just then, Grace returned from the bathroom.

*   *   *

While Andi and Grace dozed, Ed went outside. Unconsciously, he had folded his arms, embracing himself. He didn't feel as weary as he had earlier. The nap had helped.

In the evening darkness, the air remained unseasonably warm and sweet, carrying the odors of wet earth and winter-buried leaves and thawing things. Inexplicably, Ed found himself wanting nothing more than to enjoy this soft darkness. It wasn't spring yet; hard weather would return, but this gentle air called for a steak on the grill and a glass of wine, for star-gazing and quiet talk. He decided to go say good-night to Andi, buy some charcoal and the steaks and something to have with them, and take his... *daughter* up to his cabin for a peaceful evening.

He ought to be calling patients, setting up schedules, getting back into the routine. But instead, Ed simply wanted to do what he wanted to do. He went back inside and gathered Grace and whispered, "Let's get this family thing going."

*   *   *

It was even warmer up on the ridge than it had been in town. While Grace threw two potatoes in the oven and started a salad – she'd barked at him when he'd tried to take over, "I can, like, do shit in the kitchen, Northrup! Mara left me alone enough!" – Ed pulled his old grill from the shed and fired the charcoal. In the kitchen, Grace, drinking a can of Mountain Dew at the table, watched him pat the steaks dry and coat them with olive oil. He reached for the salt.

"My mom says never put the salt on until they're done."

Ed noticed the present tense. So did Grace. She said, in a smaller voice, "Or, she *said*."

Ed nodded and put the salt down. "Pepper all right?"

"I guess."

Grace watched him grind pepper onto the meat. "How do *you* know how to cook?"

He shrugged. "You pick things up, living alone. And Ted's taught me a lot."

"He's gay, isn't he?"

"And he's a good chef."

"They all are." She lifted her Mountain Dew, then put it down. "Are you gay?"

He laughed, but realized she had no experience of him with women. He shook his head. "Nope." He only hesitated a moment before admitting, "In fact, I think I might have some feelings for Andi."

"What? Like what kind of feelings?"

He raised his eyebrows. "I'm not sure, I guess. I like her a lot. And since she got shot, I wonder if maybe there's more."

"Omigod, Northrup! So if you and Andi – " She stopped, excited.

"Don't go there. I could just be feeling relief that she didn't die."

Grace looked intently at him. "Northrup, if you and Andi get together, would she be... like, my mother?"

Don't let this go any further. He raised his hand. "Let's not fantasize about something that isn't even happening yet. I think Andi and I can be good friends – and we made a hell of a search-and rescue team, didn't we?"

He'd meant to lighten things up, but her excitement shaded into a sudden look of fear. She whispered, "I was really *scared*, Northrup. I thought you guys wouldn't care if I disappeared."

He started to tell her how much he had begun to care about her, but she went on.

"I thought I was going to die." She visibly trembled, and Ed came around the table and put his arms around her. He noticed that humming sound rising very faintly in his chest. When she calmed, he stepped away. She sniffled once. "Anyway, are you going to, like, *cook* those steaks?" she said.

*　　*　　*

The T-bones were perfect, just what they needed after the horrible last few days. The strange warm darkness, the soft night air, the charcoal glowing red in the grill in front of the porch – normal, all of it. After dinner, they sat talking on the front steps. Andi's name seasoned their conversation, and they talked as if everything would be better soon, that this gentle evening was the beginning of... what?

Ed sipped his wine. "Well, it's a new road now, Grace. You and me."

"And maybe Andi."

"Don't go there, Gracie. It'll just hurt if nothing happens." He winced, thinking back to how she hated that name when Mara used it. And of his own too-cautious nature.

But Grace said nothing. In a moment, she went inside and he heard the clatter of dishes. She called out the door, "Where's your detergent?"

Ed smiled. "Forget the dishes, Grace. Come out and enjoy this evening."

"My mom always says, uh, said, don't let the dishes sit overnight, 'cause of, like, bacteria." He remembered that about Mara. He told her where the dish soap hid and, after a few minutes, went in and grabbed a dish towel.

While they'd finished, he dragged a couple of comfortable chairs out onto the porch. Only a week ago, the yard billowed in snow; tonight, although the air was cooling, it was still warm enough to bundle under blankets outside. Ah, Montana. Probably by tomorrow, there'd be another foot of snow. He poured himself a glass of Pinot Noir and a quarter inch in a glass for Grace.

After she finished cleaning the kitchen, she joined him outside. "Northrup, did you find out – " but stopped when he handed her the dash of wine. She took it, surprised. "This for me?"

"This is a special occasion," he said.

"Which one?"

"The first time we've had a nice dinner since..." He couldn't finish. Mara's death? Andi's shooting?

She drank the wine in a swallow.

"What were you asking me?" he asked.

"If you found about about my last name."

"Oh, damn," he muttered.

"Doctor Northrup, your language," she mocked. "Does *damn* mean you, like, forgot?"

His nod was dimly visible in the light from inside. "Yeah. I'll call Jerry first thing tomorrow."

After a moment, she said, "Can I have some more wine? Mine's gone."

He chuckled, passing on the chance to point out who made it gone. "Nope. You can have what I give you, and only on special occasions, till you're eighteen."

"We drink more than that in the girls' bathroom at school. Every noon."

Ed looked at her sharply. "Really?"

He could see her shrug in the darkness. "Well, not really. But geez, Northrup! My mom let me drink wine. She said I needed to learn."

"And?"

Grace snorted. "*And* she's dead and you're in charge of me. I get it." Her voice contained a tiny sob.

"I'm sorry, Grace."

She was quiet for a long time, as they sat looking into the night. Then she said, "So where do I sleep?"

It caught him by surprise. "Well, until we can get my spare... I mean, your bedroom fixed up, we'll stay at Andi's. Your stuff is already there. She won't mind."

Grace said nothing.

"Are you uncomfortable with that?"

"MJ thinks I'm afraid of you. He said I can stay at his ranch until Andi comes home."

An unreasonable anger gripped him and he had to clamp his jaw while he sorted himself out. Who was he angry with? With Grace? MJ? Finally, he said, "Are you?"

"Am I what?"

"Afraid of me?"

He felt rather than saw her warm hand groping along his wrist, seeking his hand. He clasped it gently.

"No," she said, quietly.

He took a moment to clear his throat, then said, "That's good, honey."

She held his hand a moment longer, and then went down to the grill. The glow of dying coals touched her just enough to limn her against the night. "The coals are still warm," she said.

While he dumped the ashes in a snowbank and put the grill back in the shed, Grace rinsed the glasses – so they wouldn't sit overnight – and together they pulled the chairs inside. Driving back down to Andi's house, Ed was curious.

"You didn't react when I called you *honey*."

"You did?" She was silent as he drove. Then, "Don't do it again."

THIRTY

Thursday, February 23

WAKING ON ANDI'S couch, he craned to see the microwave clock in the kitchen. It looked like five-thirty. Ed got up and began donning his running gear, then stopped. Grace would probably sleep, but he didn't want to chance her waking alone until she felt more secure with him. It was the first morning of their life in Jefferson. He could run later. *Fat chance,* he thought. It was going to be a very busy day.

After his shower, he got on Andi's bathroom scale. *Nah, that's wrong.* Twenty-two pounds gone since he'd last weighed himself? Sure, the horrible week had melted some of his waist, and he *had* been running longer distances, and maybe his morning cereal and toast regime was working. But *twenty-two pounds?*

Then again, maybe he'd be ready when Andi came home. Twenty-two pounds!

Then he wondered, *Ready?* For what?

He carried a cup of coffee onto the front porch. The sky was still dark, in fact, darker than he would have expected at five-thirty. The stars were still sharp; the unseasonably warm air had hung on overnight.

Sitting on the steps, he composed the day's to-do list.

After twenty minutes, he went in for another cup of coffee, and squinted at the clock: Six-something? Back on the porch, he sat quietly, watching the stars over the mountains. The porch looked south, facing the Coliseum at the valley's end. He ran through his list again, trying to remember all the things he had to do.

I've gotta get Grace to school! Shit! He jumped up, and hit the light on his watch. In the dark, he had to squint: It looked like *six-fifteen.* He relaxed; she could have another half-hour of sack time. He stepped off the porch.

The darkness of the sky and the stars' glitter seemed oddly sharp for six-fifteen. How swiftly, how wholly unexpectedly his life had changed. His December despair had lifted. His shoulders, if not his belly, bore *more* weight now, not less as he'd hoped – but, he had to admit, it thrilled him. Last night, when Grace had taken his hand, he'd felt a fullness in his chest that surprised him even more than his feelings for Andi. He stood at the edge of the yard for twenty minutes, soaking in the sweet air, and then went inside. He needed to talk with Jim about it all, but first he needed to get Grace to school.

When he woke her, she swore at him but he persisted, and a few minutes later she was sullenly eating the toast and eggs he set in front of her. He offered her a cup of coffee, which she slurped wordlessly. When she walked sleepily to the kitchen sink, he said, "I'll do the dishes, Grace. I won't let 'em sit. Go get ready for school."

She muttered something as she stumbled toward her room.

And then she screamed, "Northrup, you *bastard!*"

"*What?*"

"It's only ten minutes to six! You got me up an hour early!"

He'd misread Andi's kitchen clock; now, lights on, it read five-fifty. *That explains the extra-dark sky.* He sagged against the kitchen sink. *Great start on parenthood,* he thought. "I'm sorry, Grace. Go back to bed."

"You owe me one, Northrup."

That I do, he thought. *That I do.*

*　　*　　*

Grace had fallen into bed right after dinner. For both of them, the day had been exhausting. Ed's false alarm in the morning left them behind the fatigue curve and neither had caught up. During their evening visit in Andi's hospital room – Ed's third of the crowded day – their yawning had annoyed her. She'd whispered, her throat still husky and raw, "God! Go home... Sleep!"

During his earlier visits, she'd been distant, or perhaps preoccupied, but he'd repeated his mantra: Getting shot, having surgery, and working on sixty percent of your lung was enough to preoccupy anybody. On another impulse, he'd bent to kiss her goodnight, but she'd turned away. He reminded himself of her fierce "No!" when he'd suggested, yesterday, that he stay away.

On their way out, they'd stopped to say good night to Ardyss, who was fairly bubbling.

"I'm going home at the end of the week! Doc Keeley thinks this thing is almost over." She stretched out her scrawny arms toward Grace, her fingers wiggling, drawing her close. "We'll be back together again, won't we, darling?"

As Grace moved into her embrace, she looked questioningly at Ed. Ardyss didn't know about the adoption.

Ed said, "We'll talk about that tomorrow, Ardy. Grace and I are dead on our feet. But that's great news." He'd have to figure out something about Ardyss; Mara's thousand dollars would only pay two month's rent.

Grace had given Ardyss a gentle kiss on the forehead and whispered something Ed couldn't hear, then slipped out of the old woman's arms. When they'd gotten back to Andi's, she'd done homework while he cooked spaghetti; after dinner, she'd gone straight to bed. A little later, Ed had pulled the blanket over her, clothes and all. As tired as he was, his mind was restless, turning over all that had happened during the day.

He pulled a chair out onto the porch and fetched a glass of wine. Andi's coolness had begun to bother him, although he knew he shouldn't let it. She was still on morphine for the shoulder pain. As Dr. Gramment had said, it would take time for her to get past this. Still, her distance unsettled him. He told himself to get over it.

He went in for his jacket and peeked in on Grace, curled under the blanket, breathing quietly. He softly touched the hand she'd placed in his last evening, then closed her bedroom door.

A soft halo of fog was gathering around the yard light. Ed closed his eyes and laid his head back against the chair, cataloging the day. After a moment, he walked out into the yard, then up the drive into the darkness, thinking of Vic and Maggie.

*   *   *

He'd found time to drop in at the CW Ranch. Maggie had directed him across the yard to Victor's shop.

When he had knocked on the shop door, Vic had yelled, "It ain't locked."

Vic was closing a magazine on the high workbench opposite the door; with his good hand he covered the magazine with an oil-dark cloth. He turned to face Ed, leaning back against the bench. His right arm was in a sling, the hand thickly bandaged.

Ed nodded toward it. "How's the hand?"

"Worthless as a geezer's dick," Vic said, unsmiling.

"When's rehab start?"

Vic gave a disgusted look before answering. "It don't. I suppose if we had any money for rehab, they'd have me squeezin' a goddamn tennis ball till the hand's strong enough to jack off with." Ed could almost taste Vic's bitterness.

Maggie opened the door with her foot, carrying a tray with three cups of coffee and some cookies.

"We havin' us a afternoon tea party, woman?" Vic growled, displeased.

Maggie looked at him levelly. "Nope, this here's coffee, and I believe I just heard a self-pity party."

Ed laughed, but Vic glared. "Ain't *you* quick with the come-back," he grunted.

Maggie patted him on the arm, which caused him to spill his coffee cup. As she reached for the rag to wipe it up, the magazine came uncovered. It was a recent issue of *United Farm Realty*. Maggie looked from it to Vic. "Why you lookin' at real estate listings, Victor?" Her voice was steel.

Vic shuffled, and not only with his feet. "Aw, come on, Maggie, jus' getting' a fix on property values. Ain't nothin' wrong with a fella – "

Maggie cut him off. "What are you up to?"

"I ain't up to no goddamn thing, Maggie. Ed, tell her."

"Tell her what?"

Vic sagged back against the workbench, grimacing. "Well, hell. Maggie, we ain't goin' to make it, not with me all busted up like this. How'm I gonna work this goddamn ranch with one good hand."

"The surgeon thought you'd get your hand back..."

"Yeah, he *thought*. Anybody can *think*. Thinkin' don't bring back the bones and sinews and goddamn muscles."

Ed didn't buy Vic's victim-stance. "Could you run this place if you had enough help?"

Vic walked slowly across the shop to the oak gun closet. He leaned against it and folded his arms, looking at Ed. "You ever been on a horse on a hot July afternoon, ridin' fence, half-baked to death but the other half jus' lovin' that high blue sky and the sweet grass smell? You ever follow a rigged line from your kitchen door to your calving barn in a March blizzard to help a cow drop her calf? And lovin' the feelin' of makin' it through the goddamn snow to help with new life?"

Ed shook his head. "Nope, never. But tell me this: How many hands do you need to ride a horse or follow a rigged line in a snowstorm?"

Vic stood up straight, his face reddening. "Goddamn it, one of course! But when I find a busted fence line, and I will, every time, or when I gotta reach two arms up a cow's vagina to pull out a breeched calf, and I goddamn will, you can bet your Midwest ass I'll need two hands!" He turned suddenly as if to say something to Maggie back at the bench, then swung back to face Ed. "And that's why I'm lookin' at the goddamn *relaty* listings!"

"So I'll ask you again. If you had the cowboys to fix your fenceline or to pull your calf, and if you still rode the horse to find the broken lines and still followed the rigged line to share in the birthing – if you can work alongside good help, could you run this... *goddamn* ranch?" He felt entirely unsparing. It was unfair, but his anger over Andi's shooting, due so much to Vic's action, had found its target.

Vic grunted. "If. If. If. Sure. But there ain't no money to hire any cowboys, so all your questions ain't nothin' but a calf's fart."

"You say, 'sure,' You *could* do it. You *could* run the ranch?"

Vic stiffened and looked hard at Ed. He spoke very slowly. "Doc, we ain't got no money for another cowboy. Why're you fuckin' with me?"

Maggie snapped, "Victor! Language!"

"He's workin' my head, Maggie. This whole line is bullshit. I ain't playin' along. Besides," he jerked his wounded hand up, "if this asshole hadn't talked me into talkin' to Ben Stewart, none of this crap woulda happened!"

At that, Ed let go. "Vic, that's bigger bullshit than the bullshit about your hand being the problem. You went into that motel room as a free citizen, right after you told Maggie and me you wanted to, and you got shot by a guy named Stetson. So don't dump your guilt on me." He roped in his anger before he went too far.

"Guilt? What guilt?" Vic asked.

Ed had considered what to say. *The hell with it.* "You're blaming yourself for the fact that Andi Pelton got shot. Which is elephant shit."

Vic's face crumbled, though his eyes were dry. "Well, goddamn it, I did. Stetson figured out I was wearin' that microphone by how I was runnin' off at the mouth. If I'd kept my trap shut, none of this woulda happened."

Ed wanted to agree, wanted to pin his anger about Andi on Vic, but that wasn't fair, either. Vic didn't shoot anyone, or cause anyone to shoot. "More bullshit, Vic. Doc and Ben Stewart think you probably saved Andi's life." He gestured toward the wounded hand. Vic's eyes watered. "They do?"

Ed nodded.

Vic brushed his eyes clear. "Knowin' that'll go a long way, Ed. A long way."

*   *   *

He shivered, cold now, standing in the damp with an empty wine glass in one hand. He set the glass on the wet gravel and zipped up the jacket. Something seemed to be loosening inside him. He wandered a few steps farther toward the road.

Suddenly, Grace's scream rang through the fog. "Northrup! Where *are* you?!"

He dashed back to the porch. Grace, arms wrapped round herself like a farm wife, stood in the doorway, peering out into the yard. When he came into the light, she screamed again, "Where *were* you?! You left me!"

*   *   *

After apologies and calm words and her crying again in his arms, she'd gone back to bed. He looked for his wine glass, then remembered setting it down on the driveway. He should get it. In the morning. He'd stay here with Grace now. He filled a new glass and sat for a while on the couch, watching the fog thickening outside, the yard light haloed deeply now.

After a while, he readied himself for bed, still restless despite the wine and the late hour. He stretched out on the couch, but sleep didn't come. After a half hour, he went into Andi's room and lay on her bed, smelling her scent on the pillow.

It was nearly midnight, but he was wide awake. Andi's fragrance mingled with the memory of her soft skin where he'd touched her arm, her cheek where he'd kissed her good night. He imagined her sleeping here. Suddenly uncomfortable, he felt intrusive and presumptuous. He returned to the couch.

Was this restlessness about Andi? The nearness of her room, her bed? No, he'd been unsettled all evening. Wait. He'd been unsettled since the meeting with Jerry.

*   *   *

When Anne had ushered him into the lawyer's office, and Jerry had offered him coffee, he'd said, "Coffee? You have anything else on offer?" He was thinking of a Diet Coke.

The lawyer chuckled. "Ed, you are now one of my wealthiest clients. Name your drink."

Momentarily shaken by that, Ed changed his mind. "How about a good Scotch, neat." He'd seen his last patient for the day. "And then tell me about this will."

Jerry poured two fingers of Scotch into glasses, then added ice to one. He kept the iced glass and handed the other to Ed. "Well, you're a rich man."

"I believe your phrase was 'one of your wealthiest clients.'"

The lawyer nodded. Ed asked, "As wealthy as, say, Magnus Anderssen?"

Jerry laughed. "You know I can't divulge that, so let's amend it to reflect that I now have two clients who play in a ball park no one else in the valley can even buy tickets to."

"Huh." He sipped the Scotch. "Details?" Ed suddenly felt nervous.

"I presented the financials to Leese MacArdell while you were in Missoula, all names redacted, of course. I told her it was for a client outside the valley – you *were* outside, at that moment – and she worked on it nearly the whole day. She estimates the estate's net worth, after expenses, at something over five million dollars. Give or take."

Stunned, Ed muttered, "Give or take." For a moment, he found no words. Then, he whispered, "It's Grace's."

Jerry shook his head. "No, it's yours. You can set up a trust for her, and I'd recommend that, but the will is quite explicit."

He sat in the chair, slowly swirling the Scotch in his glass. "How did Mara get that rich? She didn't have anything like that when we broke up."

Jerry shrugged. "She was divorced, what, five or six times? Manny said she married wealth and took it when she left."

"Huh." After a moment, he said, "I've heard the same thing, but Jesus! Five million."

"Give or take."

He took another sip, slowly shaking his head. Suddenly he knew how Ardyss could stay in the valley. And how Vic could hire the cowboys he needed. Then, he remembered Grace's name and asked Jerry whether it could be changed.

"Sure," he said. "All it takes is paperwork and a court appearance and she'll be Grace Northrup. Not a problem."

Ed shook his head again. "The problem is figuring out what having so much money means." He left the office feeling unsettled. His picture of himself had never included wealth.

*   *   *

Ed drowsed, then again snapped awake: He'd forgotten to check the voice mail. The only message was from Ben, whose growl sounded as weary as Ed felt. "Hope you're gettin' more sleep than I am. How about on the corner tomorrow. Five-thirty? See you then."

Ed smiled. Good friends all around. He quieted, then dozed off.

THIRTY-ONE

Friday, February 24, the next afternoon

ED SAGGED ONTO the corner stool beside Ben, grateful for the break after last night's meager rest and the long day of therapy sessions. As Ted poured his beer, the bartender nodded toward a new row of gleaming draft handles.

"Take a look, Edward." He was beaming. "Three new beers coming in next week, all from the Bitterroot Brewery in Hamilton."

"That's where you get that Single Hop IPA, isn't it, Ted?" His voice came out tired and flat.

Ted's face instantly fell, and he said, "I'm sorry, Edward. I forget that my good fortune doesn't ease *your* troubles. How are Andrea and Grace?"

Ben broke in. "Andi's doin' pretty good. I just saw her. Doc says she maybe goes home middle of next week, if she keeps suckin' on that breathing gadget."

"When did she find that out?" The news upset Ed. "I just visited her before coming over here, and she didn't say a word." Ted cocked an eyebrow at his tone.

Ben also looked startled. "Oh, she don't know yet. Doc told me on his way out. I reckon he don't want to rock her boat till he's sure she's steady."

Ed tried to cover his reaction. "Sorry, guys. Guess I've just got a small case of the after-action blues."

Ben snorted. "After-action blues, eh? Me, I'm about as messed up as I've ever been. Even Marlene's bein' nice to me."

Ted tapped lightly on the bar and moved discreetly away. They looked his way. Ben put a five spot on the bar. "Buy yourself a beer, Ted, and bring it over." Ben had never done that before. Changes all around.

Ted poured himself a pint and leaned back against the new draft handles, folding his arms. "So Andrea'll be all right?"

Ben and Ed each waited for the other to say something. Ben spoke first.

"Naw. A shot cop's a messed-up cop."

"You're worried about losing an employee? That sucks."

Ben stared over Ted's head at the back bar. "You know better than that." A long silence ensued.

Ed broke it. "I'm sorry, Ben. The shooting has me tied in knots." He didn't add that Andi's coolness and distance did too.

Ben stirred himself at last and turned partway to glance at Ed. "When you came in, I was telling Ted here, I talked to Andi a little while ago. She believes she blew the entry and figures we're all thinkin' she's just a woman, she don't carry her weight, that sorta bullpucky. Most cops get muddled up when somethin' goes down on their watch, but she's got it all bunched up with the gender stuff." He swallowed some beer. "I'll tell you, Ed, she handled that entry by the book. If Stetson – by the way, his name's Michael Stewart, how's that for twistin' your shorts? Anyway, if Stetson don't get trigger happy, it's clean and by the book. We got Crane and the other two goofs in the room. As it is, it ain't turned out real good for Andi and Victor, but this is a huge feather in her cap."

Unexpectedly, Ed's eyes moistened, embarrassing him, and his throat felt too full to speak. He coughed a little. "I'm starting to think you might be getting your way, Ben."

"Meanin'?"

"My feelings for Andi have surprised me. She means more to me than I think I'd let myself know."

Ben sighed, looked away. Ed was puzzled, having expected Ben to be pleased. Ted said, "The Sheriff also talked about you with Andi, I would guess. Am I correct, Benjamin?"

Ed frowned. "How the hell do you *know* these things?"

Ted looked around mock-conspiratorially and stage-whispered like he had when telling Ed Leese wanted his body, "Don't tell, but gay folk have a *sense*, you know. We can *read* people. It's so fun. Ben's like a daddy to Andi and he just has to check out what she feels about you." He paused. "Besides, he just told me."

Ben just stared at Ted. Ed recalled Ben's confession about the daughter he'd never had. Ben gave a fake growl. "Screw you, Ted."

"As I endlessly remind you, Benjamin," Ted said lightly, walking down to pour them two more, "my heart belongs to Edward. After Lane, naturally."

"Or unnaturally," Ben said, and they all chuckled.

Ed nudged him. "So, what'd you two talk about?"

Ben sent an appeal to Ted, who threw up his hands. "Why is it you heteros leave all the hard stuff for us gay folk to say?"

Ben said, "Because you can *read* people."

Ed said, "What hard stuff?"

Ted sighed. "Very well. Benjamin wants to tell you that you better hurry and do something about those feelings of yours." He looked daggers at Ben.

Ed turned to Ben. "Meaning?"

As he shifted on his stool to look at him, Ben's face reddened. "She's thinkin' about goin' back to Chicago." He gave Ed a quick grimace, wrinkling his eyes as if to ask, *You able to handle that?* Then he said, "I gotta go melt some ice."

Ed felt empty, hollowed. What would this mean to Grace? What would it mean to him? He could feel his face redden.

After a few moments, Ted said, "Edward, listen to me." He mock-slapped Ed's cheek with two fingers, and Ed looked up at him. "Andrea will only go to Chicago if you allow it."

He shook his head. "Not my call. We're friends. I don't have any power over her."

Ben returned from the men's room. "What's that about power?"

Ed repeated, "Ted says Andi won't go if I don't allow it. I don't have that power."

Ben sat down and stared at the back bar. "If she asked you for something, you'd do it. Even something hard."

It was true. Since that night in the blizzard, searching for Grace.

Ben kept his eyes forward. "You got feelin's for Andi. We've all seen it since the shooting. And she cares about you too. That's power, buddy."

"Not if she wants to go back to Chicago."

"Uh-uh," Ben said. He spoke solemnly to the back bar, pipelining his words into Ed's heart. "She whispered to me that her only reason to stay in the valley is you and Grace."

*   *   *

Later, when he and Grace visited Andi, he'd watched every facial gesture, seeking confirmation of what Ben had said, but she just looked tired and sore. She kept working the little gadget, lifting the blue ball. Around eight o'clock, having annoyed her with their yawning, he and Grace went home. Feeling half-buried in quicksand, Ed said goodnight to Grace.

"Don't wake me up early. You still owe me one," Grace said on the way to her room.

"Yes, I do. And no, I won't."

"Northrup, I need my own alarm," Grace called from her room.

"Use your phone."

"I do. I want a real clock."

"Right," he answered. "Tomorrow."

*   *   *

After Grace had gone to bed, Ed sat on the front steps. He felt a change in the air. The breeze gusted occasionally, ringing Andi's wind-bell. Wrapped in a heavy blanket, he wasn't cold yet. People were predicting snow, maybe another storm tomorrow night, and the turmoil in the air promised it. The gusts felt moist.

He was shaken by Ben's news. What Ted and Ben advised – telling Andi to stay – went against every instinct. He stood up suddenly, angry with himself. *Am I going to be passive about this, too?* A gust chimed the wind-bell.

He'd always avoided direct confrontations. *Like my old man,* he realized. Weak. Afraid to fight for what he wanted. *No, be fair.* Not weak, just too cautious. A sound came behind him, the door opening. "Why are you sitting out here?" Grace asked, sleepily. Once again, she'd folded her arms against the cold, like a farm wife.

"I'm thinking."

"About me?"

Ed looked back at her and smiled. The narcissism of the insecure. "No, about Andi. I heard she's thinking of going back to Chicago and-"

Grace's hands jerked up to her cheeks and she let out a long "Noooo." He jumped up and took her inside. He sat her on the couch and went back and shut the door against the wind and joined her.

What to say? Shouldn't he shelter Grace, rather than tell her about another abandonment? *Or does* shelter *mean cowardice,* he wondered. Grace didn't need that sort of shelter. This girl, deposited so roughly in his care, had lost her mother, lost her old life, but she was tough. He pictured her loyalty to Ardyss in the hospital. She deserved the truth.

"Ben thinks Andi will stay if I tell her to."

"Then tell her! Jesus! What's your problem, Northrup? I *need* her!"

"Ben also says that she mentioned you, too. The only reason she'll stay is you and me."

"Then I'll tell her too. We gotta fight for her!" Again, as was happening so often now that her mother was gone, her eyes welled, and she let him hold her.

After Grace went back to bed, he prepared for sleep too, resolved. The wind continued to bump the windows.

*   *   *

Ed lay on the couch, listening to the wind and thinking about his father's weakness. Something nagged him, but before getting it, he fell asleep. And woke suddenly. From a dream? No. A memory.

*　　*　　*

Summer of 1999, a few months before his father's unexpected death. Ed's in Minneapolis visiting the parents, and he and the old man sit on the patio. His mother is inside, taking a nap after her visit to "the beauty." He's made the old man's gin and tonic and grabbed himself a beer. They sit on the patio watching the battered TV his father brings up onto the patio each summer and back down to his den in winter. His mother avoids both places. On TV, Tom Brokaw is reporting something about President Clinton, whose picture appears on the screen.

"What a fucker," his father mutters.

Surprised – his father has always deferred to his mother's Democratic orthodoxy – Ed asks, "You don't like Clinton?"

"I'm jealous of the prick. Imagine getting a twenty-year-old Jewess to blow you! Thirty years I've had to settle for fifty-year-old whores."

Ed cannot tell if he's more shocked by the word "Jewess" or by his father's crude infidelity. He leaves the patio, going out into the tiny yard, pretending to inspect the roses.

His father calls to him from the patio. "Come back here." When he sits down, the old man says, "I suppose I shocked you. Get over it. Men are men."

Ed says, "You might have taught me that when I was 18, not 43."

His father hands him his glass. "Make me another G-and-T. And don't be shy with the gin."

When Ed brings it back, his father tastes it and sighs. "You're catching on."

"To what?"

The old man gestures with his glass toward the TV. "To what Clinton knows. What men know: Make your drinks strong and fuck 'em when you get the chance."

He says nothing, irritated; the old man continues. "You've always been timid." He lowers his voice, glancing at his wife's bedroom window. "Your mother's a powerful influence on you. You turned to her too much, but of course I couldn't interfere with that. A mother's love, that sort of thing. And that ex-wife of yours. A bitch — though if she would've let me fuck her, she'd've been a ride."

Ed wants to strike him. *"You tried to have sex with Mara?"*

"Tried. She was a bitch about it. Threatened to tell your mother."

Now Ed bolts upright, almost raising his hand. He wants to leave, but his father reaches up his glass, empty again. *"Get me another G-and-T."*

Ed, salvaging some resistance, says, *"Maybe you ought to slow down."*

"I'll slow down when I'm going too fast." He's already slurry. *"Make me the fucking drink."*

Ed goes light on the alcohol, so his father sighs and carries the glass back into the kitchen and slops in more gin. He sits down clumsily. *"You were always a coward, never spoke up."* He's slurring badly. *"If you don't want to make me a real drink, say so, damn it. Don't water the fucker down."* The old man peers intently at the TV, as if he couldn't quite get it in focus, then points at Tom Brokaw. *"Now there's a man's man, if you ask me."*

Ed is seething, but says nothing. Out of the blue, his father says, *"Why'd you quit the seminary?"*

"It wasn't right for me."

"It broke your mother's heart, you know."

"She got over it."

Silence. The old man gulps his drink. *"You shouldn't take that attitude."*

"Because?"

His father glances at the bedroom window and leans closer. Ed smells the alcohol. The old man lowers his voice to a wet whisper, still glancing at the bedroom window. *"Because your mother's the Bitch Queen from Hell. Don't ever cross her."*

Ed absorbs this for a moment. *"So if she's the Bitch Queen, why have you stayed with her and fucked fifty-year-old whores?"*

Tears run down his father's cheeks, and Ed thinks he's ashamed of his weakness.

But then he realizes, No, he's just drunk, feeling sorry for his wasted years with the Bitch Queen.

*   *   *

Alone on Andi's couch, Ed relived the anger, but recoiled from his passivity. The old bastard was right, though. He'd always avoided conflict and power plays, always tried for reconciliation. He'd promised Grace he'd fight for Andi, but he'd never fought for anything before, not really.

Where would he learn, now?

THIRTY-TWO

Saturday, February 25

IT WAS WINDY when they climbed in the truck next morning, scattered snowflakes dancing in the air. As Ed turned onto the highway toward town, Grace said, "Let's go fight for her now, Northrup."

"No, remember? She's got physical therapy and respiratory therapy all morning, and we agreed to finish your shopping this morning. The alarm clock, right?"

Grace folded her arms. He thought she was going to pout, but she only said firmly, "Well, yeah. But we're fighting for her when we see her."

He nodded. "Right," he said, but doubts swirled through him. He thought of his father, who hadn't fought his Bitch Queen. Or lived a real life.

"What?" Grace asked.

"Nothing. Just thinking about our fight."

*   *   *

At the Ace Hardware, they found an alarm clock and a cartful of materials Ed could never have imagined a girl would need – batteries of all sizes, large and small bags in a rainbow of colors, brushes, different brushes, boxes of assorted sizes, and flowered leather cases for her cell phone. When he'd said, "You need *three* cell phone cases?" Grace had sighed, as if he were oblivious to fashion.

Which, pretty much, he was. She merely dropped the cases in the cart.

After checking out, he said, "That about it?"

Grace merely rolled her eyes. As they were leaving, two girls burst in from the cold parking lot.

"Omigod, Grace! We were just talking about you!"

"About me?"

"You never told us you're spending all that time at the hospital with Ardyss Conley. That's so sweet!"

Ed stood back as the three girls chattered, then said, "Grace, how about some introductions?"

"These are, like, my girls. From school." She lifted her eyebrows at the girls. "This is my, uh..." She looked helpless.

Her tallest friend giggled. "We know who he is. Hi, Dr. Northrup. I'm Jen Fortin. This is Dana Harvey." They all shook hands.

Jen said, "Yeah, MJ Anderssen goes, like, 'She visits Ms. Conley whenever she's not in school. She's real devoted.' That's so cool."

Grace blushed. "How does MJ know what I'm doing?"

Jen giggled again. "MJ's dad knows everything that goes on. He pretty much owns the valley."

Dana said, "Grace, come with us to Missoula! My folks are driving and we're going along. There's room in the van."

Grace's eyes lit. "Northrup, can I?" She hesitated, added, "Please?"

He said, "What are you girls going to do in Missoula?" He thought about the coming snow. While they explained about shopping and something about a skateboard park near the college – which Ed translated as "boys" – he took out his phone and called the radio station, asking about the weather report. All clear, he was told; the storm was holding off till tonight. Through the window, he saw that the flurries had stopped. He pocketed his phone. "I suppose it's okay." To Jen, he asked, "When will you be coming back?"

"About seven-thirty. That all right?"

"Sure, that's fine. I'll be at the hospital."

"And then we fight," Grace said fiercely. Jen and Dana looked confused; Grace would fill them in on the trip. And then some.

*   *   *

Ed checked his watch: ten-fifteen – a day to himself! He went to the hospital. Walking down the corridor to Andi's room, he thought about last night's memory of his father. Ironic. A guy chooses things, acts in certain ways, lives his life trying not to become his father, and one day, he realizes he's failed. You're him all over again. Different in lots of ways, but at heart, you're just as afraid to take a stand and just as resentful as he was. That's what brought about the terrible Sunday on the Coliseum. Resentment. *The same resentment that made my father weak, because he wouldn't do anything honest about his Bitch Queen. Just slink off to fifty-year-old whores.* An empty soul, filled with gin-and-tonics.

He stepped into the family lounge to get ahold of this before seeing Andi.

Ed considered his own weakness. Professionally, he'd been honest, sometimes fearless, confronting in his patients what needed to be confronted. Other people he'd helped face up to their own personal *black dogs*, but his own he'd skittered around. He'd barricaded himself against the story about Elizabeth Murphy, about Mara, about the troubles in Minnesota. Lately, maybe thanks to Grace, he'd started to turn that story around. So now, at the first real test of this new story, should he be his father, too afraid to upset the woman he was starting to care about?

He stood up and left the waiting room. He'd tell Andi. He could either upset her and win, or lose her. Time to ditch the old story, write the new one.

But she was sleeping. *Damn.* He left her a note and quietly left, but for the first time, he felt ready to fight. On the way out, he stopped in Ardyss's room for a minute.

She sat on the side of the bed, her feet dangling a foot above the floor.

When she saw him, her face flushed. "Ed, we gotta talk. Loretta Tweedy invited me to come live with her – I guess since Oliver passed the house is too big for her alone. Anyway, I told Loretta I'd come live with her, without thinking. How could I forget Grace? I don't know what I was thinking." She looked up toward the ceiling, suddenly looking cross.

"Tell the truth, Ardyss Conley," she muttered. "Ed, I was thinking selfishly. I was thinking that living with Loretta, I'd get to stay in the valley after Grace leaves."

Ed smiled. "She's not leaving, Ardy. Grace is coming to live with me. You can go live with Loretta."

The old woman's head tilted. She looked bewildered.

He explained about Mara's death and the adoption. "So Grace is mine to bring up. I'm her..." He hesitated. *No weakness.* "I'm her father now." Walls did not fall in.

Ardyss's hands went to her mouth, which formed a silent O. "My word, Ed." She closed her mouth, and then she stood up off the bed and came to him and put her spindly arms around him. "I do believe in all my years I've heard no sweeter words, except maybe the day Price Conley asked me to marry him." Her frail chest heaved against his. "No sweeter words on earth."

They finished their embrace and he helped her back onto the bed. She whispered, "Let me just lie here and let all that sink in. Grace growing up here in the valley, imagine that! I'll see her become a woman." She folded her hands and lay back on the pillows. "You go. I want to savor this."

*   *   *

After eating lunch, thinking about telling Andi to stay, Ed felt a ripple of doubt. He checked his watch. She would be sleeping now. Maybe Ben had some ideas, if he was in on a Saturday. He brushed aside the obvious: *You're avoiding it.* He was, but Ben might help anyway.

When Ed checked in at the department, the old bear looked up from his paperwork. "You got 'er figured out?"

"Well, I'm thinking of just telling her I want her to stay and pushing her on it. But maybe you have a suggestion or two," he said, embarrassed.

Ed pulled up a chair and sat down. Just as Ben cleared his throat to say something, Pete Peterson knocked on the door. "Got a minute, Sheriff?" He saw Ed. "Oh, sorry. Want me to come back?"

"Hell, no. What are you doin' here, Pete? Your furlough ain't up for a week and a half."

"It's about Andi, sir." He paused. "Sir, I heard something from Chicago, and, well, me and the guys don't know whether we oughta tell her we heard it. We need your opinion, sir."

Ed's heart had sped up when Pete said *Chicago*, but he sat quiet.

Ben chuckled. "Pete, you ain't never *sirred* me three times in one breath. What's this thing you learned?"

The deputy looked uncomfortably between Ed and the sheriff.

"Ed's good, Pete. C'mon in and grab that other chair and tell us this Chicago news."

Pete, plainly uncomfortable, dragged a chair next to Ed and sat. "Good to see ya, Ed." He took a deep breath. "Well, sir, I got an old friend in CPD – " He turned to Ed. "That'd be the Chicago Police Department, and I was tellin' him about the entry and what went down. I mentioned it was a girl from – " He looked uncomfortably at Ed. " – a *female* from Chicago who went in first and got shot. Then my friend, he tells me there was a similar situation maybe ten, twelve months ago in Cook County. A female sheriff got shot during an entry. So I say, 'What's her name?' My friend is, like, 'Hell, I got no idea, but I heard she quit the department and moved out west.' And so I say, 'Bill, where out west?' And Bill says, 'Someplace near you. Utah. Idaho. Where cops go.'" Pete scratched his neck with one finger, just below the ear. "So I ask him who to call in Cook County for more info and he gives me a name. I'm talkin' to this guy, a county police lieu, and when I say Andi's name he goes, 'Fuck me, it's Andi!' Seems last spring they ran a motel entry just like ours, and Andi was first in. This lieu, Hansrud's his name, a real nice guy, he says they had a four-man team – "

Again he looked quickly at Ed, who said, "Don't worry about it, Pete."

Pete went on, "So Hansrud says, Andi kicks in the door perfect. Just as it busts open – I guess she's got a hell of a kick, Ben – "

"Back to Hansrud's story," Ben growled.

"Yes, sir. Well, just as the door busts open, somebody takes a shot that nicks her right earlobe, and she takes the shooter down without flinching. Hansrud says it was one of the biggest prostitution busts of the year."

The notch in Andi's ear, the one *a boyfriend bit off.*

Ben asked, "The hooker shot her?"

Pete shook his head. "Nope, it was the pimp's crib. Anyway, Hansrud said everybody figured Andi was good to be promoted to county police sergeant, so when she quit the force and came out here, they were all shocked."

Ben leaned back in his swivel chair, which creaked. "I'll be damned. That girl's got *cojones* to take the lead again!" He shook his head. "And you and the boys want my opinion about what, exactly?"

"Yes, sir. About whether to tell Andi we know about it. Is she well enough?"

Ben turned to Ed. "Your thoughts, Ed?"

His heart was ringing. He collected his thoughts quickly and turned to Pete.

"What do you and the other deputies think of this Chicago story?"

Pete looked puzzled. "Not sure what you mean, Doc."

"Well, what does it tell you guys about Andi?"

"She's got balls of steel." He frowned. "Sorry, sir. Figure of speech."

"Yeah. You and the guys admire her?"

"Absolutely. Getting shot in the ear'd make me happy to sit in the back on an entry, but she pushed to go in first. That's balls, sir." He looked down. "Figure of speech."

Ben looked at Ed. "So bottom line: Should the boys tell her?"

Pete interjected before Ed could answer. "We got us a little schedule. One guy visits her every morning and I go in every lunch hour, and a third guy goes in every evening. I'm on my way there now."

Ed recalled running into various deputies at the hospital, not realizing they'd all been looking in on Andi on a schedule – more good friends. Ben lifted his eyebrows playfully. "And your wife thinks what about that?"

Pete smiled. "Lu sometimes comes with me. She says she's my chaperone, but it's ten minutes, period. And Lu likes Andi."

"Exactly what time do you go in, Pete?" asked Ed.

"One o'clock, give or take a few minutes. It's real important to me."

Every day at one. Ed noticed Pete's reddened, sad eyes. He took an uncalled-for stab in the dark. "You're feeling pretty bad about this, eh?"

Pete blushed. His eyes dropped. "It shoulda been me." He stared at his hands twisting in his lap, and nodded. "I'm taller and wider than her. That asshole's bullet would've hit my vest, or worst case, my arm." His guilt glimmered in the red rims of his sleepless eyes.

Ben said, quietly, "I made that call, Peter. You were exactly the man I needed in second position. You performed professionally and you prevented further bloodshed. You and me and the whole department are sick about what happened to Andi, but the call's on me and there ain't a one of you I ain't proud of."

Pete hauled in a shuddering breath. When he'd controlled himself, he said, "I can't help thinkin' if I'd'a been in first." The big man gulped back a sob, then got himself together. "Sorry," he whispered, roughly wiping his eyes.

Ben said, "Peter, I been breakin' into tears five times a day since this went down. You go on home and have a couple beers and tell your sweet Lu you jus' need to let 'er rip and she'll hold you tight while you cry 'er out. Hear me?" Pete shrugged, struggling for control.

Ben waited. "That was an order, Deputy." His voice, before as gentle as an uncle's, was now the Sheriff's. "One objective of administrative furlough is to give the officer time to cry it out. It's the only way to get past this kinda shit. Ask the doc here." Ed nodded into Pete's questioning glance.

The deputy hoisted himself up. "So, do we tell Andi?" He looked at Ed.

Ed nodded. "Yeah, but it's gotta come from you, Pete. You were there.

She knows you saw what she did. Pride from you will mean a lot."

And then he realized he had a plan. He said to Pete, "Do me a favor? Could you visit her at eight tonight?"

"Sure. Why?"

He told them his plan.

After Pete had gone, Ed smiled. "You handled him perfectly, Ben. But I've got a question."

Ben lifted his brows, inviting it.

"Do you really cry five times a day?"

Ben shrugged. "Figure of speech."

*   *   *

Just back from Missoula, Grace and her girls were chattering in the hospital room. It was seven-thirty, Ed's third visit of the day. Andi had been sleeping at his first visit, and in physical therapy the second, moving her arm. The girls were giggling about something when Ed walked in, and Andi was smiling. The spirometer was on the bed beside her. Grace said, "Ed, it's time." He shook his head.

Andi looked at them curiously, and whispered in her raspy, sore voice, "Time for what?"

Ed thought fast. "Time for Grace and me to talk about something."

Grace started to argue, but Ed took her arm and lifted her from the chair. "Come with me." He winked at Andi, who looked puzzled. Dana and Jen said goodbye, made a flurry of hugs with Grace, and left.

In the corridor, Grace said, "What the fuck, Northrup? You're not wussing out, are you?"

He ignored that and guided her outside the front doors. "I've got a plan," he said. "Tell me what you think about it."

"A plan for what?"

"For telling Andi. We're going to wait – and I mean it, we don't say anything – until ten minutes to eight." He checked his watch. "That's fifteen minutes from now. I'll say I'm going to the men's room, and you'll have five minutes to tell her you want her to stay, then I'm coming back in. Five minutes. When I come in, if you told her, say, 'Well, it's about time!' If you haven't finished, say, 'Well, if it isn't the late Northrup,' I'll know you need more time. Got it?"

He made her repeat the codes. "Then you leave and I'll have five minutes to tell her, and by then, it should be eight o'clock. Deputy Peterson is going to come in then and he'll tell her the other deputies want her to stay."

Grace repeated the codes again, delight in her voice. "This is awesome."

Approaching Andi's room, Ed checked his watch. "All right, showtime in twelve minutes." He squeezed her shoulder, and she paused and looked up at him. "Just don't, like, mess up your part, Northrup," then turned and trotted the rest of the corridor to Andi's room.

*   *   *

At ten to eight, Ed stood up. "Potty break." Andi pointed at the toilet in her room, but he went out anyway. He waited outside Andi's door for five minutes, then knocked softly and stuck his head in.

As he came in, Grace said, distinctly, "Well, it's about time." Andi, whose eyes were red, looked at Grace, then at Ed.

Grace said, again quite distinctly, "Can I go see Ardy?"

"Sure," Ed played it out. Grace left, flashing him a *mission accomplished* look. He crossed the room to Andi's bed. Without having planned it, he instinctively reached out for her hand. She frowned, but let him take it.

"What's going on?" she wheezed a little. Her voice was still raw, but smoother than it had been yesterday.

He took a breath and jumped off the cliff. "The word is you're going back to Chicago. Everybody tells me when cops get shot they feel they've lost control and aren't any good anymore. Well, let me tell you, you're – "

She started to interrupt him, but he leaned in swiftly and touched her sore lips as gently, but as quickly, as he could, smothering her words. Her eyes widened, shocked.

He continued, "You're staying right here in the valley. I want you here. I need you to help me with Grace. No, let me finish," he said, as she started to speak, "I don't know what exactly they are, Andi, but when you got shot, I realized I've got feelings for you. The department's proud of you. I'm proud of you. Grace needs you. She just lost her mother and I'm not going to let her lose you. If you're serious about leaving us, I'll pack Grace up and we'll follow you to Chicago or wherever you go. Just take in what I'm saying. You're part of us and you're staying." He was sweating when he finished.

Just then came a knock on the door. Pete Peterson, a couple minutes early, stuck his head in the door, and his wife, sweet Lu, was behind him, smiling. "Am I interrupting?" Pete asked.

Ed quickly squeezed Andi's hand and said to Pete, "No, come on in." Andi's face darkened as she tilted her head, looking from Ed to Pete and back. She was not smiling. Ed avoided her direct look and gave a *go-ahead* nod to Pete, and without lingering, said, "Back in a few minutes."

*   *   *

When he returned, getting a thumbs-up from Pete and a kiss on the cheek from Lucy, Andi glared at him. Grace came in a few moments later. For a while, she did not acknowledge them. They waited, side by side. Grace leaned a little against Ed.

Finally, in her smoother but still sore voice, she said, "Did you have a focus group to rehearse your lines?" Her words sounded somewhere between annoyed and resigned, but to Ed's ear, there was no tone of pleased.

He plunged in. "True, we planned it. Everybody wanted you to know how we feel."

Andi was silent. Her eyes betrayed nothing – they were hard and unyielding, like steel balls – but there was something else he couldn't decipher, despite all his years of reading people's eyes.

At his side, Grace suddenly sobbed and dashed to the bed and threw her arms around Andi, whose face went slack at the sudden explosion of pain. Grace's words were muffled against Andi's neck, but Andi seemed to make them out. As the pain released its grip, she settled herself and the girl back against the pillows amid the rush of Grace's words. Her eyes softened, and then moistened, and then slow tears tracked down her cheeks, like the wake of a small ship leaving on a journey to some wide new world.

THIRTY-THREE

Sunday, February 26

THE WARM AIR and soft fog had given way overnight, the gentle promise of spring collapsing under the assault of plummeting mercuries and roaring winds in the night, a driving midnight snowstorm that began heavy and wet, then turned dry and stinging cold.

At dawn, flakes still filtered out of the pale-gray sky, the storm's last brush as it departed the valley, leaving six new inches. Last night, Ed had told Grace he thought they were going to win their "fight," – though Andi had refused to talk about it – and had asked if she minded if he went for a run before she got up. She hadn't. The new snow would make the running tough, but as he stepped down from the porch, he felt good. He started jogging slowly down Andi's drive toward the small road out to the highway.

He'd barely gone fifty feet when his foot stumbled against something under the snow. He stopped and kicked the snow – a wine glass shattered, scattered in the snow. The glass from the other night! A wonder his tires had missed it. He picked up the pieces he could find, and left them on the porch. Breaking the glass left him uneasy.

He decided to dog it out to the highway and back, maybe a half-mile. The winds had drifted the snow, and slogging through the drifts wasn't fun. Although he felt strong, by the time he reached the highway, enough was enough. After the trudge back, he found Grace curled on the couch, sipping a cup of coffee. She looked comfortable.

"You all right with me out running?"

She smirked. "I watched you through the window. You weren't running. You looked like an old man."

"I'd like to see *you* out there struggling through the snow, young lady," but when her face fell, he realized he'd hurt her. "Oh, damn, Grace. I'm sorry."

She said, "Whatever," then looked oddly at him. "Why'd you go, did I mind if you, like, went for a run?"

"I don't want you to be scared if I leave you alone."

She looked thoughtful. "If I know where you went, I don't get scared. It's not knowing, like when my mom left me here." But her voice faded at the end, as if she felt she mustn't speak ill of the dead. For a moment she looked terribly sad, and her eyes moistened; she took another sip of coffee. "Shit. This is cold."

She started to get up, but Ed said, "I'll warm it up. I need a cup myself."

When he returned, she was again curled up on the couch, and had pulled one of Andi's quilts over her shoulders. She said, "I've been thinking."

"What about?"

She looked very shy. "Northrup, can I tell you something?"

"Sure."

"I want my mom buried in one of those caskets they make up at that monastery you told me about. She'd like that – she liked beautiful things."

Ed's heart sank. He'd entirely forgotten to follow up about burying Mara in the Jefferson cemetery. She'd probably already been buried somewhere. He said nothing about that to Grace. Instead, he said, "We'll go up to the monastery soon and pick one out."

Later, before his shower, he took his cell phone into the bathroom and quietly left Jerry Francis a message about what he needed.

*   *   *

The last remnants of the storm drifted east and gashes of blue sky were opening in the clouds over the Monastery Range. Bands of light played across the mountainsides, gleaming under the feathering clouds. The fresh snow draped like white flags in the green-black trees. Grace dozed in the passenger seat as they drove to the hospital. Jerry hadn't called back, and Ed dreaded telling her that his absent-mindedness had cost them their chance. Maybe they could exhume her.

*   *   *

Andi was working the Spirometer. The little blue ball was almost three-quarters of the way to the top. When he came in, she let it drop and lay back. "Whew! But I'm getting... it up there," she wheezed. "Doc says when I... consistently get it... to the top every time for a full day... I can go... home." For a moment, she paused to catch her breath. "And I'm walking... ten minutes every hour."

"You're looking better than you did yesterday. So you're coming home soon?"

"Next few days... If all goes well."

"That's fantastic!"

They talked about Ardyss's moving in with Loretta Tweedy. Andi was interested in Ed's plans for Grace.

"We've been staying at your place. Mine's not ready for her yet, although I'm planning the remodel." It had just popped into his head.

Grace's cell phone rang. She listened for a moment, then said, "Northrup, it's Jen. She wants me to come over and watch movies. Is that okay?"

"Sure."

She looked at Andi. "Do you mind?"

Andi shook her head, and Grace blew her a kiss.

*   *   *

After Grace left, Ed immediately said to Andi, "Grace needs you, Andi. She's started getting attached to you and another abandonment, well, you know." Andi closed her eyes.

Ed pushed on. "*I* need you, Andi. I need your advice."

They were interrupted by the lunch delivery. When the young woman left, Andi closed her eyes again.

When she opened them, she looked straight ahead, not at him. "I'm different, Ed." She looked at him. "I get it that you guys... want me to stay." She waited a moment. "But I don't know what *I* want. You've got to give me time."

"Time's not a problem. Place is the problem. Take all the time you need, but you've got to stay here to figure things out. If you end up being sure you want to leave, well, we'll face that then. If you've changed and you don't know what you want, now's not the time to make that big a decision."

She looked annoyed. "Don't tell me what to do. I had a father, I don't need another one." She lifted the plate cover off her meal, and frowned. "This food sucks."

He backed off. "I'm sorry." Then he thought, *New story*, and said, "I'm not your father. I'm the man who's started to care about you."

She closed her eyes again, then opened them and picked up the little breathing machine. Before she started inhaling through it, she looked steadily at Ed and said, "I know you think you care." She began to inhale, but stopped and removed the tube from her mouth. "I was starting to care too before this... and maybe I still do." She coughed a few times. "I just don't know... who I am now."

He started to reply, but she waved him silent. "Just don't argue with me about it any more." She looked at him hard.

"I'm not giving up, Andi."

She frowned. "I need to exercise." She started working the machine. At her first attempt, the ball hit the top.

She smiled around the blow tube.

*   *   *

After her exercise, during which he'd thumbed a magazine, she rested. To Ed's attempts at conversation, she responded with one word answers or grunts, pleading fatigue. But at eleven o'clock, she started to climb out of the bed. "Time for my walk." She rang the nurse's call button, and a few moments later, the nurse came in.

"We ready for another walk?" Andi nodded.

As the nurse helped Andi out of bed, Ed saw pain flicker across her face as she straightened up. She smiled wanly, and they started down the hall, the nurse steadying her with an arm around her waist. Ed walked behind for a few steps, then said, "I can walk with her if you have things to do."

The nurse glanced at him. "That all right with you, Andi?" she asked.

Andi nodded. "Just fine." The nurse let Ed take her place.

They walked in silence up and down the corridor. Andi clung tightly to his arm, and when he looked at her, she smiled, but from the tension in her arm he could feel that her pain was constant.

After ten minutes, she said, "Five more minutes," but her voice sounded strained. They walked a few yards, and she admitted she was tired, and they went back to her room. Ed helped her into bed.

Andi looked up at him. "Just give me time, Ed. But now I need a nap."

*   *   *

After her nap, Andi was scheduled for an afternoon of therapy and rest, so Ed crossed Division Street to St. Bernard's rectory. Jim answered the door.

"Ah, the long lost Dr. Northrup. Come in. My toilet's broken again."

Ed stomped snow off his boots, stepped in, and hung his coat on the correct hook. Hamilton closed the door.

"I fixed that toilet two weeks ago," Ed protested. He wanted to talk about Andi, not fix the toilet.

"You fixed the guts. Now the handle's broken. I can't flush the darn thing."

Ed swallowed his frustration and lifted the tank lid to examine the breakage. He showed Jim how to pull the stopper chain to flush.

"You want me to reach *inside* the toilet to do that? It's, it's *impure.*" But he was laughing.

Ed snorted. "That the best you can come up with?" When Jim just looked pious, Ed went outside and grabbed his smallest vice-grip pliers from the tool box and came in and clamped it onto the handle shaft. "This'll do until I can get a new one."

"Much better," Jim said. "So what's going on in your eventful life, pal?"

As Ed caught the priest up on all that had happened since the night of Andi's shooting, Jim interrupted, "Talk to me while I do some dishes." Ed leaned against the counter and told him about Missoula and Las Vegas.

Jim lowered a pile of plates into the sudsy water. "How're you doing, bud?"

"Where are your dish towels?" Jim pointed to a drawer. "I think I'm getting emotionally involved with Andi Pelton."

"Whoa! *Emotionally involved?*" Jim turned to face him, suds on his hands.

"What's that mean?"

Ed shrugged. "I like her. A lot."

"Good for you. Finally letting yourself go."

"Trouble is, she's talking about leaving the valley."

"Why?"

"Getting shot has really upset her, naturally, and she thinks she's changed. Anyway, I told her I didn't want her to leave."

"Not like you to stand up for yourself."

"Ouch."

"Come on, Ed. You've always been shy about pushing for what you want."

Jim seemed irritated, which wasn't like him. He finished the last dish and banged it into the strainer.

"You annoyed about something?" Ed asked.

There was no answer. Instead, the priest pulled the plug and watched the water swirl around the drain. When the last water gurgled, he said, "Let's run over to the hardware store and get that toilet handle."

Ed started to object, but stopped. Grace would be gone all afternoon. Plenty of time to talk about Andi.

In the truck, Ed told Jim about the first salvo in their fight. "Hmm. Not exactly Machiavelli," said Jim.

Ed feigned hurt. "I thought it was clever."

"Clever, maybe, but what's your follow-up?"

"I guess now I wait till she figures it out for herself."

"You *wait*? My God, you're as dense as Superman's balls." The priest still sounded annoyed.

Ed was embarrassed, although *Superman's balls* made him chuckle. "Well then, great sage, tell me my next move," he said, as they walked into the Ace Hardware.

"Figure it out. Right now you're starting to like the woman, but if she leaves, it'll hurt for a while, then you'll claw your way back to normal, depressed as usual. So why sit around while she thinks it over? Do what *you* want to do. *That's* your next move."

They bought the toilet handle and made small talk with the clerk, then went back to the rectory. When he finished installing the handle, he said, "Do what I want to do, eh?"

"Think about it." Jim spoke curtly. "If you push her and she stays, you win. Do nothing and you'll get nothing."

Then, surprising Ed, the priest snorted, looking very uncomfortable. "Hah. The celibate speaks," he said, rubbing his eyes. He studied Ed's face for a long moment. "I'm not being honest here. I need to tell you something, and I don't like it."

Ed waited.

Jim looked at his watch. "Is it too early for a drink?" Ed suddenly tensed: Bad news.

Jim paused a minute, then said, "I've leaving the valley."

"No!" Ed's heart pounded. "Your bishop's transferring you?"

"My checkout person came home."

The two men simply looked at one another for a moment, and embraced.

"So you're doing what *you* want, finally," Ed said, softly, stepping back. "But do you need to leave?" Suddenly, he felt immensely lonely.

Jim nodded, brushing at his eyes. "I asked her to move to the valley and she was willing, but the bishop said I couldn't do that to the parish."

"Ask your people, Jim. Fuck the bishop."

Jim cocked his head quizzically. "Now that's an unpleasant image."

*   *   *

Ed sat alone in his truck, watching long shreds of cloud rolling slowly across the blue, waiting to find pleasure in his friend's good fortune, but it eluded him. His chest felt full. He rested his forehead on the steering wheel. Too much loss. He raised his head and started the truck, drove out of town toward the Coliseum. For an hour, he sat below it, staring at nothing and everything. Finally, he went back to the hospital.

His friendship with the priest had filled a deep well in his life in Jefferson, and a large part of him would empty out when the man left. *Losing Andi at the same time might be too much*, he thought. An image brushed the edges of his memory – standing atop the Coliseum, looking into the void through the toe of his snowshoe.

She isn't leaving. I won't let her. The intensity of his feelings staggered him, and they banished the image of the snowshoe.

He smiled. *Want something bad enough*, he thought, *you get rid of the black dog.*

*   *   *

Andi was watching TV and working her Spirometer when he returned after dinner. After coming back to town, he'd spent the afternoon sketching plans for a remodel of his spare bedroom for Grace. Yesterday, Andi had only been able to raise the blue ball a few inches; now, she blew it to the top every time.

She put the instrument down and for a few moments, coughed, pressing her hand hard against her side. When the coughing ended, she whispered, "Grace's still with Jen?"

"Yep. Movies and dinner. She'll be here in a half-hour or so."

She nodded, then resumed working the machine. The blue ball hit the top on every attempt. After nine or ten rounds, she put the machine down again, wheezing, but not coughing. "Let's walk," she said, when her breathing had slowed to normal.

As he helped her from the bed, her gown inched up her lap and Ed glimpsed her pubic hair, almost gasping at his rush of arousal. They didn't talk much on the walk, but when they got back to the room, she said, "You took a peek."

"And liked what I saw."

She gave a brief laugh, but grimaced at the pain. "Sorry. My shoulder... hurts like hell, the incision stings... and this rib's still broken." She breathed a moment.

Ed began to tell her about Jim's departure, but they heard giggling voices in the hall, and Grace popped into the room, Jen behind her. Grace rushed over to the bed, but stopped just before hugging Andi. "I'm back. Me and Jen saw, like, an awesome movie. And her mom cooked the best dinner."

"What was it?" Andi wheezed.

"'Silver Linings Playbook.' About this mental guy who falls in love with a weird girl and she teaches him to dance and – "

"I meant dinner," Andi said, smiling.

"Whatever," Grace said, her face abruptly turning serious. "And you can't leave me. You're staying here in the Valley with me. I need you." She was so suddenly intense that Ed almost laughed, but Andi put up a hand and gestured Grace quiet.

"Not now, Grace. We'll talk about it another time. Tell me about the movie."

The girls described it. Then, Jen said to Andi, "I just want you to know how proud the whole valley is of you and what you did for us."

Andi winced. "I was just doing my job." She coughed. "Any deputy would've... done it."

Jen nodded. "Anyway, we're all pulling for you. And we're glad you're one of us."

She turned to go, and at the last moment gave Grace a pert nod, as if to say, *There*.

*   *   *

Later, as Ed drove them back to Andi's place, she chattered about Jen and Dana and the Junior Search and Rescue and algebra and Andi's recovery. After a long stretch during which Ed said nothing, she looked over at him.

"Northrup, you look sad."

Off guard, Ed's voice caught. About to brush off her question, he said, instead, "You're right. My best friend is leaving the valley."

"*Andi?!*"

"No, Jim Hamilton. He's been my friend since I came here. I'll miss him a lot." He felt bleak.

"Can't you make him stay too?"

He shook his head. "He's leaving to be with the woman he loves."

THIRTY-FOUR

Monday, February 27

A T A LITTLE past seven in the morning, on the way to school, Ed and Grace stopped at the hospital, and found Andi walking on her own in the hospital corridor. She led them back to her room. She said, "Doc Keeley said I might be able to go home tomorrow or Wednesday."

When Grace started to speak, Andi held up her hand. "Wait. I want to tell you two something."

Ed's heart raced.

After she settled herself in bed, Andi said, "I've been thinking about what you said." She paused and breathed quietly a moment.

Grace didn't wait. "We *need* you. *I* need you. You gotta – "

Andi lifted her hand again, silencing her. "I know you do." She closed her eyes for a moment, then looked at Ed. "And you too. I know."

Although Grace smiled tentatively, Ed, his pulse still fast, stiffened.

She continued gazing at him. "You two are... a family now. But I'm... not. I – "

Grace interrupted her, shaking her head. "No! It's, like, the three of us. I want you guys to be my family now."

Andi frowned. "Let me talk, Grace." She took a deep breath, which made her cough for a moment. Back under control, she started. "The adults in a family... have to love each other." She looked again at Ed. "Your father and I don't love each other."

Grace's eyes glistened, but she stayed quiet. Ed said, "Not now. Love needs time to grow, and I want that time with you."

She closed her eyes. "Stop interrupting me. Talking's still hard... Give me a minute." She gasped a few breaths, coughed a couple of times. "I'm not who you... thought, Ed." He started to interrupt, but she sighed. "Please, *listen* to me." She looked at Grace, who had two tear-tracks on her cheeks, and her own eyes moistened. She caught Ed's eye and nodded toward Grace; he moved close and touched the girl's shoulder, but she leaned away, then collapsed onto Andi's bed beside her, groaning. Andi winced at being jolted, then reached over and stroked her hair.

Ed kept his hands quiet in his lap, studying them, recalling the night Mara had left. That had staggered him, left him breathless, an abandonment like falling off a cliff. Andi's leaving wouldn't bring that hollow helpless terror, but it would bring sorrow. He'd be all right, eventually, although he'd always wonder what might have been. All right, but alone, and he no longer wanted to be alone. His eyes were dry.

Ben and Ted's advice: Fight. He'd tried and... failed. He looked at his hands.

Then he looked up at Andi.

Stroking Grace's hair, she was watching him intently. Her eyes were angry.

Stung, he bridled. "Look, dammit, go if you have to, but quit talking about time. We were starting to be friends before you got... before this happened, and friendship takes time. It still does, wherever it ends up. You getting shot doesn't change a damn thing about that." His voice rose. "Maybe you feel different, I'm sure you must, but I don't. I'm still your friend. More than friend, damn it. Unless what you're saying is you don't *want* the valley anymore, stay with us!"

Grace was struggling to get upright and brushed her eyes roughly as she chimed in, "Yeah! Me too, Andi! I'm not letting go."

Andi shook her head, still angry. She pulled in a long and painful breath and said, "Shut up, both of you!... *Listen* to me!... Let me finish what I need to tell you." She coughed, hard.

Grace didn't wait. "You said you're going away. I can't – "

"Stop!!" Andi spanked the bed hard. "You *heard* that, I didn't say it... I said care, friendship, family need *time*... I said I'm *different*. I never... I never said I'm *leaving*."

Ed held his breath.

Grace said, "So are you staying?"

"I need time to get through this – " She waved, exasperated, at the hospital walls, at her own chest. Her eyes filled. "Through this...shit, and I need your help to do it. Maybe someday I'll want... to be a family with you... but not till..." She took a ragged breath that ended with a sob. Tears ran freely down her face. In a moment, she collected herself, roughly rubbing her face with the bedsheet. "Not till I know what *I* bring... what I can still give you both." She sank back against the pillows, out of breath.

Grace said, insistently, "So you're staying with me?"

Andi looked momentarily angry again, but then grimaced, shook her head, and let a wan smile touch her lips. "Yeah, Grace," she whispered. "I'm staying with you." Then she looked at Ed, and her eyes said, *And with you, too.*

PART FIVE

THIRTY-FIVE

A month later, Sunday, April 1

A VOICE CALLING from a great distance. An insistent pounding. "Get up, Northrup! Get up! We're late! Let's *gooooo!*"

Ed surfaced from deep in a dream. He tried opening an eye, but saw only black. The pounding came from nearby. His bedroom door. He craned his neck, and forced both eyes open to find the clock. Red numbers: seven-twenty-five. He jolted awake and sat up. Grace was pounding on his door.

"Come *on*, Northrup! We overslept! You gotta get me to *school!*"

Darkness cloaked everything but the crack of light beneath the door. "I'm coming," he groaned. *School starts at eight! Jesus. No time for a run. No time even for coffee.* Stumbling toward the door, he felt his erection bounce, and groped on the floor for his pants. *Must've been a good dream.* After he'd fumbled on his pants and stepped into the hall, there was light under the bathroom door. *Damn, Grace's in there.* Needing to pee, he stepped outside and went off the porch. *Desperate times, desperate measures.*

He hurried back in, threw on a shirt and shoes and checked the bathroom again. The light was still on behind the closed door. He glanced at the clock again: seven-thirty-two. He knocked on the door. "Hurry up, Grace. We gotta hustle."

No water ran inside. She didn't answer. "Come on, Grace! I need to brush my teeth," he said to the door. Silence.

Muttering, he went into his kitchen and grabbed coffee grounds, then stopped. No time. *I'll pick up a couple of Americanos at Alice's and take one to Andi,* he decided. It was a ritual they had gotten into since Andi'd come home. He went back to the bathroom. It was still closed.

He knocked again, hoping he didn't seem like a stalker. No answer. He turned the handle and opened the door a crack. The bathroom was empty. Alarmed, he called out, "Grace? Where are you?!"

A scream of laughter and then "April Fools'!" pealed from Grace's room. "It's Sunday and it's only five in the morning! And you forgot I'm on spring break." She hooted again. "I got you *good*, Northrup!"

In her doorway, he looked at his watch. *Seven thirty-six.* Then he got it. "You changed my clocks."

She squealed again. "Gotcha."

*   *   *

Grace returned to bed after texting her girls about her prank, but he, thoroughly awake, went for his run. During the unseasonably warm weather in the weeks since Andi came home, his runs had stretched longer and grown easier. His belly had flattened. Without stepping on the scale since he'd seen the lost twenty-two pounds, he knew he'd seriously dented the rest. *Nothing like your friend getting shot and adopting a kid to knock some pounds off. I'll call it The Dr. Ed Diet. I'll be rich.*

Then it occurred to him that he *was* rich.

Running smoothly in the pre-dawn dark, he let his thoughts meander. Spring meltwater gurgled in the ditches. Grace's April Fool's joke tickled him. *Is that how teens treat their fathers?* He felt a smile playing on his lips. *Have to tell Andi about it.* They'd developed a comfortable routine, him bringing her coffee most mornings, helping her get about as she grew stronger. *Today*, he thought, *is going to be interesting*.

Jerry Francis had discovered, last month, that Grace's mother's body was being held in Las Vegas. Clark County required that non-residents who die there alone be kept a month, to allow outstate family time to claim the body. Being a minor, Grace couldn't claim Mara's body, so they'd had to wait the month before Ed, as Mara's adoptive father, could do so. Tomorrow, Mara's body would be arriving in the valley. So today, he and Grace were driving up to the monastery to select her casket; Andi had made sounds about joining them. Running easily, Ed felt himself beginning to smile.

*　　*　　*

Thanks to Grace's April Fool's trick, Ed was in town earlier than usual. He carried an Americano coffee in each hand as he approached Andi's front door. He put one on the porch floor to open the front door, then picked it up, only to put it back on the floor outside her bedroom door. He knocked softly, then stooped to pick it up.

"Ed? That you?"

"Yep," he answered, then realized he couldn't open the door, so he put the coffee cup down a third time and turned the handle. "You were expecting someone else?" he asked, as he swung open the door and stooped for the coffee.

She shook her head. "I called your house to see when you were coming over, but I woke Grace. I forgot it was Sunday. She said I owed her big time for that." She chuckled, then winced.

"The shoulder hurt?" he asked, sitting gingerly on the foot of her bed.

"Mostly the rib, when I laugh. And it's a lot better." She patted the bed beside herself. "Sit by me."

"Did she tell you about her April Fools' joke?" He settled himself, careful not to jostle her.

"No."

He related it, and she braced her hand tightly against her side to chuckle.

They sipped their coffee and talked about the day. Ed asked, "Do you feel up to going to the monastery with us this morning?"

"Can't. I feel stronger, but I agreed to have coffee with Callie and the other deputies, remember?"

"Right, I forgot. You're healing faster than the surgeon predicted."

Andi looked curious. "What'd she predict?"

"Two or three months. It's been, what? Just six weeks?"

"It's the mountain air."

* * *

While Andi showered, Ed read the paper. His cell phone buzzed.

It was Grace. "Northrup, can I invite MJ for lunch at the Angler today?"

"We're going up to pick out your mom's casket, remember?"

There was a pause. "Oh, yeah. Did you tell Andi about me getting you up?"

"I did. She laughed."

"She woke me up, so she owes me one."

Andi came in from the shower and pantomimed, *Who's on the phone?* He mouthed, *Grace.* She smiled, toweling her hair. He said to Grace, "And I'm sure you'll make her pay."

"What's up?" Andi asked him when he ended the call.

"Grace has a crush on Magnus Junior. She wanted to invite him to lunch today, but I reminded her we're going up to the monastery."

"Does MJ return the crush?"

"I doubt it. He's just being nice."

"Oh-oh."

* * *

In the parking lot at his office – he needed to do his billing before they drove up the mountain – he saw Leese's car. He knocked on her office door.

"Come on in, Ed."

"How'd you know it was me?"

She gestured at her window. "I saw you drive in."

"Ah, duh. You're working on Sunday?"

"Tax day is only fourteen days away. Burning the midnight oil."

With a grimace, he remembered his numbers. "Damn, I forgot all about my numbers. Look, I'll – "

She cut him off. "No worries, Ed. I filed for an extension when Andi got shot. I figured taxes wouldn't be high on your priority list."

Ed was puzzled. "Why'd you think that?"

"I figured you'd be preoccupied with Grace. And Andi." She smiled. "And I was right, wasn't I?"

"We're just friends, Leese."

The accountant laughed. "Bullshit. Everybody's talking about you two. 'Just friends' don't have lattes every other morning at one friend's house."

Ed felt himself blushing. "Word's out? What exactly are people saying?"

"That you've got your line in the deputy's water. Wrong?"

He smiled. "I hope not." He started to go.

"Whoa, there, cowboy. Even with the extension, I need your best guess whether you'll owe anything this year."

"Does the inheritance count?"

"Not this year."

"Well, last year was pretty much like the last six or seven years, I'd say. About the same income, same expenses. I paid the quarterlies you estimated."

"We're good then. You'll probably get a few dollars back, nothing much. But I'll need your numbers by July fifteenth. No later."

"You'll have them." At the door, he turned and said, "I had a talk with Vic and Maggie the other day. Thanks for your help on that IRS plan. And Vic said Marty Bayley was willing to give him good terms on the operating loan if he had a co-signer."

She lifted her eyebrows. "Who'd he find to co-sign?"

Ed blushed. "Me."

She studied him for a moment. "Isn't that ethically shady for you shrinks? Not that I don't approve, but your Psychology Board, aren't they – "

He surprised himself. "If a man can't help his neighbors, what's the point? If the Board doesn't agree, we'll talk." *And I could be the first psychologist in history to lose two licenses.*

Leese smiled. "Ballsy. I like it. And you'll be able to afford that attitude in a while." She chuckled. "Hell, you'll be able to afford any attitude you like."

Ed smiled. "Funny how financial security makes good neighbors."

*   *   *

Where the highway ends on the mountain, turn left and you're at the Coliseum trailhead; turn right, you're on the monastery driveway, under the great pines. Ed drove through the log headgate, with its carved legend, "*St. Brendan's Monastery – 1847.*" Grace looked apprehensive as they approached the monastery walls. Ed opened the massive gate. They crossed a cobbled courtyard and pushed through the high oak doors of the church.

"This place is weird," Grace whispered as they waited in the dim, echoing vestibule. The stone floor and the dark paneled walls gave off a clean waxy smell. Ed smiled at Grace as he pulled on the bell rope three times.

"Is it haunted?" Grace whispered, as a distant bell chimed somewhere deep inside the building. She sucked in her breath and pulled a little closer to Ed when the door from the monastery opened and a short round monk came through. He was bald on top, with a narrow crown of hair fringing his head at the ears. His face was creased in a smile, and ruddy.

He held out his hand, which Ed shook. "Nice to see you, Ed."

"Abbot, it's been a while."

The monk smiled at Grace. "And you must be the young lady who'd like to see our caskets."

"I'm Grace Ellonson, uh, Northrup." She glanced at Ed, then back at the monk. "Who are you?"

The portly monk smiled. "I'm Abbot Timothy. Call me Tim." His voice was as warm as his face was red.

Grace looked intently at the abbot. "What do you do here?"

He paused a moment, then said, "I'm kind of in charge."

"No, I mean, like, what do you, uh, people do up here?"

He chuckled. "We devote our lives to God through study, prayer, and work."

Grace frowned. "Sounds boring."

He laughed. "It is, sometimes."

"I meant, how do you guys make money?"

"Oh. We build and sell our wooden caskets."

She thought it over. "This is *very* weird." She turned to Ed. "Can we see them?"

The Abbot said, "We have Sext in about ten minutes. You're welcome – "

Grace interrupted, "What's Sext?"

"Ah. It's our midday prayer service. Anyway, you're welcome to join us, and afterwards you'll tour the workshop. Let me call Brother Anselm – he'll be the one showing you around after prayers." He reached for the bell-rope and pulled three times, then paused, then pulled twice more. The bell chimed far away, three, then two. "Each of the monks has his own bell code," he explained.

"Like a username," Grace whispered.

A few moments later, a handsome young monk came through the door. The Abbot said, "Brother Anselm, this is Grace Northrup. After Sext, I'd like you to show her the workshop and help her pick out a casket."

The young monk smiled. "You'll love the caskets," he said to her.

"They're for dead people," she said, doubt dripping.

The Abbot said, "Grace, while we get ready for the service, feel free to look around the church. We have some beautiful things in the side chapels, real treasures. When you hear us singing, you'll know the service has started." He stepped past them and opened the massive door to the church and gestured them inside. It was cold, and the squeak of the hinges echoed in the long space. A monk far up in the front was lighting candles. A lingering scent of incense met them. "Anselm and I will meet you back here after the service is over. Okay?"

"Sounds good," Ed said. He ushered Grace into the cold church.

*   *   *

Colored light poured through the high vaulted windows, playing on the stone wall, shadowing shapes and figures in high spaces. Grace looked up, pointed, whispered, "What are those?"

Ed looked up. "Statues of saints. You've been in a church before, haven't you?"

"No. Are they alive?"

They could hear voices far away inside the monastery. "No," Ed said, "they're statues. If we could see better, they're beautiful."

Grace shook her head, still whispering. "They're, like, scary up there, looking at me." She pointed at an archway to their right. "Where does that go?"

"It's one of the side chapels. It's probably got some of the treasures."

Ed smiled as Grace's mercurial "Awesome!" echoed in the stone cavern of the church. The candle-lighting monk turned and frowned at them. Grace walked after Ed toward the side chapel; he went in, feeling with his hand along the wall till he found a switch. Suddenly, the chapel blazed with light, revealing rows of golden vessels gleaming on ornate wooden shelves along each wall. Despite the cold, the air smelled musty.

They faced an altar of polished pine, on which rested five gleaming golden cases. The two on the left and the two on the right were miniature churches, each three feet high and a foot wide. The vessel in the center, however, was different, gloriously different. Grace, enthralled, approached it slowly, Ed following behind. She stopped, peering at it. "It's the sun!" she breathed. And it was.

A fan of golden shafts radiated down from a sunburst of alternating gold and silver blades that resembled flames. In the center of the sunburst, a dark orb, six inches in diameter, glowed amidst the gleaming blades. Grace peered up at it, then stirred herself. "There's something inside," she whispered.

"Let's take a look."

Ed dragged a heavy wooden bench across the stone floor, the legs screeching on the flagstones; when he pushed it up to the altar, Grace climbed up to peer into the orb.

She suddenly screamed and fell backward off the bench. Ed broke her fall.

"Are you all right?" he asked Grace after she'd calmed down. "What happened?"

"It was a *finger*! A black finger!" Grace howled, accusingly. "This is, like, *gross*!"

They heard voices, and feet running on the polished flagstones. Brother Anselm rushed into the chapel. Behind him, a group of monks peered in, but kept a respectful distance.

Ed explained what had happened.

Anselm's look of concern dissolved into a smile. "Oh, it sure is a finger in there! This is the reliquary."

Grace frowned. "What's a relicarry?"

"Pieces of saints, in all these holy vessels. The finger is our best one – it's said to be St. Brendan's right index finger." He was amused.

"*Pieces*?! Body parts?! What *are* you people?" The Abbot ran into the chapel, breathing heavily.

Grace turned to him, accusingly. "You keep dead bodies in here! It's a reli – " she looked quizzically at the younger monk.

"Reliquary," he said, still amused. "And not whole bodies, just the leftovers."

The Abbot frowned. "Brother, our monastery humor is a bit out of place at the moment."

"Sorry, Father." Anselm wiped the smile from his face. He turned to Grace.

"I'm sorry. I realize you were frightened."

Grace looked up at the golden sunburst. "Can I see the finger again?"

*　　*　　*

After the service, which lasted fifteen minutes, Anselm took them to the workshop. As they followed the carefully shoveled path from the monastery to the barn outside the wall, Ed looked up. The Coliseum soared above them, bold against the blue sky, blazing with sunlight. Anselm held open the door.

"The workshop's quiet just now," he said. "The monks are at lunch."

Grace looked at him. "Are you missing your lunch?"

He laughed. "No, they'll save some for me."

Two rows of large work benches stood ten deep, some empty, some supporting the large coffins in various stages of construction. Along the far wall, completed caskets rested on massive wooden shelves built of whole logs.

"Come look," Anselm said. He led the way across the huge workshop.

Grace gasped. Even in the dim light, the caskets radiated their own luster. One in particular stood out – simple, its edges softly rounded, with two sturdy branches affixed as handles along the sides.

"That's the one, Northrup. That's Mara's."

THIRTY-SIX

Monday, April 2

WHEN ED GOT back to Andi's after picking up their morning Americanos, she was already up, although Grace slept. "What time does everything start today?" she asked, as he handed her a cup. He and Grace had spent last evening at Andi's, talking about the monastery and the beautiful casket and Mara's funeral. It had gotten late, so they stayed. Ed hadn't slept well on the couch.

"Noon. The Abbot is bringing the casket down this morning. Mara should arrive around three."

Andi looked surprised. "The Abbot delivers caskets?"

He laughed. "Usually it's FedEx, but for Grace he wanted to deliver it personally. And he might have to lead the funeral service, if the bishop refuses permission for Jim to do it."

"This bishop sounds like a book prick." When Ed looked surprised, she added, "My dad's name for bosses who use rules to fuck with people."

"Some of your cop talk is really entertaining. And right on."

Grace came out on the porch, her hair spiky and wild. Her face looked puffy, her eyes red. She looked like she'd come straight from bed, but she'd poured herself a cup of coffee. During their conversation last night, she'd cried a few times, and Ed had heard sniffles, later, from her bedroom. "Good morning," he said.

She ignored him and tasted the coffee, and muttered, "Your coffee is weak, Northrup."

He smiled. "And a good morning to you too." *Good sign.* She complained about his coffee almost every morning. Even when he didn't make it.

"Why are you two sitting out here in the cold?"

Andi looked at her kindly. "We were talking about your mom coming today."

Grace grimaced. "Don't remind me. I'm scared."

Her phone rang in her bedroom and she jumped up and ran in, splashing coffee on Andi. A few moments later, they heard excited conversation, then a few moments later, a peal of laughter. Andi smiled. "Sounds like that storm has passed."

Ed remembered something. "I ran into Vic and Maggie at the Village Inn. They want to invite you for coffee."

"Really?"

"Yeah. They want to apologize to you."

Andi sipped her Americano. "No apologies needed."

Ed looked out at the mountains. "Maggie's invited Jim and his girlfriend for coffee, too."

"Sounds like the Welcome Wagon Lady's back."

Grace came back out. Ed said, "Who called?"

"Jen. Northrup, can my girls come with us to see Mara's casket?"

*　　*　　*

The casket fairly gleamed, the yellow pine burnished to an almost-reddish hue. Along the sides were fixed the two sinuous branches as handles, stripped of their bark and polished till they seemed to exude light. The lid was gently rounded, and its edges melted seamlessly into the sides. Perimeter holes dotted the rim, six inches apart. Resting on the lid was a plastic bag of two-inch pine dowels, each fitted to the holes and hand-polished to the same glowing shine as the wood.

"We don't use screws," Brother Anselm explained to Grace, who had looked quizzically at the plastic bag, "These dowels seal the top."

She stepped away from Dana and Jen and approached the casket. Her hand caressed the curving branch-handle, then softly drifted along the top. She looked up at Anselm. "Is my mom inside?"

The young monk shook his head.

Behind them, Rick Bayless, the funeral director, a genial man dressed in gray, discreetly cleared his throat. "She'll be arriving at three o'clock. We'll need about three hours to, ah, prepare her."

Grace stiffened. "What's that mean?" Ed said, "They'll make her look her best."

"What for?" Grace snapped.

"For you to say good-bye," he answered softly.

Bayless cleared his throat again. "Ahem. I should say that a viewing may not be advisable after this length of time."

"Why not?" Grace's voice was pitching higher.

The Abbot touched her shoulder. "Grace, with your permission, I'll help Mr. Bayless. If it's at all possible, we'll see to it you can see her. If not, I'll tell you the truth."

Grace stroked the lovely wood, then let her fingers rest on the lid. "Make her comfortable in there."

*   *   *

The call came that evening during dinner. Abbot Timothy told Northrup that Mara's body had been well cared for in Las Vegas and that there could be a review at nine in the morning. "Afterward, we'll have the service and burial."

When he told her, Grace smiled for the first time since last night. "Mara'll be so pissed. She hated church."

*   *   *

Next morning, standing beside the open casket, Grace simply gazed a long time at her mother's face, then touched the withered cheek as softly as a baby reaches up to touch its mother's lips. After a long moment, she stepped back, and Rick Bayless and Brother Anselm slid the lid in place. The Abbot brought an earthenware bowl filled with the short dowels and two wooden mallets, and laid it on the center of the casket cover. He handed the mallets to Grace and Ed. "Use these to pound the dowels in place. Insert them *firmly*," he said.

Grace lifted the first dowel and slipped it in a hole. She tapped it. Nothing moved.

The Abbot whispered, "Pound the living hell out of it." Her friend Dana giggled.

Grace looked surprised, then lifted the mallet and swung it hard against the wood, and the dowel slid solidly into place. She smiled grimly.

Ed followed suit. At first, he felt little emotion, but after a few moments' pounding, his eyes welled and he began to weep silently. He continued pounding dowels into holes, his face like a rain-streaked window. Andi watched him.

Finally, the box was sealed. He wiped his eyes.

Grace looked curiously at him. "Why were you crying, Northrup?"

He handed his mallet to the Abbot. "Once upon I time, I loved your mother. A little of that hangs on."

Grace looked at the lovely wooden casket. "Yeah," she whispered. The men grasped the curved handles and carried the casket to the hearse, and everyone got in the black van reserved for the family for the short ride to St. Bernie's.

Abbot Timothy sat beside Ed on the back seat. Brother Anselm sat nervously with Andi in the next bench, and Grace and her girls, Jen and Dana, sat erect and adult in the first row, behind the driver.

Timothy said quietly, "This is Jim's last service."

"Why? There's talk of him staying on as a deacon."

The monk shook his head. "Bishop Probst will never allow it. He'll cover his ass with the pope."

"Damn! Can Jim appeal?"

The Abbot snorted. "Appeal? To Vatican bureaucrats? They look away when kids are abused, but let a priest start a real relationship with an adult woman, they feed him to the fish. There'll be no appeal."

"You're pissed, Tim."

"Astute observation."

The van rolled up to the door of St. Bernie's as Rick Bayless was opening the rear door of the hearse. The beautiful casket caught Ed's eye. As they piled out, the Abbot whispered to him, "Where are the pall bearers?"

"Good question. Who arranges that?" He was watching Grace approach the hearse slowly, trying to gauge her feelings.

"Generally, the family does, but there'll be plenty of fellows."

"Doubt it," Ed said, still gazing at Grace. "No one knew Mara. Nobody'll be here."

The monk arched an eyebrow and gestured toward the parking lot behind the church. It was full of cars. Intent upon Grace, Ed hadn't noticed.

The front door of the church opened and a line of men came out. Magnus Anderssen, Ben, Ted, Pete Peterson, Jerry Francis, and lagging behind, Vic Sobstak.

Ben approached Grace. "Miss Grace," he said, "we'd be honored if you'd allow us to carry your mother in."

Grace looked at Ed, then back at Ben and the others. "Thank you," she said, simply. Ed put an arm around her shoulder.

As they carried the casket to the front, its polished wood glowed in the multicolored sunlight filtering through the stained glass. They brought it up the aisle and laid it gently on a trestle before the altar. Rick Bayless began draping a white cloth over it. Standing between Ed and Andi, Grace said politely, "Please, don't cover her up." Rick turned and looked at the Abbot, who had gone to a chair near the altar. Timothy nodded, and the director folded the cloth and took it away.

When everyone was seated, Jim came out and a rustling passed through the church. Ed looked back. The pews were almost full of people. *To honor me*, he thought, touched. *And to see Grace.*

After leading the prayers from the altar, Jim came around and stood in front, looking down at the casket. He spoke as to a departed friend.

"Mara, we never knew you, but we have you to thank for bringing Grace to us. As we get to know your daughter, we will come to know the best of you." Then he looked down to Grace. "Grace, your mother is as welcome to rest in Monastery Valley as you are to live here. Whatever story she had started writing for your life, you are now going to finish. And we will be around you, to help you write."

Grace's free hand found Ed's and she squeezed, and made a soft sound.

Ed wondered about Jim's *we will be around you*. Was he staying after all?

Jim smiled and walked down the steps to the casket. He laid his hands on it, and his fingers softly caressed the gleaming wood. His eyes closed.

"Mara Northrup Ellonson Hertz, may your memory, known through your daughter, be a blessing for us all. We will love and protect your girl, and she will be another blessing on this valley. Go now, Mara, and may you rest in peace."

Grace leaned hard into Ed's shoulder and he could feel, rather than hear, her very small sobs; his own eyes were damp. Andi reached her good arm across to Grace.

Jim stepped back and nodded to Rick Bayless, who decorously gestured the pallbearers to the casket. Ted Coldry stepped out of line and approached Ed and Grace, and whispered, "You two take my place and carry Mara home."

*   *   *

Danny Millert, the cemetery custodian, leaned on his shovel behind the open grave and the mound of earth. He nodded politely to Ed as they guided Mara's casket carefully onto the framework that supported it over the hole. Grace, standing back, looked pale and small, and Ed came around and offered her his hand.

She looked at it and said, "I'm okay, Northrup."

They gathered around the grave. Tendrils of high cloud were filtering over the mountains. The air was warm. The monks' handiwork shone, the polished pine wood reflecting the blue and sunshine-yellow sky. Grace edged close to Ed and whispered, "Mara loved beautiful things."

He whispered back, "And you gave her one." He wrapped his arm around her, expecting her to pull away, but she leaned into him. Jim opened his book and said the final prayers, and splashed some blessed water on the casket. The drops glistened dark on the shining wood. Rick Bayless and Danny Millert stepped to the ends of the casket and lowered Mara into the ground.

Grace stepped to the grave's edge and stood utterly still, looking down. Everyone waited. The only sound, a raven's far-off cry. Her shoulders rounded and her head bowed.

After a long time, she turned slowly, looking strangely at Ed. Concerned, he stepped forward.

She said, "I hope you're not waiting for *me* to shovel all that mud."

*   *   *

After the lunch in the church basement, when most of the crowd was breaking up, Grace said to Ed, "Can we go climb the Coliseum?"

Ed frowned. "Boy, it's still pretty snowy up there, and Andi's tired – "

Andi jabbed him. "Speak for yourself. It's a beautiful day. Let's go for it."

THIRTY-SEVEN

That Afternoon, on the Coliseum

FOR ANDI, THE climb was arduous, so they went slowly. After mud on the lower trail, the footing grew solid when they reached the snow, and they ascended from warm and budding spring into the quiet solitude of winter. As they approached the cedar grove, heavily tracked snow shrouded the high meadow in long blue-white swells. The dark green trees intensified the azure of the sky. The morning's fingerling clouds had drifted away, leaving the sky open and wide, radiant with sun.

Ed led the way through the cedar grove and up to the meadow, then across to the summit's edge. Standing again on the brink of the Coliseum, he marveled.

Below, the monastery glowed in the sun. The long valley ran north, piebald fields reaching to a distant mountain range hazy in the warm spring air. In the middle distance, an eagle turned slowly on thermals. Ed watched, rapt.

Grace said, "You guys remember how I, like, wished my mom could be here?"

"Yeah, I do," Andi said.

Ed was quiet for a moment, then said, "Mara's coming here seemed like a bad dream."

Both Andi and Grace looked at him, Andi with some alarm, Grace with a crooked smile. "Your, like, worst nightmare, Northrup?"

He realized why Andi looked alarmed. "Not because of you, Grace, because of her. But, yeah, my worst nightmare." Then he thought of Elizabeth Murphy. How little Grace reminded him of her now. He smiled, thinking of Elizabeth's gold coin flashing in the sunlight as it fell. *Rest in peace, little one.*

At that moment, the sun blazed on the long westward arc of the Monastery River, making it shine like a rope of molten gold flung across the green-tinged fields.

Grace whispered, "I've never seen a place as beautiful as this."

After a few minutes, the shining river faded as the sun moved west, and Ed put his arm around Grace's shoulders and drew her close. She pulled away.

"No mushy stuff, Northrup. That's fine for funerals, but if we're, like, going to be a family, don't be a mushy-head." Andi laughed.

There was a sound behind them, no, not a sound, a movement of air or a brush of pine needles falling on crusted snow. They turned. Across the meadow at the forest's edge, the bull elk stood, ears flared. His dark soft eyes fixed on them. No one moved or made a sound. They all simply gazed at one another, and then the bull turned and went back into the trees.

They watched the valley a long time, until the sun gilded the western crests, and Ed whispered, "It's probably time to start down."

Grace turned back to look out over the far Valley. "Well," she sighed. "I got my wish. Mara's here. And I'll never forget that elk as long as I live."

They worked across the meadow and down into the trees, and as they passed into the cedar grove, Ed said casually, "That sounded mushy-headed to me."

Grace didn't answer until the first switchback. She went ahead of him, and when she rounded the downward turn and looked up at him, she smiled sweetly and said, "Looks like *I'm* your worst nightmare now."

The End

ABOUT THE AUTHOR

Bill Percy draws on his experience as a psychologist to write vivid, engaging tales of real people confronting timely mysteries—child neglect, political conspiracies, clergy sexual abuse, sex trafficking. Bill has written numerous psychologist training programs and psychological documents, and turned to fiction in 2009. The result is the Monastery Valley series: *Climbing the Coliseum, Nobody's Safe Here,* and *The Bishop Burned the Lady.* He and his wife, Michele, live in beautiful north Idaho.

Thank you so much for reading one of our **Mystery** novels.
If you enjoyed our book, please check out our recommended title for your
next great read!

K-Town Confidential by Brad Chisholm and Claire Kim

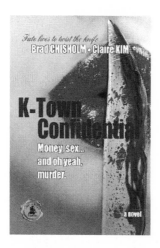

"An enjoyable zigzagging plot." *–KIRKUS REVIEWS*

"If you are a fan of crime stories and legal dramas that have a noir flavor,
you won't be disappointed with *K-Town Confidential*." *–Authors Reading*

Made in the USA
Middletown, DE
16 January 2020

83318077R00241